HIDDEN PLACE

BY SHAWN SHIFLETT

AKASHIC BOOKS
New York

This is a work of fiction. All names, characters, places, and incidents are the product of the author's imagination. Any resemblance to real events or persons, living or dead, is entirely coincidental.

Published by Akashic Books
©2004 Shawn Shiflett

ISBN: 1-888451-50-5
Library of Congress Control Number: 2003109536
All rights reserved
First printing
Printed in Canada

Akashic Books
PO Box 1456
New York, NY 10009
Akashic7@aol.com
www.akashicbooks.com

ACKNOWLEDGMENTS

Special thanks to John Schultz, the originator of the Story Workshop approach to the teaching of writing, and to my mother, Betty Shiflett; their counsel was invaluable in the writing of *Hidden Place*. Thanks to Johnny Temple, Publisher and Editor in Chief of Akashic Books, for adding me to his list of discovered writers. To Don De Grazia, for going to bat for the manuscript, and to Jaimee Wriston Colbert, a trusted reader of my work. To Irvine Welsh and Carolyn Chute, for their generosity in support of the manuscript, and to *F Magazine* for publishing excerpts from it. To my father, the Reverend James Shiflett, who kept the faith that one day this story would meet the public. To Patricia Olalde and Gabina Mora, my always-on-call consultants on Spanish wording. To Judith Kelly, my "team player" publicist, and her student intern, Nicole Chakalis. And to Johanna Ingalls, the patiently helpful voice on the Akashic end of the phone line. A posthumous thanks to Margaret Johnson, Prayer Line Director at the First Liberated Baptist Church of Hyde Park, Chicago. And much gratitude for the personal and professional support over the years from Randy Albers and my entire literary family in the Fiction Writing Department at Columbia College Chicago.

For Jac, Maggie, and Cole

But that pipe, poor whale, was thy last.
—Ishmael, *Moby Dick*

CHAPTER 1

PARADISE

I stood knee-deep in the foamy surf, shading my eyes and looking out over Escondido Bay for any sign of a dorsal fin. A strong rip-tide pulled on my ankles, burying my feet in sand. Up and down the glistening beach along the overgrown weedy foothills of the Sierra Madre Mountains, *Norte Americano* "hippies"—so called by the Mexicans—bodysurfed, riding monster waves toward shore. Mila bounded past me in her green paisley bikini, skip-running and splashing straight ahead for a swim. Then, just as a wave was about to wipe the pug-nose-cute off her face, she knifed into the curling wall of water. Her blond head reappeared bobbing and floating on the surface.

"Come on, Roman!" she yelled over the thundering breakers. "It's like bath water!"

"Didn't you see *Jaws*?" I yelled back. "I don't plan on being on the short end of any Great White's feeding frenzy."

A huge wave blindsided Mila and knocked her somersaulting underwater. Her head popped up again, and she whipped her long tangled hair out of her eyes.

"You big baby! I'll protect you!"

"Yeah, right," I muttered. I may have been on the greyhound side of lean, but I also come fully equipped with broad shoulders and a nine-inch height advantage on Mila. I took a few hesitant steps. Somewhere in the sea, I heard a shark ringing a dinner bell. The undulating tropical heat helped me to make up my mind.

Come and get it, I thought, then ran full blast ahead and dove underwater. Reaching bottom, I kicked off the sandy floor and shot into the air.

"Man, that feeeeeeeels good!" I said. A couple of yards away, Mila was staring at me with an intent dreamy look.

"What?" I asked.

"Your eyes," Mila said, moving closer. "They're so blue against the water. And the way your hair looks so dark and your curls fall around your face. You are *so* incredibly handsome."

"Oh yeah?" I batted my eyelashes. "How'd you get so lucky?"

Since 3 a.m., when we'd rolled out of bed in our one-bedroom apartment in Chicago and argued about first dibs on the bathroom, we'd been bickering tit for tat. By dawn, the Jefferson Park bus had dropped us off at O'Hare Airport. After we'd checked our backpacks at the Mexicana Airlines counter, passed without a hitch through a metal-detector test, and realized that our K 16 gate assignment must have been at the very end of an endless corridor, Mila was raising her voice—"Roman, will you quit rushing me! You are such a pain in the . . ."

A connecting flight in Acapulco and a dozen petty arguments later, we arrived in Puerto Escondido on a small prop plane that chased goats off the dirt runway.

Same as many other North American college students on semester break, we had come to Mexico to soak up some rays and vegetate in Escondido—a small rural town, good-bang-for-your-tourist-buck, 300 kilometers southeast of Acapulco. Six days of fun in the sun to look forward to, or so I thought. Here, Chicago's arctic cold, stress of finals, and media hype over the upcoming presidential primary elections belonged to a different planet. The bicentennial—not a good year for Gerry Ford, I'm afraid.

* * *

Waves rocked us, and sea gulls circled and swooped overhead in the rich clear sky. Mila wrapped her legs around my hips and her twiglike arms around my neck, kissing me long and hard.

Recognizing one of her 180-degree mood swings, I cradled her ass in my hands. Sultry and mean, she said, "Fuck me."

I forgot all about sharks. "Here? Now?"

"Yeah, fuck me."

Up on the beach, one of several bronzed sunbathers rolled onto her stomach. Out past the lighthouse that towered straight as a candlestick on the promontory at the tip of the bay, a fishing boat, a hazy speck near the ocean's horizon, faded in and out of sight.

Mila must have sensed I was game. She smiled coyly in a way that would break any man's heart, and said, "Well, maybe not *right* here—in salt water. Wouldn't be healthy." She combed her fingers back through my hair, all dreamy again. "Soon . . . I need you inside me." She licked the length of my neck, running the sharp edge of her teeth lightly over my flesh, giving me goose bumps. In the secret recesses of my cut-offs, an awakening hard-on reared its head. Mila squeezed me even tighter between her legs and began to rhythmically grind her pelvis up and down against my cock. A gull dive-bombed into the water, snagged a small fish in its beak, and swallowed it whole. Time and sound stood still. Everything so simple. *Why can't it always be like this? Why all the bullshit?*

A few hours of swimming, sunbathing, and decompressing into vacation mode later, the sun had lowered into the blazing contentment of early evening.

"Been out here a long time," I said, lifting my cheek off a stars-and-stripes beach towel spread on the sand. "Better get back to camp."

Mila ran her fingers across my shoulder blades. "Oooo, you're red all right."

We flapped the sand out of our towels and slung them over our necks. A small territorial crab darted about us as if to show who was boss. I was looking out over the sunbeamed ocean, waiting for Mila to slip on her flip-flops, when I saw something happen that should have warned me of what would come to pass during our little stay in paradise. This short skinny Mexican, about my age, shirtless and wearing gray pants cut off mid-calf, came easy-as-you-please down the beach, leaving a trail of perfect footprints along the wet edge of the surf. Suddenly, a pony-tailed gringo—bulky as a moose, with a neck about as big around as another man's waist—jumped up from his towel maybe twenty feet to the right of us toward the water, sprinted at the *muchacho*, and took him down with a flying tackle. Before I knew it, the white dude was on top, pummeling the other guy's face with his fists. My own cheek flinched in sympathy.

"Where's my nine thousand pesos, Jorge?" the gringo yelled.

"*No hay*!" the one called Jorge said, trying to throw punches and push his enemy off of him at the same time.

Mila grabbed my wrist and must not have realized how tight she was squeezing. I couldn't take my eyes off the fight. Blood was on the line. I realized without looking that the other sunbathers had stopped whatever they were doing.

"Great," I heard one woman tell another. "Just what I came to Mexico for."

A few of the guys hopped up from their towels and ambled over for a ringside view. From his shorts, big guy pulled a pocketknife, flicked his wrist to open a mean-looking blade, and put the tip of it within an inch of Jorge's throat. Nothing like a little incentive to make a man drop his hands and stop struggling.

Everything in my vision was bleached out, unreal, static. The last gasp of a wave washed through Jorge's black hair. From beyond the line of palm trees and the trailer park just off the beach where Mila and I were camping, a restaurant jukebox in town played a Spanish version of "The Night Chicago Died."

"Whoa!" I heard myself saying. As I started forward, Mila yanked back on my arm.

"Roman, don't you dare!"

I suppose I should claim I was driven by an altruistic impulse that comes from being a Presbyterian minister's kid, but the truth is I've just got a bad habit of sticking my nose in where it doesn't belong.

"Someone's got to break it up," I said, prying Mila's fingers off me. Already moving, I threaded my way through what had grown into a dozen or so longhaired gawkers.

"Roman, if you go over there I swear I will never speak to you again!"

I stopped beside the imposing gringo, squatted down level with him, and didn't have the slightest idea what to say.

"*No hay, no hay*," Jorge whimpered.

"*No hay*, my ass!" the gringo yelled. "Where is it?"

Jorge glanced at me with so much pleading terror I caught myself thinking, Glad it's not me. One of his eyes was swelling shut into a nasty shiner. Keeping my voice lowered in a conversational I'm-OK-you're-OK tone, I told my fellow gringo, "You don't want to do this. He probably fucked you over big-time and you're mad."

"No *probably* about it!" Moose said without taking his eyes off Jorge. "Two weeks ago he walks up to me on the street in Acapulco, talking about how he's hungry. I buy him dinner and let him stay in my hotel room. Morning comes and he's long gone with my money belt. One in a million I'd ever see him again. You're looking at one sorry-ass, about-to-die motherfucker."

"You don't want to do this," I said again.

"The hell I don't!" To show he meant business, the white guy lowered the blade-tip against the soft spot on Jorge's trachea and punctured the skin. Blood trickled, pooled, and then slithered down the side of his neck. Jorge seemed to be trying to flatten out and press himself into the sand—a futile effort, but also one that was far less dangerous than swallowing.

"You want to rot in some Mexican jail for the rest of your life? You're mad. Think about what you're doing. It's not worth it."

I played the silence. Water lapped up to my feet, then receded. One of the guys close behind me said, "Listen to him, man." Then another voice, "I'm going for the cops."

"Fuck that noise," someone said with a cowboy twang. "Beaners need to learn they can't mess with us."

An asshole, I thought. That's all we need. Then another cowboy twang behind me, "Jay, butt out. We're a long ways from Oklahoma. For once in your damn life, don't go lookin' to start . . ."

"Otto, you know as well as I do that the sorry som'bitch did something to deserve it. Ain't a beaner alive ain't out to dick gringo."

I was hearing all of this without turning around, when the next thing I knew, someone as tall and lanky as me knelt down on the other side of the combatants. His thin-lipped grin, partially hidden by shoulder-length stringy hair the color of dishwater, suggested that he played by his own set of rules.

"Go ahead. Fuckin' cut out his gizzard. You know he's got it coming."

I figured he must be the one called Jay. Under the circumstances, his nonchalance threw me for a loop.

I told the aggrieved *Norte Americano,* "Put the knife down."

"Slice and dice," Jay said folksy-like. He leaned closer to Moose. "Kill him."

I looked over at Jay, thinking, What's your fucking problem? He stared back at me, that grin turning as slippery as it was crooked. He and I went into an angel-devil routine, fighting for Moose's conscience.

"Don't do it."

"Stick him good."

"Use your head."

"He fuckin' asked for it."

"Think."

"Do it!"

Didn't the big guy have sense enough to care about witnesses? Not by the looks of the subtle tick in his clenched jaw. Jorge stared off into space, no longer whimpering. I figured him for a classic example of the mind escaping even when the body can't.

From somewhere behind me, Mila yelled, "Roman, get away from there!"

I thought about lunging at gringo and wrapping him up long enough for Jorge to make his getaway. Then I'd hope to God that for those who belong to the brotherhood of tourists, one slit throat wasn't as good as another. Poised on the brink of playing hero, I heard someone down the beach yell, *"Policía!* Do not move!"

Looking up, I saw a couple of blue-uniformed policemen, both sporting mustaches, running toward us. They must have seen the goings-on from what I would later learn was the station up on a hill in town.

"Cops," I said.

Jay and I got up quickly and faded into the crowd, while the gringo tossed the knife away like he couldn't understand how it had found its way into his hand in the first place. One of the cops yelled in heavily accented English again, "Do not move!"

I distinctly remember that my first impression of the man I would come to know as Roberto Sánchez was that the harsh glaring reflection in the lenses of his mirror shades bore no resemblance to the day itself. Close behind him, his partner had his hand at the ready to draw a pistol from a hip-holster.

"OK, OK," Moose said, and slowly stood up just as Sánchez reached him. Without any hope of escape, he offered no resistance when his arm was twisted behind his back and a handcuff slapped on his wrist. Jorge, taking advantage of his new lease on life, jumped to his feet, pointed accusingly at his adversary, and started screaming in Spanish what must have been his side of the story. He dabbed at the small wound on his throat, then held his bloodied fingers out as proof that he was indeed the victim.

"*Cállate!*" Sánchez yelled. Then to his partner, "*Espósalo!* Cuff him!"

In a matter of seconds, Jorge, too, was handcuffed. The identical sobering, loser expression on both prisoners said it all: *Busted.* Sánchez rescued the knife from the surf for evidence and snapped the blade shut.

"*Usted está detenido,*" he told Jorge. Then to the gringo, "You are under arrest."

Fingernails dug into my arm, and without looking I knew that they belonged to Mila.

"Hey, the gringo's the one that got ripped off," Jay called out.

Sánchez let his partner and the prisoners go ahead of him up the beach toward town. Then with arms akimbo in a puffed-up macho pose that exaggerated his medium build, he took a slow, deliberate sweeping glance over the crowd like he was making a mental note of everyone there. His dark, challenging face with its broad nose, high cheekbones, and look of withering confidence was shaded more Indian than Latino.

"I am Roberto Sánchez," he told one and all, "*Jefe de Policía.* The men I arrested will tell me why they do this."

"And pay you off," Jay mumbled.

"What was that, *muchacho?*" Sánchez abruptly moved a few steps forward, cutting in two the space between him and Jay.

"Maybe you wish to join your friends?"

Jay must have thought better than to open his mouth again. Sánchez kept his eyes on him, giving him ample opportunity to change his mind. Then he smiled, a gold cap on one of his front teeth. "Welcome to Mexico," he told everyone. "I no like knives on my beach. Have a nice day."

We all watched the *Jefe* saunter boldly away down *his* beach. When he was more than twice the distance needed to be out of earshot, the bravest among us shared profound comments.

"Bummer."

"Dude isn't playing."

"Beaner pigs," Jay said, "they're all on the take!"

Mila hit me in the chest with her fist. "Scared me half to death, you jerk! What am I supposed to do in the middle of Mexico if you get yourself killed? And for what? A thief?"

"You can say that again," Jay said. "Fuckin' beaner ripped that gringo off sure as shit." I did my best to ignore him.

"Relax," I told Mila. She simmered, obviously tempted to punch me again.

A guy with buffed muscles and sun-bleached hair came over to Jay and said, "You're one big dick, ya know that? Always got to make bad into worse."

"Aww, Otto. Don't go gettin' all mad," Jay said. "Just havin' a little fun. Wanted to see if I could make the Mex shit his drawers."

"Could have fooled me," I said.

"I fool a lot of people," Jay replied. That grin of his made me bristle inside, but I tried not to give him the satisfaction of letting it show.

"Is that right?"

"Yeah, that's right. No hard feelings, I hope."

I looked into Jay's sizing-me-up brown eyes. With his long tapered face and smooth chin, I admit there was an oily sex appeal about him.

"Jay, one of these days you're going to start somethin' you can't stop," Otto drawled. It seemed like every move Otto made flexed a different set of muscles.

"What goes around, comes around," Jay replied. "You never know when they might have to find that out the hard way."

"Who's they?" I asked.

Jay looked at me like it was high time I wised up. "Fuckin' beaners! Who else?"

"Just think about how the hell we're going to get home stone broke, OK?" Otto said.

Others joined us, gathering around the impressions made in the wet sand by Jorge and Moose. No one stepped on them, like we were all afraid of contaminating the crime scene, until a wave lapped over and dissolved the evidence.

"Man, what the hell was that all about?" asked a guy with a scattering of freckles across his burnt cheeks.

"Something about getting ripped off," said a dude with his head covered in a blue kerchief tied in the fashion of a pirate.

"It's a drag." This from a small gringa who looked like she belonged in junior high. "There's been bad vibes from the locals ever since I got here a week ago."

"Really," said another hippie, and, "Really," someone else echoed.

"Hell, yes!" Jay said. "I talked to a gringo yesterday told me his backpack got stolen from his campsite while he was gone for a swim. Happened in broad daylight! Finds it on the beach, clothes scattered all over the place, wallet empty. *Adios* traveler's checks. Fuckin' locals want us to spend our money and vamoose. If they can steal it before we spend it, that's fine, too. Then there's always the federales. They sure didn't mind helping themselves to our cash."

"Well, if you had dumped the damn ashtray out the window

like I told you to before we drove up to that roadblock, they wouldn't have had any excuse to bust us," Otto said.

"Three measly seeds," Jay said. "I'm tellin' you, they planted them so they could shake us down to our last centavo."

"What happened?" Mila asked.

Jay looked her over. "Long story. Let's just say I don't much trust these taco-breath fuckers. It's time us gringos took out a can of whup-ass."

"A can of whup-ass," Mila giggled. "That's a good one." The way she smiled at Jay made me feel like I wasn't even there.

"Come by our campsite sometime, *señorita*, and I'll teach you some more good ones free of charge."

"Teach them to me, huh?" Mila said.

"Yes, ma'am. It'd be a pleasure."

I played it cool, adjusting my towel so that it hung evenly from my neck. People began to move on, no one interested in rumbling with the Mexicans.

"Let's go," I said, tugging on Mila's elbow for us to head back to our campsite.

"See ya later," Mila singsonged at Jay. I swear she would flirt with a eunuch just to prove she could give him a hard-on.

All Jay's talk about Mexicans ripping off gringos had put a whisper in my ear. Pretty dumb leaving our wallets at camp. I expected the worst.

2

A moment, please. Let's talk about how I process trauma. Let's start with when I was five. Either one of my two older sisters or I would sometimes accidentally leave the backyard gate cracked open. Quick as you please, Penny, our red dachshund, would squirt through to freedom and haul ass on those stunted legs up and down Oriole Street. She'd whip by you just beyond your grasp, only to do a wide, banking-with-her-whole-body turn in a neighbor's yard and come at you for another pass.

One breezy autumn day, I'm watching her through the screen
door, taking a sip off a sweaty tumbler of chocolate milk. Faster
than a speeding sausage, she rips up and down the block and cuts
back and forth across Oriole like there's some kind of method in
her madness. On the other side of the street, she goes into a bank-
ing turn around the O'Conners's front yard, and just as she starts
to tear back my way, I see the car. It's one of those big jobs—blue
with fins on the back—and it's coming a little too fast for what's
acceptable on a side street in a neighborhood full of kids. For some
reason I'm like this detached observer. There's the screech, then the
dull solid thud as Penny, not quite clearing the chrome bumper, gets
hit and spins 360 degrees. Everything goes quiet, like the whole
world's listening, and then there's Penny's desperate, high-pitched
yelping. She keeps on running with her back broken, dragging her
collapsed hind legs. She makes it to our curb, rolls onto the lawn on
her side, tries to right herself with a couple of spasmodic flops, then
gets quiet and lies still. I press my nose against the screen for a
closer view, but I can't say I'm upset, just very, very attentive. It
hasn't occurred to me to run out to Penny, like I'm still waiting for
a punch from reality that can't seem to find me. The driver—he's
got one of those Richard Nixon five o'clock shadows—looks out
his window at Penny as if to say *oops*. Then he glances around,
doesn't see any witnesses, stutter-steps the gas pedal, and drives off.

Celia and Dawn must have heard the yelping, because they
race downstairs from their bedrooms to the door, take one look
out the screen, and start bawling. Dawn fumbles with the door
handle, but my mother's not far behind and yells at us, "Stay put!"
She's one of those dark, green-eyed beauties who can still give guys
whiplash when she walks by. She goes flying out the door to see
how badly Penny's hurt. Usually, my sisters and I—only three years
apart in the pecking order—do nothing but fight; but right then
I'm trying to act adult, telling them everything's OK. I think I even
give Dawn—the oldest and by divine right the bully of our happy
trio—a consoling pat on the shoulder, but both of my sisters are so
upset they can't even see me. They keep bawling, stepping away
from the screen only to be drawn back to it. Neighbors come from

their modest brick houses: old Mr. Eiserson, who once used a broom to help my mother shoo a robin out of our house; Mrs. O'Conner, who always rang a bell when she wanted her kids to come in from playing; Tony, the grease-monkey high school boy whose hands were usually black from working on his car. I don't see any of my friends; they must all be off playing in the park a block away. Dad's at Saint James Church, doing whatever it is ministers do on a weekday. The grownups, including Tony, huddle around my mother kneeling over Penny, everyone staring and Mr. Eiserson shaking his head sadly. Penny dies.

Not happy enough for you?

Fast-forward three and a half months to the day before Valentine's Day. I'm at kindergarten. Miss Caffey hands out pieces of folded pink construction paper for us kids to make our mothers a valentine. She talks to us in a syrupy voice and is a dead ringer for Mrs. Santa Claus. When you're bad (anything from running in the classroom to talking out of turn), she sends you to the corner to read *The Rules*. They're written on a posterboard that's propped up on an easel. None of us can read, but to please Miss Caffey we mouth words and point at each one until she thinks we're sufficiently versed in them and ready to retake our places among the law-abiding kindergarten population.

We all love Miss Caffey.

Anyway, I'm at one of the tables with some other kids, I've got my piece of folded construction paper, and I grab the red Crayola out of the box before anyone else can get it. I draw a heart on the cover, then jazz it up with an arrow. At 3:15, I start home across the playground with my valentine clutched in my hand. I get a great idea. I'll think of something to say in the card, something real important so that my mom knows how much I love her, and I'll have one of my sisters write it for me.

When I get home, I recruit Celia for the job. I tell her what I want to say and Celia, all too eager to show off her first grade writing skills, goes right to work with a pencil at the dining room table.

The big day arrives. I'm the last one downstairs for breakfast. Everyone else is already at the kitchen table. I slip onto my stool next to Mom. There's a plate of fried eggs and toast cooling in front of me. Beaming, I present her with the card.

"Ooooo, pretty!" Mom says, then flashes the card at my dad at the other end of the table and at Dawn and Celia across from me.

"Pretty!" Dad chimes in. My sisters are too busy eating to take much notice. I can hardly contain myself.

"Open it, Mom!"

It takes her a moment to decipher Celia's bad spelling, but then she smiles bittersweet, like she's so touched she's about to cry. Instead, she reaches over and gives me a hug.

"I wrote it for him," Celia says, probably expecting a piece of the glory.

Mom passes the card to Dad. He's real tall and looks like JFK, except my father's hair is darker than the president's. When I see Kennedy on TV, I get the two men mixed up. Dad reads the inscription, gets this reflective sad expression, and says, "Son, we'll get another dog."

His concerned tone piques Dawn's interest. She grabs the card from him, takes one look at the inscription, and says, "That's stupid." Then to Celia—"And you misspelled *dead*."

"No, I didn't!" Celia says defensively.

"You're the one who's stupid!" I tell Dawn.

"Hey," Dad jumps in. "It's Valentine's Day. None of that."

I reach across the table, snatch the card out of Dawn's hand, and open it to make sure the words haven't magically changed overnight. Nope. Everything's fine. It reads:

End of story? This ain't no *Disney*. We get a new puppy—a half-cocker-spaniel-half-mutt. The pet store owner tells us it's a girl, so we name it Honey. A few days later, we figure out that

Honey's really a *he*, but the name sticks. Honey likes to grab my mom's used Kotexes that are neatly wrapped in toilet paper out of the bathroom trashcan. He goes and finds someone and drops the bloody *gift* at his or her feet. Then he stands there wagging his tail as if he's done something nifty and deserves a reward. Honey's odd habit never amounted to that big of a problem, except for a couple of times when my parents were entertaining company.

So much for Honey. Meanwhile, Dad becomes active in the nonviolent civil rights movement. No one, and I mean *no one*, is talking national holiday when it comes to Martin Luther King Jr.'s birthday. "Treat everyone equal" isn't such a difficult concept for a seven-year-old boy to grasp, but for other people, well, it's a little harder. Dad starts taking trips all over the country. Add a pinch of jail time for civil disobedience in Albany, Georgia, to a teaspoon full of freedom marches in Selma and Montgomery, Alabama, and before you know it, people in Saint James' congregation are saying, Uh-uh, Reverend Pearson. You stay home where you belong.

"It's not just the ones that hate you that make you tired," my father told me years later. "It's the ones that know better but won't take a stand."

There's no immediate drastic change in my life as a result of my parents' "liberal" politics. By the time I reach the fifth grade, I'm obsessed with baseball, Celia is falling in love with the piano, and Dawn is bumping up against puberty, fighting with Mom and Dad about how high she's allowed to "rat" her hair, or whether or not she can wear black nylons. Then one day, a kid on the playground calls me a "nigger lover" during recess. He's one of these big, miserable bully types who spends a lot of time cooling his heels in the principal's office for sassing his teacher. I haul off and give him a fat lip—not because he insulted me, but because he *thinks* he insulted me.

A few weeks later, the phone rings, and I answer it in the kitchen. A woman's voice is tense, commanding, and vaguely familiar.

"Let me speak to your mother."

Strangely, I want to please this voice.

"Moooooom!" By the time she comes up from the laundry room in the basement, I'm already back to playing with my electric road-race set in the living room. I can hear her through the dining room, a doorway, and over the whine of my racecar zipping around a small oval track.

"What? . . . Oh, is that so. Well, let me tell . . . My family can live wherever we damn well . . . *You* get out of the neighborhood! Who *is* this?"

I hear the slam of the receiver just as I push my thumb down a little too hard on the speed control, and the racecar wipes out on a curve.

"Who was it, Mom?" I call out.

"A sick person!"

Mom sounds angry at me, so I let it drop and listen to her tramping down the basement stairs. I pick up my racecar, fit its pin back into the track's groove, and press my thumb on the speed button again. As the car accelerates to a steady, whining rhythm around and around the oval, I keep hearing that vaguely familiar voice in my mind.

Dad holds out until the end of the school year. Then he says *fuck you* and resigns from Saint James. OK, those aren't his exact words, but don't let that long black robe fool you. He's thinking *fuck you*. Dad takes a job as a fundraiser for a community theater organization, and we move from the far northwest side of Chicago into Lincoln Park, a neighborhood on the near-north side.

I adjust to living in a gray stone Victorian house that's in good shape except for the leaky roof, rusted-out plumbing, faulty electrical work, busted furnace, and rotten window sashes. By the time high school rolls around, Dawn chooses to go to a public school outside our district, Celia is lucky enough to get into a private school on a scholarship, and me, well, the shit hits the fan across the country with school integration plans just as I turn fourteen. I end up at Waller, a mostly black and Latino public high school that's also fourteen percent white. Martin Luther King's barely cold in the grave. Black kids are so pissed off about everything from A to Z, they don't give a damn what my father or any other honky did during the civil rights movement. In four years, I've gone from giving a kid a fat lip for calling me a nigger lover to having members of the Cobra Stones and Latin Kings routinely shake me down for "chump change."

I survive high school without any scars—the kind that show, anyway—and minus the white guilt. Then I get a burr up my ass about how I've got to figure out what I want to do with my life, and I end up at Everett College, located just north of downtown on Lake Shore Drive. It's an alternative Arts and Communications school of several hundred students that thumbs its nose at more traditional institutions of higher education. There, I rub shoulders with the young, the hip, and the restless.

One day I'm in my ceramics class, throwing a pot on a wheel. Seated at several other wheels around me, students are hunched over lumps of clay at various stages of transformation. I can feel the heat from the huge gas kiln not far away in the corner of the double-story room. I've already "centered" the spinning wet clay, and I'm oh-so-carefully squeezing my fingers against both sides of an elastic mud wall. The pot begins to grow, taking on a wide, pregnant belly shape. If I let the clay get too dry, my fingers will rip the wall apart; apply too much water, the whole thing collapses. Suddenly, in the middle of all that concentration, I hear a woman's commanding voice somewhere deep in the instant-replay of my mind. *Let me speak to your mother.* And then it clicks. A stretch of the imagination after all those years? I swear I put the voice together with the face. It's Miss Caffey, my kindergarten teacher. Too unrealistic? OK, then someone just like her. And as the pot, guided by the steady pressure of my hands, nears completion, I think, Dad broke one hell of a rule.

CHAPTER 2

¡FUEGO!

Almost everywhere you looked in the trailer park—not much more than a shady grove of palm trees on the edge of town—a ragtag army of North Americans rocked in hammocks, fried fish in skillets over smoky campfires, and strung up wet clothes on lines. VW buses and pickup trucks, armed with eight-track or cassette decks, pumped out Carol King's melodic "You've Got a Friend," the acid rock of Deep Purple, Crosby Stills Nash and Young harmonizing in "Déjà Vu," James Taylor's "Fire and Rain." A syrupy, Spanish love song drifted from the open-air restaurant across the dirt road. Tucked along a barbed-wire boundary of the trailer park furthest from the entrance, a row of five mobile camper homes—one of them with a TV antenna sprouting from its roof—stood out like an exclusive suburb.

Sunlight cut through the canopy of palm fronds in irregular designs that skimmed over me and Mila as we reached our campsite—not much more than her green fishnet hammock and my red one strung to a triangle of palm trees in the middle of the trailer park. I quickly went over to my backpack propped against a tree, opened the top flap, and rummaged through it. Pulling out my wallet, I checked to make sure that the pesos and traveler's checks were still there, then gave a sigh of relief.

"That asshole had me all worried for nothing."

"He's right, you know," Mila said, digging her wallet out of her pack. "Mexicans think we're all rich, so why not rip us off?"

She opened the wallet. Nothing missing.

"That'll teach you not to generalize," I said.

"Hey, the Mexican busboys at work are always trying to swipe my tips. And people have the nerve to say whites are racist. Makes me sick. Better play it smart and always take our wallets with us." From her pack, Mila grabbed a change of clothes and a plastic bag containing a bottle of shampoo and Dial soap still in the wrapper. "I'm going for a shower."

I pick and choose my battles, and right then I chose not to be the great white defender of the Mexican people. That said, if Hispanic bus-boys ever got fed up with their slave wages and went on strike, I don't think there would be a rush of non-Hispanic job applicants lining up to take their place.

As Mila headed across the trailer park toward a roofless shower house built out of cinder blocks, I contented myself with admiring her beautiful ass. I needed a shower, too. I'd buried my other pair of cut-offs, shampoo, and shaving kit at the bottom of my pack. To get to them I was in the process of dumping out my multiple pairs of underwear and socks, tie-dye T-shirts, and other assorted essentials, when I heard a twanging "Hola, amigo."

I turned around and saw Jay at the other end of my hammock, his thumb hooked on a pocket of his frayed cut-offs as he leaned with one shoulder against a palm tree. The slant of its trunk looked like it was due to his weight. He must have followed us from the beach. In spite of his laid-back facade, I had the gut feeling that at any moment he might do something as lightning quick as snatch a fly out of the air. He probed me with his stare and asked, "Where'd you get these cool-lookin' hammocks?"

"Acapulco." Mila and I had killed time between flights shopping at touristy stores inside the airport. Hoping Jay would take a hint and buzz off, I grabbed the things I needed out of my pack and began reloading the things I didn't.

"How much you pay?" he asked.

"A hundred and forty pesos."

"Damn, amigo. Guess I just come from a long line of hagglers. Only paid eighty for mine."

"Really," I said.

"Really," he said.

I found that bargain-basement price hard to believe. Two could play this game.

"Picked up a hand embroidered Mexican wedding shirt for thirty-five." In truth, I'd paid fifty.

"Got me one for thirty."

"Really," I said.

"Really," he said. "Bought some *huaraches* for forty."

"Forty, huh? That's exactly what the lady I bought mine from at the airport tried to get me to pay. I got her down to twenty."

We went on comparing prices, the list of goods we'd bought almost identical to that of every other college-age, tourist pilgrim in Mexico. At the height of our one-upping each other, I noticed a butt-naked, tow-headed kid—not more than three years old—cutting across the trailer park past the campsite. He stopped, squatted, got a strained look on his face, and took an impromptu shit. Then he continued on his way, eyeing me with such demon-child insolent hatred that I dared not reprimand him.

"Lemme show you something, amigo," Jay said.

"To be honest, I was just on my way to the showers and . . ."

"*Un momento*. Won't take long."

I watched Jay dash down the lane that separated one row of campsites from another, his limber body moving with gracefully deceptive speed. He stopped off at a site a couple of lanes closer to the beach on the edge of the trailer park, then returned just as fast as he'd gone. Not even breathing heavy, he showed me something in the palm of his hand. It was an Indian face carved out of olive-colored stone.

"Bought it off a black-market guy at the Palenque ruins," Jay whispered secretively. "Solid jade, genuine Indian artifact. Illegal to take what they call national treasure out of the country, but shoot, I say that if possession ain't nine-tenths of the law, it oughta be. This thing's worth a thousand bucks easy. Paid three hundred pesos."

"Really," I said.

"Really," he said.

I reached down to a side pocket on my pack, opened the flap and took out an identical stone Indian face. This time I didn't have to lie.

"Bought it in a store from a guy who had boxes of them on a display table. Thought it might make a good paperweight. Twenty pesos."

I handed Jay my replica of an artifact. When he'd finished comparing it to his, the thought of telling him to pick his jaw up off the ground crossed my mind.

"Lying beaner som'bitch!" he yelled. "If I ever catch . . . Well, I bet it's jade."

"Don't count on it, amigo." I gave Jay a friendly pat on the shoulder. "See ya."

I hadn't gone far toward the showers before he finally got around to what he was really after.

"Say, what's the name of that pretty little *señorita* you were with on the beach?"

I stopped.

"Mila. Why?"

"Just askin'." Jay had already regained his folksy cool.

"She's with me." I stared at Jay so that my drift would put a crimp in his plans. If I succeeded, he did a superb job of not showing it. Then I went on. All the way to the men's entrance of the shower house, I felt his brown, cagey, deep-set eyes burning a hole in the back of my skull.

2

After our showers, Mila and I hoofed it into town for dinner. Picture a section of dirt road about a block long lined with small establishments, many of which looked as if they'd been slapped together with spit for nails. At the east end of town, directly across from the trailer park, a thatched hut (dubbed the Coco Cabana by the tourists) was already filled to capacity with hippies, all of them no doubt starving after a hard day at the beach. They shouted to hear each other over a jukebox playing the already dated hard rock tune, "Born to be Wild." Further along, on the other side of the road, *campesinos* in straw cowboy hats, their open shirts exposing sweaty chests, worked overtime on a new two-story brick hotel. They hammered, sawed, hauled mortar in buckets tied to ropes up to scaffolds, and, in the tradition of construction workers of many races and nationalities, occasionally blew kisses and gestured lewdly to women passing by in the street. Beyond the work site, a few restaurants—open-air thatched-roof shelters or canvas canopies with card tables and metal folding chairs underneath—catered to still more tourists and a few locals. The only building that didn't look like it could fold up and disappear overnight was the stucco *farmacia*, and past that, crossing the street again, a hut tripled as a grocery/hardware store/juice bar. Leaving town, the road climbed steeply, made a sharp bend that overlooked white-caps surging toward shore, then wound up the dry foothills past the airport and, as I would later learn, into the lush cloud forest mountains beyond.

As Mila and I entered "downtown," a rooster strutted in front of us like he thought he owned the right of way. Mongrel dogs, their rib cages protruding, slunk into restaurants and curled up on dirt floors under tables, waiting for bleeding-heart gringas and gringos to feed them scraps of food. We passed out of the range of "Born to be Wild" and into the sphere of another jukebox playing Mexican *umpa-umpa* music that was heavy on the accordion and trombones. A short way ahead of us, a dour-faced Indian girl, no more than ten, her braided hair trailing down her back same as all the local women, leaned out from the entrance to a restaurant and tossed a bucket of sudsy water into the street.

The aroma of frying red snapper, shrimp, lobsters, and other tasty creatures of the deep teased my nostrils. Taxicabs hauling people to the airport bounced through a pothole obstacle course, kicking up clouds of dust. One of the drivers slowed his cab down as he came from the other direction, stuck his head out the window at Mila, and imitated a long juicy kiss. Then he stepped on the gas. I suppose I should have been ticked-off instead of amused.

"Pig," Mila said. "Like I'm gonna jump in his car and give him a blowjob. In his dreams."

"There's always a chance," I said.

"Yuck! Just the thought."

"You know you want him."

"Shut up, Roman. Don't start, you'll give me one of my damn headaches."

"I'm only kidding."

She mimicked, "I'm only *kidding*. Do you have any idea how often you say that to me? Wears me out."

It is true that in the prime of my youth, I considered myself too funny for words. Bad mood again, I thought, the only explanation for her biting my head off that I could think of. We continued at a slow pace in silence. An ice-cream vendor pushing his freezer-on-wheels yelled out, "*Paletas de leche!*" A small Indian boy smiled at us as he passed carrying a chicken nearly as big as him upside down by the feet.

A longhaired dude eating with friends at one restaurant yelled to a group of hippies at another restaurant across the street, "You guys ready to party tonight?" Somebody let out a whoop, and both tables of gringos raised bottles of *cerveza* in salute to each other. All in all, Escondido had the feel of a boomtown on the move.

A voice called to us over the railing of a restaurant built only a single step above ground level. "Hey, Mila! Amigo!"

I turned and saw Jay motioning with his open palm to the two empty seats at his table. Otto, sitting across from him, casually waved hello as he swigged on a longneck bottle of beer.

"Care to join us?" Jay offered. "I guarantee you'll have trouble finding a table. Every gringo and his mother are in town for dinner."

Before I could turn down the invite, Mila was already stepping through the railing's doorway. Shit, I thought, following after her. This Jay jerk was becoming a bad case of static cling.

"Sure you don't mind?" Mila asked. "I'm starving."

"Take a load off your feet," Otto said. "If me and good-old-boy here have to look at each other much longer, I'm liable to get squirrelly."

"Squirrely?" Jay said. "Damn, Otto. Ain't we got enough problems on our hands without you goin' homo on me?"

"*Squirrely* don't mean no homo, dickhead. I'd fuck a knot-hole in a fence before your skinny butt any day."

"Uh, maybe we should come back some other time," Mila said.

"Yeah, we don't want to intrude," I added.

"Beg pardon," Jay apologized to both of us, doffing an imaginary hat. "Don't let any talk of butt fuckin' fool ya none. Otto and me are buddies—that's all. Anybody gets on your nerves when you've been stranded together for a whole fuckin' week."

"You can say that again," Otto said, brushing a curly lock of bleached hair off his sunburned face. His bulbous raw nose was peeling on top of its peeling. He glanced up at me. "Come on, man. Have a squat. We won't bite."

The cowboys were beginning to seem harmless enough. Mila and I pulled out chairs across the table from each other and settled into them. A couple of young Indian waitresses—sisters, judging from their similar looks—worked the five or six tables, tolerating customers who butchered the Spanish language trying to read off menus. To my right, past another table and below the bottom of a drab gray curtain, I saw the thick calves and feet of a woman moving about a kitchen no bigger than a closet. Every once in a while she called out just loud enough to be heard, and one or both of the waitresses would snap to and come running. A few feet to the right of the curtain, a man with a genial expression on his boyish round face sat in a chair holding a coconut on a wooden soda-crate in front of him, hacking away at the husk with his machete. I surmised, just as I would when entering Escondido's other restaurants, that the business was a ma-and-pa family-run operation. The father noticed me staring at him.

"*Hola!*"

I nodded, finding his broad, gold-tooth smile infectious. He must have been the tenth local I'd seen with a precious metal tooth in his or her mouth, a phenomenon I chalked up to some serious tooth decay in that town. Later in life, I would learn that the Indians thought of their dental work as a status symbol. Behind the father, out over the back railing of the restaurant and past a stand of palm trees, the beach, and several docked fishing boats, the waning sun threw a golden shimmer over the ocean.

Mila and I each grabbed a menu stuck between a sugar shaker and a bud vase with a plastic yellow rose. One of the waitresses fed some pesos into the jukebox and before long mariachi music soothed the soul.

"Uh-oh," I said, scanning the menu. "*No comprendo Español.*"

"Just say, *Numero dos*," Otto recommended. "Red snapper and french fries. Can't beat that with a stick."

"So what's this about federales planting dope on you?" Mila asked Jay. "Sounds like quite an adventure." She'd turned so far toward him in her chair, she seemed to be excluding Otto and me from the conversation. In her white tube top that left her shoulders and midriff bare, she'd never looked more self-aware of her physical beauty.

"Don't get Jay started on how the damn Mexicans fucked over us poor innocent gringos," Otto said, oblivious to Mila's body language. "He's goddamn obsessed is what he is."

"What happened?" Mila asked again.

"Well, maybe you can let what they did slide right off your back," Jay told Otto. "Me, that just ain't my natural disposition."

"Nothin' we can do about it now, Jay. It's *their* goddamn country."

"Shoot, you call this armpit a country?"

Discreet was not Jay's middle name. His raised voice had drawn the attention of a few tourists at other tables. I glanced around to check for a waitress within earshot, embarrassed, then remembered that they probably didn't understand English any more than I understood Spanish.

"I could be wrong," Otto said, "but last I looked at a globe, Mexico was on it."

"*What happened?*"

"Yeah, Jay, will you tell my girlfriend here what happened before she dies of an aneurysm?"

Mila flipped me the bird. I saw our tiffing register in Jay's keen opportunistic eyes. The weight of his forearm made the wobbly card table tilt his way.

"Well, *señorita*, like I was tellin' you on the beach, me and Otto here were drivin' down to Guatemala in our camper-truck, mindin' our own business . . ."

"Y'all wake me up when he's finished," Otto said. He slumped his chin to his chest, closed his eyes, and let out a snore.

"Mindin' our own business," Jay repeated, not letting Otto rattle him, "when five miles from the border we run into this federale roadblock out in the middle of nowhere. Must have been twenty of them. They make us pull over so they can search our truck. When they can't find nothin', one of them takes a second look-see. He runs his hand around inside the ashtray, then comes back out of the cab grinnin' big-as-you-please with three fuckin' seeds in his palm. Puts them right under my nose and says all snotty-like, '*Qué está?*' Shoot, *what's this* my ass. Som'bitch can suck on my *qué está*. He planted them sure as shit."

"You don't know that," Otto said, dropping all pretense of sleeping. "We *think* he planted them. It's not like you and me haven't been known to throw a few seeds away into the ashtray now and again." With a wink in my direction, Otto finished off his beer. He held up the empty bottle and yelled across the room at a waitress carrying a fried fish on a plate, "*Señorita, cerveza, por favor.*" Then to himself, "And keep them comin'."

"If I had licked that ashtray clean," Jay said, "he'd have still found those seeds. Next thing we know we're being hauled to the local police station in some scrawny town. They charge us with possession of narcotics and throw us in a cell with a stopped-up shitter. Smelled so bad I thought I was gonna puke. Things looked mucho bad, all right. We're talkin' ten years minimum in a beaner prison."

"For three lousy seeds?" Mila asked.

"Three seeds, three pounds, makes no difference in the land of *frijoles*," Jay said.

The waitress, midget-tall but sturdy, appeared and banged a fresh bottle of Sol beer on the table in front of Otto. She looked at us sullenly, pen and pad in hand, waiting for our orders. A chicken pox scar on the side of her nose blemished her otherwise flawless dark skin.

"Ladies first," Jay said.

"Why, thank you," Mila replied. "Such a gentleman."

I hoped my face didn't betray that this round with Jay wasn't going nearly as well for me as the last. We all ordered *numero dos* and a *cerveza*. The waitress wrote it down, then moved on without a word to another table.

"Stupid fuckin' peasant," Jay said. "She could at least say *gracias* for our damn business. Watch her screw up the order. She always does."

"Will ya give it a rest?" I said. "How the hell would you like to live in a town that's invaded by a bunch of people who can't even speak your language?"

"Just callin' it the way I see it, amigo. Besides, my money speaks Spanish just fine."

Mila gave me a do-you-always-have-to-be-such-a-liberal look. I couldn't help it; I'd been welcomed into many a Mexican friend's house while growing up in Lincoln Park—before the yuppies took over Chicago's near-north side.

"Face it, Roman," Mila said. "She's being rude because we're white. Did you see the way she banged Otto's beer down on the table?"

"Maybe she understands English more than we think." I had started out speaking to Mila, but finished my point with a hard-ball stare at Jay.

"I doubt it, amigo," Jay said, not even fazed. "Believe me, beaners don't need an excuse to be assholes. Give yourself another couple of days down here and you'll be singin' a different tune, I guarantee it."

"Ain't no big deal," Otto said. "I got me my beer, that's all that counts." He lifted the bottle to his lips, took a long swig, then set it back on the table half-empty.

"So go on," Mila told Jay, her tone buttery-pleasant.

"Where was I? Yeah, we'd been coolin' our heels in that cell for most of the day, when I decide it's time to make my move. I slip one of those beaners a fifty—American, that is—through the bars. Old-boy took one look at Ulysses S. Grant and his eyes popped open big as ping-pong balls. Next thing you know, it's *adios*, and we're back on the road. Fuck this vacation shit. We tear ass north toward the U.S. of A. just as fast as our truck can eat up highway. Could have been worse. We still got us $350 in traveler's checks. Home free, right? Shoot, free ain't nothing but a state of mind in old Mexico. I hadn't even had time to pass gas before we run into another federale roadblock out in the middle of nowhere. Som'bitches back in town must have radioed ahead that a couple of gringos with some tall cash were coming their way. Federales search our truck from top to bottom, then dump all our shit out in the middle of the road and search through that, too. When they come up empty, they go back to the truck for a second look-see. Well, what do you know; one of them just happens to find the burnt end of a roach in the crack of the seat. He smiles right at me, and then damn if he don't say, '*Qué está?*' I almost spit in his face. He planted it, but what can we do? It's his word against ours."

"He *probably* planted it," Otto said. "We can't be sure."

"Otto, whose fuckin' side are you on, anyway? You know something I don't?"

"I know you're a damn hot-head when you get yourself all wound up. Me or you could have dropped that roach any number of times we smoked a joint. It's as simple as that."

"I'll tell you what's simple," Jay said. "Them damn federales fucked us comin' and goin'." He looked over at Mila, his eyes narrowing as he leaned even closer to her. "Next thing you know, we're hauled to another police station. This time I know the score, so when the beaner in charge is taking us to a cell, I slip him a twenty-dollar traveler's check. Som'bitch rubs his fingertips together for me to fork over another check, and another. He cleans me out and then Otto except for one last twenty, just enough money to get us the hell out of his jurisdiction. Shoot, how we gonna make it to Oklahoma

City on twenty bucks? We aim for Acapulco—might have to push the truck the last hundred miles, but we'll deal with that problem later. Things could be worse; we could be eating beans and rice and gettin' butt-fucked for the next ten years, right? And it ain't like them federales ever did find our stash."

"You mean you *did* have dope on you?" I asked. "Where'd you hide it?"

"Trade secret," Jay said.

"Aww, don't go actin' like no one else knows how to hide a little dope," Otto said. "I taped the baggie to the underside of the spare tire. Can't deprive a man of his smoke."

"I'll second that," Jay said. "Once we got to Acapulco, we could go to the American Express office, tell them we lost our traveler's checks, and get new ones. There we are cruising up the coast, everything peachy, James Gang rock'n'rollin' on the tape deck, when just as we get a few miles outside of Escondido, some beaner on a tractor runs a stop sign and plows right into us. We go flying off the road and end up wrapped around a tree. We're OK, but the truck's totaled."

"See," Otto said, a beer-buzz smile on his face as he pointed at a long gash on the veiny underside of his forearm. "Musta caught it on the dashboard. My own damn fault for not wearin' my seatbelt."

"If we'd kissed that tree head on instead of slammin' into it sideways, it would have been *adios* gringos," Jay continued. "Truck's worth eight hundred bucks. Otto and I went in on it fifty-fifty so we could see the world. We can collect the insurance money and use it to fly home, right? Wrong."

The waitress returned with four bottles of Coke on a serving tray. She banged each one of them down in front of us on the table, then started away.

"I believe we ordered *cervezas*," Otto called out, but the waitress must not have understood that he was talking to her and didn't stop, disappearing behind the kitchen curtain.

"Told ya she'd fuck it up." Jay smirked at me.

Nice timing, I wanted to tell the waitress, and felt bad more ways than one.

"What a bitch," Mila said. "She probably did it on purpose."

Otto picked up his bottle of Coke, turned it back and forth in his hand like he was totally mystified, and drawled, "What the hell am I s'posed to do with a bottle of sody pop?"

"Drink it," I said. "I'm so tired a beer probably would've put me to sleep, anyway."

"Told ya," Jay repeated, not about to let me off easy. "These stupid fuckin' peasants can't find their way home, much less remember your order." When he'd made sure I'd gotten *his* drift, he turned back to Mila.

"Hell, it was a clear-cut case of whose fault it was. The beaner plowed right into us. He thinks, Uh-oh, and takes off running down the road quick as a jackrabbit. Me and Otto thumb a ride on an old hay truck that backfires all the way into town. Then we go right to the police station up the hill yonder and describe the peasant and the tractor that hit us to Sánchez—the *Jefe* himself. He listens all polite and everything, then laughs and tells us that the peasant works for some rich landowner that owns half the state of Oaxaca. His advice is to forget about trying to collect from Mr. Big, and that we better call our *seguro*—that's Mex for insurance. See, when you drive down here, they make you buy *their* insurance. We call the main office in Mexico City, and some woman says they'll fly out a claims agent right away. A day goes by. We call the lady again. '*Mañana*.' Same thing next day. Shoot, whole damn country operates on the *mañana* system. Tomorrow will be eight days. If Alberto hadn't put us up for free in his trailer park we'd a starved to death."

"Now that was damn nice of him, don't you think?" Otto asked.

"Shoot, Alberto only charges ten pesos a day to camp out," Jay said. "Ain't no skin off his rich butt. He owns the *farmacia* and half the town. He just feels guilty cause he knows his beaner brothers fucked us over. Can't wire home for money 'cause both our parents are on vacation. We're down to thirty-eight pesos between us. Livin' lean, if you know what I mean."

"You poor guys," Mila said, patting Jay's hand resting on the table.

"Hell, least we're stuck where it's awfully pretty," Otto said. "I keep telling Jay to kick back and enjoy the scenery. My folks will come through soon as they get home in a few days."

"Let me and Roman buy you guys dinner," Mila said. "That's the least we can do."

I gave her a look.

"Fine, Roman. I'll pay for them myself."

"It's not like we're rollin' in dough," I said. We both had another semester of school before we graduated from Everett College—Mila as an art major, me in liberal arts with a creative-writing minor. On my part-time bartender's salary and her waitressing, we'd scrimped to pay for a bare-bones vacation.

"Don't be so cheap," Mila said.

Before I could defend my frugal spending habits, Jay accepted Mila's offer.

"That's real kind of you, *señorita*. Appreciate it."

Great, I thought, tapping my fingers on the white oilcloth. Fucking great. My eyes traveled across the room to the father swinging his machete, the blade cutting decisively into a coconut husk. Otto seemed like a nice enough guy to help out, but as for Jay, if every word of his story were true, it couldn't have happened to a more deserving low-life. My legs felt cramped under the card table. No matter which way I moved my feet, they bumped into someone else's.

"Oh, look at the cute dogs," Mila said. She snapped her fingers down by the floor. "Here, pooches."

I looked over my shoulder and saw a couple of mongrels slinking closer to our table. One of them, a bitch whose tits hung low from too many litters, wagged its tail. Suddenly, the father of the family-owned establishment jumped to his feet, machete in hand, and charged across the dining area, hissing at the dogs. They cowered, ears pulled back, but didn't opt for the easy escape out the doorway. Instead they hunkered down closer to the dirt floor, probably driven by hunger. The Mexican owner reared his foot back and gave the bitch a solid kick to the belly. Mila gasped and threw her hand over her mouth. Without so much as a yelp or a snarl, the dog absorbed the blow, then slunk with its passive-resistance partner around the father, all the while staying out of reach of his machete thrusts. They retreated under a table, protected by a jungle of tourists' legs. Every conversation in the restaurant had come to a halt as horrified gringos and gringas waited for the man's next unpredictable move. On the jukebox a lovesick crooner poured out his heart. The owner glowered at the dogs, machete poised. Then, as if realizing he was upsetting his patrons, he grudgingly went back to his chair, sat down, and picked the coconut off the floor. He set it on the crate and began hacking away with his machete again.

A woman with a mooning, blue-eyed face reached her hand below her table and stroked the head of the bitch. "There, there, it's OK, you're with friends now."

The dog lifted its head, laid its snout on the woman's knee, and stared up at her with a victimized look so convincing the dog must have practiced it in front of a mirror.

"Aww, you're just hungry, aren't you, girl?" Moon Face cut off a piece of fish on her plate with her fork and let the dog eat from her hand. The other dog inched closer to nose away the first in the event of another hand-out.

"What did those poor animals ever do to him?" Mila asked. "I'll never eat here again, that's for sure."

"Mexicans don't respect life," Jay said. "Dogs around here would starve to death if it weren't for us tourists, I guarantee it."

"Sure could use another beer," Otto said, looking bummed.

I reached for my Coke and grasped the sweaty coldness in my hand. The father had violated my middle-class sensibilities as much as the next gringo's. I was hungry. I wanted to eat.

3

After dinner, Mila and I had just stepped out into the street with our cowboy companions, when I felt my gut squeeze into a cramp. Damn, I thought. Ate too fast. A little Indian girl in a white cotton dress approached us carrying a heavy tin bucket that made her walk with a starboard list. She pulled back a cloth inside of it and revealed steaming packets individually wrapped in cornhusk.

"Tamales," she said, soft as a squeak. "*Dos* pesos."

"Oh, you are too cute for words," Mila said, stooping with hands on knees to meet the girl on her level. "What's your name, sweetheart? *Como se llama?*"

The girl hesitated, her brown eyes as savvy as they were innocently curious. Then she rewarded Mila with a shy smile.

"Consuelo."

"Consuelo," Mila repeated. "That's a beautiful name. What a gorgeous braid. Bet that took a long time to grow. You are just too adorable! Can I wrap you up and take you home with me?"

With a kid's natural inclination for the limelight, and a sale to be had, Consuelo offered Mila a bigger smile.

"I'll buy one of them tamales," Otto said.

"We just ate," Jay said. "Like we got money for dessert?"

"Aww, the kid's gotta make a living." Otto shoved his hand into one of his cut-off pockets and fished around for a couple of coins. "I can use a tamale for a late-night snack."

"I'll take three," Mila said, reaching into her purse. "I mean, *tres, por favor*. Isn't she adorable?"

"Extremely," I said, and meant it. As Mila peppered Consuelo with more compliments that the girl couldn't possibly have understood, I saw Jay mouth the words *stupid fuck* to Otto. Then Otto's look of *Wha'd I do?* Sale finished, Consuelo went on her starboard-listing way.

"*Adios*, honey," Mila called after her. Consuelo waved. "Did you see that? She likes me!"

"Yeah, ain't she adorable," Jay said.

My stomach wrenched with another cramp. I knew that the intestinal revolt would only worsen, and told Mila, "I don't feel so good. I better go get some Tums at the drugstore."

"Try a beer," Otto said. "Settles my stomach every time."

I took it for granted that Mila would tag along with me, but instead she said, "OK, see you at camp." Without a second thought, she started down the road with Otto and her new buddy.

I stood there in the road like an idiot holding his dick, watching them moving away. Then I hurried off in the opposite direction. From behind me I heard Jay saying, "So you're an artist, huh? My cousin's an artist. Lives in New York. He could hook you up with a few gallery owners. I guarantee it."

Give me a fucking break, I thought. Just be cool. She'll see through him. Making a mental effort to wipe any trace of jealousy off my face, I cut a diagonal across the empty street.

The glow of the *farmacia's* bright fluorescent ceiling bulbs had pulled even with the light of the diminishing day, setting off the small modern building even more from the rest of the ramshackle town. I stepped through the store's wide-open front side past three old geezers sitting in chairs near a magazine tree-rack. They all wore straw cowboy hats, their faces buried in comic books, a form of entertainment popular with young and old alike in Mexico. Two short aisles of sundries took up half the store, a counter the other half, behind which a slight man wearing a pharmacist's jacket sat on a stool reading a newspaper stock index. Castillian light skin, thinning dark hair slicked back, sharp nose, and impeccably trimmed mustache, he looked like a refined gambler.

I went up to the counter, paused awkwardly because of the language barrier, and said, "Medicine, stomach, *por favor*." I broke into a pantomime, rubbing my hand in circles over my belly and affecting what must have been a near-death expression.

"What kind of medicine?" the druggist replied in fluent English. "Lomatil? Tums? Pepto Bismol?" I felt like a fool.

"Tums."

He hopped off the stool and pulled a bottle from below the counter.

"*Seis* pesos."

I took out my wallet and gave him the money. With my stomach screaming for instant relief, I flipped the plastic lid off the bottle, poured out a couple of tabs, and downed them. The druggist leaned his elbow on the Formica counter top, propped his chin in his hand, and looked at me as if amused.

"*La Turista*?" he asked.

"No, la eat-too-fast."

"Been in Escondido long?"

"Got in today."

"It is hard not to eat fast here," the druggist said. "The food is so good—fresh from the ocean. And cheap."

I nodded. Then, thinking about how Mila and I had footed the bill for Jay and Otto—"Could have been cheaper."

"Cheaper?"

"Never mind," I said.

"This town is a good deal for you *Norte Americano* kids. You can live like a king for next to nothing."

"I'm not complaining," I said.

Already the Tums had begun to reverse the tide of battle in my stomach. The druggist asked me where I was from. When I told him *Chicago*, he pretended to hold up a tommy-gun and shoot me full of lead—"A-a-a-a-a-a-a."

"Yeah, Al Capone, that's me. You better give me these Tums for free if you know what's good for you."

The druggist belted a hearty laugh, then reached out and offered his hand for me to shake.

"Alberto Huerta, at your service."

Him, I thought, then said, "When the heat's not on, I go by the name Roman Pearson."

The firmness of Alberto's grip as we shook hands surprised me, like he believed in making a manly first impression in lieu of his small size. Suddenly, I heard a barking racket in the road. A pack of dogs had surrounded an Indian man passing by the *farmacia*. He kicked at the mongrels, barely keeping them at bay while their fast paw-work sent up a cloud of saffron dust. I recognized the bitch from the restaurant, her canine teeth bared as she snarled and lurched, threatening to take a chunk out of the Indian's leg. The dogs' turn-the-other-cheek philosophy must not have applied in the street. Two of the senior citizens reading comic books didn't even bother to take notice of the confrontation, but the third glanced up just long enough to dismiss the dog nuisance as old hat, then went back to his comic. A longhaired gringo came out of a restaurant across the road. The dogs, immediately recognizing the difference between a local and a tourist, broke off their attack and followed merrily after the potential benefactor with their tails wagging.

"What's with man's-best-friend around here?" I asked.

"Ah, yes, the dogs," Alberto said. "You think we are mean to them, no?" He waited for an answer but got only my polite smile. "They are a filthy health hazard. Con artists, every one of them. Always begging off the tourists. Tell me something. If a dog wandered into a restaurant in Chicago and sat by your feet, would you give him some of your food, or complain to the owner?"

He had a point.

"Complain."

"You would be outraged. But here for some reason these pests are considered cute. I do not understand. Believe me, they are not cute. They carry diseases, bite children, and multiply like rats."

"Strays, huh?"

"Yes, that is the problem. If we do not do something about them soon, they will overrun the town."

I noticed one of the old men holding out his comic book to another seated next to him, apparently offering a Donald-Duck-for-a-Woody-Woodpecker swap. The second geezer kept shaking his head, arms folded stubbornly across his chest. He was driving a hard bargain.

"This town must be doing all right from all the tourism," I said. "People are calling Escondido the next Acapulco."

"Oh, really." Alberto indicated the entire town with a sweep of his hand. "I would say we have a ways to go."

"Yeah, but the tourism's probably already pumped some major bucks into the local economy, don't you think?"

Alberto shrugged. "The tourists are good for the economy, but they are mostly spoiled college kids who cannot afford Acapulco and are used to Mommy and Daddy paying for everything. They do not understand how things work around here. These people are Indians—very poor, very ignorant, very Catholic. The tourists just want to have a good time drinking, smoking marijuana, skinny-dipping in the ocean. Do you have any idea the effect a naked white woman has on these men? And better not let the police or federales catch you with illegal drugs or you will find out just how far away from home you really are. No, when in Mexico, it is up to the *Norte Americanos* to understand *us*. Otherwise, there are problems."

"Like what?"

"Misunderstandings. Believe me, I am constantly coming to the rescue of kids who are—how you say?" Alberto snapped his fingers a couple of times as if that would help him to recollect the words he was after in English.

"Wet behind the ears," I suggested.

"Hmmm, yes, that will do," Alberto said. "They think they are immune to our laws and customs. Mexico justice is much different than in your country. Here you are not innocent until proven guilty; you are guilty until you give the right people some money. We call it *la mordida*—the bite. It is not such a bad way of life once you get used to it."

I thought of one gringo I wished Alberto hadn't taken on for a charity case, but I let it ride.

"You grew up around here?" I asked.

"Me?" Alberto looked perturbed. "Of course not. I am from Mexico City. We are not all peasants. I am only putting in time here. Five years."

"Five years?"

"Why, by then Escondido will be the new Acapulco, and I will make lots of money and buy a mansion in Mexico City and a summer home in Connecticut and live happily ever after." Alberto laughed. "Escondido, the next Acapulco. That is a good one."

He was having fun at my expense, but I liked him anyway. I picked my bottle of Tums off the counter.

"These did the trick. Thanks a lot."

As I turned to leave, Alberto smiled, showing off a set of pearly white, straight teeth.

"Come back anytime, Big Al."

When I got to camp, Mila wasn't there. I climbed into my

hammock, rocked back and forth, and did a slow burn. We'd planned this little trip in a last ditch effort to work out our differences and avoid breaking up, and here she was traipsing off with a racist hick like Jay—not exactly a promising start to our "new beginning." What the hell did she see in that redneck? If I were to play junior psychologist, I'd say her attraction to Jay had something to do with her fucked-up relationship with her father, but I'm not into dwelling on all that Freudian shit. Overreacting, I thought. Harmless flirting. No big deal.

Cocooned in the hammock, I tried to relax. Tape decks had all fallen silent, many people still in town for dinner, off to the showers, or on the beach to watch the tail end of the sunset. I watched the sun going down in all its glory beyond the palm trees and last row of campsites, a day-glo pink orb dipping lower and lower beneath the rim of the silvery ocean, the entire western sky brushed in red, orange, yellow, and lavender. I stared for a long time, the sun surrendering, colors slowly fading. Stars popped out one by one. An hour later they were thick as a bowl of celestial Cheerios.

I thought I heard Mila's laughter once or twice, stabbing above the diminishing chatter of campers inside tents or gathered around the last embers of cooking fires. In the "suburb," a mobile home's screen door banged shut, then a mother's shrill voice in English, "I thought I told you to get in here before dark!" I refused to go looking for Mila. This is bullshit, I thought. Fuck her. Betrayal nestled in a tight ache behind my eyes. Something had to give between us, give soon, but not wanting to think about what that *something* might be, I escaped into sleep.

I was awakened by Mila climbing into my hammock. It must have been late, the trailer park dead silent, a high three-quarter moon shining down through the fronds of palms like a soft floodlight. Still within easy reach of the dream world, I let the distant crashing surf lull and comfort me. Mila didn't say a word, just threw her leg over mine, ran her fingers in and out of my curly locks, and kissed me gently, then harder. I suppose I could have ruined the moment by asking her where the hell she'd been, but I didn't and instead wrapped my arm around her waist, losing myself in the familiar, lemony shampoo scent of her hair. Each slow, prolonged kiss and nuzzle pulsed with meaning. The need to fuck took a back seat to the need to hold. I interpreted her sudden passion as *I love you,* but now, looking back years later, I should have read it more as *Stop me.* It didn't last long, this final, perfect, one-with-each-other-and-the-universe gasp between us, before we drifted off to sleep.

I awoke to shouts of *"Fuego! Fuego! Fuego!"* coming from someone running down the road. The moon must have completed its arc and disappeared.

Mila started awake and lifted her head off my chest. Then a gringo's voice a few campsites away, "Fire! Fire!"

I smelled smoke. Beyond the custodial hut at the entrance to the trailer park, and through the last of the palm trees in the direction of town, flames lashed up, glanced about opportunistically above the fronds, and then ducked out of sight again. Already, dark silhouettes of gringos rushed past our hammocks, their footsteps hushed by the sand.

"Come on, let's go see," I said, not wanting to miss the excitement.

Mila's head fell to my chest again, and she groaned. I shook her, repeating, "Come on."

She must have been weighing whether or not to give up the security of our snuggling for the thrill of fire. She let out a long exhale, then a reluctant, "OK."

We reached the road and immediately saw that the restaurant where we'd eaten dinner a hundred yards away was ablaze, downtown lit up bright as day.

"Look at that!" Mila said.

Angry curtains of flames enveloped the kitchen and dining area, swarmed over tables and chairs, and breathed in and out between railing spindles along the open walls. The last untouched side of the conical thatched roof ignited with a *whooosh!*

"Man!" I said, standing in the road mesmerized for a moment by the fire's greedy hunger, power, and beauty as it shot higher and higher into the starry night. Then adrenaline kicked in. *Should help!* Assuming Mila would follow, I sprinted as fast as I could in flip-flops to join a bucket brigade of locals and gringos organizing into a line across the road. The closer I got, the more I heard the fire's crackling, sucking draft. Frantic voices yelled out in Spanish and English:

"*Ándale!*"

"Hurry up with the water!"

"Doesn't anybody have a fuckin' hose in this town?"

I reached the human chain and plugged a hole between an Indian man and a gringa just in time to help pass a heavy bucket filled with water. When the bucket reached a tall longhair at the front of the line, he heaved a stream into the inferno. The fire beast let out a scornful hiss and a burst of smoke, then instantly healed itself, raging.

"Keep it moving!" someone yelled.

The gringo ran with the bucket across the road to a water spigot sticking up from a pipe. Everyone in line rotated forward. Other locals, men and women alike, rushed down the road from nearby homes carrying buckets, dish pans, and pots filled to the brim with water. They handed them to people in the bucket brigade or threw the water onto the flames themselves.

"And to think I was asleep five minutes ago," said the gringa next to me, an eerie incandescent light on her ruddy, eager face.

"No shit," I said, and for some reason it struck me that I was far, far, far away from home.

We kept the buckets moving, my cheeks feeling more and more toasted the closer I got to the fire. Overhead, billowing smoke drifted inland, and somewhere out in the vast darkness of foothills a couple of dogs howled a lonesome duet. It was my turn.

"Let her rip!" the gringa said, handing me a bucket. I swung it aiming for the center of the dining area, water flying. There was another scornful hiss, then sizzling on a charred metal table top like spit on a hot iron. A mob of flames parted, hemmed and hawed, worked up its courage, and swooped in to reclaim lost territory. *Die!* I thought, running for the spigot with my empty bucket.

Soon it became clear that our voluntary-fire-department effort was too little too late. With a loud *snap,* the roof caved in, some-one shouting, "Look out!"

A sea of sparks shot up, and we all stepped back, some people shielding their eyes. Sparks turned to ash, settling. A tin bucket clanked on the ground. The fire beast, having smothered its own draft, mellowed into a steady burn. Folks called it quits: "Kiss that one good-bye." "That's all she wrote." "At least we tried."

A few more Mexican men tossed buckets of water into the blaze, then stood aside. The human chain dissolved into small seg-regated groups of locals and tourists. I joined a few gringos in the middle of the road.

"A shame," someone said.

"No big deal," added another guy. "Won't take more than a week to rebuild—tops."

"Easy for us to say," I put in. "It's not our livelihood."

Suddenly I thought of Mila. In my haste to play good Samaritan I'd forgotten all about her. It took several quick glances around before I spotted her with Jay past the crowd and over by the *farmacia.* Perfectly framed in the store's metal shutter that reflected the fire's ominous light, they were locked in conversation, leaning close to each other, not touching but violating each other's space with the intimate permission of lovers. I felt something plunge in my chest and gut, then go dead. *Please don't do this.* What was the matter with her? Missing a marble when it came to men? At that moment I loved and desired her more than I could bear. Naked defeat no doubt smeared all over my face, I sup-pressed an urge to kick some cowboy ass. Easy, I thought. Take it easy.

A loud angry voice distracted my attention. Nearer the burn-ing restaurant, the father of the family who owned it was vehe-mently explaining something in Spanish to several other men. A friend put his hand on the owner's shoulder to calm him down, but the ruined man turned away in a huff, flinging the plastic bucket he held into the fire. It landed on top of the collapsed roof and half melted, curling into a fist. Locals began to debate something that all of us tourists could only guess at. Casting an accusing eye at *Norte Americanos*, the owner yelled in a challenging tone, *"Quien hizo esto?"*

"What's with him?"

"Pissed about something, that's for sure."

"Poor guy, I'd be pissed too."

The owner stepped up to the tall hippie who'd helped on the bucket brigade and shoved him with both hands.

"Hey, man!" the gringo said, catching his balance. "What's your problem?"

Jefe Sánchez, dressed only in a white T-shirt, blue police trousers, and worn leather sandals, moved quickly out of the crowd of locals and separated the two. Other Mexicans were giving confused tourists a piece of their mind. A squat Indian woman, no taller than my chest, rushed up to me and began ranting, flicking her hands to shoo me away. I made out the words *Estados Unidos*. She was telling me to go home to the United States?

"Cállate!" Sánchez shouted. *"CÁLLATE!"*

Everyone stopped. In the ensuing quiet a corner of the restaurant's roof collapsed further and smashed a card table. Sánchez addressed the locals in Spanish, the gist of which I took to mean, *I'll handle this.* Then in English he said, "Restaurants do not burn with no help. If anyone has *información* who made the fire, I am in the *policía* station up the hill. I will find him."

"You think one of *us* did it?" said the moon-faced woman who had fed the starving dogs. She stepped forward but kept a respectful couple of yards away from Sánchez, staring at him with the astounded look of the wrongly accused. "That's bogus, man. We're out here helping just like everybody else."

Other tourists pleaded their case with Sánchez.

"It takes one bad person to cause the trouble," Sánchez said. He looked around at tourists like we were all suspect. Then, "It is late. There is no more to see. Everyone go."

Torched? I'd assumed a gas leak. Sánchez said something more in Spanish, and the gathering broke up, people heading both ways down the road. The restaurant owner started arguing with him again, stomping around, gesticulating wildly. Sánchez kept his cool, repeatedly shaking his head. And then a creepy feeling traveled up my arms and neck, my eyes pulled toward the *farmacia*. I saw Mila slowly coming toward me, but Jay hadn't moved, watching the flames across the road with an expression of barely disguised, intoxicating power-run-amok. A ridiculous theory took root in my head. Whoa, I thought. Revenge against Mexicans? Then why target that particular family? Jay had taken the waitresses' bad attitude and lousy service personally? The theory kept knocking around in my head like it needed more space.

"Guess what Jay thinks?" Mila asked as she approached me.

"Something brilliant, I'm sure."

"He says that police chief, Sánchez, set the fire just to blame it on the gringos."

I looked at her, mad as hell.

"That's the stupidest fucking thing I ever heard."

"Jesus, what's with you?"

"I'm not blind, Mila, OK?"

The way she looked a touch too perplexed let me know that she knew exactly what I was talking about. I started down the road toward camp without her, but she hurried to catch up, grabbing me by the arm.

"You mean Jay? I was just talking to him. What's the big deal?"

"I'm not blind," I repeated. As we walked in silence, she nudged against me with her shoulder—a peace offering. Headlights rushed toward us, the driver honking for people to get out of the way. We leapt aside as Alberto roared past in a red jeep with a roll bar. From his house somewhere in the hills he must have seen the foreboding glow illuminating the night. He screeched to a halt in front of the burning hut, cut the engine, and jumped out with a fire extinguisher. Flitting about, he blasted the fire from all sides with retardant. The town grew darker and darker, until there was only the blanket of stars above to guide people home. Mila and I felt our way down the road, the murmur of conversations and feet scuffing dirt all around us.

"Can hardly see," Mila said, staying close again. "This is scary."

Her fear and reliance on me to lead the way gave me hope.

"I'll get us there," I said.

Not far behind, I heard a woman telling someone else, "Follow the voices." Others were counting on me. I strained to make out the tall wooden fence posts that marked the trailer park entrance by the side of the road.

"Jay's interesting, that's all," Mila said.

"Yeah, real interesting. A regular artist when it comes to playing with matches."

Looking back these many years later, the jury in my mind was far from returning with a verdict as to Jay's guilt or innocence, but my jealousy made it convenient for me to accuse him of the crime, anyway.

"What are you talking about?"

"Fucking open your eyes, Mila."

Her not responding told me that I'd given her serious reason for pause. I moved toward something tall and straight . . . reached out and touched one of the rough fence posts. Looking directly overhead, I saw the crossbeam of the entrance against the stars.

"This way," I said, loud enough for others to hear. Mila hesitated.

"Are you sure?"

"Yeah, I'm sure." We entered an even darker blackness under the canopy of palm trees, the hard ground changing to soft sand. Slowly my eyes adjusted, and rows of campsites emerged out of shadows.

"Not much further. Don't let go."

In the morning, before Mila awoke, I took a quick dip in the ocean to wash off the stench of smoke. But the real smoke from that night would prove much harder to get rid of.

CHAPTER 3

GIVING THANKS

A little over a year earlier, 1974, I met Mila at Everett College—an arts school crammed into a converted warehouse on Lake Shore Drive just north of the old "S curve." That hairy portion of the six-lane road spanning the Chicago River—site of many a fender-bender—is long gone now, torn down and rebuilt straighter and two lanes wider. I would leave my creative writing classroom on the fifth floor at 1:00 on Tuesdays and usually see Mila in the hallway as she made her way toward the art department carrying a large portfolio that hung to her ankles. Afraid that any woman as gorgeous as Mila was out of my league, I would sail past her without so much as a friendly nod. If my radar didn't pick up any trace of her blip, I'd sit down on the brown speckled tiles with my back against the wall, pretend to read *Sons and Lovers* or *Crime and Punishment,* and wait for her to swing around the corner. This too-shy-to-break-the-ice routine went on for an agonizing month, until one day, as bell-bottom-and-flannel-clad students navigated around my outstretched legs, I saw Mila coming straight toward me. Mustering courage, I jumped to my feet right in front of her and said in a rush, "Hi I'm Roman would you like to have lunch?"

Startled, Mila leaned away from me. Then she gave me the once-over, must have liked the merchandise even if the delivery was a little rough around the edges, and smiled.

"Sure."

Over the next couple of weeks, whenever we both had time

to kill before classes, we got in the habit of eating lunch together at Herman's, a greasy-spoon on Ontario next door to school, or taking walks along the lakefront. It was already mid-November, but a rare Indian summer held the city in a warm bubble that refused to burst. We would cross the Drive at the Ontario light and stroll hand-in-hand on the wide concrete breakwater north along Lake Michigan. The water level, at a record high, dipped and swelled, washing over the path and threatening to drown our gym shoes if we didn't stay alert and nimble. Other times we headed due east from school, passing Lake Point Tower, its brown, curvy glass walls reflecting the sun, and into Olive Park, deserted except for a sleeping wino or two who'd set up house-keeping on benches.

One particular day, we went leisurely along Olive Park's walkway, occasionally stopping for quickie make-out sessions, then continued on blissfully lost in a lovers' swoon. The inevitability of fucking each other's brains out for the first time was only a convenient opportunity away. On our left, past a wrought-iron railing and down a slanting wall of huge boulderlike rocks, the lake stretched oily calm along the shoreline; on our right, in the park's grassy field, three small man-made hills, shaped like upside-down bowls, were topped by the empty circular pools of dormant water fountains. We reached a deck overlooking the lake, and I sat on a cement bench with Mila in my lap. Down below, I heard water lapping against rocks, and far out on the lake, a pumping station, sharply outlined in the mid-afternoon light, looked tempt-ingly desolate.

Mila nuzzled her nose against mine and asked, "Wanna come over to my house for Thanksgiving next week?"

"Yeah, that sounds good." A commitment to spend the holi-day together made it official: Mila, a babe among babes, was my girlfriend.

"Just so you're forewarned, my family's a little weird," Mila said.

"Everyone's family is weird." I pecked her with a kiss. "Don't worry about it. My Texan granddaddy always says, 'Two things stink after three days—fish and family.'"

"No, Roman. I mean *really* weird."

"Weird how?"

"Well, for starters, they're D.P.'s—you know, 'displaced persons.' My mom's German and my dad's Yugoslavian, but he hardly speaks English. They came here after World War II and aren't exactly what you'd call educated."

The drone of traffic from the Drive carried out over the park. There was a light breeze.

"They were smart enough to make you," I said, rubbing the line of Mila's exquisite vertebrae through her blue work shirt. "I owe them big-time for that."

She stared at me all gushy-eyed, touched my lower lip with her finger, and said, "You are so incredibly sweet."

"Parents always like me," I bragged. "I'll charm their socks off—have them eating candy out of my . . ."

"Oh brother." Mila rested her forehead against my shoulder. "This should be interesting."

* * *

So a week later I'm at the Popovic home in West Rogers Park, at that time a mostly Jewish neighborhood. The entire block where Mila lived was made up of modest brick Georgian-style homes. I got stuck in the living room with Semo, Mila's father, while Mila and her sisters, Vera and Nada, and their mother, Hilda, finished whipping up the Thanksgiving feast in the kitchen.

Semo, a short, swarthy man over sixty, sat grim-faced at the opposite end from me on an L-shaped, sectional couch. Plastic slipcovers protected the white cushions. Lost in his own thoughts, Semo looked like one compact piece of muscle, the result of hard years slinging cargo on a loading dock. As I tried to relax, plastic crinkled with my every move. I smiled uncomfortably at Semo, clueless as to how you shmooze someone who barely understands English. Glancing around the room, on the wall behind Semo I took in the schlock print of a windmill in a golden meadow, and on the glass coffee table, bric-a-brac boy and girl figurines dressed like Swiss peasants seemed to be beckoning me to come frolic with them in the Alps. Something happening on the street outside the picture window must have taken Semo's attention, because he popped up and hobbled over to investigate.

Peering around the edge of a yellow curtain, he bent a tall rubber tree out of his line of vision, spying on a situation that I couldn't see from my angle on the couch. Soon his whole body shook with rage, a vein popping out on his thick neck. He cut the air with a fist, shouting, "Shit garbage Jew! Park my house son bitch Jew! I get gun!"

Maybe my translation was the problem. After all, I've seen many a Mexican look at me cross-eyed trying to understand my pidgin Spanish. But I could have sworn the old guy had just burned my ears with some of the worst anti-Semitism I'd ever heard. King, the family's hyper toy terrier, came flying through the arched entrance from the dining room and began barking at Semo, threatening to nip an ankle. Semo kicked at the dog—"King, shut up!"—kicked at him again, until the dog, growling and giving one last defiant bark, retreated out of the room.

Nada, Mila's youngest sister and a freshy in high school (the family called her Sweetness ever since she was a toddler and Hilda had proclaimed her the "sweetest thing on earth"), appeared in the arched entrance wearing hip-hugger denim bells and a beige stretch blouse with a collar wide enough to pass for wings. Unlike Mila, who leaned toward the German side of the Popovic gene pool, Sweetness was more of a Slavic, round-faced, babushka girl.

She flicked her head to get her scraggly brown bangs out of her eyes, glanced out the window, put her hands on her hips, and called across the room to her father, "Tati, if Mr. Goldstein wants to park his car in front of our house it's not against the law. Will ya get off it about the Jews already?"

"Shit Jew!" Semo yelled, glaring out the window.

It's not for a dinner guest to get up on a soapbox and lecture his host on the evils of discrimination. Besides, I may come from a socially activist family, but that doesn't mean I can't recognize a lost cause as fast as the next guy.

Sweetness looked at me, smirked, rolled her eyes, and ran her finger around in circles next to her head to indicate her father was loony. She wandered over to the couch and asked, "So you're a creative writing student, huh? How exciting. I love to write. Wanna come up to my room and hear my poem?"

"Sure," I said. "How 'bout after dinner?"

"No, now. Pleeeeease."

"Shoot all garbage Jew!"

"On second thought," I said, pushing up from the couch.

Sweetness grabbed my hand and led me toward the stairs in the entryway. "Better behave, Tati," she said over her shoulder at Semo as if he were a child. Then she called down the hall to the kitchen, "Mila, I'm borrowing your boyfriend."

"Don't be a pest, Sweetness!" Mila called back. I heard the scraping of a pot and the oven door banging shut.

"*Moi?* A pest?" Sweetness batted her eyelashes, giggled, and headed up the stairs with yours truly in tow.

She pulled me into the first small bedroom off the stairs, yanked open a drawer in her desk, grabbed a red spiral notebook, and plopped on the bed. Lest anyone should get the wrong impression, her inviting me into her bedroom was strictly innocent. Sunlight coming from a window across the room lit a few stray pimples on her shiny forehead.

"This poem is really good." Sweetness flipped through her notebook to the right page. "I just finished it today. Ready?"

I bounced down next to her on the bed.

"Ready."

Sweetness took a deep breath, collecting herself, then began to read lickety-split:

Your smell is like
The whispering dreams of my life
Warm misty shades of memories gone cold
Leaving me without answers
Like thundering rain in a night full of confusion
Forever alone in your shadow of despair

Forever full of lost hope without emotion
Forever crying
Blinded by your essence
Maybe someday I will heal

She looked up at me expectantly. "Did ya like it?"

"That's real nice, Sweetness."

"Wha'd ya like about it?"

"Everything, Sweetness." I got a blast out of saying her nickname. "You're talented. We better go see if they need any help downstairs."

"Wanna know what it's about?"

"A boy, Sweetness." Then I couldn't resist adding, "Probably an arrogant dick who fucked you over."

She looked genuinely surprised.

"How'd ya know?"

"Just a lucky guess."

"He's *such* a dick—tells me he loves me one day and then never calls again. I hate his goddamn guts." Sweetness burst into laughter—a lousy attempt at hiding her bruised feelings.

"Want me to go kick his ass?"

Sweetness seemed to think over the big-brotherly offer.

"That'd be cool!"

"Forget about him," I said, waving off the idea. "He's not worth it. At least you got a good poem out of him."

"Yeah, but that's the last ink I waste on him. Thinks he's such hot shit."

"Look at it this way." I laid a little positive mental attitude on her. "Ninety-five percent of the people in the world are assholes. Our job is to find the five percent who aren't."

"That's a depressing thought," Sweetness said. She studied me for a moment. "You sure aren't like Mila's other boyfriends."

"Is that good?"

"Well, let's just say they were definitely in the ninety-five percent category."

We both laughed like we'd come to an understanding. Then

she furiously flipped through her notebook. "One more, it's really, really good."

"Sweeeeeetness," Mila called up the stairs. "Mom says for you to set the table right now."

"OK, OK, OK," Sweetness yelled out the doorway. Then to me, "I'll show you some more of my writing after dinner—if you survive."

"What do you mean?"

"Like you haven't picked up on how wacky things are around here?"

"Maybe a tad anti-Semitic," I said, following her out the room.

Sweetness giggled, then under her breath—"Believe me, it gets worse." She flounced down the stairs, skipped the last step, and hit the floor with a two-footed *boom!* Tossing her head back and opening her arms out wide, she waited for applause.

"No jump!" Semo screamed from his chair in the living room.

King raced out of the kitchen and through the hallway, his nails clicking a drum roll on the linoleum until he hit the gray shag carpeting in the entryway. He pulled up short and began barking like a maniac at Sweetness. Ignoring Semo and King, Sweetness exuded a spunky, center-of-the-universe confidence as she pranced down the hall, on her way to cutting through the kitchen to get to the dining room. King growled vigilantly at her heels, and I tagged along behind him.

I helped Sweetness set the table. The doorbell rang.

"I'll get it," said Vera, the overweight middle sister, and I heard her snappy footsteps going from the kitchen to the front door. The new guest, a short bookish boy with wire rimmed glasses and an Afrolike head full of hair, was led by Vera from room to room and introduced to all of us simply as "Ralph," her friend from nursing school. And then it was turkey time.

"Sit, everyone!" Hilda ordered, rushing into the dining room from the kitchen wearing a lime-green dress for the holiday occasion and carrying a platter of carved meat. She placed it on the center of the table. Though Hilda was in her mid-forties, her face was prematurely lined and matronly. Bitterness and some hard experience had taken their toll. "Food's getting cold."

With the table leaves extended, there was little dining room left to spare. Never one to be shy when it comes to good grub, I grabbed a seat closest to the turkey. Just as Mila reached for the chair to my right, Vera quickly slipped into it. Take away fifty pounds, she could have passed for Mila's carbon copy.

"Vera, do you mind?" Mila said. "You have a boyfriend here. Why don't you go sit by him?"

"Ralph's not my boyfriend," Vera said. "He's my *friend*. I can sit wherever I want."

Ralph chuckled good-naturedly, scootching a chair up to the table across from Vera.

"You pull this every time," Mila said, moving around to my other side.

Semo took the place of honor at one end of the table, Hilda claimed the other end, and Sweetness got stuck next to Ralph by default.

"Eat already!" Hilda commanded. "Eat! Eat!"

We began to pass the dishes clockwise. I recognized the green-bean casserole, mashed potatoes, gravy, and stuffing, but when a plate of gelatinous glop called "head cheese" came my way, Mila whispered, "You don't have to eat it."

"Oh yes he does," Hilda said, overhearing Mila. "Look at him, so skinny. Head cheese thickens the blood!"

"Mom, he doesn't have to if he doesn't—"

"No, I'll try it," I said politely, cutting off a chunk of glop with a serving fork. "My blood's been a little thin lately."

Sweetness and Vera laughed, Ralph chuckled good-naturedly again, and Semo ate with his mouth open, his glasses cockeyed on his face.

"Just leave it on your plate if you don't like it," Mila said.

"Cranberries?" Vera asked, bringing her face close to mine and pressing a hand on my forearm. She passed me the bowl, then grabbed the spoon. "Here, Roman, let me."

"Vera, why don't you take care of your own boyfriend," Mila said.

"He's not my boyfriend, he's my *friend*. More turkey, Roman?" Vera reached for the fork on the turkey platter. "A big guy like you needs his protein. White or dark?"

"White, thanks."

"That's what I thought," Vera said. She dropped a nice big slice of meat on top of the one I already had on my plate. "You look like a breast man."

"Roman's *not* your boyfriend, Vera," Mila said.

"I'm just helping. Will ya get off my back?"

"Vera, you've always got the hots for Mila's boyfriends," Sweetness said.

"Shut up, Sweetness."

"No arguing," Hilda chided. "Eat!"

"You too, Mom," Mila said. "You cooked everything, it looks great. What's with the empty plate?"

"I'm happy vatching everyone else eat." Hilda passed the green beans on to Sweetness without taking any for herself. The rest of us chowed down. Then, as if wanting to get the ball rolling on some stimulating table talk, Hilda said, "So, have you all heard? The Jews have taken over Channel 2."

Mila bowed her face into her hand, obviously embarrassed. "Come on, Mom. Don't start in about the Jews, OK?"

Ralph chuckled louder this time and stared down at his plate like there was something humorous on it.

"It's true," Hilda went on. "Valter Jacobson is the new anchor man on the 5 o'clock news, and he's Jewish. That means the Jews control Channel 2."

Knives and forks continued to scrape plates. The constraint I felt as a boyfriend trying to make a good first impression on my girlfriend's parents was nothing short of astonishing, but I did ask, "Are you sure about that, Mrs. Popovic? Ya know, Channel 2's a pretty big operation. I'm not so sure the Jews can handle it."

Sweetness nearly spit out her food laughing, and covered her mouth with a napkin. Mila kicked my ankle under the table, a signal for me to stop egging her mother on. Semo, totally out of it because of the language barrier, took a slurp of red wine. A low growl came from under the table—"*Grrrrrrrr*." Mila threw King a scrap of turkey below the tablecloth.

"Big operation, hah!" Hilda said. "Are you kidding? Channel 2 is small potatoes to the Jews. They run the vorld. Vake up and smell the coffee. They got so much money; I don't know how they get their hands on it, but they always do. Yah, Hitler did a lot of bad things, but he sure vas right about the Jews."

"Well!" Ralph mumbled. That *something* on his plate was becoming more and more humorous.

"Mom, really, I don't want to hear about Hitler right now, OK?" Mila said.

"I do," I said, interested. "What was it like in Germany back then?"

Mila huffed, stabbing a fork into a pile of mashed potatoes on her plate.

"At first it vas so beautiful!" Hilda began. "Ve vere all in the Hitler youth—same thing as the girl and boy scouts—and ve vould march around and sing songs and have so much fun. Everyone vas vorking and happy. And then that stupid Hitler had to go and get us in a var!"

"And kill six million Jews," I added.

"But it vasn't just the Jews that vas sent to the concentration camps—it vas all kinds of people. If you said bad things about the government the Gestapo vould come in a truck and take you away and you are never heard from again. Ve vere all scared. It vasn't just the Jews!"

"*Grrrrrrr*."

Vera tossed another scrap of turkey under the table.

"Look, Mom," Sweetness said, "I've got lots of Jewish friends who aren't rich, OK?"

"Oh yes they are," Hilda assured her. "They hide their money. They got it under the mattress or under the floor."

"Well!" Ralph said, chuckling giddily.

"No, they don't!" Sweetness said.

"Vat do you know? You're still young!"

"Well! Well!"

"*Well* what?" I asked Ralph.

"I'm Jewish!" Ralph said. "And my family definitely isn't rich. I'm putting myself through nursing school."

He shoveled green beans on his fork and began politely eating again, like he regretted, no matter how justified, over-stepping his bounds. Semo, evidently not even trying to follow the conversation, wiped the back of his hand across his mouth, then picked up his knife and proceeded to cut himself another bite of turkey. Ralph's hair fit the stereotype, but it hadn't even crossed my mind that he might be Jewish. In the uncomfortable silence I felt hot breath on my knee. "*Grrrrrrrr.*" I surreptitiously gave King my head cheese.

"Nice goin', Mom," Sweetness said.

"I didn't do nothing vrong!"

"All right!" Vera shouted. She must not have known that her *friend* was Jewish and now felt compelled to come to Ralph's defense. "I'm sick and tired of hearing about the Jews the Jews the Jews in this house. Let's just change the subject!"

While the Popovics squabbled, none of them looked at Ralph, as if they all hoped he would make it easy on them by simply evaporating. Old Semo suddenly unleashed a torrent of loud, definitive Serbian, the gist of which we all took to mean *cool it*!—all of us except King, who, galvanized into action, began yip-yapping and tearing around the table so fast I thought he'd turn into butter. The sisters yelled at him simultaneously:

"King, stop it!"

"Shut up, ya mutt!"

"Go lay down!"

King darted under the table. "*Grrrrrr.*"

Semo hunched over his food and went to work on his fruit salad. The rest of us, subdued by his lordship's outburst, glanced discreetly at each other.

"Great, just great," Mila said. "Now Tati's mad."

I looked at Sweetness and she at me. It was all we could do to keep from busting out laughing. Hilda spooned cranberries from a serving dish. Ice cubes clinked as Vera brought her water glass to her mouth. Mila fumed, done with eating in spite of her half-full plate. Years later, I realized it was her feeling responsible for her parents, and her inability to ever live them down, that drove her ambition to rise above it all.

"I certainly have nothing against the Jews," Hilda said, looking at no one in particular. "I remember how vhen I vas young, I used to run errands for different shops. Vhenever I delivered a package to this house vhere Jews lived, the voman vould always give me a thick slice of the best cheese. Hmmm, I can still taste it. They had such a beautiful house—lots of expensive things. The daughter played the most beautiful music on the piano, and the son alvays vinked at me and made me blush. I had such a—how do you kids say—*crush* on him. The father told me I vas so pretty he vished he could adopt me. Such nice decent people. And then one day I ring the bell and a different lady answers the door. The Jews are gone—poof! I ask vhat happened to them, but she grabs the package out of my hand and shuts the door in my face. I stood there vaiting to hear that piano music from inside the house, but I heard nothing."

Hilda stared into space, her expression changing from worried to upset.

"I often vonder vhatever happened to that family."

The room had grown shadowy in the early evening light coming through the archway from the living room picture window. No one said anything. It was one of the most amazing social about-faces I have ever witnessed. Call Hilda's storytelling a great performance, or call me a sap, but I believe she saw no contradiction in caring about the Jewish family and talking nonsense about the Jews taking over Channel 2. Outside, a kid riding a Big Wheel rumbled down the sidewalk, and the distant, steady roar of a jet-liner grew louder, louder still, then faded.

I cleared my throat and tried to rescue us all by asking Ralph, "So, do you think you could give me a good deal on some Channel 2 stock?"

Sweetness doubled over laughing.

"Anytime," Ralph said.

Mila massaged her temples with her fingertips.

"You OK?" I asked.

"Think I'm getting a headache."

I reached over and gently kneaded the muscles on the back of Mila's neck.

"Roll?" Vera asked Semo, offering him the basket. "Come on, Tati, don't be a grump." She gave him one, then turned toward me and squeezed my arm. "How about you?"

It occurred to me that I hadn't yet heard Hilda or Semo speak a single word, in any language, to each other.

2

After dinner, Ralph didn't waste any time thanking the Popovics for a "lovely meal," said he had a big test to cram for, and let Vera fetch his coat from the entryway closet. No sooner had Vera shut the front door behind him than Sweetness, helping Mila and Hilda clear the table, called out innocently, "Oh, Ralph, do come back anytime. Think of us as your home away from home."

"Hush up!" Hilda said, sweeping through the kitchen doorway with a stack of dirty plates. "Always think you're so funny." From my chair in the dining room, I watched Sweetness shrink out of Hilda's way, then make a face and scoot into the dining room.

Stranded again with Semo at the table, I started to get up to help the women, when the old man says to me, "Roman, you good boy. Come, I show guns."

Sweetness, traipsing back into the kitchen with several wine glasses in hand, announced, "Tati's taking Roman to show him his guns."

As I followed Semo through the living room to the stairs, I overheard the women's conversation on the other side of the wall.

"Tati and his guns again," Vera commented.

"Mom, stop him," Mila said. "He's embarrassing me."

"You think your father listens to me—hah!"

Sweetness imitated Semo's voice. "You like gun, Roman? I shoot you balls you touch daughter."

"Vatch your mouth, Miss Smarty Pants!" Hilda said.

If Semo understood them, he must not have given a damn, already climbing the stairs. I tagged along, amused, and, weirdly enough, honored: Semo and I were about to share a moment with guns, man to man. He led me to the master bedroom next to the bathroom at the end of the upstairs hall, hobbled over to his bureau, and opened the top drawer. With an agitated look of excitement on his elfish, weathered face, he pulled out a sizable handgun.

"Good gun. Very good. Made Austria. Shoot big hole thief, he rob me."

Semo placed the weapon in the palm of my hand. I'd never held a gun before, and as I tentatively curled my finger on the trigger, I was surprised by the weapon's heft.

"Real nice," I told Semo, nodding politely. "It's a really, really nice gun."

He took the pistol out of my hand, put it back in the drawer, and pulled out a smaller, nickel-plated gun.

"I carry work. Protection. Lot nigger work. They fuck me, I kill nigger."

I nodded politely again. This wasn't the moment of male bonding I'd been hoping for. I kept telling myself that in Semo's own pathetic, ignorant, uneducated, fascist, anti-Semitic, racist sort of way, he wasn't such a bad guy.

"Nigger want money. Boom! Dead nigger."

The more animated he became—taking aim above the bed at the picture of Hilda and him forcing smiles at the photographer's command, or pointing his gun at the window that overlooked the tree-lined street—the more his language shifted to Serbian. The room started to close in on me. All of his gun waving made me nervous, my armpits moist inside my maroon V-neck sweater.

"OK, Tati, that's enough."

It was Mila, come to save me. She grabbed my hand and started tugging me out of the room.

"Thanks for showing me your guns, Mr. Popovic."

"You good boy, Roman," Semo called after me.

"Tati's so proud of his fucking guns," Mila said as we headed down the stairs. "I wish he'd shoot himself."

"Mila, he's your dad. Give him a break. He doesn't know any better."

Mila pulled me into the living room, shoved me onto the couch, and sat next to me.

"You'd think he could find something else to be proud of," she said. "Like my mother. Why doesn't he try being proud of her for a change instead of always making her miserable. God, my head hurts." She snuggled closer, putting her head on my shoulder.

"They don't get along, huh?"

"Are you kidding?" Mila lowered her voice to a whisper and said, "My mother can't even go to a restaurant with him because he embarrasses her—always eats with his mouth open. Backwoods hick. Used to come home drunk every day when I was little. He lied to my mother about his age. Now he's an old man and she's stuck with him for life. He's missed three months of work already this year because of his bad feet, so she's got to make ends meet working as a nurse's aide emptying bed pans at Augustana Hospital."

"How do you know he lied about his age?" I asked. Mila lifted her head off my shoulder.

"She told me. She tells me everything. This one time we're sitting at the kitchen table, when Tati comes in with this silly grin on his face. He keeps walking all over the house like he's so excited he can hardly contain himself. The next thing I know he goes up to their bedroom and yells down the stairs, 'Hiiiiiilda.' I say, 'What's with Tati, Mom?' She has this look like she's sick to her stomach and tells me, 'He wants to do it. I can't stand it when he touches me.' I'd thought they'd stopped having sex together years ago and was shocked! She's like his slave. I watched her slowly get up to go and give him what he wanted." Mila shivered. "My poor mom."

"They must have loved each other at some point," I said, trying to think of the bright side for Mila's sake.

"I doubt it. My grandfather used to beat my mom, and with Germany in such a mess after World War II, she married the first man she met with enough money to take her to the United States.

Tati's too damn lazy to learn English—leaves that to my mother. If he keeps missing work, he'll get fired before he makes it to retirement and collects his pension. Then where will we be?"

I didn't know what to say, so I squeezed her hand. Just then Sweetness and Vera left the kitchen clean-up work to Hilda and made their escape through the hallway and into the living room. Vera immediately plopped down on the couch next to me so that I was once again sandwiched between two Popovic sisters. Sweetness leaned over the armrest, crowding Mila.

"Roman, will you read another one of my poems now—please, please, please?"

Mila pushed Sweetness away, then told Vera, "Get away from my boyfriend."

"He's my guest, too," Vera said. "This isn't *your* living room."

"Pleeeeeease."

"Not now, Sweetness," Mila snapped. Then to Vera—"I said, get away from my boyfriend."

"I can sit wherever I want."

"Pleeeeease."

"That's what you think, Vera," Mila said.

"Pleeeeease."

"Sweetness, Roman's not going to read your poetry right this second, so get lost," Mila said. "Vera, find someone else to fuck you, because Roman's not interested."

I admit it—as the lone, male center of attention, I found the sibling rivalry highly entertaining. Sweetness made a fart sound with her lips.

"Be that way. I wouldn't show him my poetry if he paid me." She sulked toward the stairs.

"I'll read it next time, Sweetness," I said, hoping her feelings weren't hurt too badly.

She pounded up the stairs, and then her bedroom door slammed shut.

"Good-bye, Vera," Mila said with a cool intensity.

Vera didn't budge.

"I don't have to leave."

"Yes, you do."

"No, I don't."

"Yes."

"No."

"*Good-bye*, Vera."

I thought the claws were going to start flying from either side of me at any second. The sisters stared each other down. Finally, Vera got up, went over to the entryway, and lingered there.

"I hope I see you again, Roman," she said. "I'm sorry your girlfriend's such a bitch." She disappeared into the hall. I heard her footsteps descending the basement stairs to her bedroom. Mila let out a long exhalation and put her head on my shoulder again.

"Maybe if I didn't have such a back-stabbing, bulimic slut for a sister, I wouldn't have to be a bitch."

"Bulimic?" I asked.

"Yeah, Vera's lost thirty pounds in two months. Didn't you notice how she excused herself from the table after dessert? She went up to the bathroom and stuck her fingers down her throat. She admitted it to me in the kitchen. Only one halfway normal around here is Sweetness. Give her a few more years and she'll be as crazy as the rest of us."

I stroked my fingers through Mila's hair, having difficulty registering that things could possibly be as bad as she painted them. The dishwasher clicked on in the kitchen. Hilda bustled into the room and turned on a lamp next to the couch. Stepping over to the window, she pulled the drawstring on the curtains. Then she picked up a short plastic rake leaning against the wall by the rubber tree and began raking the footprints out of the shag rug, making sure that all the long carpet strands lay in the same organized direction. Mila straightened up, letting go of my hand.

"Mom, why do you do that? No one cares how the rug looks."

"Just vant everything neat and clean before I go up for my nap. You know me—can't sleep othervise."

Hilda worked fast, finished the whole room, and put the rake back against the wall by the rubber tree.

"OK, kids, be good."

"Nice meeting you, Mrs. Popovic. It was a delicious meal."
Jesus, I felt like that brown-nosing creep, Eddie Haskell, on *Leave
it to Beaver*.

"You're velcome," Hilda returned, her voice icy, not even
looking at me. And then she was gone up the stairs to join Semo
in their bedroom. They both worked night shifts and would have
to leave the house in a few hours.

Alone.

"I don't think your mom likes me."

"Don't worry about it," Mila said. "She's not big on trusting
boys. I like you. A lot."

We wrapped our arms around each other and started trading
some serious spit. As our groping intensified, Mila straddled my
lap and yanked her cream-colored sweater over her head. She wasn't
wearing a bra, and her small, perky, teardrop breasts said howdy
to me.

"Mila, you crazy? What if someone walks in?"

"Let 'em," she said, tossing the sweater onto the coffee table
behind her. We'd made-out plenty of times, but this was different,
like she was out to prove her value in spite of her D.P. family. Still
worrying that someone might barge in on us at any second, my
hands explored and fondled the soft contours of her boobs.

"You like them?" she asked.

"Yeah, I like them."

"Not too small?"

"More than a mouthful's a waste," I said.

She giggled as I brought my tongue to a nipple and—how
should I put this—feasted. All the while she was bumping and
grinding on my stiffening cock, our breathing heavy in the silent
house. A floorboard creaked above us in her parents' bedroom. I
quickly came up for air.

"Did ya hear that?"

Mila teased a slobbery nipple over my lips.

"Don't worry. Once they go up, they stay there till it's time for
work."

"You sure?"

"Yeah, I'm sure."

She began pulling up my sweater. Unconvinced, I tugged it down.

"Mila!"

She pulled up my sweater again, calling the shots. I thought about it. My dick thought about it. Who were we to argue? She worked the sweater over my head and tossed it onto the coffee table next to hers. Then she ran her hands possessively over my flat chest. We kissed long and hard. I felt myself sinking deeper and deeper into the hot, tireless, can't-get-enough-of-each-other lust that comes with a new relationship. *Fucking dangerous*, I thought, then, *Incredible bod.*

I'm not sure how long we'd been going at it, when Mila lifted off my lap, reached down, and palmed the crotch of my Levi's.

"Come on, my diaphragm's upstairs."

I tensed, disengaging my hands from anything incriminating. "No way!"

Mila stroked my cock tenderly through my Levi's.

"Be real quiet."

"Yeah, I'll end up quiet all right."

"Fuck Tati and his guns," Mila said. "Thinks he owns everybody." She got off the couch, not about to take no for an answer. It occurred to me that I wasn't her first boyfriend, and that she knew the drill in her own house. Besides, call me weird, but there's an erotic, gonad-hormone-pumping excitement in knowing you're about to poke a woman whose daddy, armed and dangerous, is asleep right on the other side of the wall. I lurched off the couch and put my sweater back on just in case I had to make a quick exit, but Mila, brazen to a point, didn't bother with hers, letting me carry it. I tiptoed up the carpeted stairs after her, staring at the smooth skin of her shoulders and the way her long fine hair cascaded down to a small waist. When we reached the top, the hallway was dark. Light shone under the bottom of Sweetness's door, and from the other end of the hallway, behind the master bedroom's closed door, I heard Semo's loud measured snoring. We stepped straight ahead into the middle room. Street-lamp light, sliced neatly by the venetian blind slats, lit a desk against the wall opposite from her tall dresser. Mila shut the door carefully so as not to make a sound, then moved across the shadowy room to her single bed.

"Help me with the mattress," she whispered.

Tossing the sweater on a dresser, I went over to her. We each grabbed an end of the mattress—Mila at the foot and me at the head—and slid it off the box spring to the floor. I understood that this way we wouldn't squeak any springs with our humping.

We kissed, simultaneously working each other's belt buckles, and soon our pants and underwear were puddled around our ankles. When we were completely undressed, Mila knelt down and pulled back the bedspread and sheet. Then she looked Mr. Cock in the eye, stroked him delicately with her hand, and without further ado popped him in her mouth. A shadow cast on the wall bobbed with pistonlike precision. Mila tickled my balls with her sharp fingernails, put on a show of running her tongue up and down the hard bowed shaft and flicking it over the mushroom head.

"Feel good?" she asked.

"Ummm."

I dropped to the mattress and rolled onto my back. Then I folded the pillow in two and propped it under my head because, well, I like to watch. She curled herself around my groin, grabbed hold of the base of my veiny missile, and continued to bob and lick. After a while, I tried to pull her up for a kiss, to diddle her clit, or to reverse our positions and return the pleasure by performing the fine art of cunnilingus, but she always brushed my hands away. It would take a few more times in the sack with Mila before I realized that what made her the turn-on of all turn-ons, what gave her a lovemaking advantage over other women, wasn't simply her superb fellatio technique (in the proverbial language of the boys' locker room, that girl could suck the chrome off a bumper); no, it was the fact that giving head made *her* hot. It's the kind of obsessive, need-to-please, oral-fixated, twisted behavior from a woman that men dream about.

Spoiled me for life.

Mila stopped and looked up at me with my dick tucked oh-so-cutely against her cheek.

"Do you want to come in my mouth or fuck my pussy?"

Tough decision.

"Pussy," I said, respectfully.

She gave my cock a few more bobs for good measure, then turned away from me onto her side, reached for the bottom desk drawer, and opened it. The beam from a car's headlights roamed across the ceiling, down a wall, illuminated a porcelain clown doll staring at us with a creepy leering smile from its perch atop the dresser, then vanished. Mila pulled a round, plastic, blue container and a tube of spermicidal jelly from the drawer. I spooned her body with mine, nibbling on her neck, massaging a breast, watching the meticulous birth control preparations over her shoulder. She took the diaphragm out of the container, uncapped the tube, squeezed the jelly onto the rubber surface of the diaphragm, and smeared it around, making sure to cover the entire rim so that no athletic sperm could make an end run. Ah, the sickly sweet, perfumed scent of that jelly. Just the memory of it turns me into a horn-dog. With a well-practiced move, she flipped onto her back, spread her legs, and slipped the diaphragm into place. Then she rolled on top of me.

"Fuck me," she whispered, shoving her hands under my shoulder blades to hold on tight.

My cock toyed with her wet pussy—slipping, sliding, poking, withdrawing, and I'm thinking, Semo . . . this is crazy.

"Quit teasing," she said.

I eased in. Her whole body shuddered. Grabbing hold of her firm ass with both hands, I pumped furiously.

"Leave it deep and don't move."

I didn't mind the stage directions—whatever got her rocks off. She buried her face in my neck. I felt her subtle internal adjustments as she worked her pussy on my cock, searching for that elusive combination to the promised land. I drove deeper. She moaned softly, focused, trembling, riding me faster. It didn't take long.

There's always that magnificent moment when a woman's entering the nether-nether world of the almighty female orgasm. Mila bit my neck to gag herself, breathed a windstorm in my ear, and dug her fingernails into the valley between my scapulas. I almost screamed in pain. Then, suddenly, I couldn't hold back, resumed pumping, and came with her. Both of us broke out in a cooling sweat. With her chest smashed against mine, I couldn't tell the hard, rapid pounding of her heart from my own. The rhythm of our fucking slackened, then stopped. Breathing slowed. I heard a muffled sob, then another one. Something wet dripped on my shoulder.

"Are you crying? What's wrong?"

"Don't know. Too . . . too . . . intense."

"Oh," I said, but couldn't relate. My once-proud member shrank apologetically out of Mila. She dismounted and snuggled next to me in the crook of my arm. I listened to her sniffling, then it subsided. I kissed her on top of her head.

"You all right?"

"Yeah, I'm fine," Mila said.

I hope I wasn't fishing for post-coitus compliments when I asked, "Headache gone?"

"It's killin' me."

I couldn't help thinking about Semo.

"We better get up. I told my mom we'd try to make it to my house in time for dessert."

"Let's just lay here for a while," Mila said. "You smell so good."

"Yeah, you smell good too. What if your dad wakes up?"

She nuzzled her pug nose against the soft underbelly of my chin.

"He won't for at least another hour."

"Mila, I really think we should . . ."

"Stop worrying, will ya?"

"I don't think this is a very good—"

"OK, OK!"

"Shhhhhh," I said, sure that Semo was going to crash through the door at any second with both guns blazing. Mila sat up, let out a loud exasperated breath, and began pressing her temples with her fingertips. I felt bad about rushing, but it didn't stop me from scrambling to my feet and snatching my Jockey briefs off the floor.

"I'm so sick of living here," Mila said.

We dressed, lifted the mattress back on the bedsprings, made the bed, and were out of the room in a minute flat. Mila stopped off at the bathroom at the end of the hall while I took the stairs down staying light on my toes. I grabbed my army jacket from the closet by the front door, threw it on, and began impatiently shifting my weight from foot to foot in the entryway, waiting for Mila. Upstairs, I heard a door creak open, then shut. A pair of nursing shoes and the stout legs of a woman appeared near the top of the stairs, then as she descended, the hem of her polyester beige uniform, and finally her lip-curled, cynical face. I nearly shit a green brick as Hilda's cold stare bore through me.

Trying to play off my nervousness, I smiled and asked, "Up so soon?"

Hilda reached the threshold and stood there.

"Couldn't sleep." Her lip curled even more. "I kept hearing things."

The smile dropped as I felt myself blushing. So that was it. She'd purposely waited for us to make a clean escape from the bedroom so things wouldn't get too *messy*.

"I'm not as stupid as you think," Hilda said.

"Mrs. Popovic, I certainly never thought you were stupid. I have absolutely nothing but respect for you and your family."

Hilda advanced toward me. I involuntarily stepped backwards until my heels hit the wall next to the archway leading into the living room. She stopped in front of me.

"You listen and listen good. You can do anything you vant with my daughter, but don't you dare get her hooked on drugs. Is that clear?"

Drugs? What the fuck was that woman talking about?

"Mrs. Popovic, I'm not into drugs—honest. What makes you think I would ever—"

"Don't play games with me. I vasn't born yesterday."

"I'm not playing—"

"Boys—they're all the same no matter vhat country. I draw the line with drugs. Believe me, you don't vant to cross it."

My back was against the wall—literally and figuratively.

"Right," I said. "No drugs. I wouldn't do anything to . . ."

She humphed, as if telling me to save my worthless, skirt chasing, male breath. I heard the toilet flush through the ceiling, then shortly after that Mila's footsteps on the stairs—thank fucking God.

When she saw Hilda and me, she didn't miss a beat, looking no more than pleasantly surprised as she asked, "Mom, what are you doing up so soon?" She went over to the closet and opened the door. Hilda's hard-ass demeanor magically dissolved as she turned away from me.

"Too vound up, I guess, so I thought I might as vell get a head start fixing something for Tati's lunch box." She watched Mila grab her camel-colored, wool jacket from a hanger. "You leaving?"

"Yeah," Mila said, slipping an arm into the jacket. "Me and Roman are going to his house. I'll probably stay there tonight. They've got an extra room."

It was a lie. I'd already explained to Mila that my parents were "cool" and always let my girlfriends sleep with me in my room.

"OK, sweetheart," Hilda said. "Be careful."

"Don't worry, Mom." Mila kissed Hilda on the cheek. "Bye." She pulled open the front door, then pushed the handle of the storm and stepped onto the cement porch. I edged past Hilda.

"Thanks for the meal and everything, Mrs. Popovic."

"You're velcome," Hilda said flatly. "For everything."

Chilly autumn air felt good on my hot face. Mila grabbed my hand as we headed down the steps, then the walkway.

"She knows," I said.

"Who cares," Mila said. "I'm twenty, give me a break."

"She told me not to get you hooked on drugs. Do I look like a fuckin' drug dealer?"

"Oh, God." Mila hung her head, then shook it. "How embarrassing. My mom thinks every boy I meet wants to turn me into a heroin addict. If I don't figure out a way to move out, I'll go nuts."

"You'll think of a way."

"On a part-time waitress salary? Won't have any money left over to buy toilet paper, much less pay rent."

We fell into a brisk pace down the sidewalk. Call it a character flaw, but I basically like people to like me, and it bummed me out that I'd made such a bad first impression on Hilda. Oh well, she hadn't exactly measured up to *my* high moral standards, either. Lights from inside copycat Georgian houses spilled through bay windows and over front lawns that were carpeted with dry maple and elm leaves. A crisp breeze smelled of approaching winter.

"Look." I pointed at a full, burnt-orange harvest moon suspended in the eastern sky just over the roofs and tree tops.

"Ooooo," Mila said. "It's huge!"

I knew that I would save this moment, mark time with it, always. And then for no particular reason, like a tension release, we both started cracking up laughing and could hardly stop collapsing into each other for the entire four-block walk to the bus stop.

3

We'd taken the Lunt Street bus to the Morris El stop and were riding a practically empty train south to Lincoln Park, when it dawned on me that all in all I'd had a pretty damn good time at Mila's house. I sat closest to the window with her snuggled next to me, our feet propped up on the single seat that's at the front of every Chicago El car. Below us, the streets and lights of Northside neighborhoods glided past. I chalked up my poor showing with Hilda to experience and even began to feel cocky about getting laid behind enemy lines, so to speak. Not long after we pulled out of the Wilson station, I started entertaining myself by imitating Popovics.

"Read my poem—please please pleeeeeeeease. It's *really* good, I wrote it five minutes ago.

"Have some more white meat, Roman. You look like a breast man.

"So, did you hear the news? The Jews have taken over Channel 2. Just ask Walter Jacobson.

"Shit garbage Jew park my house!

"Ahhh, it was so beautiful in the Hitler youth.

"Good gun. Boom! I shoot nigger."

My talent for mimicry was hitting on all cylinders, when suddenly I noticed Mila glowering at me.

"I'm just kidding."

"Ha, ha," Mila said.

"I like your family. They're interesting characters."

I heard how patronizing that sounded right after I said it and knew I'd fucked up on top of fucking up. Mila continued to glower, letting me feel the heat, then said, "*Interesting characters?*"

Somewhere behind us, one of the few passengers—probably the half–passed out, slumped-over drunk I'd seen when boarding the car—hacked up a hocker. The train's wheels screeched as we took a hairpin turn above Graceland Cemetery.

"Let me tell you something, Roman," Mila said, raising her voice. "My family's had it hard—real hard."

"I didn't mean to sound like I was making fun of your family."

"Oh, really? My mother stacked bricks from buildings destroyed by the Allied bombing for a dollar a day until her hands were too bloody to pick them up any more. After she and my dad moved to Chicago, she heard an air-raid siren, grabbed me out of my crib, and ran like a mad woman down the street looking for a bomb shelter. It took a neighbor two blocks to catch up to her and God knows how long to convince her that it was just the city testing the sirens."

"Mila, I'm sure that your family—"

"That's the problem," Mila interrupted. "You're a little *too* sure. Like you have the slightest idea what it's like to wake up one day and find yourself in the middle of World War II. My father was in a Nazi work camp—one cut above a concentration camp. No one even knows how he scraped the money together to get him and my mother to America—probably something illegal. The only thing he hates more than the Nazis are the Jews, but my parents are so out of touch and in such a hurry to buy a house, they don't even realize it's in a mostly Jewish neighborhood until we've already been living there for a week. Tati works like a dog. The other men on the loading dock tease him because he can't speak English. 'Hey, D.P.! Hey, Polack!' Serb, Pole, Czech, Martian, it's all the same to those idiots."

"Mila, I'm really—"

"And when you're ignorant like my parents, people constantly rip you off. Like the lawyer they used to close the deal on our house. He overcharged us five hundred bucks. Or the butcher. It's two years before my mom realizes he's giving her the shitty cuts of meat. My parents buy an extra-big car they can't really afford because they think it makes them more American. They've never had an extra dime between them that someone didn't find a way to steal. They work hard, and they're *my* parents, so don't you ever, ever make fun of them again, understand?"

I'm feeling like Mila's just handed my balls to me on a paper plate as the train eases into the next station. I look away from her and out the window at the wooden platform. The train stops and the doors fold open.

"*Sheridan*," says the scratchy conductor's voice over the intercom, "*Sheridan*."

No one gets on or off the train, the doors shut, and we begin to move again.

It hit me plain and simple. I was utterly and madly in love with this woman. I put my arm around her shoulders and looked right at her. She was staring through the emergency door window and into the next car.

"I'm sorry," I said. "I'm a real asshole. It won't happen again."

Mila didn't respond, gone to that place I would never learn

how to reach. I wanted to tell her how much I loved her and that she was the only one for me and all that shit, but something told me to just keep my mouth shut for the time being. I mobilized for the fight to win her back.

CHAPTER 4

ALL FALL DOWN

The morning after the fire, I'm heading along the surf toward camp, recharged from a cool dip in the ocean. Down the beach, I spot a bowlegged, muscular figure slowly coming my way out of the hazy humidity. It's Otto. I'm all set to pump him for information about good-old-boy Jay, when he gets close enough for me to notice an inch-long ragged gash running through the corner of his left eyebrow.

"Whoa! What happened to you?"

Pale around the gills, eye swollen half shut, and hair a matted mess, Otto had definitely seen better days. He glanced evasively off at the ocean, then down at his feet, and drawled, "Oh, guess I partied a little too hardy last night." He began shoveling a hole in the wet sand with his big toe. "Went into town for a few more beers around 10 o'clock. Next thing I know I'm wakin' up on my sleepin' bag at camp—blood all over my damn face. Don't remember nothin'. Maybe I tripped and fell on the way home. Kinda scared me."

Otto's drunken blackout reminded me of a supposedly true story I'd heard from a friend of mine. A lush stops off at a bar for a few drinks after work. The next thing he knows he wakes up in a bedroom he's never seen before. He rolls over in bed and finds the biggest, fattest, ugliest naked woman asleep next to him. Oh shit, he thinks, what have I done? Then he rolls over the other way and finds the biggest, fattest, ugliest naked man. It occurred to me that Otto might not appreciate the story right at that particular hungover moment. I grabbed hold of either side of my beach towel draped around my neck and peered closer at the gash.

"Looks nasty. You might need stitches."

"Awww, I'll be all right," Otto said. "Not like I had the prettiest mug to start with. Better lay off the partying for a while, that's for sure."

We both gazed at the surf. The ocean had mellowed overnight, the whitecaps wimpy compared to the day before. Nearer to town, where the beach curved toward the rocky peninsula topped by the lighthouse, men unloaded baskets of fish from a couple of wooden skiffs pulled up on the sand.

"So who you think lit that fire?" I asked.

"Fire?" Otto looked confused.

"Yeah, last night."

"Don't know nothin' about no fire."

"Pretty hard to miss it," I said. "Jay didn't say anything?"

"Uh-uh. He's still sleepin' like a log. What fire?"

"That place where we ate. Someone torched it."

"Really?"

"Really. To the ground. Nothing left."

"Must have slept through the whole thing," Otto said. "Too much partying." As he reached up to scratch his scalp, he inadvertently flexed a grapefruit-sized bicep.

"Wouldn't have any idea who the hell would do something like that, would ya?" I asked.

"Do what?"

"Ruin an entire family's livelihood. Must have been someone with a grudge."

"Wasn't very nice whoever did it," Otto said. "People sure can be dickheads."

I started shoveling sand with my toes, adding to Otto's pile.

"So you weren't with Jay last night?" I asked.

"Nah, I needed a little break—all that damn bitchin' he does drives me nuts."

"Yeah, he sure sounded mad about what those federales did to you guys."

"Awww, he's just full of talk. Long as I tune him out, we get along fine."

Otto kept digging a hole, but the look on his face let me know he was chewing on something, weighing possibilities.

"Seemed to me like he was ready to do a lot more than just talk," I said.

"Wouldn't know nothin' about that. My bet is he was out tom-cattin'. That boy could sniff pussy on a dead lady a mile away. Why you so interested?"

"No reason." Then I changed the subject. "Mila should be done taking a shower by now. Guess she and I'll head into town for breakfast."

"Food, huh?" Otto said. "That's a concept I'm learnin' how to live without. Say, what time you figure that restaurant burned down?"

"Must have been three, maybe four."

Mulling something over, Otto used the bottom of his foot to smooth out the mound of sand we'd built.

"Later," I said.

"Yeah, see ya."

I hadn't gone ten steps before Otto called out, "Mind if I give you some friendly advice?"

I stopped and turned around. "Sure."

"You seem like a nice enough feller. I wouldn't go tangling with Jay too much. We're good friends, but I've seen him get a little crazy, if you know what I mean."

"Oh yeah?" I pulled the towel tighter around my neck. "Like how?"

"Trust me," Otto said.

"Can't very well trust what I don't know." I wandered back over to him. "Spit it out."

Otto hesitated, stroking his chin with his fingers. "It's like this. Jay comes from what you might call a long illustrious line of white trash. One day his old man drills for oil on their rundown farm south of Oklahoma City. What do you know, it's a gusher. Jay goes from barely havin' enough money for shoes to being sent to prep school for fifth grade. Those snobby rich types try to knock the redneck out of him, but all they do is scramble his brains. Next thing you know he's got what they call an authority problem."

"Authority problem?" Deciding that our sand pile was a castle in need of fortification, I began to use my big toe to excavate a moat.

"Yeah, that's what they call it when you punch a teacher in the face in front of the whole class. Doesn't take him long to get kicked out of that school and three more before he ends up at Capital Hill—a public high school. I met him there on the wrestlin' team. Not to brag, but I was state champ in my weight class and mentioned in the *Daily Oklahoman* newspaper as someone with a chance to go to the Olympics."

Impressed, I glanced up from my moat-in-progress and said to Otto, "No shit."

"Yeah, I had what they call potential. Anyway, Jay takes a shine to me and tells me his whole damn life story. Problem is, when Jay wrestles, he's got a habit of dislocating his opponents' shoulders and elbows, so the coach kicks him off the team."

"You trying to tell me something?" I asked. A shovel full of sand had slid off the side of my toe prematurely before I could add it to the castle. I decided to turn the construction site mishap into a crude guardhouse outside the moat and began to scrape more sand together for that purpose.

"Just friendly advice is all," Otto said. "If you can handle Jay, fine. I'll say this for him, he's generous with his reefer. We must have smoked the entire country of Colombia in his bedroom. There we'd be every day after school, gettin' high as a kite off his bong. Stuffed a towel under the door so that his born-again Baptist mother wouldn't smell nothin'. You always knew where she was in the house, because she'd be singing hymns about Jesus this and Jesus that. Jay's old man would try to whup Jesus into him. Hell, what the rich types didn't scramble in that boy, his old man and Jesus did. About the time we graduate from high school, Jay tells me he's planning on shooting his parents with his old man's shotgun. I suggest to him that he put off murdering his folks for the time being so that we can go looking for adventure as roughnecks."

"Roughnecks?" I'd moved on to scraping another pile of sand together for an army barracks to go outside the guardhouse.

"Yeah, that's what you call people working on oil rigs," Otto continued. "Can't beat the pay, but it's dangerous work. When you're using heavy machinery and equipment like that, you can lose a finger, hand, or your pecker if you don't look sharp to what you and everyone else is doin'. Jay and me end up near Maysville living in a bunkhouse with twenty other roughnecks. The hole we're drillin' hits high-pressure gas two miles down. Never know when that sucker is going to blow our pipe and take everyone's head off. Then again, a spark from the engine or some idiot smokin' a cigarette can ignite the gas and charbroil the whole crew. Next thing I know, Jay's volunteered to be derrick hand. Let me explain. When you're working on a hole that's got high-pressure gas, derrick hand is the equivalent of an army suicide mission in Vietnam. He's ninety feet up in the rig, walking around on a few crisscrossed boards, the biggest one not much wider than a diving board. I ain't gonna get all complicated on you, but basically his job is to help me and another floor hand sixty feet below on the rig platform. The three of us lift and lower long sections of pipe connected to the drill bit in and out of the hole. That gas blows, those of us on the platform only got a thirty foot jump, but if Jay was to jump from way up where he is, wouldn't be nothing left of him but the splat. All he's got is the Geronimo line."

"*Geronimo line?*" I asked. Whether from imagining myself ninety feet up in an oil rig, or from a growing leeriness, I felt a moment of swirling vertigo. I steadied myself by starting to toe-dig a second moat to go around the army barracks, outside the guardhouse, the first moat, and the castle.

"Yeah, the Geronimo line is this t-bar attached to a steel cable running to the ground. When the gas blows, the derrick hand is supposed to sit on the bar, ride that cable down, and slingshot to safety. You'll break your legs when you hit the dirt, but at least you'll be alive. 'Course, if somebody parked their car where they shouldn't have, you'll smash into it and end up in a body cast. That hole came so close to blowin' a couple of times, I looked up and saw Jay climbing onto the Geronimo line. Then he'd realize it was a false alarm and climb off. Funny thing is, I've never seen him happier—worked like a dog helping to lift, swing, and lower those sections of pipe. Didn't hurt none he was always stoned. Company brass loved him—paid him a big fat bonus.

"After a couple of months, we figured we had enough foldin' money and quit. Went our own ways—me to O.U. on a wrestling scholarship, Jay to dealin' dope. Thought my major was *partying* until I flunked out second semester. So much for the Olympics. Hooked up with Jay again and been roughnecking with him on and off ever since. He's kept his nose fairly clean the last couple of years, except for the dealing, and that time he got thrown in jail for bashing out a feller's pickup truck windows with a baseball bat. Did it one morning right in front of the guy's house where all the neighbors could see him. Some kind of misunderstanding."

"*Misunderstanding?*" I was all ears. No matter how many lines of defense I built for the castle, it was just a matter of time before a sneak attack from the surf obliterated it.

"Yeah, something about a girl," Otto said. "Jay's old man bailed him out and hired a hotshot lawyer who got the charges thrown out of court on a technicality."

Fuck, I thought. Then to Otto, "So what are you telling me?"

"Just that you might want to be careful."

I stared at Otto, hoping for a shred of good news to go along with the mountain of bad, but he just looked at me with an expression that implied he would hate to have to stand over my dead body and say, *I told you so*. Then he turned away and slowly walked into the ocean to take a dip. Up against a psychopath? I wondered. Not afraid. As I cut across the beach toward the trailer park, hot sand stung the soles of my feet.

* * *

"I'm telling you, he did it."

"How can you be so sure?"

"Otto all but told me it was a good bet."

Mila and I kept our voices down in the small establishment—little more than a jerry-rigged canvas canopy over several card tables. A short, dark, round-shouldered proprietor busied himself loading soda pop bottles into the slushy ice of a cooler, and behind him, a woman, probably his wife, was cooking food orders on a gas stove for a scattering of hippies just now getting in gear for another day of fun in the sun. Directly across the road, a couple of Indian townies stopped to gawk at what was left of the torched restaurant—a heap of charred support beams, overturned tables and chairs with the paint burned clean off, and a smoke-blackened stove and refrigerator. A burnt stink contaminated all of Escondido.

"You just don't like him because of what happened on the beach during that fight," Mila said, cutting into her *huevos rancheros* with the side of a fork. "He was probably just using reverse psychology so that the guy would drop the knife."

"Bullshit."

I took a few slugs off a bottle of Squirt. Afraid of contracting amoebic dysentery, I hadn't drunk anything but pop and beer ever since leaving Chicago.

"He's scum," I said.

"He's interesting," she said.

"Nothing but a hick manipulator."

"What the hell do you know? His cousin lives in New York, and Jay's going to ask him if he can connect me with an art-dealer friend of his in Soho."

"Let me get this straight," I said. "The friend of a cousin of an Okie you've known for less that twenty-four hours is going to help you launch your art career in New York? Smell the fucking coffee! The only thing Jay's interested in is his dick in your pants."

Mila screwed her face into a frown like she always did whenever I crossed into the realm of too blunt, too negative, too crude, or all of the above. Giving slow, equal emphasis to both words, she said, "Fuck you."

We ate in silence. I felt her wanting-her-freedom vibes from across the table. Won't work, I thought. Losing her.

After a couple more bites of chili-drenched eggs, my mouth burned like a three-alarm fire. Just as I reached for my bottle of Squirt again, I see Jay heading down the road at a leisurely pace. Mila goes right on eating, lost in her own little mad-at-me world. Without missing a step, Jay lifts an Indian necklace trinket off the nail of a vendor's display board not far from the burnt-out restaurant. The vendor, haggling with a gringo over the price of a hammock, doesn't even notice Jay casually slipping the necklace over his head like he's owned it all his life. Next, two things happen almost simultaneously. Jay spots me watching him from across the street and—talk about nerve—winks. Then, as a boy rides past on a bicycle with a case of Coke strapped to the back fender, Jay nabs one of the bottles easy-as-you-please, never changing stride. With split-second timing, he palms a mango from the table of yet another vendor who's engrossed in reading one of those soap opera comic books. It's like Jay's moving through the middle of town in a pocket of invisibility that only I can see. His sheer gall leaves me speechless until he's passed from view.

"Did you see that?"

"See what?" Mila asked, buttering a piece of toast. I gave her a blow-by-blow account of Jay's petty-crime spree.

"So?" she said.

"*So?* He's a fucking asshole!"

"Look, Roman, he doesn't have any money. He's probably hungry. Besides, the Mexicans Jew us every chance they get."

"*Jew us?*" In the year I'd known Mila, she'd never once let on that her parents' anti-Semitism had rubbed off on her.

"What do you mean, *Jew us?* I suppose the next thing you're going to tell me is that the Jews control all the money in the world."

She looked at me as if wondering why I was stating the obvious.

"They do, don't they?"

I took a deep breath. Who or what was I in love with, anyway?

"Is Rockefeller a Jew?" I asked. "Is DuPont or Howard Hughes a Jew?"

"Well, you have to at least admit Jews are cheap. How about the family I babysat for in high school? I accidentally let the kid eat ice cream with one of their precious kosher spoons. I should have just kept my mouth shut, but no, I have to be honest and I tell the mother and father what happened. You'd have thought I'd murdered their little brat the way they both went off on me. How could I be so careless, so irresponsible, so disrespectful of their fucking culture? The father orders me to take the spoon out to the backyard and bury it. Then the mother takes a dollar out of my fifty-cents-an-hour pay to cover the spoon. Tell me that's not cheap."

"So those people were jerks," I said. "In case you haven't noticed, jerks come in all shapes and nationalities."

"Jews are definitely worse."

I thought about laying the usual guilt trip on Mila about how twisted opinions like that led to the Holocaust, but I hadn't been getting anywhere with her that day.

"Mila, stereotyping Jews is beneath you. And giving a creep like Jay the time of day is beneath you, too."

"That's for me to decide," she said, sopping her plate clean with her toast.

"Oh, really. Hating Jews, or having the hots for Jay?"

"Whatever."

I took her response as a threat.

"You fucking go right ahead." We both knew exactly what I was talking about. All she had to do was tell me that she didn't mean it, but she said nothing, staring off at the burnt-out restaurant like she wished she were somewhere else. My whole body suddenly felt heavy and lethargic. From down the road, I heard the sharp ringing of a construction worker's hammer finishing off a nail in the new hotel. It's an age-old story: The less Mila wanted me, the more I wanted her. I was worthless.

We made our way down the road to the trailer park, giving each other the silent treatment. Total drag, I thought. Can't be happening. Fuck her. Once inside the gate, Mila hung a left to go to the john, while I cut through campsites toward our hammocks. Practical matters popped into my brain. Who was going to move out of the apartment? Who would get to keep our cat, Wrigley, or the Eastlake antique mirror we bought with both our money at a garage sale? We'd also split paying for a new diaphragm and a month's supply of spermicide jelly. If some other guy's sperm was going to have the pleasure of getting killed instead of mine, didn't I deserve a refund?

Lost in serious thought, I stumbled upon three new arrivals setting up camp to the noise of Black Sabbath, acid rock coming from the tape deck in their truck. We're talking longhair bad-asses, all of them wearing wraparound shades, tank tops that showed off their buffed muscles, biker chains looped on their cut-offs, and rolled-up kerchiefs for headbands. They moved and flexed in time to the music's beat—unloading gear out of the truck's camper cabin, hammering a tent stake into the ground, firing up the Coleman stove. Every now and again they paused and glanced about to check if anyone was checking them out. Instinct told me to veer around their campsite.

"Say!" one of them called and came over to me. "Know any broads need a ride to Oaxaca?" He had one of those gravelly voices like he'd been kicked in the throat during a bar fight. Two of me would have fit inside one of him. A tattoo of a coiled cobra ready to strike decorated his sculpted arm. "We're leaving tomorrow," he said. "Free room and board for any broads."

It took me a moment to realize he didn't intend to eat me for breakfast and just wanted a lead on women. Bad-asses Two and Three stopped whatever they were doing to listen in. Those boys definitely had pussy on the brain.

"Sure don't," I said.

"Free room and board," the first one repeated. "Sweet deal. Spread the word."

"Yeah, I'll do that." I continued on my way. Nothing but a treacherous, rocky dirt road through the mountains connected Escondido to Oaxaca. Some sweet deal, I thought. Getting gang-banged in a camper bouncing all over the place for ten hours. Women would be trampling each other for the honor of that job, all right.

I reached camp, climbed into my hammock, and stared past the shady palm trees and glaring beach to the ocean. A screechy guitar riff erupted from the Bad-asses' tape deck only a few campsites away. So much for tropical-paradise ambiance. I lay there brooding, when some guy passing by whispered, "Narcs!" He kept hustling down the lane warning people. It took a moment for what he'd said to register, then I looked around. About halfway across the trailer park, these three Mexicans were fanning out and moving from campsite to campsite. They'd appeared out of nowhere, flashing badges at hippies, searching through gear. They looked a little too fashionable in their Levi's, polo shirts, and baseball caps for Escondido locals; maybe Sánchez called in backup from Acapulco. Word of the narcs traveled like a subtle breeze.

"Cops."

"Look out."

"Ditch your weed."

No one made any sudden moves. Getting caught with so much as a joint in Mexico can mean spending the best years of your life in a prison cell. People, including the Black Sabbath boys, turned down the volume on their tape decks. A hush hung in the air. Across the lane, I saw a woman squat next to a palm tree and discreetly bury something in the sand.

"*Policía.*" A young debonair narc flashed a badge in my face. "Got any drugs?" He spoke perfect English.

"No, sir." I climbed out of the hammock feeling guilty by suspicion even though I damn well had had enough sense not to travel with any illegal drugs in Mexico. I assumed Mila knew better, too.

"Those yours?" he said, pointing at the two backpacks leaning against a tree.

"Yes, sir."

He opened the canvas flap on my pack and started pulling out my belongings, dumping them in the sand.

"You have a visa?"

"Yes, sir, side pocket."

"Seen anyone with drugs?"

"No, sir."

"Heard of anyone selling drugs?"

I kept kissing his Gestapo butt with a lot of *Yes, sirs* and *No, sirs.* I felt the eyes of other campers watching the proceedings. Just as he unbuckled a strap on Mila's pack, a cop at a campsite up the lane called out, "*Mira!*" Kneeling over a backpack on the ground, he waved for his partners to come quick. He held something in his hand that I couldn't make out from that distance—maybe a head-shop pipe that he'd already found in the pack.

Without so much as a thank you for my cooperation, Officer Debonair hightailed it over to his friend, as did the third cop from the other end of the trailer park. Uh-oh, I thought. A couple of scrawny bearded hippies in a white VW camper must have had their heads in the sand. They stood aside feigning disinterest as the narc trio fine-tooth-combed their camper and belongings. Soon, the cop rifling the backpack found a sandwich baggie and held it up to the sunlight to inspect the contents. Oregano, perhaps? I don't think so. Busted. I expected some kind of reaction from the hippies, but it must have happened so fast they didn't seem to realize they were totally up shit creek. Probably under orders from the narcs, they started breaking camp, slowly collecting their boxes of food, cooking utensils, and other stuff, loading it all into the van. My guess was that they were in for a ride to the police station in town.

"What's going on?

Mila, the free-spirit princess, hath returned from the john.

"Narcs," I said. "One was just here. They busted those guys. Found a baggie of dope." Still pissed at her, I stooped over and began restowing my things into the backpack.

"One was *here*?" Mila asked. "*Now?*"

"Yep."

"Did he look through my stuff?"

"Started to."

After a long pause, I heard her shaken voice.

"Close."

"Close what?"

"I've got a joint in my pack," Mila whispered.

"You've got a *what*?"

"Shhhhh. Jay gave it to me last night. I thought it might be fun."

"*Fun*?" I got right in her face. "You picked a fine time to want to have fun! Don't you read the newspapers? Mexico does not play when it comes to—"

"Will you relax, Roman?" Mila backed away a few steps like my anger was more than she could handle. Ten years minimum of getting butt-fucked by Mexican prisoners flashed before my eyes. No thanks. I went into survival mode.

"Where is it?"

"Will you calm—"

"Where the fuck is it?"

Mila got the hint I meant business.

"In the pocket of my cut-offs."

I undid the second strap on her pack and opened it. Inside, the cut-offs lay folded neatly on top.

"Are you nuts?" Mila hissed. "Not now!"

Shut up was on the tip of my tongue. I found the joint, glanced down the lane to make sure the narcs were still busy with the two loser gringos, and popped it in my mouth. I chewed vigorously. That was that. Mila went over to her hammock and fell into the fishnetting womb like she didn't want to think, much less hear, anything more about how stupid she'd been. Good, I thought. It pains me to admit this, but she scored on one point. I almost made our worst nightmare come true by insisting on disposing of the joint right then and there, for I heard, "*Buenos días, muchacho.*" I turned around and damn near pinched a loaf in my pants. Sánchez, puffed up into a macho stance with his arms folded across his chest, stood in front of me. He must have snuck up on us. I swallowed the incriminating evidence in one gulp.

"Morning, officer," I said, then licked my lips to make sure they were clean. "How goes it?"

Mila, rocking gently in the hammock, kept quiet, playing it cool. I saw my guardedly neutral expression in both of Sánchez's mirror lenses.

"Not good, *muchacho*," Sánchez said. "I am telling everyone I will find who start the fire last night. Anyone with *información* must talk to me. Otherwise"—he pointed in the direction of where the narcs and busted *Norte Americanos* were piling into the VW camper—"you have fun at the *policía* station up the hill with your friends."

"I'll be sure to let you know if I hear anything, officer."

I can't say for sure, but I suspect it was my bogus, overly solicitous manner that must have forever marked me with Sánchez, a cop with an intuitive bullshit radar if ever there was one. He slowly took off his mirror sunglasses, leaned in close to me with squinty laser eyes, and rummaged around inside my brain, testing one door after another to make sure none of them were suspiciously locked. Finally, he said, "Hmmm," as if he were making a mental note to check the locks again at a later date. Then he moved off toward some other campers across the lane, continuing his rounds.

I climbed into my hammock, stared up through the canopy of fronds high above, and concentrated on stemming the flood of adrenaline in my veins.

"Told you not to take it out," Mila said.

Like she had any right to lay an *I told you so* on me.

"Fuck you."

"No, I think it's more like fuck *you*, Roman."

"*Au contraire*, darlingest one, fuck *you*."

"The pleasure is all mine, honey-bunch—fuck *you*."

We'd reached a new level of mutual respect for each other.

"I'm going to turn Jay's ass in," I said.

"Don't you dare!"

"He's a scumbag."

That's what I told Mila, but in truth I felt caught in one hell of a moral dilemma. Mexico wasn't exactly what you'd call a "free" country that's big on constitutional rights, and I'd have had to think long and hard before I turned in even a pus-pocket gringo like Jay.

"You better not," Mila said. "It's not your business."

"Maybe." I left it at that.

The VW van pulled out of the campsite with a hippie at the wheel and a narc riding shotgun. As it headed past campsites toward the gate, people stopped whatever they were doing as if solemnly watching a hearse. Screwed, I thought. Could have been us. It occurred to me that neither the narcs nor Sánchez had gone close to the exclusive "suburb" end of the trailer park, leaving the privileged class untouched. My eyes drifted to the Bad-asses' campsite. Lo and behold, Jay was there talking up a storm with three new buddies gathered around him. A victim's angry righteousness written all over his face, he occasionally gestured in the direction of Sánchez several campsites away. Great, I thought. Here we go. The head hooks up with the brawn.

2

We'd been in our hammocks for only a short while, and the day's heat threatened to roast me.

"Going for a swim," I said.

"Me, too," Mila said, her tone subdued, like she wanted to call a truce. "Wait for me to change into my suit, OK?"

Mood swing, I thought. Who cares? She can go swim with Cowboy.

"Hurry up," I said.

She must have known that I'd reached the limit of my patience with her, because without another word she swung out of her hammock, plucked her bikini from the clothesline, and headed off to the john.

Soon we were cooling our heels in the ocean. The waves had picked up again. Ranks upon ranks of them swelled, dipped, rolled, and lurched toward us, slapping me in the chest before continuing on their merry, kamikaze way to the beach. Mila and I hadn't said much of anything to each other, when all of a sudden she turned and gave me a long desperate hug. I took it as an act of unconditional surrender.

"I want us to work," she said.

The hug, genuine and needy, melted my unmeltable defenses, and I wrapped my arms around her, too.

"You got a funny way of showing it," I said.

"That's because I'm scared."

"Of what?"

She laid her cheek against the narrow track of hair that split my breast plate.

"That you don't love me."

"Give me a break, Mila."

"It's true!" She socked me in the kidney. Any harder, and it would have hurt. She resumed hugging me and accusingly said, "You only love the great sex."

"Bullshit." That's what I said, but already Mila had me questioning how shallow I could be.

"Then prove it. Be romantic. You're never romantic."

I thought about it. What was the point? Romance is a lot of jive-ass talk to get in a woman's pants.

"OK, OK. I love you more than the moon and the stars and the entire universe," I said. "Satisfied?"

She socked me in the kidney again.

"You're not even trying."

"This is stupid."

"God, you're a dull fuck." She had me in a goddamn death grip. What choice did I have but to suck it in for another attempt?

"OK, I love you more than love itself. I love you so much that without you, I would be nobody. Without you, I would die a big-time death."

I waited for my romance grade. Mila pushed away, submerged up to her neck, and moved her supple arms gracefully like she was treading water. She looked at me, intrigued, radiant, encouraging.

"More."

It occurred to me that maybe *romance* was important to her. Years from now in the happily-ever-after, we might tell our kids a bed-time story about how Daddy laid it all on the line, bared his soul, went where no other man was man enough to go, and captured Mommy's heart. Besides, if Willy Shakespeare could give an evil asshole like Richard III the wherewithal to woo Lady Anne into marrying him even though she knew he'd had his henchmen off her husband, I could certainly sweet-talk a babe like Mila into forgetting about a loser like Jay.

"More, huh? OK, try this," I said. "When I'm on the El train or taking a walk along the lakefront by myself, I'll feel your presence so strongly it's like if I reach out, you'll materialize right in my arms. Even if you were to break up with me tomorrow, the memory of your touch, the perfect fit of your lips against mine, and the love we've shared would stay wrapped and protected in the inner me forever."

I was getting a little too heavy for my own taste, so I struck a dramatic pose looking off toward the horizon, and in a deep announcer's voice, said, "All this and more from the book of *Love*."

Mila splashed me in the face.

"Just had to ruin it, didn't you," she said. "Blew the whole goddamn mood."

Down but not out, I wiped the salt water from my eyes. The key to success had come into focus. I knelt face to face with Mila and took hold of her hands in mine.

"OK, no more jokes," I said. "The truth. Sometimes I'll go to the corner store, fork over a dollar for a newspaper, then be so ridiculously happy thinking about you that I'll leave without the paper or my change. Sometimes, like when we're at a party, and everyone's dancing and drinking and having a good time, I'll stop whatever I'm doing, spot you across the room, and think to myself, I can't believe she's mine. Sometimes, in the middle of the night, when we're in bed and I'm too wired with love to fall asleep, I'll match the steady rhythm of your breathing with my own so that we become one. You always spoon me tight as a vise, like you're afraid we might get separated from each other in your dreams. There's no one but you for me, only you and always you."

I brought her hand to my face, nuzzled my cheek against it, and then planted a kiss on her knuckles.

"That's how I feel."

Staring at me all lovey-dovey, Mila said, "That was beautiful."

Either the truth was working, or I was taking one hell of a

masochistic pleasure in hanging my butt out to dry. I reasoned that to win the undying love and affection of a woman in Mila's league, you had to pass a few survival-of-the-fittest tests, so I plunged on.

"When I read *War and Peace*, I see your face for Natasha's. Tracy and Hepburn ain't shit compared to Pearson and Popovic. If you were miles and miles away from me, I could find you with only my love for a compass. Every inch of your body—from the bean-size mole on the small of your back, to the vaccination scar high on your thigh, to the cute dimple in your smile—is permanently etched in my heart. If I didn't hear from you for years and years, and then you called me on the telephone, I'd know it was you before the first *hello*. To fear me is to fear being loved. That's the truth, the whole truth, and nothing but the fucking truth, so help me God."

Damn if I hadn't rendered that woman speechless, but I can't say I was exactly sure who had whom in the palm of his or her hand. We stopped to watch a paraglider, towed by a motor boat, sail past like a prehistoric bird. He pulled the cord, floated down from the bluest blue, and landed with a soft touch just up the beach toward town. A couple of Mexicans, probably partners of the two men on the boat, ran over to help the gringo out of the harness, and a small group of tourists, some of them waiting a turn at dangling through the air for a hundred pesos a pop, gathered around.

"Must be a rush," I said. "We should try it."

"Yeah, that'd be fun." Mila leaned forward to embrace me, but still holding her hands, I gently restrained them, at the ready with an encore.

"I will be the man behind the great woman; make love to you morning, noon, and night; satisfy your every desire; adore you until death do us part and go right on adoring you in the hereafter. Ours is one motherfucker of a love. So do me a favor, will ya, and get used to it."

I'm not sure who made the first move, but before I knew it we were locked in each other's arms. Not far away, I heard the power boat rev, about to pull another paraglider into the heavenly heights.

"I do love you," Mila whispered, and peppered my face with kisses. "I do I do I do I do."

If we didn't find a private place to fuck soon, we'd burst. Won't last, I thought, holding onto Mila for dear life.

And why did I feel so lost?

* * *

I awoke in the hammock from a mid-afternoon snooze. As I gazed out over the ghetto of campsites, my vision jiggled like the picture from an unsteady movie projector. *Dream?* I blinked hard, trying to shake a light-headed anxiousness. Sounds flowed out of my ears instead of in—a cooking pot clanging against a grill, a toilet flushing, the squealing of kids playing over by the suburb. *Do I exist?* I checked. Naked except for my damp cut-offs. Hours in the sun had bleached the hairs on my arms and legs and cooked my skin to a taut, sore red-brown. A tall skinny guy wearing nothing but well-worn Levi's passed by and glanced lazily my way. *Why's he looking at me? Acting weird?* Then, on the verge of a panic attack, I recognized the problem. I was stoned off my ass. The joint I'd eaten must have packed one hell of a wallop. Fuck, I thought. Grass always turned me into a paranoid basket case. Mila lay sacked out in her hammock, curled up with the peaceful aura of a child. I decided to go into town and buy something at the drugstore to take the edge off my buzz.

When I got there and started across the cement floor, Alberto, seated on his stool behind the counter, must have heard the heel-slapping approach of my flip-flops, because he looked up from reading something on a clipboard. His gambler-cool facade instantly changing to one of terror, he leaped to his feet, reached for the ceiling with both hands, and shouted, "Don't shoot! The money is yours!"

In my stoned state, the Al Capone joke flew right over me. I jumped back a step and held up my own hands to show I meant no harm.

"Name's Roman. I came in here yesterday for Tums, remember?"

Alberto collapsed over the counter in a fit of laughter. I lowered my hands. *Did I say something wrong? Funny?* When Alberto caught his breath, he managed to brace one arm on the counter and pointed at me.

"You make a lousy gangster, my friend."

Gangster? Seated over in the corner by the magazine rack, the three old geezers—evidently permanent fixtures in the store—looked up from their soap opera picture books and began to titter. Did my being stoned somehow allow them to understand English? The buzzing voltage in my skull cranked up another notch. *Act normal!* Careful not to make any sudden moves, I stepped up to the counter that was just beyond the sharp border of sunlight creeping ever so slowly across the floor from the open-air entrance. Alberto straightened himself and turned all businesslike.

"What can I do for you?"

"I need something to help me sleep."

A lot of drugs that take a prescription in the States are over-the-counter in Mexico. Alberto looked at me with mild disapproval.

"Judging by your heavy eyelids, sleeping pills are the last thing you need."

"Can't sleep," I insisted. "It always takes me a few days to get used to a new place."

I'm a lousy liar straight, much less stoned. Alberto knew, that I knew, that he knew I was high. In fact, aided by a newly acquired ability to read minds, I knew that he knew my entire life's rap sheet right down to the piece of Bazooka bubble gum I'd ripped off from the corner store when I was five. Fingering his thin mustache, he held my fragile psyche in the balance. Then, as if deciding, *What the hell, a sale's a sale*, he reached beneath the counter, slid open a cabinet door, and searched around inside for something with his hand. Retrieving a small box, he set it on the counter.

"Try these. Same as what you call Darvon. But please, no taking them all at one time. I do not want to have to scrape you off the street. That will be thirty-six pesos."

I took out my wallet, fumbled pulling the correct change in bills for what seemed an eternity, and slid them across the counter.

"You know, to be honest, how can anyone sleep?" Alberto said, ringing up the register. "All this trouble in town. It is bad for business. I am telling you, *Jefe* Sánchez is not a man to fool with. If he says he is not going to rest until he finds who burned the restaurant, he means it. I hope people stay calm instead of everyone blaming everyone else. Reason must prevail. Can I count on you?"

"For what?" I asked.

Alberto closed the register box with a firm shove.

"To be a soldier of reason."

The impact of a moral crusade descended upon my shoulders. This was no mere druggist across the counter from me; this was my blood brother.

"Yes," I said solemnly. "Never doubt you can count on me."

Alberto looked at me queerly. "Are you *always* this serious?" he asked. "You need to—how do you say—lighten up."

Shit, I thought. Can't do anything right. Cutting my losses, I grabbed the box of downers, then rushed out of the store and into the road. I hadn't gotten ten feet before I slapped my hand against my forehead. *Oh, I get it—Al Capone.* I took one of the pills out of the box and cellophane wrapper. Too paranoid to stop at a restaurant for a Coke, I popped the pill in my mouth, made do with saliva, and swallowed. Feel better soon, I thought. It was still a good two hours before the gringo dinner rush, the town fairly deserted. Up ahead, several men loaded charred beams and planks from the burnt-out restaurant onto a flatbed truck. I just wanted to lay low in my hammock.

Then something happened, the meaning of which I would have understood stoned or straight. As I was about to pass a *campesino* standing with a beer in his hand just outside the restaurant where Mila and I had eaten breakfast, he spit right in front of me, barely missing my toes. I hesitated. Straw cowboy hat low on his forehead, beefy arms, and skin black from the sun, he never looked directly at me, taking an insolent slug off his *cerveza*. Didn't see me coming? Bullshit. Anger prickled the hairs on the back of my neck. The advice of Jesse Wilks, a friend of mine in high school, has always stayed with me. "*White boy, a good fight lasts three sec-*

onds. Longer than that, and you fucked up." Using Jesse's rule of thumb, I'd already fucked up by hesitating. I wasn't in any shape to get physical; besides, I wouldn't exactly call flip-flops proper ass-stomping attire. Fine, I thought, moving down the road again. See if I help put out the next fire.

But that prickle stayed on my neck all the way to the trailer park.

3

I'd been lying in my hammock, spacing for I don't know how long, when Mila stirred in her hammock, stretched, and yawned. Probably still under the spell of my undying love declaration, she smiled at me contentedly.

"Hey, sweetie," she said.

"Bad news," I said.

"What's bad news?"

"That joint I ate is freakin' me out. Too stoned. You gotta help me get through this."

Genuine concern crossed Mila's face.

"Help you how?"

"Can't think," I said. "Feel like I'm losing control."

Without my having to explain anything more, Mila swung out of her hammock, came over to mine, and squeezed in next to me. Cuddling, she kissed me tenderly on the cheek.

"It's all my stupid fault. Good thing you're always looking out for us. Now it's my turn to take care of you."

The worst of the day's heat had come and gone, the trailer park's comfy shade slowly deepening. The shower house next to the toilet stalls must have been full up, several people waiting in line out front.

"Ummmm, love you so much," Mila said. "Almost time for dinner. Hungry?"

At the suggestion of food, the munchies laid claim to my gut and cottony dry mouth.

"I went into town for some downers to soften the buzz, but it's not helping. Can't deal with anyone when I'm like this. How about you bringing food back here?"

"Relax," Mila said. "We'll be at our own table and I'll do the ordering. Leave everything to me."

And so I turned my fragile psyche over to Mila's loving care. Damn if she didn't take her job seriously. She held onto my arm as we headed out of the trailer park and down the road into town like she was leading a blind man.

"Doing fine," she said. "Try to enjoy the high. Almost there."

By the time we reached the Coca Cabana, my break from the responsibility of *being* didn't strike me as half bad. Sunlight stabbed from the doorway but quickly died in the dim interior. The conical thatched hut with its seven candlelit tables and wall decorations of seashells tangled in fishnets reminded me of a cheesy nightclub. *Born to Be Wild* cranked from the jukebox for the umpteenth time in two days. Arriving just under the wire of the dinner rush, we took the last empty table in a corner. Ravenous sunburned tourists gabbed as they waited for their food. Mila began deciphering a Spanish menu, while I stared into the candle's red glass container at the hypnotic flame.

"Isn't fire cool?" I asked.

"Uh-huh," Mila said.

"I mean, really, really cool."

"Uh-huh."

"I mean, it's like so fucking cool."

Mila giggled and glanced up from the menu. "You're wasted."

I leaned over the table and kept my voice down.

"Am I acting weird?"

Mila patted my hand reassuringly. "You're fine."

A young Indian waitress glided over for our order. Pen and pad in hand, she looked at us in the sullen manner I'd come to expect from most of the locals. Pointing at an item on the menu, Mila ordered for the both of us.

"*Tres, por favor.*"

Miss Happy went off to another table without so much as a friendly nod.

"What are we getting?" I asked.

"I think it's shrimp and fries. Thought you'd like it."

So this was how women feel when men coddle them. Not bad. The downer finally kicked in, and as marijuana frenetic buzz passed the baton to barbituate drowsy happiness, I got the slouches and felt myself sinking into one mellow fellow. The music changed back and forth from dated rock to Spanish schmaltz. Surprisingly, I had no problem grooving to the beat of either cultural flavor. Before I knew it, our waitress was slamming plates of food on the table. Then, right in the middle of Mila trying to politely order a couple of Cokes from her, she raced off toward the kitchen doorway at the back of the hut.

"Gee," Mila said. "Think she's trying to tell us something? If you want a good tip, you give good service. I should know, it's what I do for a living."

"Life is so cool," I said.

"Let these people try and last five minutes working in a restaurant in Chicago."

"Wouldn't it be cool to eat fresh seafood and swim in the ocean and live on the beach every day for the rest of our lives?"

"Roman, did you hear anything I said?"

"Huh? I love you so much. I mean, I really, really love you. Do you love me?"

"Yes, sweetie. I really, really love you."

Starved, I picked up a piece of shrimp and peeled the shell. It was becoming a conscious effort to keep my tipsy head balanced on my neck.

The family that owned the Coca Cabana lived in the small quarters connected behind the kitchen. A wide-eyed chubby toddler, dressed in only a cloth diaper, waddled out of the kitchen doorway and started chasing after a mangy mutt that was prowling the dining room for food scraps. Fido, not interested in being a playmate, slunk in and out from under tables and between customers' legs with the boy always hot on his tail. Finally, Toddler lunged for the dog's bony rump in the middle of the dining room, fell short, and smacked his face against the dirt floor. He bawled bloody murder.

"Awww," said a gringa at another table. "Poor kid."

Consuelo, the tamale girl, hurried out of the kitchen where she and a sister, not much older than her, had been assisting their mother in preparing meals. She helped her baby brother to his feet, brushed dirt off his cheek, and gave him a hug. The wailing stopped so abruptly you'd have thought she'd flipped a switch on the kid. Then she aimed him in the direction of the kitchen doorway, patted his diapered butt, and sent him on his eager way.

"*Hola*, Consuelo," Mila said. "So this is where you live."

Consuelo wandered over to Mila. By the looks of her shy smile, she seemed to want something. With a child's brave innocence, she reached out her hand and began petting Mila's hair.

"Oh, you like my hair?" Mila asked. "Fair's fair, let me touch your braid. Ooooo, it's so thick! Wanna trade?"

They shared a hair-petting moment that I'll admit was sweet to watch. Curiosity satisfied, Consuelo darted into the sanctuary of the kitchen.

"*Adios*," Mila called after her. Then to me—"Isn't she the cutest?"

"She's beautiful. Most beautiful kid I've ever seen." I bit into a shrimp. "This tastes great. Best shrimp I ever had. What a great vacation."

After dinner, in our hammocks again, evening light reflected off the beach beyond the palm trees in a luxurious crimson. Mila read her paperback copy of *Fear of Flying*—a book on the best-seller list then; I attempted spiritual and intellectual growth by reading *Moby Dick*. Talk about a lost cause. Only those who have ventured to plow through Melville's masterful prose while stoned know the true meaning of futility. Six passes on the same paragraph later, I gave up and tossed the book underhanded in the direction of my pack. Hell, if one downer made you feel all drowsy-wonderful, why not two? As I climbed out of the hammock, my foot caught on the edge of it. Tripping and spinning with the grace of a loosey-goosey drunk, I landed on my back in the sand.

"You all right?" Mila asked.

"Yeah." A human rubberband feels no pain. I picked myself

up and dusted off. "That downer's a killer. Think I'll have another one." I went over to my pack to get the box of pills and my canteen filled with warm flat Coke. "Want one?"

"Sure," Mila said. "We deserve some fun."

The evil deed completed, I restowed the canteen in the pack and fell clumsily into my hammock again. Eyelids growing more and more heavy, I fought off the dreamy lure of sleep. The sun went down, its panoramic blaze of color searing the ocean. In the thickening twilight, Mila came over to my hammock, climbed in, and pulled her sleeping bag on top of us for privacy. Kissing, licking, nibbling, stroking, and diddling, I felt as if we were melting into each other like wax. We managed incredible acts of physical dexterity in those close quarters, not the least of which was helping each other wiggle out of our shorts and underwear. When it was good and dark, we attempted to sneak a fuck, but each time Mila mounted into position above my hard-on, some idiot would come down the lane casting a busy-body flashlight beam, or show a complete lack of decorum by cutting through our campsite. We had to face facts. Humping in a public place attracts an audience.

"This is ridiculous," Mila said. "Let's go find somewhere on the beach."

"Yeah, this bullshit." I was starting to economize the effort it took to talk by leaving out words and must have sounded like the Lone Ranger's faithful Indian friend, Tonto. "Need fuck bad, sweetie."

We struggled to get dressed again. Drugs and horniness blunted my common sense. I didn't stop to think that maybe a beach at night in a desperately poor country isn't the safest place for a couple of moving-in-slow-motion *Norte Americanos*.

We left the trailer park behind us and lugged our sleeping bags about a couple of hundred yards into the inky darkness. Sufficiently alone on the beach, we stopped. Waves crashed in the surf. At the tip of the bay, the lighthouse beacon pulsed in intervals of two blinks at a time. Up above, a multitude of stars—so close and big I could have plucked one out of the sky and used it for a baseball—

marked our earthly coordinates. We laid out the unzipped bags, peeled off our clothes, and crawled into bed. Within seconds we're fucking, Mila on top. Profundity of the universe above me, Mila's ass in my hands, my cock at long last tucked safely inside her pussy, what more could any son of mortal man ask for? But alas, a word of warning to all men: The penis does not—I repeat, does not—appreciate downers. To put it delicately, my hard-on takes a powder. Our pelvic gyrations grind to a halt.

"What's a matter?" Mila asks.

"Drugs," Tonto answers. "Sorry."

"That's OK. Don't worry about it. No biggy."

She could say that again. We both yawn.

"Take break," I say. "Rest little while."

The next thing I know, Mila's still on top of me, shaking my shoulders and yelling, "Roman, wake up! Wake up! Someone's here!"

"Huh?"

It's all I can do to pry my eyes open. Mila slides off me, and there towering over us is a bare-chested, built-like-a-squat-bear figure who's holding a machete at his side. He says something in Spanish, like he's calmly telling us the way it's going to be, and reaches for Mila.

"Don't touch me!" She sits up, clutching the sleeping bag to her breasts. I'm so wasted it's all I can do to roll onto my side and hold out my arm, more like I'm offering to shake hands than to ward him off.

"Amigo. What you want?"

I make out his inscrutable eyes in the darkness. Again the low-key conversational Spanish as he reaches for Mila. I brush his arm away, confused as to what he's after.

"He wants to rape me!"

I'm expecting him to deny Mila's accusation in one language or another, but he just stands there, the inscrutability in his eyes tipping toward anger. I sober up fast. A Mexican with a machete has the jump on us, we're butt-naked, fucked-up on downers, and there's no cavalry on the horizon. He pulls back his arm with the machete just enough so that I get the message, then with his free hand he makes another move for Mila. I knock his arm away.

"No!"

Responsibility for the defense of Mila's body is mine alone. He threatens with the machete again, this time not so subtly. I envision my decapitated head spurting blood as it rolls to a stop in the sand. Something tells me to play dumb.

"We amigos. No trouble, amigo. Me, you, amigos."

He's not buying any of this *amigo* shit, looking at me like it's my last chance to get out of the way of what's his. A part of me feels as if I'm a casual observer watching the outcome of someone else's fate, the other part bluffing for dear life.

"No, amigo. Why you want hurt us, amigo?"

In the prolonged standoff, the rumbling surf takes on an omnipotent presence.

"*Diez* pesos."

He wants to pay me less than a dollar for my girlfriend?

"No!"

It's his move. If looks could kill, I'd be fertilizer for daisies. Then, like he decides that things have gotten a little too complicated for his own good, he moves away into the darkness. A few steps later, he stops and spins around. *Changed his mind?* My gut pops into my throat, but I stare back at him, making sure he can't read any trace of fear. He takes off again at a brisk walk across the beach.

"That was—"

"Shhhhh!" I tell Mila. Not until the Mexican has gone up a dirt road, disappearing into the blackness of the hilly countryside, do I feel the fist of tension loosen inside my chest. I let out a long breath.

The space around me slowly expanded to normal.

"That was close," Mila said.

"Scary shit," I said.

"I would have let him rape me if I had to. It's not that big a deal. I'd survive."

The frank glimpse into her strength as a woman startled me for an instant.

"This is dangerous," I said, consciously not slipping into Tonto-talk again. "We better get back to camp."

Recreational drugs always bring out the stupid in me. I groped around for my pants but couldn't find them anywhere.

"Sonofabitch stole my clothes. That's my wallet, traveler's checks, driver's license—shhhhhit!"

Mila searched on her hands and knees for her clothes.

"He got my clothes, too."

We must have been so conked out we didn't hear our *bandido* friend sneak up on us, steal our stuff, take it some place for safe keeping, and then return as an afterthought to get some nooky from Mila.

"Let's get out of here," I said.

Wrapped in our sleeping bags, we looked like a couple of mummies hustling toward the trailer park. It must not have been that late; the flickering glow of several small campfires, at that distance not much bigger than the flames of matches, guided us homeward.

"Un-fucking-believable," I said. "What the hell are we going to live on for the next four days?"

"Relax, Roman. I left my wallet and traveler's checks in my pack. Seventy bucks oughta be enough to get us through."

"I thought you said we should never leave our money at camp."

"Be glad I forgot," Mila said. "Might as well look at the bright side."

"Fuck the bright side. You think there's an American Express office around the corner where I can get my checks replaced? How much you wanna bet the closest one is in Mexico City? If we don't watch every penny, we're up shit creek."

Changing the subject, Mila asked, "Did you get a load of the size of that guy's boner?"

"His *what*?"

"You didn't see it stickin' out of his fly? Hard to miss. Must have been a foot long."

Mila sounded more awed than anything else. I'd been so intent on always meeting the *bandido's* eyes, I hadn't noticed that formidable below-the-belt detail. Growing more pissed-off by the second, we approached the outskirts of the trailer park. Call it the luck of the draw, but whose campsite should we choose in the darkness to cut through than that of the cowboys. Perhaps hearing the jingling zipper tab on Mila's sleeping bag, Jay poked his head above the edge of a hammock strung between two trees.

"Looky what the wind blew in," he said, grinning.

Otto, sitting with his pack for a cushion against one of the tree trunks, hit us with a sloppy buzzed smile and lifted a bottle of beer in salute.

"*Hola*," he said. "Just in time to party."

So much for Otto's fling with sobriety. On the sand beside him was a wooden case of beer, more than half the bottles already missing from their pigeon holes. Mila and I stopped by a tarp laid out with a couple of sleeping bags. The harsh light of an incandescent lantern from a few campsites away cast the four of us in ghostly-goblin shadows. Otto picked up a beer from the case and offered it first-come first-serve.

"No thanks," I said. "That's a lot of beer. Thought you boys were short on cash."

"Let's just say this alcohol is compliments of a delivery truck parked all by its lonesome in town," Jay said. "Shucks, I forgot to leave an IOU." He gave our mummy attire the once-over. "What's this, the latest style from Parie?"

"Fucking asshole stole our clothes and Roman's wallet while we were asleep on the beach," Mila said. "Wanted to rape me. I hate these people."

"Fucked us over, that's for sure," I added.

Jay lifted a beer to his lips, drained the last of it, and swung himself out of the hammock. He hurled the empty bottle far out onto the beach, then sauntered over to us. He was wearing only cut-offs, and the lantern from behind him lit his tall sinewy outline.

"Can't say I didn't try and warn ya," he said. "Give a beaner an inch, and he thinks he can take our women."

"What all happened?" Otto asked.

"You deaf, Otto? Fuckin' beaner tried to rape Mila."

"Now, just hold on, Jay. No one's hurt. Let's give these folks a chance to calm—"

"Calm my ass, Otto. They been robbed."

"Not like we can go to the cops," Mila said. "Everyone knows these people all stick together."

"You sayin' that beaner shouldn't pay?" Jay asked, leaning his goblin face in close to Mila.

"Sure, he *should*," Mila said.

"He's long gone now," I said. "Could be anywhere."

I was about to chalk the whole fiasco up to experience and ask Otto for that beer after all, when Jay said, "This ain't no time to be chicken-shit." He moved quickly over to a machete stuck like a sword in the sand next to the tarp, grabbed the rawhide handle, and pulled the weapon free.

"Hey, that's mine," Otto said. "Where the hell you goin'?"

"Come on, *señorita*," Jay said. "I'll defend your honor. Let's go find that damn *hombre*."

By the flattered expression on Mila's face, I could have sworn she was contemplating taking Sir Cowboy up on his gallant offer. Something in me snapped. I learned firsthand that the flip-side of a happy-go-lucky downer's freak is a mean nasty one.

"Gimme that!" My arm shot out from the mummy wrapper, and in one fell swoop I snatched the machete out of Jay's hand. Raising it over my head, I shook it like a saber, shouting, "I'm gonna fuck me up a Mexican!"

"Whoa!" Otto said. He got to his feet so fast he seemed yanked by some invisible force. He came toward me, gesturing up and down with his hands for me to cool off. "Might want to just hang on there a minute, friend. Believe me, this all will look a whole lot less serious in the morning."

"The fuck it will!" I shot back. "Don't worry, I'll bring your machete back."

"Hey, the machete's the last thing I'm worried about," Otto said. "Why not just stay awhile and have yourselves a nice warm beer."

I wasn't big on being Alberto's "soldier of reason" right at that moment.

"Come on," I told Mila. "Let's go get dressed."

"Then what?" she asked apprehensively, but I heard her foot-steps in the sand as she followed after me.

"You'll see."

"Now you're talkin', amigo," Jay called after us, and he let out a war whoop that split the night—"Whaaaaaaow!"

At our campsite, under the cover of darkness, Mila and I each threw on jeans and a T-shirt. Befitting the vigilante occasion, on the front of my powder-blue shirt was a huge badge logo of the Chicago Police Department, sponsor of a city baseball league I'd played in. As I knelt down to tie the shoelaces on one of my Adidas, I heard fragments of a conversation coming from the bad-ass hippies' campsite not that much further in the trailer park. I made out Jay's animated voice among several others.

"Beaner tried to rape . . ."

"No shit."

"Stole their clothes, money . . ."

"Fuckin' bogus."

"Oughta teach these . . ."

Great, I thought. Everyone knows. To say I felt the need to save face is putting it mildly.

Soon Mila and I were heading across a stretch of beach that lay before us like rumpled black velvet. Never have I felt so capable of so much ugly as on that beautiful starlit night. I had the machete grasped resolutely in my hand, and not even the sand fill-ing my gym shoes could slow me down.

"What are we going to do?" Mila asked, having trouble keep-ing up with me. "Go door to door?"

"If that's what it takes to find him," I said. "Fucked with the wrong guy."

The whole idea of male-ego anger is to maintain it long enough so that common sense can't derail the serious mistake you're about to commit. I made out a break in the tall grass and scrub weeds where the road that the *bandido* had taken led into the hills. We veered to the left and started up it. Soft sand gave way to firm dirt underfoot. As we came over the lip of a small hill, the crash and roar of the surf faded into the cricket-singing, hushed countryside.

"Sure you know what we're doing?" Mila asked.

"Fuckin' *A*."

Not much further, we came to a lone, windowless thatched hut on the side of the road. From inside I heard people gabbing in Spanish. I led our way around the hut and into stark light spraying out the open doorway. About a dozen or so teenage boys made themselves at home on bunkbeds or sat on stools playing cards at a table in the center of the room. Most of them wore raggedy pants without any shirts. My guess is they were field hands. We're talking poverty—not a sink or a toilet in sight. A kerosene lantern, white-hot bright, hung from a rafter. Surprised by a pair of sleepy-eyed, stoned *Norte Americanos* this far off the beaten tourist path, the boys dropped their cards, comics, or stopped whatever else they were doing, swarmed to the doorway, and stood looking us over, neither ruffled nor threatened by the machete held at my side.

"Been robbed," I said. "Where is he?" I attempted to enter the room but immediately ran into several of the boys' hands against my chest.

"I'm comin' in."

A wall of hands shoved me back again. For some strange reason, they weren't the least bit impressed with the police-badge logo on my T-shirt. A mop-headed boy, who in a parallel universe might have been a high school buddy of mine in Chicago, stepped forward and explained something to me in Spanish.

"Get out of my way!" I reached to push him aside, but he and others immediately slammed their hands against my shoulders, chest, and ribs so hard I stumbled out of the doorway and had to catch myself from falling in a dirt clearing. Mila quickly followed after me and gave my elbow an urgent tug.

"Let's get out of here, Roman."

"Fuck that!"

She looked at me like I was supposed to pick up on her signal.

"What's your fuckin' problem?" I asked her. The spokesboy stepped out of the hut and over to me. Without raising his voice, he again explained something to me in Spanish that in hindsight I would translate as follows: *This isn't your house, this isn't your town, and this isn't your country, so get lost.*

Between the impact of the shoves still throbbing on my body, the now-or-never weight of the machete in my hand, and the amused looks on the boys' faces crowding the doorway, I came to the enlightened realization that something wasn't kosher. I did the math. A dozen Mexicans is greater than one stoned white dude. They seemed all too willing to let my actions dictate the extent of my own demise. If not for their patience and sense of fair play, I would have already been dead meat.

"We better go," I told Mila. I didn't hear any argument from her.

As we retreated back down the road, I heard an explosion of laughter from behind us—no doubt at my expense.

"Fuckin' assholes," I said, and stopped. "Let them come out here and laugh."

"Go," Mila ordered, pushing me forward.

My career as a vigilante nipped in the bud, we continued toward the beach. Not until sand squished underfoot did Mila say, "You could have gotten us killed. *That* was my problem."

"They got the message," I said, but already I was beginning to wonder how the hell I had landed so far on the wrong side of the common-human-decency fence. My vague mental picture of the *bandido's* face blurred with countless other Indian men I'd seen in Escondido. With my anger dissipating, the pillowy myopia from the downers laid claim to me with a vengeance. We stumbled along in the direction of the trailer park, so much empty, lonely blackness before us. I wanted to erase all that had happened that night by collapsing into my hammock and sleeping the sleep of the dead.

"Never shoulda taken downers," I said. "Shoulda known better than to fall asleep on—"

"*Shoulda* won't change anything." Mila was pulling away from me again. I felt it in my face and stomach sure as a sudden drop in barometric pressure. We trudged on. Several times I came within a hair of accidentally slicing a gash in my shin or calf with the machete dangling uselessly at my side. About halfway down the beach to the trailer park, something caught the corner of my eye. Not far away, a small group of shadowy figures separated, merged, and separated again from the dark, in a state of black-on-black dreamy flux.

"Look," I whispered, and we stopped. Instinct told me to keep a low profile. Some kind of ritualistic dance? Four of the shadows had surrounded a smaller fifth that was bouncing between the others like a dishrag. I heard the smack of fist on cheekbone.

"Oh," Mila said, reacting to the raw violence by shielding her eyes with a hand. "What are they—"

"Shhhhh." I knew the score. Street-gang mentality. They fuck with one of yours, so you fuck with one of theirs. Doesn't matter which one; leave it to the enemy to sort out the particulars. The dishrag shadow absorbed a few more punches, then fell in a lump on the sand.

"That's enough," said a shadow with a gravelly voice.

Another shadow, tall and lean, got down and became one with the lump. It didn't take long. Even at that distance I heard a cracking pop, like someone twisting a wing off a roasted turkey. Then a yelp of pain. With a shudder, I kissed good-bye any last doubts about who had torched the restaurant.

"I said, that's enough!"

The tall lean shadow separated from the writhing lump and stood over it as if admiring his handiwork. Not my fault, I kept telling myself. Never asked anyone to fight my battles. But a heavy guilt damn near paralyzed me.

"Come on," I whispered.

Mila and I skirted past the group unnoticed. When we were definitely out of earshot from the shadows, I couldn't resist: "Still like your cowboy?"

"What do you mean?" Mila asked. "Jay?"

"No, Roy fucking Rogers. Who do you think I mean?"

"Jesus, Roman. Do you always have to assume the worst about everybody? What makes you think Jay was over there?"

"Can't imagine," I said. Then I wondered, *That naïve?* "Didn't you hear him talking to those biker types? Otto told me Jay has a talent for dislocating people's joints. Wha'd you think that *pop* was? Anyone that mean wouldn't think twice about burning down a restaurant."

"It's dark," Mila said. "Like a *pop* proves anything? Maybe Otto's the one causing trouble, and he's telling lies about Jay to cover his own ass. Ever think of that, Einstein? And who cares if some Mexican gets jumped; I've been around this place long enough to know he probably did something to deserve it."

Just then, a shooting star zipped over the mountains from the southeast to far out over the ocean in the northwest, so bright and long and sharp as a jeweler's cut I thought the speckled sky would break in two and reveal what lay beyond.

"Did you see that?"

"What?" Mila followed my gaze upward, but it was already too late. She'd missed it.

* * *

I awoke in my hammock to the early, reprimanding light of morning, immediately flashed on the night before, and thought, *Roman, you should be dead.* I glanced over at Mila still asleep in her hammock. From her troubled expression, I wondered if she was having a bad dream. An inner voice attempted to pierce through my obsession to keep her: *Fuck it. Let her go.* Not a chance. The things that would make life easier aren't always easy to do. Past Mila and several other campsites, the Bad Asses were long gone, nothing left but a curlicue of smoke rising from their spent campfire. Their dirty deed done under the cover of night, I doubted the victim could have identified his assailants any more than I could have identified the *bandido*.

Consuelo approached my hammock carrying that bucket almost as big as herself. Thin arms sticking out of a sleeveless white dress, she lifted the bucket by its handle to just under my chin and looked at me with huge eyes that were as savvy as they were innocent.

"Tamales?" she asked in a soft voice. "*Dos* pesos." She pulled back a towel covering the top of the bucket, and the smell of hot, steaming corn meal, like the secure embrace of civilization itself, greeted me. I looked from her to the tamales to her again, that brown face so endearing. I reached into a pocket of my jeans, but felt not a single centavo. My days of throwing pesos around like they were manhole covers were over.

"Sorry," I said, and held up my hands to prove they were empty.

Downcast by the sure sale that had somehow slipped through her fingers, but nonetheless ready to persevere, Consuelo lugged the bucket off to another campsite.

Like a good middle-class kid, I silently vowed never to tell my mother how stupid and ignorant I had been that night.

CHAPTER 5

FREEDOM

Let's be honest. A good blowjob is often a sure-fire way to a man's heart, but that said, my undying love for Mila was far more complicated than my fearing life without her carnal talents. It's the horrific story Mila told me about her family that tugged at my sympathy and carried me into my downward-spiraling effort to hold on to her.

The winter before our trip to Mexico, you'd have to say living together was my idea. She constantly bent conversations around to how she felt suffocated by her family, and this led one Friday night to my spontaneous, "How about I move out with you? That way we can both afford it." Facing her in a vinyl booth at the Far East restaurant on Diversey, I dished a patty of egg foo yung onto her plate. Just a few weeks after the holidays, the reality of three more months of bitter Chicago cold seemed unfair. Mila looked at me like the thought of us going dutch on rent had never even occurred to her.

"That's sweet of you, Roman, really. But four months together is hardly enough time to—"

"I know you better than anyone I've ever known in my entire life."

A waiter rushed past us down the aisle, up to his ears serving the "date night" crowd. As he burst through the swinging doors to the kitchen shouting something in Chinese to the cooks, I heard the loud hiss of food sizzling in woks. A paper lantern hanging over our booth cast a shadow of a dancing dragon that looked like it was about to bite Mila's neck. I reached out across the table and squeezed her hand.

"Do you have any idea how much I love you?"

Gazing into her eyes, I sensed, just below the surface of her caution, a strong undertow of relief. She didn't take much convincing.

And so I kissed a cozy set-up at home good-bye, where, since my eighteenth birthday, my parents had allowed me to bring home a steady girlfriend for the night.

"Better that than sneaking around behind our backs," my mother had told me. "Just remember, I don't need any shotgun marriages in this family." Then from my father, "It's not just the girl's responsibility—*always* use birth control."

Cool, I thought. My older sisters, Dawn and Celia, already into the sexual revolution and living in their own apartments with boyfriends, quickly pointed out that they had never had it so good while at home. They chalked up my conjugal-visitation-rights as another one of my parents' long list of flagrant double-standard treatments of me. No matter. At the ripe old age of twenty, armed and ready with a babe for a girlfriend, I wanted some *real* freedom.

It took awhile for the two of us to squirrel away a cash reserve. Then around the middle of spring, just about the time the trees in Chicago are fooled into opening their buds only to suffer the consequences of a freak snowstorm, Mila spotted an ad in the *Reader* for a one-bedroom apartment in the Lake View neighborhood on Belmont Avenue above a Polk Brothers appliance store. The rent was a whopping $250. With the help of a kind-hearted buddy of mine ("It's on the fucking third floor?" he yelled at me over the telephone) and a U-haul trailer hitched to my father's Plymouth Fury, Mila and I made the big move in May and set up playing house.

A typical day during summer vacation might go something like this: Wake up and fuck. Cook bacon and eggs for breakfast, then fuck. Work on a Kafka-wannabe short story for a few hours at my desk in the bedroom, while Mila stands at her easel in the dining room painting a naked fat woman mysteriously hiding in a room behind a couch. Then break for lunch and a fuck. Take a bike ride for a mile or so through the neighborhood streets of Victorian houses and apartment buildings to the park along the lakefront, stop off at Fullerton Beach for a cool dip in the breakers and some sunbathing, then ride home and fuck like bunnies again.

No nook or cranny in our humble abode escaped the sweet scent of our lovemaking. Up against a wall; on top of the dining room table; in the shower; on the throw rug in the living room; bent over the kitchen sink; in front of the full-length mirror on the bathroom door; in the pantry with Snap, Crackle, and Pop smiling down at us from a box of Rice Krispies on the shelf. And, lord have mercy, on our bed. We put the *Kama Sutra* to shame. Who gives a shit that all our silverware didn't match, that we bought furniture at Salvation Army stores, or that we seldom paid the bills on time. Life was a fucking utopia.

Around 4 o'clock, Mila would tear away from my lascivious clutches, shower, and head off to her part-time waitress job. Recently, she'd graduated from a *Wimpy's* hamburger joint to a new classy French restaurant in Lincoln Park called *Amour*—a hokey name that was in sync with the culture at the time. On a good night, she brought home seventy to ninety bucks in tips—no small chump-change. I counted myself rolling in dough if I pulled in twenty-five bartending at Bismarck's, a neighborhood hole-in-the-wall on Sheffield Avenue just a few blocks away from our apartment.

Thursdays through Saturdays, an hour sharp after Mila's departure, my gratified cock and I left for work. Bismarck's catered to college kids, struggling actors, artists, and assorted other members of the inner-city, urban-renewal vanguard, most of whom contented themselves swilling the gut-rot beer we kept on tap.

A word or two is probably in order to explain how I landed a bartending job before I turned twenty-one. For several years, the Illinois State Legislature lowered the legal drinking age for beer and wine to eighteen, the argument being that if you're old enough to die for your country, you damn well ought to be old enough to drink. The legislature reversed the law again because of all the human roadkill at the hands of drunk teenage drivers, but that's beside the point. I caught that window of lowered-legal-age-drinking opportunity. With the Vietnam War slowly winding down and the Selective Service draft put on hold the exact year of my eighteenth birthday, I also avoided the tough moral decision between fighting Communism halfway around the world or taking a permanent vacation in Canada. Instead, I firmly established myself as a regular at Bismarck's with a talent for nursing a single beer longer than it took most people to earn a Ph.D. One night, tired of the insufficient-funds routine, I approached the crowded bar and asked Carl Steiner—owner, proprietor, former pastry chef, and switch-hitter in his sexual preference—for a job instead of a brew.

"So you vant to try life from this side of the business, yah?" Carl asked. With his German accent, wavy red hair, handlebar mustache, and dashing, rugged good looks, more than a few customers had thought themselves original by calling him *The Red Baron*. People two deep at the bar were clamoring for beers. "OK," Carl said. "You start right now."

I spent the rest of the night learning how to correctly slant a beer mug to prevent too much foam head on a draw from the tap, the right glass for a Tom Collins as opposed to a Whiskey Sour, the intricacies of operating a cash register with a drawer that had a bad habit of sticking, and when to tell impatient drunks, "Hey, buddy, do I look like I've got three hands?"

Perhaps my employment with a "good German" helped to lessen the blow Hilda must have felt when her eldest daughter confided to her that she intended to openly live in sin with yours truly. "Who am I to judge?" she asked Mila. "If you're happy, I'm happy." But whenever Mila and I visited the homestead for a free meal, I always felt Hilda watching me with her permanent cynical sneer, ready to jump in my shit the moment I proved to be a typical brute. As for Semo, he heard from his wife and three daughters only that Mila had gotten her own apartment, and not a peep about sharing it with me.

"You good boy, Roman," Semo would say, and slap me on the back like I was the son he never had. "You come." Once he led me with those mincing bad-circulation steps of his up the stairs to the same master bedroom closet where he kept his guns. This time he stooped down, picked up a pair of wing-tip shoes from a shoetree, and proudly showed them to me.

"Shoes twenty year old. Like new. Italian, lot money."

"Wow," I said, taking one of the shoes from him and politely inspecting it. "Great-looking shoes, Mr. Popovic."

Another time he took me out to his backyard vegetable garden, plucked one of the grapefruit-sized tomatoes off a vine, and dropped it in my hand.

"Big tomato. Fert'lizer."

"Wow," I said. "That's really something, Mr. Popovic. Bet it's real juicy."

"You like, take."

"Thanks, Mr. Popovic. I'll be sure to use it on my cheese sandwiches."

From the relative safety of not being Jewish, I found the old man's childlike need for approval endearing.

Later, as I rode the El home with Mila, I asked, "Can't we just tell him we live together? I'm not into all this lying. You're twenty. He'll get over it, won't he?"

Mila looked at me from her side of the seat as if to say, *Please tell me you're not that naïve.* "Get it straight once and for all, Roman. Don't even think about telling Tati we live together unless you want to wake up one night with one of his guns shoved up your nose. I know him a whole lot better than you do, all right?"

"Whatever you say, sweetie. Do you see this tomato? Semo gave it to me as a token of our undying friendship."

"Ha, ha, ha," Mila said. "We'll see how *undying* you are if he finds out you're shacked up with his daughter."

Around mid-July, when a sauna-like humidity beat down on Chicago by day, only to swelter up from the streets by night, Carl and I manned the bar on a slow evening. A slip of my tongue (something about how Mila intended to treat me to a night out on the town to celebrate my upcoming twenty-first birthday) alerted Carl to my half-boy-half-man status in the eyes of the law. He had long since given up trying to flirt his way into my pants and settled for taking a fatherly shine to me.

"You mean to tell me you vere nineteen vhen I hired you?" Carl asked, narrowing his eyes angrily. "Ve serve hard liquor here, too, yah? I could lose my license just like *that!*" He snapped his fingers right in front of my nose. Without giving me a chance to respond, he grabbed a dishtowel on top of the beer cooler and began wiping down a spill left behind on the bar by a customer. I quickly busied myself washing out beer mugs with the electric bristle scrubber in the sink, expecting the old heave-ho any second. Across the room, a bell on the bowling machine went off as an anorexic-looking woman—the latest girlfriend of a scruffy tortured poet who could always be found at the end of the bar downing shots and guzzling beers—threw a strike. Barry Manilow crooned from the jukebox about how he writes "the songs that make the whole world sing." Soon, Carl stepped over to me again and put his hands on my shoulders.

"You look good behind the bar and the customers like you, Roman," he said. "Until you are twenty-one, just make sure you disappear out the back door vhen the cops come to break up a fight."

"No problem," I said. "Consider me never here."

Hell, we're talking pre–Ronnie Reagan and George Bush Senior era, and back then people were kinder and gentler to each other. Carl, already on his fourth Rusty Nail of the night and feeling no pain, started one of his off-color stories—something about how he and another prominent pastry chef in Hamburg once beat off in a vat of blintz filling that would soon end up in a culinary gift from the West German government to Buckingham Palace. He paid me strictly in cash, and I figured the I.R.S. wouldn't mind me using their share to help pay for school.

Bismarck's closed at 2 a.m. With a slurred, "Drive safely," Carl locked the front door behind the last customer. Then he counted the till and poured himself another Rusty Nail while I collected and washed beer mugs, wiped down the bar, mopped the floor, and sprayed all the baseboards with a small tank of insecticide that sent the hordes of cockroaches scurrying up the walls to safety.

I got home long after Mila had already crashed in bed. Kissing and nibbling her awake, we shared one last glorious fuck of the day, then lay side by side with her cooling in sweat and, so I thought, harmony. Flat-gray light from a street lamp in the alley washed under the half-open windowshade and illuminated my trusty typewriter and a mess of manuscript pages on the desk in front of the window. Through the doorway and out another open window in the dining room, I heard a lone car swish past on Belmont Avenue, that major city artery all but deserted. Wrigley, our mellow tabby, hopped up on the foot of the mattress, double-checked to make sure that the coast was clear of our tumultuous lovemaking, and curled into a ball against Mila's ankle. Soon his contented purring filled the room.

"What are you thinking about?" I asked.

Mila stared at the ceiling.

"Nothing."

"Has to be something."

Not until she rolled away from me did I sense something different, something wrong. Wrigley lifted his head and meowed plaintively, then edged close to Mila again, curled into another ball, and resumed his purring. I reached around Mila, my fingers traveling lightly over her ribs and up to her small wonderful breast.

"Stop." She brushed my hand away.

"Why?"

I waited for an explanation. When none came, I tried my luck again and gently rubbed the ball of my thumb over her nipple. This time she spanked my hand, and I quickly retracted it.

"What? Are you mad about something?"

"I'm just not in the mood."

Not in the mood? Was this the same woman who daily allowed me to deposit enough sperm in her to overpopulate the planet Jupiter? Fuck her mood. I rolled away from her, determined to win the snub contest. Soon I heard sniffling. Was she crying?

"It's not you," she said, her voice weepy as she rolled toward me.

"*Raooow*!" Disturbed one too many times, Wrigley sprang from the bed and dashed out the door. Mila pulled me closer to her, our faces inches apart on the pillows.

"I'm just depressed."

"Depressed about what?"

"I don't know. I just get like this, always have, but lately it's worse. What am I doing with my life, anyway? I'm no artist."

"Sure you are," I said, rubbing her back. "Don't be silly."

"I'm not like you, Roman. I can't stay home and paint every day the way you're happy writing. I need something more."

"More what?"

"I don't know, just *more*. I keep telling myself that there's no reason to feel this bad, that it'll go away, but these . . . these waves keep hitting me, like I'm slowly dissolving and I can't stop it."

"Are you getting close to your period?" I asked, never a smart move.

"Right. Why didn't I think of that? Guess I'm just not a genius like you."

"I'm only trying to help." Aware of my own breathing, I felt our soul-mate connection drifting apart. "Then what is it?"

"I don't know *what*." Mila's sniffling started again. "Don't you think I wish I did? Maybe then I could get rid of *this*."

At best, I found it difficult to identify with her problem. I mean, when I'm depressed, I always know *why*. My hand came to a rest on the small of her waist, and we lay in silence for what seemed a long time. Maybe she'll feel better in the morning, I thought. I had all but dozed off, when Mila, in a voice distant and nakedly revealing, as if she were confessing to acts of unspeakable butchery, started telling me the story of her family.

2

"My grandfather in Germany was a pig who got his jollies beating my mother and aunt. They lived in a small village just outside of Berlin. House not spotless, they get beat. Laundry not ironed the second it's dry on the line, they get beat. Eggs from the backyard chicken coop not collected before they're even laid, the girls get beat. And I'm not talking love taps; sadistic fucker broke my mom's jaw and gave her so many black eyes she still has no peripheral vision in one of them."

"That explains a lot," I said, and sat up to better catch a rare breeze coming through the window. "Guess I can stop taking it personally that she hates me."

"Yeah, *men* aren't exactly high on her list of things to like. Can you blame her? The more my grandfather drank, the more he beat her. She could wake up in the middle of the night with him bashing her with his fists for no apparent reason, or during the day he might sneak up and kick her in the kidneys just to see her hop. And my grandmother—talk about spineless—always looked the other way, scared she'd be next. Between my grandfather's rages and the Allied bombing, all Mom knew by the time she turned sixteen was fear and more fear.

"The Nazis confiscated everything to feed the army and didn't so much as leave a bread stick in town. One day, after the war's over, the pig throws my mother down the stairs for not folding his shirts exactly the way he likes them. She wakes up on the floor with a bad headache and thinks to herself, Why the hell get beat to death before I starve to death? So she slips out the bedroom window at night with nothing but the clothes on her back and hitches a ride on a truck to Berlin."

"Probably better off," I said. Clasping my hands together on the top of my head, I aired out my dripping armpits.

"That's what my mom thought—at first. She lands a job stacking bricks from bombed-out buildings. A Serbian working alongside her can hardly speak German, but he's no fool. My mom might look worn-out now, but back then she was gorgeous. Tati gets someone to teach him how to say, 'Will you marry me?' and tries his luck. There Mom is, all alone, nothing but a country girl. At least the guy's got a few deutchmarks—probably robbed a German as payback for the three years he spent in a Nazi work camp. Mom says yes and goes back to stacking bricks. A year later, she and Tati catch a boat to the U.S. in search of a better life and end up in Chicago. You know the saying about D.P.s?"

I stretched out onto the damp sheet. It felt as if it hadn't lost any of my body heat from when I was lying on it before.

"First a D.P. is your neighbor, then he's your janitor, then he's your landlord. They take that American-dream shit seriously. My parents work like dogs—everything from washing other people's laundry by hand in the bathtub to selling pencils door to door—and within five years they scrape up enough money to buy a six-flat on Bissell just a few blocks away from your parents' house. Back then Lincoln Park was a rough neighborhood—lots of hill-billies and other poor trash like my parents—but they owned their own place, and so what if the El tracks run right over the alley behind their backyard. Tati finds steady work on a loading dock, and after a few more years and a few more bucks socked away, they start a family."

"They must be proud of themselves," I said. Then I moved my cheek over on the pillow in search of a cooler spot.

"*Proud*?" Mila repeated. "People like my parents are too busy worrying that everything will be taken away from them again to waste time being proud. There they are living in America, the six-flat paying for itself, three beautiful girls. Instead of relaxing and enjoying life for a change, Tati starts hitting the bottle. Mom thinks it was a delayed reaction from the living hell the Nazis put him through. He worked on an assembly line building tanks until his hands bled, and never knew if a guard was going to shoot him or the guy next to him for the fun of seeing someone's brains splatter all over the floor. Whatever, he starts downing a fifth of whiskey a day. A few drinks when he comes home from work, a few more during dinner, a couple for dessert, and before you know it, he's sloshed. Here we go again, Mom thinks. She sailed all the way across the ocean to get away from an alcoholic, only to end up in the lap of another one. I remember the time she hid Tati's precious bottle. I must have been four or five. They're in the kitchen screaming at each other in two different languages. Me and Vera, scared to death, are watching the whole thing from the dining room doorway. Sweetness starts wailing in her crib back in the bedroom because of all the noise. Tati whips his arm back to slap the shit out of Mom, but before he can do it, she's already on her knees, bawling, hands up to protect herself, pleading, 'No, no! Please don't hurt me! It's in the china cabinet!' Talk about pathetic. She just snapped, probably from what my grandfather did to her all those years. You should have seen the smirk on Tati's face—total control over Mom. Vera and me get the hell out of his way so that he can stumble past us. Then we go and comfort Mom, but what can a couple of little kids do besides put our arms around her? I think I asked her something like, 'Is Tati sick?' And she's probably thinking to herself, I should never have had kids, now I'm stuck. Can you blame her?"

I started rubbing Mila's back again, trying but unable to grasp the scope of the family's tragedy. "I'm sure your mom looks at you and your sisters as the good that came from the bad."

"Don't count on it," Mila said. "How would you like to waste almost your entire young adulthood with three hungry mouths to feed and a husband you're scared to death of? It's not that Tati ever actually hit her, but we always knew he was capable of it. In the summer, he'd take his bottle out to the picnic table in the backyard after dinner and drink until he passed out. Mom, so embarrassed, would have to ask tenants to help her carry him inside our first-floor apartment so that she could put him to bed. One time, she and a couple of men were struggling to lift Tati from the table. The men grab him under the arms, Mom takes him by the legs, and they lug him like a sack of potatoes over to the porch stairs. I'm watching all of this, but I'm more busy playing with Vera and Sweetness—so cute and barely old enough to walk—back by the chain-link fence where Tati's vegetable garden has gone to weeds. We've each got one of these fairy-princess wands that Mom bought us at the Community Discount store, and we're using them to poke through the weeds and hunt for monsters. I look down, and there's this pumpkin about the size of a cantaloupe, bright orange. We'd thrown our seeds in the yard after making jack-o-lanterns for Halloween, and somehow a few of them survived the winter and sprouted. We find another pumpkin and another one, and we're all excited. I pick one off the vine for Sweetness, and then Vera and me each pick one for ourselves, and we run across the yard, holding them up for Mom to see—'Look! Pumpkins! We've got pumpkins!' But she's trying to hang on to Tati's legs, and the men in front, already on the stairs, look like they're thinking, What a pain in the ass. She drops one of Tati's ankles and swats the pumpkin right out of my hand, screaming, 'Not now!' It bounces halfway across the yard and rolls under the picnic table. Then she and the men haul Tati up to the porch and inside the screen door. Vera and me are like, What did we do? Sweetness keeps showing us her pumpkin—'Pumin! Pumin!' I come this close to swatting it out of her hand just to be mean. Then I go and fetch my pumpkin. It's cracked and dented. I remember concentrating on the noise from an El train. Welcome to my happy childhood."

"But you did become the woman I love so much," I said. Under the delusion I could cheer her up with a little flattery, I rested a reassuring hand on her shoulder. "A childhood that produced someone as beautiful as you wasn't all bad."

"Yeah, a real barrel of laughs," Mila said, ignoring the compliment. "And don't worry, it gets worse. The next thing you know, Tati turns into an old man overnight. My mom said, 'How was I to know he lied about his age?' She finds his birth certificate hidden in his dresser drawer. Surprise, he's closer to fifty than forty. His feet hurt, his back, shoulder, you name it. Believe me, arthritis and bad circulation are a bitch. He racks up the sick days at work, and the big question—the one that to this day hangs over my family like a dark cloud—is will he or won't he get fired before he can collect a full pension? By this time I'm in second grade, Vera's in first, and Sweetness goes to a neighborhood church for daycare so that Mom can pull in a few extra bucks steam-pressing clothes at

a dry-cleaners. Vera and I would come home from school, let ourselves in with a key, and find Tati in his favorite living room chair,
soaking his feet in a pan of water. He'd already be passed out, chin
in his lap, a half-empty whiskey bottle on the table beside him.
What did we know? We'd use him like an over-sized teddy bear,
walking our Barbie and Ken dolls up his legs.

"'Hi, Tati. I'm Barbie.'

"'And I'm Ken. Wanna go to the beach with us?'

"Tati might lift his chin long enough to groan, '*Uhhhh*,' then
slump over again. Talk about worthless. But I'll say this for the
man. The second he feels up to it, he's right back on that loading
dock earning a paycheck."

Shifting around on my side of the bed, I'd run out of any dry
spots. "Sounds like your dad has his faults. But you have to at least
give it to the guy that he kept a roof over your heads."

Mila made a disgusted *Pffff* sound and rolled her eyes up at
the ceiling. "More like a roof over our jail," she said. "Something
had to give.

"Enter Antonio. He was a customer at the dry-cleaners.
Whenever the owner was out, Mom would fill in for him at the
front counter. Antonio liked to stick around after dropping off his
clothes and flirt with her. One day, he asks her out for lunch. Why
shouldn't she say yes? It's not like she's in love with my father.
Talk about the perfect man for her—too-good-to-be-true looks,
sharp dresser, educated, comes from a rich family in Argentina
that lost all their money when Peron nationalized the railroads.
Six years after immigrating to the U.S., he's already finishing medical school at the University of Chicago and ready to start hauling
in the big bucks. He and Mom would pick Vera and me up from
school in his car and take us to Roma's Pizzeria for ice-cream sun-
days. Sweetness needs new shoes? Antonio buys her a pair at
Buster Brown's. He knew all of that proper-manners stuff that
Tati is clueless at—always opening doors for Mom and scooting
in her chair for her at restaurants. Next thing you know, she loses
twenty pounds and looks beautiful again. Tati's so plowed he
doesn't even notice the change in her, or that his three daughters

are running around in dresses bought with another man's money. 'Don't ever tell Tati about Antonio,' my mother warned us, and by now even Sweetness knew to keep her mouth shut. I can remember being at Antonio's apartment. Mom and him usually disappeared into the bedroom, while me and my sisters watched *Lassie* on TV in the living room. I once asked Mom, 'What was sex like with Antonio?' She said, 'Oh, it was so beautiful, like floating.' Then I asked, 'What's it like with Tati?' You should have seen the face she made. She told me he's so rough, she just lies there till he's finished."

"I can't believe you talk to your mom about that stuff," I said, doubling the pillow under my head. "You have to admit, it's not exactly your typical daughter-mother relationship."

Mila lifted her head off her pillow and looked right at me.

"I'm the only friend she's got, Roman."

I suddenly felt like I was on thin ice. "I'm not trying to say anything. I mean, it's good you're so close."

"Very close," Mila said, making a point. She rested her head on the pillow again. I moved my hand down and up her arm. Then, as if choice were not an option, Mila continued.

"After about an hour in the bedroom, Antonio and Mom would come out looking happy. He'd drive us home before Tati got there from work. One day, after Tati leaves in the morning, my mother tells us, 'That's it!' She throws as much stuff as she can fit into a few suitcases, scribbles a note to leave on the kitchen table, and takes us in a cab to another apartment on Fullerton. She must have had it all planned and gives us strict orders to run the other way if we ever see Tati again.

"A few days later at school, I'm on the playground near the monkey bars during recess. Right in the middle of chasing this boy I like, I see Tati and stop. He's not more than ten feet away on the sidewalk, leaning over the chain-link fence with his arms held out— 'Mila, come Tati.' He looks so sad, like he's about to cry. I remember what my mom told me, and I hesitate—only for a second, but that's all it takes to break his heart. Then I go to him and say, 'Hi, Tati, what are you doing here?' Kids are running all over the place, screaming, having a good time. I'll never forget that look on his face, like I'd betrayed him."

Reaching over, I ran my fingers through Mila's hair above her temple, but she didn't react in any way to my touch, staring past me at the wall across the room. "That must have been awful."

"Not half as awful as Tati must have felt," Mila said. "He gets permission from the principal's office to walk Vera and me home. On the way there, we pick up Sweetness from daycare. When we all get home, he makes us go play in our room with the door shut while he calls my mom at work. Think about it. The man hardly understands English. He must have gotten a neighbor to read the note and somehow explain to him that his wife's leaving him for another man. Talk about humiliating. English or no English, Tati gets it across on the phone that if she doesn't change her mind quick, he'll shoot us and then go looking for her."

"Shoot you?" Withdrawing my hand from Mila's hair, I waited for an answer. Either I'd misunderstood or I was going to nix any more sympathy for Tati.

"That's Mom's version, anyway," Mila said. "I never asked Tati for his version, because if you don't mind, I'm taking a pass on finding out whether or not he's really got it in him to murder me.

"In the end, my parents strike a deal. Mom agrees to come home and never speak to Antonio again, and Tati agrees not to go balistic on her and to cut way down on his drinking. Next thing you know, we're all living together again. Mom quit her job to avoid seeing Antonio. For months he would show up at our house while Tati was at work and stand on the sidewalk staring up at the front window. If he caught a glimpse of my mother, he'd mouth *Please*. She always shut the curtains. Then after a few weeks, he stopped coming around, and we never saw him again.

"Soon after the whole Antonio episode, my parents noticed 'beatniks' moving into Lincoln Park and thought the neighborhood was going down the tubes. They sold the six-flat for peanuts and moved to Rogers Park. That's right about the time your family moved into Lincoln Park, and we all know what happened next—real-estate values there skyrocketed."

"Mila, hindsight is always—"

"Yeah, yeah, yeah," she interrupted. "Mom and Tati have stuck to their truce even though you can cut the hate between them with a knife. I'm sure Tati still sneaks a nip now and then and hides it with breath mints, but he knows better than to get shit-faced. Mom's so miserable. I keep telling her, 'Why don't you try to find Antonio?' She just hangs her head and says, 'He's probably married with kids by now. I missed my chance.'

"So now you know all about my cursed family. I was my father's favorite before that day on the playground. Now it's Vera. Whenever he looks at me, the way I hurt him is always in his eyes. How could I hesitate like that? It's not his fault he was brought up in the backwoods in Yugoslavia and nearly worked to death by the Nazis. He'll never forgive me."

"You've got to be kidding," I said. I turned onto my back and my soaked hip peeled from the sheet. "You were just a kid and must have felt torn between—"

"He's my father, for Chrissake."

"Mila, if only half of what you've just told about him is true, it doesn't sound like he deserves all that much love and affection."

"What do *you* know about it?" The bedsprings jolted as she flounced away from me.

"And your mother," I went on. "Give me a fucking break. She doesn't strike me as being anyone's fool. I'd say she lays it on a bit thick with playing the victim."

Facing the window, that combat-weary distance in her voice again, Mila said, "Roman, you're a spoiled asshole brat who grew up with liberal parents that let you do whatever you fucking damn well please. Don't even think about judging my parents."

"Look, I'm just—"

"Well, *just* don't."

It takes me a while, but with the right encouragement I usually see that I've dug my own deep-shit grave. Nice move, I thought. Already I couldn't remember why it had been so important to share my big-mouth opinion about a sore subject for Mila like her *parents*. Sagging into the mattress, I stared at a large patch of raw plaster on the ceiling directly overhead. In the darkness, it looked like a crab about to lash out with one of its claws. In spite of the landlord letting us slide on half a month's rent for decorating expenses, we still hadn't gotten around to painting. We never would. I reached toward her, then stopped my hand and let it fall to the bed. A worlds-apart silence separated us.

In the morning, I awoke to Mila crawling on top of me. With the sun already above the window, the promise of another scorching-hot day pressed down through the flat tar roof and into our top-floor apartment. Mila bumped and teased my morning boner.

"Come on, fuck me," she whispered in my ear, sultry and desperate. "Please fuck me."

There's nothing like a little *morning delight,* and grabbing hold of her ass with both hands, I let my cock take aim. Mila's denial did have its perks. Thank God things were back to normal.

CHAPTER 6

HIGHER GROUND

In Escondido, the locals' revenge for the mugging on the beach was random, brutal, and swift.

Not long after Consuelo lugged her bucket of tamales away from my hammock, I was jolted out of any lingering effects from the downers by the staccato of gunshots in town. I pushed my hands against the stretchy fishnetting and sat up, ear cocked. Mila lurched up in her hammock, too, blinking away sleep.

"What was—"

"Shhh."

"Roman, that sounds like—"

"Shhh!"

A few campsites down the row, a tangled mess of dark hair poked out of an orange pup tent. A woman in cut-offs and a tie-dye T-shirt stopped on the path to the johns and stared intently across the trailer park in the direction of town. Here and there, campers in sleeping bags stirred like caterpillars on ground tarps. In the "suburb," the screen door of a mobile home creaked open. The whole camp held its breath, everyone looking to everyone else for an answer to the same question.

"Roman, what if they—"

"Be quiet."

The gritty crunching of footsteps came up the road from town. Then ten or so straw cowboy hats bobbed above the tall weeds and brushes that intertwined with the trailer park's flimsy wire fence.

One of the peasants shouted something in Spanish. The long barrel of a rifle appeared pointing straight up and—*boom*!

"Get down," I said.

As Mila and I both slid low in our hammocks, I was all too aware that our suspended butts made nice fat targets. The peasants let out a burst of aggressive laughter, the kind that men find contagious after a long night of drinking. They continued slowly down the road, a profound silence left behind in their wake. I looked off toward Jay and Otto's campsite along the edge of the beach. Otto slept the hungover-sleep of the dead in his army-green mummy bag, but Jay was nowhere in sight. Figures, I thought. Then I heard voices from all over the trailer park.

"Holy shit."

"What was that all about?"

"Got me."

"Nice welcoming committee in this town."

"Hey, I surrender."

"Think it's over?"

Fear took one last spin inside my chest, then gave up the ghost. Mila peeked over the edge of her hammock at me.

"Scary," she said.

"What did you expect? A kiss on the cheek after what Jay and his boys did last night?"

"Roman, it's the first thing in the morning and people are shooting guns. Can't you at least make sure we're not going to die before you start in with Jay, Jay, Jay, Jay, Jay? Lots of guys around here could pass for him in the dark. And if you ask me, neither of us was in any shape last night to be sure about anything."

"Yeah, right," I said, swinging out of the hammock. "Can't imagine why I keep wrongly accusing poor innocent Jay." I stripped off my T-shirt and went over to my pack leaning against one of the palm trees. Deciding it might not be a bad idea to show solidarity with the locals by going native, I dug into the pack and pulled out my white Mexican wedding shirt beautifully hand-embroidered down the middle of the chest in bright red stitching. As I slipped it on, I reluctantly began to have second thoughts about what Mila had just said. That whole fiasco of a night seemed as agonizingly unreal as much as it did real. How could I trust my gut instinct if that same gut had been swimming in downers?

"Jesus!" I said, climbing into my hammock again. "Were we two dumb somebodies or what?"

"I don't even want to think about it," Mila said. She rolled onto her side and curled up like she wished she were still asleep. "At least that asshole didn't rape me."

"Yeah, well, you sounded awfully damn impressed with his dick last night."

"Not *that* impressed. And who the hell did you think you were with the machete—Zorro?"

I tried to summon up a single ounce of the rage that had justified my acting the fool the night before, but came up empty. The real culprit, the machete, lay in the sand not far from my hammock. In the light of day it looked rusty, dull, and irritatingly smug. Fucker, I thought. I gazed up through the palm tree fronds at a blue so creamy it must have belonged to someone luckier than me.

"So what do we do?" Mila asked. "Think it's safe?"

"Got me. Better stick around here for a while until we know for sure."

In the false hope that danger is but a passing circumstance, it's amazing how quickly people can bury themselves in the normalcy of their every-day routines. Just ask survivors of the Holocaust, or the man who chooses to live in a house built near the San Andreas Fault. In spite of the occasional tremor that shakes the foundation beneath his feet, he prefers not to dwell on the probability of the Big One coming anytime soon. Likewise, the rag-tag trailer park inhabitants went back to the business of lining up for showers, building fires for cooking breakfast, stuffing sleeping bags into carrying sacks, and performing other Joe-camper chores. The young Mexican who ran the trailer park for Alberto—nicknamed Tarzan by gringos because of his chiseled physique, his habit of wearing nothing but short-shorts, and his monosyllabic command of English—lumbered out of the thatched hut where he lived next to the entrance gate. A slow-moving, soft-spoken, wary stud by nature, his habitual grave expression was even graver than normal as he started methodically going from campsite to campsite, collecting the ten-peso daily rent from his clientele. He usually waited until the afternoon to put the squeeze on us for *dinero*, but evidently worrying that *Norte Americanos* had plenty of reason to immediately pack up and split for more hospitable parts, he was getting while the getting was good.

A bad sign.

Someone slipped a couple of pesos in a jukebox in town, and that now familiar *umpa-umpa* Spanish music beckoned people to come on down the road for breakfast.

A good sign.

A few longhair brave souls began trickling out of the trailer park gate. Three guys passing by our campsite jokingly took turns pushing each other to the lead.

"You first," one said.

"Oh, no, by all means, be my guest."

"Hey, I hear they only shoot ugly gringos. Don't worry, I'll see to it you get a proper funeral."

I watched them until they'd gone out the gate and disappeared down the road. No more gunshots. Apparently, people were making it to restaurants alive.

A very good sign.

I rolled out of the hammock and stepped into my flip-flops.

"Come on," I said to Mila. "I'm starved. Let's ditch Tarzan before he gets here. If he wants his money, he can get it from the asshole who ripped me off last night."

"Probably half the town knows who has your wallet," Mila said, kicking her legs out from under her blanket. "Not like Mexicans give a damn." She paused, as if she were reconsidering something. Already, the heat of a new day threatened to stifle an easy breeze off the ocean. "Maybe we should just skip breakfast," she said. "I'm scared of what these crazies will do next."

"A growing boy like me needs his food."

"Your growing days are over, big guy."

"Really?" I held out my arms, looking them and my legs over

closely as if genuinely surprised to find out that I was indeed a man. "Well, I'll be damned. Must have snuck up on me."

I had coaxed a grin from Mila. It's disgusting how so little a response from her could give me hope.

"Can't stay out of Dodge forever, " I said. "If I don't eat soon, I might shrink back into a boy." Then that famous line from the movie *Little Big Man* popped into my head. "It is a good day to die."

* * *

Seeing is believing. For supposedly ignorant peasants, the locals showed a remarkably sophisticated logic in their choice of revenge. As Mila and I hedged our way down the road toward town, what at first looked like a scattering of large gray lumps up ahead turned out to be the corpses of many dogs. We stopped, absorbing the sharp blow to our precious sensibilities.

"In-fucking-credible," I said.

"Killed the dogs?" Mila asked, stunned. "Why?"

My feeling grossed out and sorry for the mutts didn't stand a chance against my weird curiosity. I started to move on for a closer look. Mila grabbed my arm.

"Roman, don't! Those men could come back any second."

"Relax."

"Relax? Look at those poor dogs!"

"Nothing we can do to help them now," I said, pulling away from her.

"Roman!" Mila quickly caught up to me, muttering, "Can't believe we're doing this."

The jukebox in the Coca Cabana flipped over a new record— one of the lovesick, Spanish, male ballads that gave the macabre spectacle before us a disconcertingly humorous touch. We side-stepped a dog with bloody, wormy intestines hanging from a hole blown out of her soft underbelly; side-stepped another dog missing half a skull, chunks of his brain and other crimson pulpy tissue splattered in a trail across the baked dirt.

"Think I'm gonna puke," Mila said. She grabbed hold of my

arm again like she was afraid the dogs might snap to life and take their revenge on us. A cute little mongrel, blasted just outside the charred ruins of the torched restaurant, lay with legs pointing up like she was waiting for her master to come and lovingly scratch her torn-apart, gory chest. On the other side of the street, in a grassy ditch between two more restaurants, a dog peppered in buckshot wounds had gone to his maker curled in a ball. Head bent to the side at an unnatural angle, his long, abnormally thick, purplish-pink tongue hung out of his mouth. Over near the *farmacia*, past several more contorted corpses, another former member of the canine club lay stretched out as if sunning himself. Blood dripped from his snout, and he stared cock-eyed up at the sky with a glazed peaceful acceptance to his fate. Need I go on? There must have been at least two dozen in body count—a regular bow-wow My Lai massacre.

"How could they do this?" Mila asked. "What's the point?"

"Seems pretty obvious to me," I said. "How about, *Dogs today, you tomorrow. Think twice before you fuck with us again.*"

"Well that's just fine," Mila said, "but who's here to tell them to think twice before they try to rape and rob us?"

Good question, I thought, but said nothing. The town was open for business as usual. None of the locals—a man unloading wooden cases of Coca-Cola bottles from his truck, a construction worker hitching on a tool belt in front of the new hotel, an Indian woman sweeping out a restaurant—gave the dogs more than a dull glance. Waitresses took food orders from the few tourists willing to risk life and limb for *huevos rancheros* or other delicious menu choices. A scruffy-looking gringo with a three-day-old beard and a permanently stoned look in his sleepy eyes sat at a card table under one of the makeshift tent roofs, greedily shoveling pancakes into his mouth with a fork. He saw us passing by in the street, grinned, and called out, "Hey, don't worry, everything's cool. There's a special on dog tacos."

Out of friendly habit, I waved to the sick fuck.

"Dog tacos," Mila said. "Aren't we the funny one. All this sure does wonders for my appetite. Isn't anyone going to clean up these dogs for God's sake?"

We stepped under the white canvas canopy of a small establishment right next door to the *farmacia*. A muted dusky light fil-
tered down through the canvas and over four empty card tables,
two on either side with a narrow dirt aisle in between. I pointed at
the nearest table and told Mila, "Sit with your back to the street.
That should help."

"Not like I can't *feel* them there," she said, scrunching her
shoulders and rubbing her hands over her arms as if struck by a
sudden chill. Before a host of gross images could play havoc with
my intestinal juices—including the time I saw a boy pick up a dead
rat in an alley and show off to his circle of buddies by flipping it
back and forth between his bare hands—I slammed the door shut
on that particular trip down memory lane.

The obligatory young Indian waitress stepped out of a cur-
tained doorway to the kitchen at the back of the restaurant, past
several high stacks of soda pop cases, and over to our table.

"*Buenos días.*"

She seemed pleasant enough; no sign of a grudge against *Norte
Americanos*. Through the half-open curtain, I saw the equally
obligatory heavyset mother scrubbing dishes at a sink. We ordered
scrambled *huevos* and "hot cakes." No sooner had we been served
our food, than I heard a metallic, rumbling clatter coming our way
down the street. Looking up, I saw Alberto pushing a wheelbarrow
with a couple of dog-stiffs heaped inside it one on top of the other.
He spotted me, set the wheelbarrow down right in front of the
restaurant, and flashed his sparkling toothpaste-commercial smile.

"*Hola*, Big Al. *Cómo estás?*"

I must have been downwind of him, because a liberal dose of
lime-scented aftershave on his baby-smooth cheeks drifted my
way. Dressed in a starched whiter-than-white pharmacist's coat,
pressed dark trousers that defied the heat, and spit-shined shoes,
he'd blown all the time he'd spent primping in front of the mirror
that morning by also donning a pair of latex surgical gloves.

"Don't . . ." I was too late. Mila had already looked over her
shoulder to see who was calling me Big Al and glimpsed the dogs
lying in Alberto's wheelbarrow in a pool of blood. Groaning, she

jerked back around and lowered her forehead into her hand. I looked from my squeamish girlfriend to dapper Alberto to the hard-luck dogs in the wheelbarrow, and with that lovesick crooner still wailing from a jukebox down the block, I damn near busted out laughing.

"*Estoy bien*," I said, one of the few lines I'd memorized in high school Spanish before flunking the class. "*Y tu?*"

"Could be better, Big Al. As you can see, I—I mean, we—woke up with a little *problema* this morning. I was wondering, with your permission, *señorita* . . ." Alberto had changed his address to the back of Mila's head ". . . if I could borrow Big Al, a man of principle, a man of character, a man who, if he helps me get rid of these dogs, can have all the free Tums he wants in our beautiful Puerto Escondido, the next Acapulco." His gaze fell a notch and lingered on Mila's tanned delicate shoulders left bare by a delightfully naughty red-and-white-striped tube top.

"Big Al?" Mila whispered. "Who is this guy?"

"My apologies, *señorita*," Alberto said, overhearing, and he bowed with so much exaggerated graciousness that the gesture bordered on mocking us. "I am Alberto Huerto—pharmacist, real-estate tycoon, unofficial mayor of Escondido, emergency sanitation commissioner, and friend to Big Al Capone from Chicago—at your service! And you are . . ."

"Mila," I answered for her, guessing by the way she kept her forehead in her hand that she wasn't about to turn around and risk another snap-shot of the dogs.

"Ah, I see. Such a beautiful name. Different. You are married, no?"

"No," I told him.

"Ah, I see," Alberto said again, and paused briefly to contemplate our openly-living-in-sin status. It should be noted that in 1976, the free-love movement did not enjoy the same following in predominately Roman Catholic Mexico as it did in the U.S. Alberto seemed on the brink of inquiring as to how one publicly navigates the social and moral turbulence of a sexual relationship not sanctioned by the Pope, then stopped himself and shrugged as if to say, To each his own.

"Do you think you could take your dogs somewhere else?" Mila asked, still not turning around. "We're having breakfast."

"Ah, my apologies." Alberto quickly grasped and lifted the handles of the wheelbarrow. "These unfortunate *perros* do not wish to upset your delicate stomach. Come, Big Al, we have little time, many dogs."

"Not like it's your job," Mila said to me under her breath.

"Save my food. This won't take long," I assured her, scraping my chair away from the table. "Someone should help." But as I got up, I thought, Why always me?

I headed with Alberto toward a mutt corpse out in the middle of the road, the sun like a heating pad across my shoulder blades. A taxi flew past and showed absolutely no respect for the dead by running over the dog. It flopped and twitched to life under the weight of the bald tires, then went still again.

"Better hang on to that one," Alberto said out of the corner of his mouth like one sly ladies' man to another.

"Hang on to what one?" I asked.

"Your woman. She is a plate, no?"

"A what?"

"How you say—very good-looking?"

It took me a second.

"Oh, you mean she's a *dish*."

"Plate, dish—damn those idioms. Trust me, Big Al, you won't do better than her."

"Tell me about it," I said, but Alberto didn't pick up on the futility in my voice. He set the wheelbarrow down next to the dog, reached into one of his coat pockets, and pulled out a second pair of crumpled surgical gloves.

"Here. Wear these. I do not want you to catch a disease from your *perro* friends."

"This town sure knows how to treat its friends," I said, shaking out the gloves.

"You mean these people?" Alberto gave a wave at the entire town. "They did not do this. They depend on your tourist dollars to feed their families. Why would they want to scare you away?"

"Maybe because they think one of us gringos burnt down that restaurant," I said with a nod in the direction of the charred ruin down the street. I didn't mention anything about the latest reason the locals had for seeking revenge—the ass-whipping on the beach. Not my problem, I told myself, steering clear of getting involved. I began stretching a glove onto one of my hands.

"The town's people may not want to kiss you, Big Al, but money speaks, no?"

"*Talks*," I said. Where I got off correcting his English in his own country is beyond me, but let's just say that at the age of twenty-one, youthful arrogance springs eternal. "I think you mean, money talks."

"Exactly. You are a necessary . . ." The right word on the tip of Alberto's tongue, he reached a hand up and came within an inch of absentmindedly stroking dead-dog germs into his neatly trimmed mustache. Then he flipped his index finger into the air. "Nuisance! Yes, that is it. No offense, Big Al. It is the country peasants who work the farms and coffee plantations from morning till night that you must watch out for. They have no patience for your the-world-is-my-playground attitude. And did you not hear that someone beat up a boy last night on the beach?"

"Really?" Something cold and wet wrung itself in my gut. "A boy, huh?" I hoped I wasn't laying the surprise on too thick. "That's a shame."

"Yes, a shame," Alberto said. "Only fifteen years old. Caught him on his way home from working late on a *ranchito*. Broke his nose, dislocated a shoulder, cracked a couple of ribs. This is no good."

Busying myself stretching on the other glove, I connected the innocent, terrified face of a boy with the shadow I'd seen getting tenderized by Jay and his boys. Fucking assholes, I thought. From the hotel construction site, the screech of a circular saw cutting wood went on interminably, then finished with a dying whir.

"So you're telling me that country folk, not town folk, shot the dogs to let gringos know it might be smart to back off?"

"Country folk, town folk—you have a funny way with the

words, Big Al. Keep in mind that all of these Indians have one foot stuck in the old ways, but yes, some are more stuck than others, and it pays to be careful with them. True, the *perros* were already a *problema*, but everyone knows you tourists think these pests are cute. The *hombres* responsible for this know how to kill two chickens with one stone."

"*Birds*. Kill two birds with one stone."

"Ah," Alberto said, throwing up his hand in disgust. "A chicken is a bird, no? English is like you *Norte Americanos*—strange. If this trouble continues, it will be very bad. Grab those legs."

It amazes me to this day that a swiped wallet and my girl-friend's close encounter with a Mexican boner brought out a nationalistic side of me that would have made squealing on Jay—his infinite sliminess notwithstanding—feel like an act of treason. We squatted over a dog with a hole shot clean through its throat. Alberto grabbed the bitch's front legs, me the hind, and together we lifted and swung her on top of the other brutes in the wheel-barrow. Then we started off again with me close in tow.

"Well, if you really want to know the truth, there's plenty of blame for shit to go around in this town," I said. "Someone stole my wallet and travelers' checks on the beach last night and wanted to rape Mila."

We came to a halt next to a mutt with a rivulet of blood running from its ear and down the neck. Alberto looked at me with an expression of heart-felt concern.

"I am very, very sorry to hear that. Why did you not come to me? Ask anyone, I am always there for those who need assistance. Consider yourself and Mila my guests at the trailer park. I will inform Pedro, the man who collects the camping fees, of the new arrangement."

"Thanks," I said, relieved to stretch our money. At least now Mila and I wouldn't have to keep ducking Tarzan. I thought about advising Alberto to be more discriminate with his charity and to cross Jay off his welfare list. No, just leave it alone.

"Say, while you were on the beach, you did not happen to see who hurt the boy, did you?" Alberto asked.

"Afraid not," I replied.

"Do you and Mila have enough *dinero?* I can talk to the fishermen; they will give you fresh fish to eat every day."

"Nah, we'll be all right."

"You would do the same for me, no?"

I was beginning to wonder whether or not Alberto was intentionally working on my guilty conscience.

"Yeah, sure," I said. But I had my doubts.

"Ah, Big Al, you are a good man. It is in your eyes. You and I are citizens of the world first. Just remember that in Mexico, there are many bad people who are only too happy to rob tourists on the beach late at night. That is why I must ask you as one citizen to another, where were your brains?"

"Hey, you know how it is. Mila and I . . . well, we needed a little privacy."

"*Privacy?*" Then the look on Alberto's face changed to sly ladies' man again. "Ah, yes. Just so long as you understand the risks, my friend. If a canary is stupid enough to land on a cat's nose, the cat has the right to eat it, no?"

I wasn't in the mood for any philosophical shit. We collected a couple of more dogs, then moved up the street past the *farmacia.* Paws, tails, and snouts spilled and jostled over the wheelbarrow's edges, and as I walked along I leaned sideways to keep a hand on the top dog's bony rump so that the carcass pile wouldn't tumble to the ground. When we'd gone beyond the juice bar/hardware/grocery store, Alberto unceremoniously dumped the mutts on the side of the road. We paused for a breather, observing a solemn moment of silence over the twisted, tangled heap of victims. Then we headed back for another load.

"These people are no one to play with," Alberto said. "Ignorant, yes, but no one to play with. Do as they do when you are in their turf."

"*On* their turf."

"*Pfff,*" Alberto sputtered. "On, in, around, behind—you people make up the English preposition rules as you go along. May the blessed virgin of Guadelupe have mercy on my soul." He dropped the handles of the wheelbarrow to cross himself, then picked them up again. I noticed that our unlikely partnership was indeed drawing a few curious glances from locals and gringos inside restaurants and shops. A plump Indian woman crossing the road not far in front of us went all rubber-necked checking me out, as if for her a gringo dog-remover was disturbingly out of context. I offered her a friendly nod, but she looked away, skittish, and hurried on.

"So how come none of the town's people are out here helping us?" I asked Alberto. "Don't they care?"

"It is not my fault," Alberto said. "I do my best with the Indians. But you must remember this is not Mexico City, and here, proper sanitation is the other person's responsibility. Yes, eventually someone would clean up these *perros*, but only after they begin to stink and infest with the maggots. Such are the Indians. You do understand the difference between them and me, do you not?"

We stopped by a dog with nothing but pulpy, raw muscle tissue and splintered snout where half its face had been blown off.

"Yeah, I guess," I said. "But you're all Mexican, right?"

Alberto suddenly looked terribly annoyed.

"I am a *mestizo* from the educated class. The most powerful empire the world has ever known, one capable of building the Spanish Armada, is my heritage."

Due to the infamous demise of the Spanish Armada, I didn't think of that particular fleet of boats as any great-shakes to brag about, but hey, we're all entitled to an opinion. Alberto motioned with his hand at my wedding shirt.

"And tell me, Big Al, why do you tourists insist on buying these cheap Indian clothes?"

"Cheap?" I protested. Pinching the fabric on either side of my chest, I held it out for him to take a closer look at the hand-stitched embroidery. "Think of all the labor that went into this. Have you any idea how much this shirt would cost in the States?"

"My friend," Alberto said, shaking his head with a patronizing smile, "do not be surprised if your shirt falls apart in the washing machine. If you need clothes in Mexico, go to a real store and buy real clothes. Why do you want to dress so . . . so backward?"

I must confess that it is both an irritant and a relief to constantly rediscover that white North Americans do not have a monopoly on the racism market. The dog sprawled at our feet waited patiently.

"I wouldn't exactly call people who once built pyramids backward," I said.

"These people can hardly feed themselves, much less build pyramids," Alberto said. "Have you not read the latest research? Men from outer space built the pyramids, not the Indians."

"Men from outer space?" Alberto had laid the extraterrestrial tidbit of information on me so matter-of-factly, I thought I might have heard wrong.

"Everyone knows it, Big Al. Where have you been?"

"That sounds kooky to me," I said. "I think you're selling these people short."

"*Selling short?*"

"Not giving credit where credit is due."

"Ah, I see," Alberto said, smiling again. We dumped the mutt into the wheelbarrow, careful not to let blood drip on either of us. Then as we started off for another dog, Alberto added, "You hippies are naïve."

"*You hippies?*" Now it was my turn to get annoyed. "You can't tell the difference between me and a hippie?"

We stopped so that Alberto could double-check his stereotyped assumption by looking me over, from my bushy hair and long sideburns, to Mexican wedding shirt, to cut-offs worn out in the crotch, to flip-flop sandals.

"Why no, Big Al. Am I missing something?"

"Yeah, I'd say so. Do I look like someone so full of pseudo–love-and-peace manipulative bullshit he can't see straight?"

"Ah, I am so stupid," Alberto said. "Why did I not see you have no pseudo–love-and-peace manipulative bullshit? You must be an independent thinker, like me." From his grin, I got the distinct impression he was pulling extra hard on my leg, but before I could take any more offense, he said, "You have helped enough,

Big Al. We set an example of cultural cooperation for everyone. I can take it from here."

I'd had no idea Alberto had been using me in a civics lesson for locals and gringos alike.

"You sure?" I asked.

"Yes, I am sure. You may wash up in the *baño* at my *farmacia*. Go. It is never wise to keep a woman like Mila waiting."

And with advice that would prove timely, Alberto headed off with the wheelbarrow, whistling in a resonant, virtuoso tone that rode in high harmony with the latest love song from a jukebox down the road.

2

When I got back to the restaurant, who should I find at the table with Mila but the Oklahoma cowboys. Jay, in my former seat to Mila's right, was pouring syrup thick and heavy over *my* plate of steaming pancakes. Otto, across the table from Mila and looking droopy around the jowls, reached with his fork, not about to let a hangover keep him from his share of the pancake spoils.

"*Hola*, amigo," Jay said, smiling up at me friendly as you please. "How goes the doggies?"

Before I could think of a zinger to put him in his place, Mila glanced over her shoulder and said, "Oh hi, honey."

Oh hi, honey, my ass, I thought.

"You weren't back yet, and I didn't see any reason to let your food get cold and go to waste."

"Heavens," I said. "Waste not, want not."

"*Señorita!*" Mila called, deliberately ignoring my sarcasm. Our young waitress poked her head out from behind the kitchen curtain.

"*Mas hotcakes, por favor.*"

"Plenty of room," Otto said, and kicked out the last empty chair from the table. "Sure appreciate you helping us."

"Yep," I said, taking a seat. "That seems to be our job these days."

"Cool shirt you got there," Jay said, trying to change the subject. "Say you picked it up in Acapulco?"

"Yep," I repeated. By now, only someone deaf and dumb could have missed my zero-effort attitude.

"Hell, this is your food, amigo." Jay pushed the plate of pancakes across the table toward me. "Didn't mean to horn in none."

"Yeah," Otto said. "'Scuse us for being so pushy. Hunger will do that to a feller."

"We can all share," Mila said, shoving her plate of scrambled eggs and fried potatoes my way. The more food I had in front of me, the more isolated and pissed off I felt.

"No thanks." And I slowly pushed both plates back where they'd come from.

"Roman, come on." Mila had lowered her voice like she didn't want a scene. "Don't make this into more than it really is, all right?"

"No, it's not all right. We got enough trouble taking care of ourselves."

"Sure is something about these dogs, ain't it?" Jay asked. "Damn amigo, how'd you let old Alberto sucker you into helping with the clean-up crew? Takes nerve for a beaner to think us gringos are some kind of goddamn maid service."

"Nerve?" To hell with Jay's wrestling talent for dislocating peoples' joints. I leaned in close to the table. "Let me tell you about nerve. Nerve is when four grown men beat the shit out of an innocent boy on the beach."

Jay's easy slippery grin took a hike. Mila stopped mid-chew.

"Where'd you hear it was a boy?" she asked.

"Alberto." I kept staring at Jay. "Said they busted him up real good." Out the corner of my eye, I saw Otto's confused face ping-pong back and forth between the rest of us.

"What y'all talkin' about?" he asked. "I miss something?"

"That's a shame," Mila said. I expected her pity for the boy to translate into anger toward Jay, but she only reached for her glass of orange juice, taking a sip. Her need to stay in the dark about Jay confounded me. From behind the curtain, I heard the mother scrape a pancake off a griddle with a spatula, then the sizzle as the flipped pancake hit the griddle again. Tinny clinking, unmistakably that of silverware being sorted, explained the daughter's disappearing act.

"Shouldn't go pointing fingers and startin' rumors, amigo," Jay told me, his deliberate tone meant to warn, if not intimidate. "Alls I know about what happened on the beach last night is what little I heard from another gringo."

"Is that right?"

"Yes, indeedy."

"Wonder how he knew about it."

"Can't say I asked."

"How convenient."

"*Convenient* is my middle name."

"I just might have to find you a new name."

"Wouldn't if I were you," Jay said. "*Might* cause me a severe identity crisis, and Lord only knows what I'd do then."

"Guys, time out!" Mila held up a hand to either one of us like a traffic cop. "This is silly. No one's accusing anyone of anything. Isn't that right, Roman?"

"Accuse anyone?" I said, locked in a staring contest with Jay. "Why on earth would I want to do that?"

"Yeah," Otto said. "Y'all lost me. How's about we just relax and have ourselves some wake-up beers. I still got me a few spare pesos. My treat."

"Already awake," I said. "Tell me something, Jay. If I were to ask Otto here where you were all last night, think he'd cover for you?"

"No reason for my best friend to lie, ain't that right, Otto?"

"Last night?" Otto asked. "We partied. I think. Didn't we?"

"Don't go all mushy-brain on me, Otto," Jay said. "You know damn well we didn't do nothing but kill a case of beer. Matter of fact, you killed a lot more of it than me, ain't that right?"

"Yeah, that's right," Otto answered, but he looked troubled.

"Convenient," I added.

"There you go," Jay said, grinning again. I felt a sharp kick from Mila under the table, an irritating habit of hers whenever she wanted me to let something drop. Not a chance.

"How's 'bout me and you do a little supposing, amigo—just for grins," Jay said. "Let's *suppose* I did have something to do with what happened to that boy. Have to admit people been known to look bigger and more ornery in the dark. Why, in the heat of battle, anyone can make an honest mistake. And just between you and me and your holier-than-thou memory, you seemed awfully interested in kicking beaner butt last night when you run off with Otto's machete."

"I was wonderin' where that was," Otto said. If he didn't remember trying to reason me out of borrowing his machete, how could he possibly remember whether or not Jay had slipped away from their campsite to rendezvous with his tough-guy friends.

"I *suppose* you didn't do jack-shit with that machete," Jay continued. "And I *suppose* that if you knew I'd been man enough to pay back these beaner bastards for what one of them did to you and Mila, you'd think about it real hard and then realize you're *supposed* to say *thank you*."

"I think it's more like *fuck you*," I said.

"Roman, that's enough," Mila said.

"Hey, what the hell," Otto said. "We're all friends here, ain't we?"

"One big happy family," I said.

"Amigo, I do believe you want a piece of me," Jay said.

"Partner," I said, imitating his drawl, "if you don't stay away from me and my girlfriend, I do believe I do."

"Not your call who I stay away from."

"I'm making it my call."

"Wouldn't do that, pretty boy."

"Kiss my pretty-boy ass."

We were on our feet in a flash, metal chairs crashing to the dirt floor. Expecting Jay to leap over the table, I braced myself, ready to connect with a fist.

"Whoa!" Otto said, as he, too, jumped up, and another chair bit the dust.

"Stop it!" Mila yelled. Cautiously getting to her feet, she held out her spread hands over the table like she was declaring the air-space off limits to flying bodies. "Both of you!"

Back by the kitchen, outside my peripheral view, I heard the whisk of hooks on a dowel rod as either the mother or daughter threw open the curtain. Before Jay could make his move, Otto lunged, wrapped a steel-trap arm around his friend's chest, and started dragging him backward out of the restaurant and into the road.

"We were just leaving, weren't we, Jay?" The Red Cross insignia on the front and back of Otto's gray lifeguard tank top took on a whole new meaning.

"Let me the fuck go!" Jay said, making a show of resisting. "Come on, amigo! Here I am! Come and get it!"

I blew him a kiss.

"Yeah, you'd like that, wouldn't you, faggot!"

I blew him another kiss.

"It ain't over, pretty boy! I guarantee you that! When you least expect it! You hear me?"

"Not today," Otto said, and swinging Jay around, he shoved him in the direction of the trailer park. "Keep movin'." He shoved Jay again. "Ain't gonna be no bloodshed on my watch."

The lively chatter from a table full of gringos in a restaurant across the road had ceased.

"My word against yours, pretty boy!" Jay screamed in a twisted rage. "Messin' with the wrong *hombre*! Sleep tight tonight!"

Damn if that sonofabitch didn't keep screaming at me his whole way back to the trailer park gate, finishing off with a war-whoop that should have given me reason to buy life insurance—"Whaaaaaaow!" Concentrating on appearing the winner by remaining cool, calm, and collected, I picked my chair off its side and pulled up to the table again. My hands were trembling.

"Let him try it," I said. "Any fucking time."

Ignoring my bravado, Mila sat down and slouched into a brooding silence. She began rapidly tapping her heel in her flip-flop sandal, the knee of the same leg jiggling the table. From the kitchen doorway, the mother shook her spatula at me angrily and rattled off Spanish that I took to mean, *If you can't behave in my restaurant, get out.*

"*Sí,*" I said. As a peace offering I hopped up and tidied the area by picking Otto and Jay's chairs off the ground, tucking them into the table. Then I took my seat again. Boss *Mamacita* kept right up with her tongue-lashing.

"*Sí, sí, sí,*" I repeated.

The daughter, close behind the mother, bit her lip, holding in a giggle, finding me great entertainment. *Whisk*, and the curtain shut.

"Satisfied?" Mila asked. "I've never been so embarrassed."

"Too fucking bad," I said.

Alberto roared down the road in his jeep, the back of it loaded with a monumental heap of dead dogs. The love song coming from another restaurant's jukebox ended on a crescendoing high note.

"Was all that really necessary?" Mila asked.

"Hey, I'm not the one who invited them to breakfast. At least now you know what an asshole Jay is."

"Roman, I hate to break this to you, but he never admitted anything. Face it, all he did was a lot of supposing to get your goat."

That woman had to be kidding.

"It's him or me," I said.

"What?"

"You heard me. Stay away from him."

The table stopped jiggling as Mila frosted me with a look.

"Let's get one thing straight," she said. "I've watched my father act like he owns my mother all of my life. Welcome to a new generation. You don't tell me what to do, when to do it, how to do it, or who to do it with. Is that clear?"

"Perfectly," I said. "I had no idea your ignorant father and I had so much in common."

When something that mean feels that good to say, you should always know you've gone too far. A look of resolute indifference fell across Mila's face.

"I've got a good idea," she said. "What do you say we take an extended break from each other?" She reached into a pocket of her cut-offs and pulled out a wad of pesos. Peeling off a few bills, she slapped them onto the table. "That should last you a couple of days. See ya around."

Before I could come up with a witty retort, Mila was already pumping elbows down the road.

"Fine!" I yelled after her, but did that ever sound lame. Just then the waitress came with the second order of pancakes, set them on the table, giggled at me, and took off for the kitchen again. I surveyed my three plates of food. I snatched up the bills and counted them. A year-and-almost-four-months relationship equaled a total of 250 worn-out pesos—about twenty bucks. Three and a half more days until Mila and I flew back to Chicago. Won't that be a happy flight, I thought. Leaving thirty pesos on the table to pay for breakfast, I folded the rest of the bills and shoved them into my cut-offs. An anxiety rush, as if I were free-falling, lodged in my chest. And what had I gotten myself into with a nut-case like Jay? Better watch your backside from now on, I thought. As I sat there like a dead man trying to figure out from which direction the train had creamed him, I felt a light scratching at my calf. A ghoulish apparition with black, dilated, death-camp eyes stared up at me. From a bullet crease down the center of the dog's forehead, a bloody, ritualistic mask had dripped over its face. Revolted, I came within a heartbeat of kicking the dog away when, what should I call it—a fit of conscience? Let's just say that I knew, as sure as my name is Roman Collin Pearson, if I so much as raised a single toe to harm that dog, I'd be kicking the wrong things for the wrong reasons for the rest of my life. I grabbed Otto and Jay's plate of pancakes.

"Here you go, girl." Talk about a canine vacuum cleaner, that food was practically in her gullet before I could scrape it off the plate with a fork. "Good girl, eat it up." Then I gave her my pancakes and the leftovers on Mila's plate, too. "Yummy in the tummy. Yeah, that should keep you for a while, huh, girl?" She stared up at me longingly. "*No mas*," I said, showing her the last empty plate. "Not safe for you here. Get!"

And thanks to the mutual language of survivors, the dog fled out the side of the restaurant, scampering for the hills.

3

I left the restaurant and stood in the road under the beating sun, pausing before making my next post-Mila step in life. Hey, I held an ace. A little persuasive blowing in Sánchez's ear, and Jay would be an ex-member of the free world. But when couple-hood is snatched away from you, everything—from the lofty palm tree fronds swaying in clubby unison, to the stray pig skittering a wide berth to avoid you—conspires with the same subliminal message: *loser*. What was I supposed to do, anyway—stick around Escondido and watch Mila attract men like flies to shit? No, time to get my sorry-ass back to Chicago where I could pack my stuff, move home to Mom and Dad's, and stick Mila with the well-deserved headache of dealing with the landlord on the illegalities of breaking a lease. I asked for and got the whereabouts of the Aero Mexico Airlines office from a couple of carefree gringos on their way into the restaurant. Then, dodging a speeding taxi that must have had my initials engraved on the front bumper, I made it in one piece across the road to steep concrete stairs cut into a hill just beyond where Alberto and I had dumped the dogs. Halfway up the hill, I came to a small stucco building that, judging from the faded whitewashed walls, must have been around for Zapata's revolution. As I entered a dark room, the clerk, a teenager on a stool behind the counter, heard the flip-flop of my sandals and looked up distractedly from his soap-opera picture book. High on the far wall, a Western Union sign and a chalkboard posting the latest peso-dollar exchange told me that the teenager, plainly dressed without nametag or uniform, wore many official hats. With a mish-mash of English, pidgin Spanish, and creative gesturing, I managed to inquire about the possibility of moving my flight time up to that afternoon. Never has a human being looked at me with more disinterest.

"*No hay.*"

"Not one seat?"

"*No hay.*"

"You sure?" A wag of the boy's finger let me know that he relished his bit part in the universal conspiracy against me.

"*No hay,*" and he went back to his picture book.

"Shhhit." I flip-flopped out the door and onto the steps' narrow landing. Stuck in bum-fuck paradise. I couldn't wait to run into Mila, envisioning her already traipsing around town on Cowboy's arm. Fuck it, I thought. Go for a swim. Maybe a shark would do me a favor and take a big enough chunk out of my butt so that I'd drown.

I was about to head for the trailer park and change into my swimming shorts, when I heard, "Long time no see, *muchacho.*"

Startled, I whipped around. Not more than a few yards away on a dirt path leading further up the hill, Sánchez smiled, the shine of his front gold tooth giving the shine of the silver badge pinned to his shirt a run for its money. If fate intended to provide me with an opportunity to snitch on Jay, this was it, but something about Sánchez—perhaps the toying glimmer of advantage in his eyes—gave me the willies. He picked a fine time to forget to put on his mirror shades. I tried playing him off with a casual wave, starting for the stairs again.

"No so fast, *muchacho.* I want a word with you."

"Me? What for?"

"I ask the questions, *muchacho.*"

"But my girlfriend's waiting for me back at our campsite, and I really should be . . ."

"Come."

So much for my smooth lying technique. With no alternative but to play it by ear, I followed Sánchez up the path and around the whitewashed building. We immediately came to a dirt driveway that must have wound through the palm trees back down to the main road. Parked alongside a blue Renault squad car not much bigger than a sardine can was the VW camper van that belonged to the two hippies busted for drugs. Just beyond the driveway at the top of the hill, a stone building overlooked the beach and radiant ocean. Police station, I thought. Oh, joy.

Inside, up high, sunlight from two small barred windows did little to disturb the overall dimness of the room. Sánchez went straight to a swivel chair behind a desk, sat down, put his feet up, and folded his hands behind his head. He eyed me critically as I stood before him. I tried not to visibly squirm. At a second desk near the back of the room, a middle-aged man, unshaven and prematurely gone to seed, was hunt-and-peck typing what must have been a police report on an ancient manual typewriter. Glancing my way, Pops gave a snort of contempt that reminded me of more than a few Chicago city patronage workers I've dealt with. Then he went right back to his typing.

"So, *muchacho*, what do you think of my home away from home, eh?" Sánchez asked.

I took in the *Wanted* posters of murdering desperadoes on the bulletin board to my left, the gun rack behind Sánchez that included among other firearms a submachine gun, and the grimy ceiling fan slowly circulating a century's worth of cigarette stench.

"Very nice," I said.

"You think so? Maybe you like to stay."

"Not especially."

"Careful, *muchacho*. I am easy offended." Amused by himself, he let out loud rapid-fire laugher—"Heh-heh-heh-heh-heh. I tell you what I want. *Información*. There are people who think they can come to my town and burn a *restaurante* and hurt an innocent boy. I am asking everyone what they know about these people."

As much as I wanted to put Jay's ass in a sling, instinct strongly urged me to play it safe.

"All I know is what Alberto told me this morning." At the mention of Alberto's name, Sánchez sneered with working-class disdain for those born with silver spoons in their mouths.

"And what did *Señor* Huerta tell you?"

"Just that someone beat up a boy on the beach."

Leaving me to twist under his critical gaze, Sánchez reached into his uniform breast pocket and pulled a cigarette from a pack of Marlboros. He grabbed a lighter off his desk, flicked, lit, inhaled deeply, and blew the smoke in the direction of my face. I was beginning to feel like the railroaded hero in a B movie. Sánchez's expression turned as cold-blooded as those in the mug shots on the *Wanted* posters. "I ask you what you know."

"Nothing. Honest," and I held up my hands as if to prove they were not only empty, but clean as well. Pops continued to clack so slowly on his typewriter it pained my ears.

"And where were you last night, *muchacho*?"

"With my girlfriend," I answered, making sure not to hesitate. "Must have fallen asleep around 10 o'clock. Slept like a rock."

"It is good for the health to get a good night's sleep, *muchacho*. Do you worry about the health?"

"Yeah, I suppose," I said, attempting a smile. "I mean, doesn't everyone?" Whether from the tropical heat, the interrogation, or my new respect for B movies, a dribble of sweat worked its way down my forehead.

"You will be surprised, *muchacho*," Sánchez said. "There are a few people who no care about the health. If they no care, why I care? And who decide the few from the many? Poor, poor Roberto Sánchez." He sucked on his cigarette and blew smoke at me again. Then he added, "I think I am leaning to decide you are one of the unfortunate few."

That gaze of Sánchez's rattled inside my head. There would be no need for the bamboo-splinters-up-the-fingernails routine. I was about to sing everything I knew about Jay and also, as an added bonus, plead temporary insanity for my inexcusable, machete-armed crusade into the law-abiding Mexican heartland, when Sánchez said, "Let me show you something."

He swiveled out of his chair, came around the desk, and intentionally bumped shoulders with me on his way to a metal door across the room. He lifted a large key ring off a hook on the wall, and several keys the size of pencils jingled like chimes.

"Come closer, *muchacho*."

Sánchez selected a key and turned it in the door's lock. The loud clack of the inner bolt reminded me of a vault. He pulled heavily on the doorknob. I followed him for a step into a dark room lit only by sunlight shooting through a slit of a window in the far wall directly across from us. The acrid stench of urine assaulted my nose. I found myself in a wide center aisle lined with the bars of two cells—one on either side of me. Each was equipped solely with a plastic slop bucket. In the cell to my left, the big gringo I called Moose—shirtless and still wearing the same jeans cut-offs he'd worn when he was arrested on the beach—rushed toward Sánchez and grabbed the bars with his thick hands.

"You can't keep me here forever, man!" he yelled at Sánchez. "I'm an American fuckin' citizen!" His blue eyes, full of panic and rage, stared out from his oily, meaty face.

Sánchez folded his arms across his chest and shook his head as if it were of great concern to him that his prisoner seemed incapable of learning from past mistakes. Then he said, "How often I tell you I am so, *so* scared of American fucking citizen? Heh-heh-heh."

In the cell on my right, the two scrawny, bearded hippies busted for drugs got up from where they'd been sitting against the back wall and gravitated to the bars.

"You gotta give us that phone call sooner or later!" one of them yelled. "We know our rights!"

"Yes, your rights," Sánchez said. "I keep forgetting."

"And where's that fuckin' little weasel, Jorge?" Moose asked. "He rips *me* off, but I'm the one in jail?"

Sánchez reached into his pants pocket, pulled out a money clip, and rubbed his thumb over the edges of many colorful peso bills like he was limbering up a new deck of cards. "I almost forgot Jorge. He is familiar with our customs."

"That's my money!" Moose screamed. Jorge must have held out on him even under the threat of a switchblade tracheotomy. Sánchez grinned big as you please.

"How is it you *Norte Americanos* say—'Loser weeper, finder keeper?'"

"You won't get away with this," Moose muttered, but the look on his face said, *I'm totally fucked.*

"And where do you get off searching a van without a warrant?" asked the second longhair from across the way. He mirrored Moose with his hands on the bars. "My dad's lawyer is gonna sue your ass!"

"A lawyer?" Sánchez slipped the pesos back in his pocket, snagged me by the scruff of the neck, and pulled me further down the aisle. "Here is your lawyer."

From my view in the center of the room, the half-open metal door, only a few feet beyond reach, looked dangerously tempted to clang shut by itself. I doubt I passed for a full-fledged member of the American Bar Association, but the three prisoners, grasping for any chance at freedom, began bombarding me with desperate instructions:

"Hey, man, call my father—4154037687!"

"No, man, call *my* father—2126483751!"

"No, the American Consulate! They'll nuke this fuckin' banana republic!"

"Don't listen to those two dickwads! I been here a day longer than them—4154037687!"

"There's money in it for you! My father's loaded—2126483751!"

"No, the Consulate! Please!"

My eyes bopped back and forth from one cell to the other. I can give a blow-by-blow account of everything that happened to me in my early childhood, but remembering a new phone number until you can jot it down has never been one of my finer mental talents. Frazzled, I made a snap decision and stepped close enough to Moose to damn near Eskimo-kiss his shiny nose through the bars.

"Say the number nice and slow," I told him.

"Thanks, man." The hulking jock suddenly looked like he was going to burst into tears of gratitude. "41540—"

"Hey, what about us!" said hippie one.

"Shut your fuckin' yap!" Moose shot back.

"Who you tellin' to shut up?" said hippie two.

Moose jammed his forearm through the bars, a wasted effort to reach across the wide aisle and into the other cell, but an action

violent enough to make both longhairs flinch. "I'll break your goddamn, twerpy, little—"

"Fuck off," said hippie one.

"I am so sorry," Sánchez interrupted. "We must leave now.
The lawyer is very busy. Always remember that in a banana republic, there are more important bananas than you to defend." He
slapped a hand on my shoulder and gave me a firm prod back
toward the doorway. "*Adiós.*"

"Wait!" Moose yelled.

Then from the hippie dynamic duo:

"You can't let us rot in here!"

"Heeeeeeelp!"

Sánchez swung the door, but before it shut completely I saw
the golden aromatic contents of Moose's slop bucket arcing gracefully across the aisle toward the hippies' cell, then heard the *splat*.

"MOTHER"—*boom* shut the door, its reinforced steel muf-
fling—"fucker!"

Voices continued to scream obscenities, accusations, and over-
lapping phone numbers. The mixed-up digits slid in and out of my
brain like they were greased. I hadn't even gotten any of the prisoners' real names.

"A lawyer," Sánchez said, locking the door. "That is a good one.
And why they want to stink in piss? I should let them clean." For a
moment he seemed to contemplate allowing the inmates shower
privileges, but then he shrugged. "Maybe *mañana*—heh-heh."

The clerical worker quit typing long enough to cast a look of
condescending amusement my way. Nausea crawled up my throat,
then receded. I was temporarily reprieved from Dante's last circle
of hell. Sánchez motioned petulantly with a finger for me to follow
him. He took his seat behind the desk again, and I resumed my
place of honor in the interrogation. After a long, squinty-eyed drag
off his cigarette, he blew smoke in the only direction he knew how
to blow it.

"So, what do you think of my happy family, *muchacho*?"
Sánchez tilted far back in the swivel chair. "You want to join your
brothers?"

"No thanks."

"*Por qué?*" the *Jefe* asked innocently.

"No reason in particular."

"Why is it that ever since I meet you, I have the funny feeling you are lying? I think you want to be family. Maybe I put you in there and lose the key." Sánchez tossed an imaginary key over his shoulder and laughed. A regular riot. His expression turned desperado cold-blooded again.

"Listen to me very, very careful. If I find out you have *información*—that you wait five minutes before you come to me—you are guilty as the people who hurt my people."

I'd already waited a day and a half procrastinating on what to do about Jay. So much for any thought of fessing up to Sánchez. I looked the *Jefe de Policía* square in the eye.

"I know absolutely nothing."

At that exact moment, Pops quit typing again and let out a string of Spanish, the furious tone of which could only mean expletives. At first I thought he was offering his opinion of my false sincerity, but then he picked up a bottle of white-out off his desk and was soon dabbing a brush to a typo. With a perfectionist's delicate touch, he finished and blew on the liquid to permanently dry the cover-up. All the while that critical gaze of Sánchez never stopped probing me.

"Is that right, *muchacho?*"

"Yes, that's right."

As Sánchez weighed my fate, his office helper went back to typing. *Clack clack.* Long pause. *Clack.* I'm dead, I thought.

"Be careful," Sánchez said. "Angry *hombres* with guns want to shoot all *turistas.* I have my eye on you. Get out."

No one had to tell me twice. I was almost to the front door, when Sánchez added, "And, *muchacho* . . ." I stopped and faced that gold-toothed smile. "Know your family has room for you here."

I don't think I took a decent breath until I again set foot on the road at the bottom of the steps. Close, I thought. Too close. All the way through town, I felt like at any second Sánchez would change his mind and reel me in by an invisible leash.

Shops and restaurants once again bustled with tourists and locals, the last evidence of the dog massacre already dried and vanished into the dusty dirt. I hung a right at the trailer park gate and noticed a few more empty campsites than usual, but nothing that the continuing flood of sun-worshipping *Norte Americanos* wouldn't quickly fill. Yep, I thought, the sun still pushing the Fahrenheit. Go for a swim and hope for a shark.

4

I never did make it to the ocean that day. Back at camp, right after changing into my swimming cut-offs, I came down with Montezuma's Revenge—a.k.a., diarrhea. A dozen or so roundtrips to the toilet stalls later, I lay convalescing in my hammock. Twice the recommended dosage of Lomotil medicine had done nothing to solidify the problem. It'll pass, I thought. Sunlight coming through the fronds tattooed my naked chest and long sprinter's legs with flickering, geometric shapes. I assumed that Mila, missing in action, was off somewhere sucking the cock of her new cowboy squeeze. I raised my head to spy on Jay and Otto's campsite over near the beach. Otto, sitting Indian-style all alone on the sleeping tarp, held a can of food on his knee as he laboriously, one cut at a time, worked a pocketknife can-opener around its rim. Just by chance, he glanced my way, caught me watching him even at that distance, and gave an apologetic, no-hard-feelings wave of the hand. Not in the mood to reciprocate with a friendly wave of my own, I let my head fall to the hammock again.

The human body holds an amazing amount of liquid. A couple of hours later, as my game of running bases between hammock and toilet came to an end, a bad case of the chills had floated me into the energy-sapping, melancholy fever world. This is so fucked it's beyond fucked, I thought. Better get a doctor.

* * *

In town, I stopped off at the *farmacia* and got directions to the hospital from Alberto.

"Medical care is free in Mexico," he told me with nationalistic pride from behind the counter. I'd interrupted his using a spatula to sort and count pills in a tray. "Do not worry. They will take good care of you there."

Continuing down the road, out the main drag and around the climbing bend that overlooked a glittering ocean, I came to a small prefabricated building with sheets of corrugated fiberglass for a roof. This is the hospital? Beggars with the runs can't be choosy. I stepped through the front door and into the waiting room that I suspect smelled just as disinfectantly clean as the Mayo Clinic. Sitting at a desk across the room, the hospital's lone employee, a pretty young nurse less than a quarter my size put down one of those soap-opera picture books. I was slowly catching on that the locals were addicted to this form of schmaltzy, pop-culture entertainment.

"*Cómo le puedo ayudar?*"

Her brown eyes, soft enough to melt a man's socks, balanced the extra starch in her backbone. Assuming that she'd asked if she could help me, I began pantomiming that all was not tip-top with my digestive system. She gestured for me to have a seat beside the desk. With textbook nursing efficiency, she shoved a thermometer under my tongue, checked my blood pressure with one of those Velcro-strap gizmos, and lifted my shirt to feel around on my chest and back with a cold stethoscope. Then she took the thermometer out of my mouth to read the verdict. Leaving me hanging, she disappeared through a back doorway, then reappeared a moment later with an I.V. bottle in her hand. It's unclear to me whether she'd diagnosed me as being in danger of becoming dehydrated, or already in that condition. Either way, she had to be kidding.

"*Es necesario.*" She smiled sadly as if to add, Trust me, I know what I'm doing.

Nurse Florence, as in Nightingale, led me into another room with two metal-framed beds on one side and a supply cabinet on the other. In the bed nearest the door, a teenage boy, his swollen face

bruised and grotesquely discolored, lay with his ribs neatly band-
aged and one arm folded across his heart like he was reciting the
pledge of allegiance. Even in sleep, his grimacing expression seemed
to say, It hurts. Car accident? I wondered. I climbed onto the white
sheet of the other bed and watched Florence hang the I.V. bottle
from a tall stainless-steel rack. She'd already stuck a whopper of a
hypodermic needle in my hand above the knuckles, taped it and the
connecting tube securely to my skin, and begun thumbing the flow
switch to start a slow drip of Glucose water, before the identity of
my roomie dawned on me. It's one thing to feel your guilt from a
safe distance, quite another to have it up close and personal. My
own face throbbed with his bruises. Yeah, Jay & Company had
roughed him up good, all right. Florence made a final adjustment
on my I.V. drip, then swished in her crisp uniform out of the room
and left me, my troubled conscience, and the boy alone. In the quiet
I heard a noise on the peaked, translucent roof, looked up, and saw
the underbelly of a gecko skittering down one side. I clicked on the
what ifs: What if I hadn't come to Jay and Otto's campsite and
demanded revenge on the beach *bandido*; what if I *had* gone to
Sánchez on the night of the restaurant fire and suggested he pull Jay
in for questioning; what if I'd never met Jay by butting my big nose
into Moose and Jorge's fight; what if I hadn't been the fastest sper-
matozoa out of my daddy's dick? Any way I cut it, diced it, chopped
it, or puréed it, the finger of responsibility for the boy's wounds
pointed squarely at me. But who said guilt ever brings out the best
in any of us? Fuck this, I thought. Not that sick. I lurched up, about
to rip the I.V. out of my arm and blow that pop-stand hospital,
when a sudden one-two punch of blood to the brain hammered me
to the pillow again. The fuzzies slowly cleared from my vision.
Someone had played a dirty trick and cranked up the juice on the
gravity dial. Guess Florence knows her shit, after all, I thought.
Soon I plunged into a dizzying, crushing sleep.

   *Dressed only in my underwear. Why does this keep happen-
ing? Oh well, already at the restaurant. If I stay under this table
and act like everything's normal, maybe no one will mind. Beyond
the hem of the white tablecloth are the legs of formally dressed*

couples at other tables. *Must be a classy joint.* In the chair in front of me, I recognize Mila's shapely legs inside a slinky black evening gown. With a lover's sense of permission and entitlement, I reach my hand up under the gown and nestle two fingers into a pussy as velvety snug as a fur-lined glove.

"Excuse me."

I hear Mila's tone of displeasure from above the table, but her gyrating hips are giving me a mixed signal.

"You know better," she chides. As my fingers shrink apologetically out of her, the scraping of a knife on a plate makes me aware of someone else. Across the table from Mila are the legs of a man in creased wool trousers and immaculately buffed shoes. *If I've been replaced, what am I supposed to do with the hard-on in my Jockey briefs?* I crane my head out from under the table. The man, dressed in a Victorian three-piece suit and derby hat ignores me, cutting steak with his silverware. His table manners are impeccable.

"Just one sip of water," I implore Mila.

"Oh, all right," she condescends, and dipping her fingers into a cut-glass goblet, she flicks water in my face. I stretch my tongue out too late to catch a single drop. I'm about to ask for a second chance, when there's a hubbub of angry voices at the back of the room. A set of huge doors bursts open onto a stone patio. Immediately beyond it, Lake Michigan lies in a vibrant pinkish-mauve twilight. *I know my job.* Scurrying from under the table, I dash out the doors, onto the patio, and vault the railing. It's a short drop to the beach below. I'm just in time to thwart an intruder who, playing possum as he floats facedown in the lake, is attempting to crash the restaurant for a free meal by riding waves ashore. *Nice try, pal.* I run out into the surf, grab him by a stranglehold round the throat, and flip him over. It's the boy Jay and his buddies roughed up. He springs to life and claws at my hands, but it's no use. I squeeze his Play-Doh neck until there's only a flimsy cord keeping his head attached to his shoulders. He goes limp in the shallow tide, eyes turning as cloudy gray as spent flash bulbs. A crowd of onlookers, cocktails in hand, has come out of the restaurant and onto the patio. They must have brought the night with *them. Up and down the shoreline, the lake, now a calm sheet of black, reflects beams of light coming from heavy traffic on Chicago's Lake Shore Drive. Mila and her boyfriend (why didn't I recognize Jay before?) lean over the railing to observe the trouble I've gotten myself into. Even in death the boy struggles to get up, but his spaghetti neck can't support the weight of his lolling head. I should have known he'd play on people's sympathies.*

"See why I don't love you anymore?" Mila asks. Jay shakes his head like a father who must bear the heavy burden of a wayward son.

"You think I like me like this?" I yell up at Mila. But if murder isn't embarrassing enough, my flagpole boner still rages inside my underwear. There are some situations in life you just can't explain your way out of. The onlookers stare at me disapprovingly, swirling ice cubes in their drinks. I see past them, through tall windows, and into the brightly lit restaurant that is as big as a palace ballroom. Mila and Jay, holding hands and running with nimble grace, slip out the front door, no doubt on their way home for a night of . . . The clinking of ice cubes grows louder, and it suddenly occurs to me that the rich communicate with each other in a secret cocktail language. "Fuck you!" I scream, but no one's listening, people going back inside the restaurant to finish their rudely interrupted meals. And then I'm drifting up and out over the blackness of the lake like a helium balloon at the mercy of crosswinds. The lights of the city grow fainter and fainter . . .

I awoke to the clinking of Florence replacing my old I.V. bottle with a new one on the hook of the tall steel rack. I was still straddling the dream world, and my overheated body felt encased in lead. As I turned toward her, the gyroscope inside my inner ear tried to steady itself. The diminished light coming through the fiberglass roof told me it must have been early evening. Florence swished out of the room again. The boy, still sound asleep, had visitors. Along the edge of his bed sat a granny, a couple of pre-pubescent sisters, and a younger brother, all of them staring at me like they were watching the boob-tube. Lined up in descending order of height, they reminded me of peasant nesting boxes made to fit one inside the other. I thought it imperative to play goodwill ambassador.

"Hi there."

No response.

"Pleased to meet you folks."

No response.

"Hope he's feeling better."

No response.

"Think the Cubs got a chance in hell to go all the way this year?"

Granny reached into a *bolsa*, a Mexican shoulder bag, and pulled out a box of Chiclets. Her impressively long silver braid hung down her back and in layered circles on the bed like a ringmaster's whip. She shook a couple of pieces of gum out of the box for herself, then passed it down the line to the eldest granddaughter. Just as the tray of Holy Communion bread is passed from person to person, so went the box of gum. I wondered what it would be like to be in their family and saw myself with them around a blazing campfire in the woods at night. We stargaze, eat gamy food with our fingers from clay bowls, and exchange folklore stories that explain the mysteries of the universe into the wee hours of the night. Except for marauding bands of gringos that like to beat the shit out of us, it's a good life.

The Indians chewed their gum in unison and kept on staring like I was some kind of freak of nature. I couldn't help but laugh.

They laughed.

Progress. I laughed louder.

They laughed louder.

"Funny, huh?" Somewhere in the middle of us having a rip snortin' time, I conked out again.

A breezy sunny day for taking a walk to Lincoln Park along Chicago's lakefront. To my left, wide cement stairs slope down to the water. It's choppy and brilliantly green like in an animated cartoon. I come around the bend of the bicycle path to a grassy area just before the long stretch of beach between Fullerton and North Avenue, when who do I see lying naked on a picnic blanket but Jay, Mila, and the Indian boy. They wave for me to come join them. With Mila squeezed in between the other two, the only room left for me on the blanket is at everyone's feet.

"Care for a tuna fish sandwich?" Mila asks pleasantly, offering me one. She can't fool me. If I take the sandwich from her, I'll be accepting a demotion to third-string lover. The sandwich magically transfers from her hand to mine. I'll have to explain to her in private that tuna fish, no matter how delicious, pales in comparison to fucking. The patter of conversation goes in one ear and out the other as I'm much more aware of Mila turning one way to grope Jay's cock, then turning the other way for a make-out interlude with the Indian boy. Suddenly they're gone, and along with them the many bicyclists, roller-skaters, picnickers, joggers, and sunbathers. Day changes to night, and summer changes to bitter-cold winter. I haven't moved from the grass—huddled, shivering, and wrapped in a blanket tattered and full of holes. The lake is a frozen snowy wasteland. Then I hear the sounds of Mila's love-making, riding high over miles of lit city streets. She's at the threshold of orgasmic enlightenment, that begging-to-be-fucked moment so vital to women and pleasing to men. I'll freeze to death.

Or wake up. Talk about a psyche's talent for self-torture. Someone was crawling into my bed.

"How you feel, sweetie?" Mila asked, spooning me.

"Better." I lay in a cooling film of sweat, the fever broken. Moonlight shone through the roof. I checked my hand. Florence must have already removed the hypodermic needle while I slept. "How'd you find me?" I asked.

"Alberto," Mila said. "I ran into him on the street." She cuddled tighter, then began to sniffle. "I don't want to break up. Not ever."

With the sub-zero weather alternative still very real to me, I gladly rolled over, pecked a kiss on Mila's cheek, and said, "OK." The boy and his family had apparently gone home, his mattress and pillow stripped of linens.

"Where's the nurse?" I asked.

"What nurse? I let myself in."

Probably goes home at night, I thought. I managed to sit up without fainting, then slid both feet over the edge of the bed. They hit the floor like two bricks. I'd have to get used to carrying my own weight all over again.

I took a long overdue piss in the hallway bathroom. Then Mila and I went out onto the hospital's front porch and sat down in metal lawn chairs. She must not have liked the seating arrangement, because after we'd listened to the distant, monotonous surf for a while, she got up, came over to me, and curled into my lap. I felt as if I were breathing a lingering precariousness from my dreams in and out of my lungs. She started sniffling again. Whenever the pendulum of her mood swung in my favor, I seldom risked blowing it by asking a lot of questions, but as I held her in my arms, something didn't feel right.

"What's wrong?"

More sniffling.

"Tell me."

"I just don't want to lose you," Mila said.

Far out in the countryside, a rooster crowed. Then another one nearby echoed a response. Soon dozens of roosters were announcing the new day, each one trying to out-cockadoodle-do the other. So late it's early, I thought. That meant an awful lot of unexplained time for Mila. And then somewhere between the crashing surf and Mila's pressing weight, it all made perfect intuitive sense. Numbness outweighed my impulse to dump her off my lap. This was no dream. She'd fucked Jay.

Before I could shake the numbness, Mila jerked her head off my shoulder and stopped sniffling.

"You smell that?" she asked.

I took a whiff.

"Yeah, smoke." Then out of the darkness, growing stronger and beating sunrise to the punch, flickery ominous light haloed in the eastern starry sky, fooling the roosters into silence. We got up and went to the porch railing to see around the hospital down the brush-covered hill into town.

"Please," I said. "Not again."

Mila buried her face against my arm as if I alone stood between her and the shooting flames. The Coca Cabana was burning.

5

We all do it. *Obsessive torture,* I call it.

It's late at night. In the moonlit darkness of the trailer park, the only thing stirring is Jay's humping ass underneath an unzipped sleeping bag on the cowboys' tarp.

"You like my cock, baby?" Jay whispers.

Baby? Mila thinks. The thrill is in knowing a man wants you, not in giving a man what he wants. Maybe it was the lack of fore-play, or the fumbling of his cock before it found its dry mark and rammed home, or his wounded-animal raspy breathing in her ear, or *baby,* but for whatever reason she's most aware of his crushing weight. A mellow buzz from the joint they smoked earlier is either deadening her libido or making it possible for her to ride out the mistake she's made. She stares up at the moon directly above, just a sliver shy of full. *Why is everything always my fault?* Jay's self-indulgent thrusts push her head off the tarp and onto the sand. Ever a perfectionist, she locks her ankles around his calves and presses a hand against his sinewy ass. As hard as I shut my eyes to that self-inflicted image, I can't obliterate it.

"You like my cock, baby?" Jay asks again.

Panic stirs in Mila's lungs and throat. She runs her fingers tenderly through the stringy hair on the nape of his neck.

"Yeah, I like your cock." To win she must mean it. She pulls and wills him deeper inside of her, thinking, I will not cry.

Afterwards, Mila doesn't waste much time getting dressed. "Better go check on Roman," she mumbles, and slogs away in the sand.

"What's your hurry?" Jay calls out, but Mila's already disap-pearing behind a tent under the palm-tree canopy. Too late now, bitch, he thinks. Run on home to pretty boy. He throws off Otto's sleeping bag, his cock still hard and moist. Moon and stars so beautiful. It's as if layers upon layers of the sparkling white speck-les are multiplying and filling in the sky's few remaining spaces. Where the hell's Otto? Jay wonders. Big lummox. Probably smashed and passed out in a ditch somewhere. Who'd a thunk it.

Otto Hoffman—high school wrestling champ hero. Shoot.

It occurs to Jay that with Otto out of the picture, opportunity knocks. He stargazes awhile longer, the pride of the infinite universe swelling within him. He reaches for his cut-offs beside the sleeping bag, slips them on, and buttons the fly. Then, rolling up onto his shoulder blades with his legs high overhead, he spring-flips to his feet in a showboating gymnastics move. He goes over to his backpack lying on a corner of the tarp and reaches into it for a black or dark-colored T-shirt that will help him blend into the night. *Ready or not, beaners. Here I come.*

Trusting that the side of *right* will prevail, Jay reaches the trailer park gate. Sure enough, sitting there like it's got his name on it, is a tin bucket left by Tarzan for easy access in case of another fire. As he picks it up, the handle squeaks loudly, and he freezes to listen. Nothing but the crickets. Holding the bucket away from him so that it won't accidentally knock his leg and cause a racket, he moves like he's hurrying to market with a fragile load of eggs, his bare callused feet making not a sound on the road that's soaked and shiny with dew.

In town, a garden hose, presumably left threaded to the road-side water spigot by a civic-minded local who knows how to learn from past fire-fighter mistakes, lies neatly coiled on the ground, ready for action. He pulls out a narrow black object from his pocket, then presses his thumb against a release button that's on it. A six-inch blade flicks open. He cuts a yard off one end of the hose for a siphon, then cuts the other end just below the threads so that the hose can't be reattached to the spigot. He takes an admiring look at his handiwork, indulges himself with a cunning smile, and thinks, Shucks, how do you suppose that happened?

A taxi—red dingle balls trimming the inside of the wind-shield—is parked on the other side of the road in front of the charred ruins from Jay's first arson triumph. He puts away his switchblade, creeps across the street, and kneels beside the rear fender. Flipping open the gas tank lid, he unscrews the cap and sticks one end of the short hose down into the tank, then brings the other end of the hose to his lips. He tilts his head lower than the lid and sucks on the hose until the toxic liquid gushes into his mouth. *Nasty!* Imagining that god-awful contaminated taste makes me run my own tongue around inside my mouth same as Jay must have done. He spits several times, but a lot of good that does. When the bucket is full, he pulls the hose out of the tank and leaves it and the cap on the ground like a calling card.

Looking up and down the road at the loose string of dark huts and shops, Jay uses a scientific method for choosing a target.

> *Eenie Meeni minee mo*
> *Catch a beaner by the toe*
> *If he hollers let him go*
> *Eenie Meeni minee mo*

His finger is pointing at the Coca Cabana. Somewhere over a hill, a rooster congratulates him on his decision by belting out a cockadoodle-do. Then another rooster down the road responds to the first, and soon it's a goddamn rooster symphony. *Shit! Wake up every motherfucker in Mexico, why don't ya?* Moving fast, he angles the thirty or so yards back up the street to the Coca Cabana, the taut muscles and tendons in his arm shaking from the weight of the bucket. If he's not careful and gas sloshes onto him, he'll be all the more tagged with an incriminating smell. He stops in the doorless front entrance and stands there framed by moonlight. Beyond the small dining area and past the kitchen, he hears something in one of the two back bedrooms and freezes again. *Snoring?* Can't lose nerve now. Silently, he puts the bucket down on the floor and tips it over. A river of gas flows around the legs of tables and chairs, puddling in the low spots of the packed dirt and spreading out to the far corners of the room. From his shorts he takes out a book of matches, rips one off, strikes it, and turns the sulfurous head upside down so that it works up a strong flame. *Sweet dreams.* He tosses the match and simultaneously jumps backward out of the doorway and into the road. *WHOOSH!* A blue fireball flashes to within an inch of searing his face and, shielding himself with his arms, he springs back ever further into the road. Thatch sizzles and crackles, the entire dining room engulfed in flames. As the decorative fishnet draping the walls disintegrates into ash, seashells and starfish that were inter-twined in it fall clunking and clattering on tables and chairs. The snoring stops abruptly. Already the fire beast licks and curls out the doorway, slithers up the conical roof, and coalesces into a firestorm that whips and rages. The rooster symphony calls it quits.

"*Fuego!*" yells a man from behind the rear wall. "*Teresa! Pepe! María! Consuelo! Despierta! Fuego!*"

Standing in the lurid light, Jay can't resist shooting his clenched fist high into the air as if to shout, *I did it*! He darts off the road into the palm trees and undergrowth of an acre of land between the trailer park and the new hotel that's being built. He hasn't run more than five steps before he sees the bright spot of a flashlight in the trailer park. He belly flops for cover. The terrified shrieks of children are coming from inside the Coca Cabana, but before regret can find a toehold in him, he thinks, *Didn't name the rules*. He crawls commando-style straight for the beach, brambles snagging his T-shirt and scratching his arms and legs. Playing it close is proof that he plays fair.

"Fire!" yells a gringa from the trailer park. "Hey, everybody, there's a fire across the road!"

Breaking through the undergrowth to nothing but sand, Jay gets up and walks with restrained quickness past a couple of fishing dinghies resting on their sides. As he follows the surf away from town, cool foamy water rushes in and erases his tracks, *Hot damn!* The far reach of the lurid light reflects out over the ocean. Of the many indistinguishable frantic Spanish- and English-speaking voices he hears coming from town, a woman's panic-stricken screaming rises above the rest.

"*Consuelo! Mi Consuelo! Por favor, alguien ayude a mi Consuelo!*"

By now someone must have discovered that the hose is slashed.

Thunderous waves are applauding Jay. He is conspicuous only in his moving away from what everyone else is moving toward. Suddenly he gets an attack of convulsive giggles known to brides at weddings and mourners at wakes. *How's that for lighting a fire under someone's ass?* He laughs so hard he has to stop to bend over and clutch his aching gut. When he's finished cracking himself up, he circles back around the beach to his campsite and lies down on the tarp with his hands behind his head, stargazing again. More and more people are running down lanes toward the trailer park gate.

"A little girl's caught in there!" he hears a woman say, the news spreading faster than the fire itself.

"*Consuelo! Mi Consuelo! Por favor, no la dejen morir! Consuelo!*"

Even now, as grief flushes through me yet again, I can hear that mother's screaming going on and on and on.

Beyond the horrific brilliance piercing the night, the moon and stars are as bright as ever. Jay thinks, Can't someone shut her up? Not that big a hut. Mother and father too damn lazy to push their kid out a window? He reaches for his last warm *cerveza* in the wooden case next to the tarp, then feels around in the empty pigeon holes for where Otto left the church-key opener. Finding it, he pries off the bottle cap, takes a swig, gargles, and spits beer in the sand. He can't get rid of the gasoline taste. He'll finish his beer, then go back into town for a close-up view of his creation. So as not to arouse anyone's suspicion, he'll pitch in with the fire-fighting effort. He takes another hard swig off his beer. *Fucking gasoline.* And then like a cruel joke on himself, one of his mother's favorite hymns comes to mind.

> *Lord, lift me up and let me stand*
> *By faith, on Heaven's table-land*
> *A high-er plane than I have found*
> *Lord, plant my feet on high-er ground*

CHAPTER 7

WHERE GOD LURKS

If one's fate is indeed predetermined, I did a great job of ignoring the warning signals that foreshadowed mine.

During that long steamy summer before our trip to Mexico, I became hooked on the street theater two stories below my dining room window on Belmont Avenue. The show often starred the three transsexual prostitutes who plied their trade on the four blocks of small businesses between Sheffield and Racine. I gave each of these lovely ladies a personalized moniker: Marilyn, a gangly, six-foot-tall, platinum blonde; Chocolate, so named out of no intended disrespect to African-Americans, her svelte muscularity equal to that of any Olympian whose picture has ever adorned a box of Wheaties; and Ponytail, a striking creature with large, mysterious cat eyes and a severe brunette hairdo pulled like a tight bathing cap to the top of her head, then rubberbanded into a plume that trailed down the full length of her back. This troika of pure womanly desire was given to an excess of rouge, false eyelashes, stiletto fuck-me pumps, and an array of hot pants and halter tops designed to advertise slim-hipped butts and hormone-induced perky breasts. Stare too long, and the he/she, lounging luxuriously against a parking meter or a bus stop sign, would level an inviting stare back at you. *Johns*, identifiable from my birds-eye view only by the color and make of their cars, drove up like clockwork, paused long enough for their "dates" to hop in the passenger side, then sped off for a quick blowjob or other services too far beyond my limited life experience for me to describe. Usually, within twenty minutes of being picked up, I'd see Marilyn, Chocolate, or Ponytail lounging against a parking meter on Belmont again, lipstick perfect and looking none the worse for wear. Call me a romantic, but I'd like to think that for sheer entertainment value alone the transsexuals earned a well-deserved acceptable niche among the mainstream neighborhood population.

One day, as I lay on the living room sofa closing in on finishing that epic to end all epics, *War and Peace*, I heard someone yelling in the street, "Give me my mothafuckin' money, chump! I said, give me my money!" Interrupted just as Pierre finally, after eight hundred pages, was going to get it on with Natasha, I lurched to my feet and went to the dining room window. Down below, right in front of the Polk Brothers appliance store, Chocolate shook her finger in Mr. Dodge Dart's face, backing him up around his double-parked red car. I'd never really seen the john other than to catch his vague image through the mirrorlike reflection in his windshield whenever he picked up or dropped off Chocolate. He turned out to be a short, doughy, middle-aged man.

"I ain't paying you nothin'," he said, apparently dissatisfied with Chocolate's performance and trying to blow off paying for his blowjob. The gold wedding band on his finger caught the bright, late-morning sun. Still backpedaling, he looked worried, as if it were dawning on him that maybe he had underestimated Chocolate's ability to stay in touch with his masculine side. I heard the shower running in the bathroom; Mila often missed the juicy street action and had to rely on my secondhand accounts. Chocolate flipped off one high-heel shoe, then the other. He snatched the sandy-colored bouffant wig from his head, exposing a cropped afro, and spiked it to the street. Neon-pink hot-pants, white halter top, and all, he went into a boxer's stance, moved to and fro laterally, and began sticking Mr. Dodge Dart with a lightning-quick left-jab that would have made Muhammed Ali proud.

"Hey, watch it, ya fuckin' freak!" yelled the john, holding up his hands to ward off the blows.

"Who you callin' freak, Freak?" Chocolate connected with a

vicious combination of punches that knocked poor Mr. Dodge Dart clear off his feet and sent him sprawling on top of the car's hood. He shielded himself with his arms and drew a leg up to protect his balls. Marilyn and Ponytail, their fuck-me pumps already discarded, came loping from opposite directions on the street. The three transsexuals-turned-manly-men proceeded to pummel, kick, gouge, knee, and choke the hapless john, damn near ripping him a new asshole.

"Mothafucka," Chocolate yelled, "this ain't no charity work!"

A handful of the straight-arrow-type salesmen in Polk Brothers piled out onto the sidewalk to watch and snigger. Across the street in the used-clothing store, a woman waiting to have her merchandise rung up at the counter paused to gawk out the plate-glass window. Ponytail twisted off the car antenna and flung it to the ground. Barefoot, Marilyn kicked an impressive dent into the front door on the passenger side. "There," she yelled in a husky throaty voice. "Now you paid, ya piece of shit." Somehow, in spite of Chocolate's punches raining down on him, Mr. Dodge Dart did a rolling escape off the side of the hood, flung open the driver's door, and jumped inside faster than Batman into the Batmobile. As he slammed the door shut and fumbled with his keys, Chocolate, in close pursuit, hocked up a big hocker, leaned in the open driver's window, and spit in his battered face.

"Take your jiz, mothafucka!"

I never knew a family car could lay so much rubber, the Dart vanishing down Belmont for parts unknown. God only knows what the john's face swelled into by the time he got home to his dear sweet wife. The general message of the troika seemed reasonable enough: Don't play, if you won't pay. Maybe I'm a sicko, but I considered that a good day.

Another time, there was a bad day. Shortly after Mila left for *Amour*, I had lost myself in the *writing zone* at my desk in the bedroom, when I heard car tires screeching, then that solid thud, just like the time Penny got hit, except louder. Immediately drawn from my chair to the dining room window, I looked down below.

Something plummeted in my chest, then lapped against the walls of my stomach. "Awwww, no." In the middle of the street, a little girl, maybe five or six years old, lay on her side, curled in a fetal position, just inches in front of a white Impala's bumper. Not a visible scratch on her, she might as well have been taking an afternoon nap. The driver, a suit-and-tie businessman, jumped out of his car, square-jowled face so florid it looked like it supplied nourishment for his meticulously coiffed red hair. He rushed over to the girl, knelt beside her, and touched her cheek with a careful palm. No response. "Somebody call an ambulance!" His scream, trapped between the buildings on either side of the street, amplified straight up to me and into the pale sky.

Nothing unites a community like harm to one of its young. Before I could take a step toward the wall phone in the kitchen, the voice of a salesman called out from the Polk Brothers' entrance, "It's on the way!" A woman with a scarf covering her hair rollers ran from the currency exchange into the street, then the Hispanic grocer from down the block, followed by the owner of the Moti Mahal restaurant, her lavender silk sari fluttering like an exotic sail behind her.

The woman with hair rollers squatted down, grabbed hold of the girl's hand, and began patting it. "Come on, honey. Wake up." Still no response. The driver yanked off his seersucker jacket, wadded it up for a pillow and gingerly slipped it under the girl's head. Within minutes, a large crowd of the concerned and morbidly curious had jammed the street and stopped traffic. A block and a half away on the Belmont El platform that runs over the street, several commuters watched the drama, one of them shading his eyes for a better view.

"She ran right out in front of me!" the driver told anyone who would listen.

"Ain't no excuse," yelled a teenager from the rear of the crowd, still mounted on his ten-speed bicycle. "You're going to jail."

The wail of a squad car zeroed in from the west, the wail of an ambulance from the east. And then I noticed blood puddling in a crimson pool around the girl's blue shorts. Marilyn elbowed her way through the crowd carrying a blanket she must have gotten from her car. With a flourish she spread it over the girl. It quickly soaked through. I stayed by my window, that same irrevocable change I had felt after Penny's accident like cold dew on my face and arms. And me, unable or unwilling to change and grow with it.

Later, after the paramedics and the cops and the crowd had all gone, and a street sweeper scrubbed away the blood, and traffic once again moved smoothly on Belmont, I went off to work at Bismarck's. As I passed Polk Brothers, I asked a salesman in the doorway on the lookout for potential customers coming down the sidewalk if he'd heard any news about the girl.

"Dead. Didn't even make it to the hospital. A real shame."

2

The honeymoon of our relationship over, Mila's bouts of depression grew longer and more frequent. By late-August, everything I did—leaving my wet bath towel on the bed, chewing on ice cubes after finishing off a glass of Coke, ignoring her system of neatly stacking pots and pans on the pantry shelf—got on her nerves. Often, no amount of foreplay could warm her to my touch or prepare her for my cock.

"We're not married," she said. "I need more space. Maybe we should be friends."

Rejection sucks. Whatever happened to my tender, willing-to-please babe?

"Roman, I pick up a brush and don't have the slightest idea what to paint—not exactly the stuff great artists are made of. What's the secret, anyway? How do you know you're a writer?"

As we lay in bed that morning, I reached across the space of rumpled sheet and stroked her fine, corn-silk hair off her forehead. "I just am." Mila seemed to think about that, her eyes doing a familiar subtle, darting dance that reminded me of a trapped bird searching for an escape route. Then a long exhale.

"Must be nice," she said.

We were always short on cash. A swing through the Jewel supermarket for a week's groceries became a time for debating things like the long-term savings benefit of buying a sixteen-ounce bottle of ketchup as opposed to a twelve-ounce bottle, and the pros and cons of toughing it out with Scotts one-ply toilet paper as opposed to splurging on Charmin's snugly soft two-ply paper.

"Why do you always have to be so difficult?" Mila asked, racing ahead of me with the grocery cart down the cereal aisle. "Let's just buy what we need and worry about money later." She picked a box of Raisin Bran off the top shelf and tossed it into the cart.

"No, corn flakes," I said, snatching a box off the bottom shelf and catching up to Mila. "They're on sale."

"I hate corn flakes. Maybe if you didn't eat so much."

"It's not my fault I'm a big guy."

"Well, I don't have *big* money. Why the hell should I pay for half the food?"

"OK, then you start paying more for the phone." I put the box of Raisin Bran back on the shelf. "You yak with your friends so much you might as well buy stock in AT&T."

"I can't help it if I have more friends than you, Roman."

"Try writing letters," I said. "Stamps are cheap."

"Fuck off," Mila replied. Then wistfully distant, "I need a vacation. Alone."

"Fine. You do that."

"Next summer I should go live in France, meet other artists."

"That's a great idea." But the sudden lurch in my stomach said otherwise. "Just remember, I won't accept collect calls. Send me a postcard."

Then, without warning or fanfare, the depression would lift for a few days.

"Come on, don't stop!" Though technically it is I who rode Mila hard on the bed, her sharp fingernails spurred my flanks. "Deeper! No one's ever fucked me like you. I love your cock in my pussy."

Let the natural born, heterosexual man who can resist the pleasure of that kind of dirty talk from a woman step forward.

How about the time Mila came home from bargain hunting at a used-clothing store with a bag full of lingerie? As I lay stretched out on the olive-green couch, the *Sun-Times* resting against my chest, she stood in the middle of the living room holding up a black teddy for my approval.

"Would you like to fuck me in this?"

I looked the teddy over, savoring the joys of life.

"Sure."

"Pure silk," Mila said. "Only a dollar. I doubt it's ever been worn." She tossed the teddy onto the overstuffed chair in the corner, then reached into the bag at her feet and pulled out an aquamarine negligee.

"I could get a matching garter belt and some nylons with seams to go with this. What do you think?"

Mercy.

Sometimes, she'd prescript our lovemaking.

"When you're ready to fuck me," she said, pausing from sucking my cock during an afternoon quickie in bed, "rip my panties off. Would that be a turn-on, sweetie?"

"Sure."

No wonder I skated through the bad times with Mila, ignoring signals, legs pumping faster and faster in the hopes that the next good time on the horizon would not prove a watery mirage. And then one morning, after waking up and making love with Mila not once but twice, I thought for sure that our mutual lust/love had conquered all. Suddenly she climbed on top of me, grabbed each of my wrists tightly in her hands, and pinned them to the mattress on either side of my head. Looking all pug-nosed determined, she braced her matchstick arms and said, "Try to get up."

"Why?"

"Bet you can't do it."

"You can't be serious."

"Try!" she demanded.

With little effort, I raised my arms in spite of her pushing down on them, snapped my wrists free of her grasp, and swatted her aside onto the mattress. She lay there, hair a mess, looking at a loss for words, then miffed. She climbed on top of me again and repinned my wrists with an even tighter grip than before.

"Now try."

"Mila, this is silly. In case you haven't noticed, I'm a whole lot bigger than you."

She waited. I'm no muscle man, but I tossed her aside almost as easily as before. Looking doubly miffed, she climbed on top and pinned me again, leaning the full weight of her body against my wrists.

"Ready," she said.

"You sure?"

"Yeah."

I faked a yawn just to bug her.

"Quit stalling."

This time, I'll admit, Mila forced me to tap into my reserve strength to free my hands, but I tried not to show it, grabbed hold of her waist, and might have sent her sailing over the edge of the bed had she not snared a handful of chenille bedspread.

"Whoa!" I said. "Sorry. You OK?"

Lying in a heap with one leg dangling off the bed, Mila didn't answer.

"Are you OK?" I asked again. Still no answer. She slid off the bed and knelt beside it, arms folded on the mattress, supporting her chin. Staring off into space, her eyes did that subtle darting dance. I heard the hydraulic hiss of a CTA bus opening its door at the stop in front of Polk Brothers, then a pause, followed by the diesel groan as the bus pulled into traffic. Mila glanced my way.

"So you're always aware of being stronger than me?"

"Of course. I'm a guy."

"And if you wanted to, you could hurt me?"

"I suppose. Gee, thanks for the creepy thought."

"Not that you would, but you could."

"Mila, where've you been? Why do you think boys are taught it's uncool to hit girls?"

It's difficult to believe that at twenty she hadn't already made peace with man's brute strength advantage, but looking back I know now it was something about me or, more precisely, what she felt about me, that upped the risk. I reached for one of her breasts. She pushed my hand away, slowly got up, and went over to her dresser near the foot of the bed. Opening the top drawer, she snatched out a pair of panties and stepped into them.

"I'm going for a walk," she said.

"Awww, come on. Let's stay in bed for a while."

"I just feel like being alone." She opened the middle drawer, pulled out a white tank top with spaghetti shoulder straps, and yanked it over her head.

"Oh, honey-poochy-pie, what's a matter?" I bounced off the bed, came up behind her, and started tickling her ribs. "Daddy-kins would never hurt his wittle itty-bitty baby-kins."

"Stop!" Mila flinched away from me.

I plopped onto the end of the bed, still not getting it. She opened the bottom drawer and dug out her army-surplus bomber khakis. Then in the dresser mirror, I recognized the hard, gray, washed-out expression that belonged to the other Mila. A familiar weariness zapped me. Shit, I thought.

And so began another round of Mila's depression.

3

Chicago's blistering summers do not end gradually. One morning you wake up, and the cool-dry swoop of fall has cleansed the city. With the change of seasons came the start of our senior year at Everett. Between work and class schedules, Mila and I usually saw each other only in passing.

I lay on the couch watching the 10 p.m. news. Jimmy *who* was running for President? Get his peanut-farmer clock cleaned in the primaries next year, I thought. I hopped up and clicked off the portable TV atop the bookshelf. Too early for bed. I made my way through the apartment, snatched my army field jacket off the coat-tree in the dining room, and went out the kitchen door to the back porch. Somewhere down below in the dark alley, two cats facing off in a turf war tried to psyche each other out with eerie moans. I climbed a rickety painter's ladder left behind by the last tenants, pushed aside a wooden trap door in the ceiling, and escaped to the roof. That nippy night, I sat on the smooth tar that still held the warmth of the day's sun, hugging my jacket to my ribs. Chicago's sodium streetlights reflected a crown of pink above the city. Far to the south, the Sears Tower, John Hancock, and Standard Oil building stood tall and ruled the glittering downtown skyline; to the west, high above a sea of rooftops, Saint Alphonse's church steeple pierced the night; a half mile to the north, Wrigley Field, embarrassed by yet another Cubs' nose-dive finish in the standings, hid shrouded in darkness; and a mile to the east, the lit neighborhood streets stopped abruptly with a loose string of high-rises, then a backdrop of starry nothingness out over Lake Michigan where I suspected God lurked. The windows of the Quiet Night music club on the corner of Belmont and Sheffield must have been open to let in the cool, because even from two blocks away I faintly heard the Segal Schwall Blues Band's harmonica-jamming, screaming rendition of "Corina." I lost myself in deep life-is-a-bitch thought. What was I going to do after graduation? How was I going to keep Mila? When would I ever sell a single story? Where would I be in a year, much less five or ten? I was drawing blanks. Time flew by, the warmth from the tar and the pulse of city life slowly ebbing beneath me. Around midnight, good and tired, I climbed back down the ladder and returned to the apartment, fully expecting to find Mila home from work.

"Heeello," I called out.

No answer. I checked the bedroom. Not there. Probably went out for a drink with her waitress friends, I thought. Soon I was in bed, staring up at the familiar crab on the ceiling. Sleep? Forget it. Where the fuck was she? Wrigley insisted one too many times on trying to sleep on top of my face. I scooped him up and tossed him toward the door.

"*Raooow!*"

He hit the floor running and darted out of the room. One o'clock. Two o'clock. Images of Mila lying bruised, battered, or worse in some dark alley gave way to images of her wantonly sucking and fucking another man's cock. Can't even take a break to pick up a phone? Three o'clock. Wired, I bounded out of bed, pit-stopped in the bathroom, opened the medicine cabinet, and knew exactly where to lay my hands on a hard-core drug— NyQuil. I poured and downed a couple of nasty-tasting shots hoping they would knock me out, then fumed back to bed. Even dependable Nyquil proved no match for my anger. Tossing, turning, and crab-staring through another couple of fitful hours, I vowed that if Mila wasn't already seriously dead, I'd kill her myself. Then right about the time the neighborhood bird population announced the dawn with a chirping racket, I heard a key turn in the front door lock. My ears traced Mila's every guilty move. The open and shut creak. The careful attempt to noiselessly relock the bolt. Tiptoeing past the half-closed bedroom door and into the bathroom. Pee hitting water. No flush. I quickly plumped my pillow to lift my head so that she'd have my withering stare to greet her the moment she swung open the door. Keep cool, I thought.

"Oh, hi. You awake?"

"Fuck you." So much for keeping cool.

"Huh?"

I wanted to smack that fake, surprised innocence I'd seen her use so many times on her mother right off her face.

"Which part don't you understand—the *fuck* or the *you*?"

"I meant to call. Sorry." Without any more explanation, Mila slipped out of her *Amour* tuxedo-shirt–black-miniskirt uniform, crawled into bed, and snuggled up next to me. I smelled her stale booze breath. She had to be kidding. I moved away.

"Roman, I went out for a few drinks, all right? I'm too tired to get into it now. Let's talk in the morning."

"It *is* the morning, darling. Who the fuck were you out with?"

A long pause.

"No one important."

"Well, how about you give me Mr. Goddamn-Motherfucking-Unimportant's name?"

Another long pause.

"He's a regular at *Amour's*."

It was the kind of coming-clean honesty that only young people are stupid enough to think their significant other will appreciate. My stomach dropped.

"He's been asking me to go out with him for months," Mila said. "What can I say, it just happened." She reached over and caressed my shoulder. I picked her hand off me like it was something dirty and dropped it back onto her.

"You must think I'm a real chump."

"Roman, he means nothing to me." Mila's pulling-a-fast-one tone began to crack. "I'm really, really sorry I didn't call."

"Well, guess what?" I said. "I'm really, really sorry I'm moving out tomorrow. Goodnight." I rolled away from her.

"Don't say that! Please!" Starting to cry, she tugged on my waist for me to roll back to her. Forget it, I thought.

"I love you so much it scares me! That's why I went out with him. I can't help it! You don't know what it's like to grow up around parents who hate each other's guts. I feel so trapped! It doesn't make sense! You're everything I want! What's wrong with me? Don't move out! Please! You can't even begin to know! I'm sorry, I'm sorry, I'm sorry!"

Listening to her sob, I felt the vice-grip of her hug around me and the wetness of her tears on my arm. If it was a performance, it was a great one. She went out with another man because she feared loving me? I was having a little trouble taking the compliment, but incredibly, I already knew I would forgive her. For some masochistic reason, I wanted the details of her crime. I turned her way, and she pressed her cheek to my chest. Careful not to show any affection, I kept my hands to myself.

"Who is he?"

"It doesn't matter. I'm not going out with him again."

"Who the fuck is he?" I demanded.

"Tony."

"Tony fucking what?"

"I don't know—Marzulla, Marzullo, something like that."

"What's he do?"

"He's a professional gambler. Bets on sports."

Shit, even if she claimed she wasn't going out with him again, how could I compete with the lure of that kind of life-in-the-fast-lane? No doubt some older guy with a Corvette.

"Did you fuck him?"

"No."

"Did you kiss him?"

"Yes."

"Where were you?"

"His place. We went there for one last drink."

"Oh, nothing like going to *his place* on a first date. Did you make-out with him?"

"Roman, why get into all—"

"Shut the fuck up." The brute edge to my voice surprised even me, but hey, a man has his breaking point, and I can't say I didn't get a perverse satisfaction in feeling her go perfectly still against me. I repeated the question slowly and deliberately.

"Did you fucking make-out with the fucking low-life mother-fucker?"

"Yes."

"In bed?"

"No, on the couch."

"You got undressed?"

"OK, OK, I'm not going to lie. He unbuttoned my shirt, but that was it."

"Oh great, you let him cop a feel."

No answer. Then, "I admit I wanted to go to bed with him, but I couldn't do that to you, so I came home. There's things I need to work out. I know that now."

She started sobbing again. I'd never seen her that remorseful or broken. That's enough, I thought. Could have been worse. And she did say she was going to work on her problem. What did I expect, that she'd trust men after growing up around a winner like her father, or watched her mother "miss her chance"? With a jerk like Tony who's unafraid to break rules to get what he wants, Mila saw the opportunity to not miss *her* chance, to play it smart. She'd choose somebody she didn't care about so that she herself wouldn't get hurt.

Poor Mila. She had a serious short in her love circuit, and I had a serious need not to quit on her. Hell, I'd give her the cold shoulder for a few days, then play it by ear and work at proving it was safe for her to love me. I fought the urge to hold and comfort her.

My cold-shoulder resolve didn't last the hour. By 8 o'clock, Mila and I were fucking for a third time that morning. If I'd had Tony the Gambler's phone number, I would have dialed it and let him listen to Mila's screamer orgasm that no doubt added spice to the downstairs neighbor's breakfast cup of coffee. Wrigley, returning from exile, planted himself by the side of the bed, stared indifferently up at my pumping ass, and began to meow, wanting someone to go and pour Purina Cat Chow into his bowl in the kitchen. First things first, kitty.

Over the next few days of sexual bliss, Mila and I shed life's drudgeries in the warm afterglow of our lovemaking. Her talk of living in France changed to the more affordable alternative of taking a five-day Christmas-break vacation in Mexico.

"My friend Gail says it's dirt cheap down there. If we both work an extra day a week we can swing it. We need the change, Roman. Together."

I knew that Carl could always use the extra help behind the bar. My grades might suffer, but love conquers all. By the time Mila's mood changed again and she'd gone back into her I-need-more-space shell, we'd already made our nonrefundable flight reservations.

The DC10 slowly rose above the smoggy, limited visibility over the city and southern suburbs, disappeared among clouds covering barren farm fields, and punched free into the brilliant, heavenly blue realm of a last chance. Make it or break it, everything rode on Mexico.

CHAPTER 8

WOLF ETIQUETTE

I've heard it said that if two wolves get into a fight to the finish, all the loser has to do is roll onto his back and expose his neck to the winner. No matter how much the winner may yearn to sink his canines into the loser's jugular, he will yield to a higher wolf moral authority and grant clemency. Until further notice, Mila was in for a lot of unconditional neck exposing.

Caught in the Coca Cabana's flickery light as we stood on the hospital's front porch, I pulled my arm free from my beloved's grasp.

"You fucked him, didn't you?" I said it devoid of any real emotion. Mila burst into tears.

"From now on you can fuck all the Jays and Tonys you want. Just stay away from me." I slowly moved toward the hospital doorway, my low energy reserve fading fast.

"Roman!" Mila followed after me through the darkened hospital, pawing at my back. "Don't say that! Please." She crawled into bed behind me and repeatedly tugged on my shoulder for me to roll over and face her.

"It was awful! You were right about him! I can't even explain why I did it! You're the only one I love! Please don't hate me!"

Bitch, I thought. But I can't honestly blame my not kicking Mila out of that bed on physical sickness alone, for as she continued to spew her abject apology, I began to feel the bind of the dominant wolf. Eerie firelight coming through the translucent ceiling waffled and danced on walls. There was only one escape.

"Go to sleep," I said. Mila clamped a tight spooning hug around me, her quiet breathy crying in my ear.

It must not have been long after the crack of dawn that I awoke to nurse Florence standing beside the bed and pressing her fingertips to my wrist for a pulse. The faint warming light of a new day brought with it an even split between hope and dread. Florence seemed not the least bit disturbed by the unexplained presence of Mila, who was just then stirring awake and loosening her arm from around my chest.

"*Es bueno,*" the nurse said, giving me the OK sign.

"*Cuanto cuesta?*" I asked, digging into my shorts for the few pesos Mila had given me the day before.

"*Nada.*"

Three cheers for socialized medicine.

Other than extreme body fatigue, I'd made a miraculously fast recovery. What was I supposed to do—tell Mila she couldn't walk with me back to the trailer park? Like it or not, we were stuck together in Escondido for another three days. As I left the hospital, snail-pacing my way down the road, she stayed beside me, solicitously holding onto my elbow.

"You all right, sweetie?

"I'm not your fuckin' *sweetie.*"

"I know I can't blame you if you want to break up with me."

"No shit."

"But . . ."

"*But* my ass."

"Will you please let me finish!" Mila's voice had that quavering, trying-not-to-cry quality. "I can't expect any favors—"

"Now *there's* a safe bet."

Out of frustration, Mila let go of my arm, hauled her fist back, and socked my shoulder so hard bone throbbed and a nerve tingled down my arm. I squared off with her. I've never violated the rule, *Thou shall not stomp a woman*, but I came awfully close to decking that particular woman on the spot. I settled for going nose to nose with her.

"Don't you mother*fucking* ever hit me again." In Mila's eyes I saw both fear and a willingness to take a punch. I continued down the road.

"Roman!" She quickly caught up to me. "Will you at least do me the favor of letting me look after you until you're well?"

"Like you looked after me last night? Find yourself a new chump."

"You're not a chump," Mila said. "I'm the chump. I did something incredibly stupid, all right? Whether you like it or not, you're the best thing that ever happened to me, so don't expect me to stop caring about you even if you never speak to me again."

"You're a fucking whore cunt," I said. Had I been able to think of words that packed even more derogatory wallop, I'd have used those, too.

Mila closed her eyes as if she were absorbing the insult, then opened them. Her voice quavering all the more, she said, "Yeah, but I'm a very, very sorry fucking whore cunt."

It was a tender loving moment.

Bothered that the sap deep within me was already inching toward forgiving Mila, I tried to convince myself that I allowed her to throw a hug around my waist strictly because I needed a good nursemaid. Judging from my Gandhi-like frame, I'd dropped more than ten pounds in less than twenty-four hours, and regaining my full strength was first on the Roman priority list. Then I would decide whether or not I wanted to dish out payback to Jay.

Mila and I rounded the bend. Low on the eastern horizon, an orange-pink sun touched the tops of worn mountains that slanted every which way as if they were trying to pull back from each other's company. If that toasty ball had rolled straight ahead down over the foothills, it would have flattened both of us. At the other end of the nearly deserted town, Sánchez and a couple of Indian men milled about the ashes of the Coca Cabana, kicking at and turning over debris. Fuck, I thought. We'd have to make it past him. A burnt stink hung in the air.

"Look at that," I said. "Cowboy sure had himself one hell of a busy night. You believe me now?"

Mila slid her hand up my arm and leaned into me dejectedly.

"You're the one with the good instincts about people," she said. "Not me, that's for sure."

We passed the juice bar/hardware/grocery store hut, then came to the *farmacia*. The wide steel shutter had been rolled up to open the entrance. Inside, Alberto sat in a chair next to the magazine rack, reading a newspaper. He glanced up at us, his expression gravely somber as he lowered the paper to his lap. A smudge of soot marked his unshaven dimpled chin, but his pharmacist's coat was impeccably starched and white as usual. He must have decided to stay in town instead of going home after helping put out the fire.

"I see someone's been playing with matches again," I called out to him from the road. Alberto didn't answer. As if discretion were in order, he motioned with his hand for Mila and me to step closer.

When we'd come inside the *farmacia*, he quietly said, "I am afraid he played with much more than that. He played with a life."

And then Alberto told us of how Consuelo had died hiding under her parents' bed; of how the parents had gone into the children's room and herded the smallest two kids out a back door believing that Consuelo had already made it to safety. When they saw no sign of her in the road, both mother and father dashed into the hut again, searched every room including the restaurant, and suffered third-degree burns themselves. Who would have thought that the girl, in her panic, was hiding and too terrified to make a sound? Perhaps in all the confusion, each parent thought that the other had checked under the bed. They raced out into the road hoping that they had somehow missed seeing Consuelo there. Townspeople arriving on the scene restrained them from running into the hut a second time. "They would have died trying to save her," Alberto said. "I saw the body. Not a pretty sight. Nothing but charred flesh and raw blisters. And the smell. I will never forget. They have taken her to another town where the Indians buy coffins. The funeral is tomorrow."

How does one begin to react? Drowning in guilt, I might as well have lit the fire myself. All I could muster was a lame, "That's terrible."

"I just bought a tamale from her yesterday," Mila said, her

voice shaking. "I even had a silly fantasy about adopting her. What kind of person would . . . ?"

"Yeah," I said, my tone dangerously ironic. Mila glanced at me woundedly, then hugged her arms to her body. I noticed they were goose-bumped.

"Such a sweet girl," Alberto said, his eyes teary. "When she would come in here, I would trade her candy for a tamale. She was always so serious with the hard bargain, asking for two boxes of Chiclets instead of one. I would tease, 'Consuelo, if you will only smile for Mr. Huerta, I will give you *three* boxes of Chiclets.' I always got the best of the bargain, because a more beautiful smile you have never seen. Now there will be no more smiles to fill that place in my heart. And what did she die for, eh? Tell me that."

Had the man known how close he was to ripping the information he sought out of me, he would have paused a moment longer.

"It is out of my hands," Alberto continued. "The people are very angry. They think that only a gringo could be this kind of a butcher." He explained how the arsonist had slashed the hose from the water pipe and siphoned gasoline out of a taxi and into a can he stole from Pedro. It was Sánchez who spotted the piece of hose and the gas cap on the ground by the car. "The *Jefe* would not be my first choice for a dinner guest, but no one can say he is bad with the eyes," Alberto said. "He thinks people should bribe him for permission to breathe, and he does not tolerate anyone who—how you say— thumb their nose at his authority? Believe me, if he cannot find the person who is responsible for Consuelo's death, he will find someone else and shoot him, anyway. That is the way it is with the *Jefe*."

"Yeah," I said. "He gave me a little tour of his jail yesterday." I briefly told Alberto and Mila about Sánchez's generous invitation for me to join his family. "A real friendly guy."

"Scary," Mila said. "Someone could end up *disappeared* around here."

"You do not want to play games with the *Jefe*," Alberto said. "Take my advice and stay close to the trailer park. Whatever is to happen, I would rather it did not happen to either of you."

After leaving the *farmacia*, I walked with Mila down the road toward the trailer park, neither of us saying a word. As badly as I'd already felt about the boy getting beat up, that was but a drop in the bucket compared to the numbing guilt I felt about Consuelo's death. Can't tear yourself up, I thought. But the horrendous weight of responsibility would not go away. Up ahead, Sánchez, looking like his usual hard-ass self in his mirrored shades, stood with arms folded across his chest, holding court with two other men in front of the burnt, leveled ruins of the Coca Cabana. The *Jefe's* sidekicks—dark-skinned, no-neck, stocky peasants—each wore beat-up straw cowboy hats low on their foreheads and seemed to be hanging on the *Jefe's* every word. I navigated down the center of the road with Mila and thought, Just be cool.

"Shouldn't we go over there and tell Sánchez we think Jay did it?" Mila asked, breaking our silence.

"Forget it," I said. "He'll throw us in jail for not coming forward sooner. He told me so himself."

"But how are we going to live with ourselves?"

As much as Mila's question gnawed at me, it did my heart good to know that she had finally gotten with the guilt program. I've never mastered the fine art of looking the other way. Jay had pushed the stakes awfully high. I needed time to think, and as we approached what was left of the Coca Cabana, I whispered to her, "Don't say a fucking word to Sánchez if you ever want to see home again."

Not a single support beam of the former building was left standing—stove, tables, and chairs reduced to scorched junk. Sooty dishes once stacked on wooden shelves had crashed to the floor, many of them shattered. A dresser, black as charcoal and sagging in the middle, looked like it would collapse into a heap of spent embers if someone dared pull on any of its drawer handles. Several charred mattress springs lay strewn about, the largest of which must have been from the parents' bed that Consuelo had died under. I couldn't help but envision her curled up in the fetal position, trying to breathe in the smoke and flames.

Just when I thought we'd made it cleanly past Sánchez, a metal table leg the size of a baton landed on the road inches in front of our toes.

"Not so fast, *muchacho*."

One of the peasant sidekicks laughed, amused at how Mila and I had been startled out of our skins. As Sánchez slowly came over to us, I saw my own refracted face and dwarfed body in one of his lenses. He stopped and grinned, appraising Mila with lingering eyes.

"I see why you were in such a hurry to leave my *policía* station, *muchacho*," Sánchez said, turning to me. "Maybe next time your girlfriend come instead of you."

"Not a good idea," I said, trying to toe the line between smarting off and showing I wasn't afraid.

"*Por qué?*" Sánchez asked innocently. "You no trust your woman with a Latin lover—heh-heh-heh."

"In your dreams, pal," Mila said.

Sometimes women are awfully brave when they shouldn't be. So much for toeing lines. The grin fell from Sánchez's face, and he stepped forward, crowding Mila.

"*Muy bonita señorita,* you must always remember I am a powerful man who can make dreams come true. Do you know what I am dreaming now?" He waited as if daring Mila to open her sassy mouth again. "I am dreaming that I should arrest both of you for burning down this *restaurante* and killing one of our *niñas*."

"We didn't kill anyone," Mila said. I could tell by her pulled-back posture that Sánchez intimidated her, but she didn't flinch.

"That's right," I said, stepping in between them as non-threateningly to Sánchez as possible. "You got the wrong people."

"Was I talking to you?" Sánchez poked me so hard in the chest with his index finger it felt like he'd left a bruise. "Was I?"

Out of the corner of my eye, I saw the sidekicks move closer.

"You've got the wrong people," I repeated. "I spent the whole night in the hospital sick. When the fire broke out, Mila was with me."

"Is that right, *muchacho*."

"Yes, that's right."

"Tell me something, *muchacho*. Why is it that I always think you are lying?"

"I'm not lying. Ask the nurse."

"Why should I ask the nurse when I can ask my dream?" Sánchez said. "Do you know what my dream tells me? It tells me that you think you can come to my country, spit on our customs, and get away with murder. You are gringo shit."

Sánchez translated that last line for the sidekicks, and they let out peanut-gallery laughter. Then, moving even closer to flank the *Jefe*, they looked at me with baffling dull stares from their side of the cultural divide.

"And Yankees like you think that you are the masters of Mexico?" Sánchez asked. "How can a master be shit? Maybe I am your master—heh-heh. What do you think, *muchacho*?"

In Sánchez's sunglasses, I see the dual image of my *fuck you* expression. Maybe he's through having his fun.

"Come on, Mila." As soon as I turn to leave, a hard kick to the small of my back slams me belly-down on the road.

"Do not move!"

A knee to the kidneys and strong hands on my shoulders pin me to the ground.

"Stop it!" Mila yells. "Leave him alone!"

Someone's got a fistful of my hair, someone else pulling a wrist so far behind my back my arm feels like it's about to snap. I make the mistake of moving a leg and get kicked in the balls.

"I said stop it! Leave him alone!"

Sharp twisting pain spreads from groin to gut. Gasping for air, I am strangely detached from what is happening and aware of my cheek grinding into the dirt. A handcuff tightens and cuts into my wrist.

"He didn't do anything!"

I hear the slapping of Mila's hands against what I imagine to be Sánchez, then the grunt of a man, followed by the slip-sliding of feet and the skidding thud of someone hitting the ground.

"You want to be next, *señorita*? Shut up!"

Fucked, I think. And then from down the road, someone yells

out in rapid Spanish. It's Alberto. An argument ensues. Sánchez's voice grows more heated, but Alberto's insistent voice comes closer until he, too, is right above me. The knee is removed from my kidneys and the many hands let go, but I don't dare move. The stabbing groin and stomach pain loosens. The two sidekicks join in the argument, but as it seesaws back and forth, Alberto seems to be holding his own. Finally, there's a long pause. Then one last angry outburst from Sánchez. The handcuff comes off my wrist.

"Get up, Yankee shit."

I slowly do exactly what I'm told. Before I can catch my bearings, Alberto shoves me in the direction of the trailer park.

"Go!"

Mila comes from somewhere on my right, and together we hurry down the road just shy of running. We know better than to look back.

"I have my eye on you!" Sánchez calls out. "You are in *my* world!"

"Fucking assholes," Mila says. She's crying, and I notice a large raspberry scrape on her right calf that's starting to ooze blood. I put my arm around her waist.

"Is your leg hurt bad?"

"Fucking pig pushed me down."

"Don't worry. It's over now. Good thing Alberto's looking out for us."

"He bribed him," Mila says.

"Huh?"

"I saw Alberto give Sánchez money."

We turn through the gate of the trailer park and enter underneath the reassuring canopy of palm trees. Walking off the soreness in my groin and tracing fingertips over my roughed-up cheek, I wonder about the going rate for freedom.

Saved by *la mordida*—the bite.

* * *

Heeding Alberto's advice, Mila and I stuck close to our hammocks, recuperating, saying little to each other, licking our emotional wounds. To distract myself from having to think about the mess we were in, I reached down, took *Moby Dick* out of my backpack, and began to read. Call me weird, but I soon found myself feeling sorry for that poor, white, misunderstood whale. After an hour or so, I rested the book open-faced on my chest and keyed into bits of people's conversations. From a longhair gringo a few campsites closer to the gate:

"Hey, man, I feel as bad as anyone that girl got killed, but that's no reason for a cop to go through all my shit like *I'm* some kind of criminal."

From a gringa wearing a long Mickey Mouse T-shirt over near the johns:

"That crazy Sánchez took my boyfriend to the station for questioning. Threatened to charge him with murder!"

"Bummer," said a girlfriend cradling a load of dirty clothes in her arms.

"Yeah," Mickey said, "we're out of here."

And from one of the few elderly women in the trailer park over near the mobile home suburb:

"Did you see that new sign at a restaurant in town? 'No hippies.' I'd like to see someone *white* get away with that kind of discrimination."

By 9 o'clock, more than the usual amount of camping vehicles had pulled out of the park and left town, significantly thinning the tourist ghetto. At one point, I awoke from a catnap and saw the same naked kid who had taken an impromptu shit in the sand come waddling down the lane, terrorizing a couple of girls older than himself by flailing a piece of palm frond like a whip.

"Watch out," one girl said, both of them trying to keep a step ahead of harm's way. "That thing really hurts." With single-minded hatred, the tow-headed little boy pursued the girls all the way out of the trailer park and onto the beach. Definitely Charles Manson material, I thought. I picked up my book again. Aboard the Pequod, in the middle of a tempestuous stormy ride, Mila spoke to me softly from her hammock.

"So what are we going to do?"

"*We?*" I returned. She'd made the mistake of thinking I'd unconditionally forgiven her. "Do me a favor and *can* the *we* shit."

Fuck proper wolf etiquette. I went for her jugular.

"Tell me something," I said. "What's it like knowing you've got a murderer's sperm inside of you? Are you keeping it nice and warm? No sense punishing the unborn innocent."

I suppose the shattered look on her face should have given me satisfaction. I wanted her to say something, anything, so that I could lay into her even more, but she just absorbed my cruelty, closed her *Fear of Flying* book, and turned away. I picked up *Moby Dick* from my chest again. I was unable to concentrate on the story, and the Pequod left me behind to tread water in an ocean of mean-spirited self-pity. Sonofamotherfuckingbitch, I thought. Like this is all my fault? I lay there for I don't know how long staring up through the palm trees. Finally, I bit the maturity bullet and admitted to myself that I was a complete asshole. Swinging out of my hammock, I moped over to Mila's hammock and crawled into it with her. I slid an arm around her waist, pressed my forehead against the back of her dainty skull, and said a word that damn near choked me.

"Sorry."

Sniffling, Mila rolled my way. We lay hugging each other, our equally shredded egos once again on an even keel.

"How can someone take a little girl's life and then just walk away like nothing happened?" Mila asked.

"Good question."

"We're going to let Jay get off scot-free?"

"Not if we can help it."

"What if we tell Alberto about Jay?" Mila suggested.

Looking back, I should have trusted Alberto to have enough discretion not to tell Sánchez where he'd come across the information, but at the time it struck me as foolish to risk our fate on someone we'd only known for four days.

"We could end up doubly fucked for not going to Sánchez ourselves," I told Mila.

"So what do we do?"

Since when did Mila think I was the King of Answers? "Only thing we can do," I said. "Play it by ear and hope that a safe way for us to make sure Jay gets caught falls into our laps. We owe it to Consuelo."

As if agreeing, Mila tightened her arm around me. Soon we drifted off to sleep.

* * *

At noon, a loud diesel truck loaded with huge, twenty-gallon glass containers of purified water woke us up as the driver tried to squeeze around a turn between two palm trees and into our lane. Bare-chested Tarzan/Pedro was out in front of the cab using hand signals to help the driver navigate. A man who looked the spitting image of George S. Patton came power-walking down the lane from the direction of the suburb, where he owned a mobile home big enough to subdivide into condos. He wore a khaki-colored ball cap, the bill of which was trimmed with embroidery of gold leaves. All knobby knees and plaid Bermuda shorts, he looked to me like a well-to-do retiree. He called out to Pedro with a jaunty, "Yep, you're my man! You're my man!" He must have said *you're my man* half a dozen patronizing times. I'd never seen Tarzan be anything other than stone-faced sullen to us dirt-poor college kids, but he knew a good tip when he saw one and gave the general so broad and transparently ingratiating a smile that I thought I was going to puke.

Sure enough, the general got his water delivered to his front stoop before any of the other suburbanites. Not long after the truck roared off down the road, I heard, "Room service."

I looked up and saw Alberto approaching our campsite with a plate of tinfoil-covered food in either hand. He stopped beside the hammock.

"I did not see my favorite lovebirds in town for so long and thought they might be hungry."

The delicious aroma of *picante* chicken, Spanish rice, and corn tortillas perked up my forgotten appetite.

"Hey, that's really nice," I said. Then, thinking there must be a catch to Alberto's overboard kindness, I asked, "How much do we owe you?"

"*Owe?*" The question seemed to stump Alberto.

"Yeah," Mila said. "Including the bribe you gave Sánchez. We'll mail you a check from Chicago."

"My guests do not *owe* me," Alberto said, frowning. "Maybe you have not noticed, but you are both having a very bad vacation." He extended the plates out for us to take them. "Careful, is very hot."

Soon Mila and I were feasting, plates balanced on our laps, trying as best we could in the close quarters of the hammock not to knock into each other's elbows.

"Ummm," I said, tender meat melting off a drumstick and into my mouth. "This chicken's the best."

"*Pollo*," Alberto corrected. "Chicken is *pollo*. It is time you learned Spanish."

"*Sí*," I said. "So what did you tell Sánchez? I thought I was good as dead."

"I told him the truth—that you are a good *Norte Americano* boy who respects the Mexican people. Unfortunately, the *Jefe* does not believe that *any Norte Americanos* respect the Mexican people, so I made a small contribution to his *niño's* college-education fund."

"A guy like Sánchez has a kid?" Mila asked.

"No," Alberto said, "but that is not important. What is important is that Big Al still has the hair on his head. For what is a hippie without hair? The answer is simple. It is a very unhappy hippie."

"I'm *not* a hippie."

Repressing a grin, Alberto tipped his head apologetically. "Pardon, Big Al. I forgot."

"It's a shame all this trouble in town is putting a dent in your business," Mila told Alberto, brushing rice with her fingers onto a tortilla.

"Ah, Mila, it does my heart good to know that such a beautiful woman is worried for my business, but do you think I live off the ten pesos a day I charge the hippies? It is owning the real estate that is the investment. You are all just keeping it—how you say—warm for me. Someday I will sell to a person who wants to build a first-class hotel, but for this to happen, Escondido must not get the bad reputation. That is no good for the next Acapulco—right, Big Al?"

"You're never going to let me live that one down, are you?" I said.

"You were born for teasing," Alberto told me good-naturedly. "Get used to it and enjoy the people who enjoy you. That is the key to a long life." He sighed, shook his head, and in a solemn voice said, "Ah, today is so sad—*muy triste*. The people are preparing for Consuelo's funeral tomorrow morning. If there is trouble, it will be after that." He looked at me curiously. "Why do you think the *Jefe* has taken such a dislike to you, Big Al?"

"Just for being my irritating, teaseable self," I said.

"This is not good for you," Alberto said. "And yes, if the *Jefe* beats up my customers, I will soon have no bodies to keep my real estate warm. I suggest that you and Mila spend tomorrow afternoon as my guests on a horseback ride in the mountains." He smiled at Mila and gallantly added, "That is, if the *señorita* would do me the honor. I already know how interested Big Al is in the Indians."

"Sounds exciting," Mila said.

"I'm up for it," I put in. "Do us good to get out of town."

"That is the idea, my Chicago friends. And away from the *Jefe*. I will come for you when the funeral is over." Alberto turned to leave, then stopped. "I almost forgot." Reaching into his pharmacist's coat pocket, he pulled out a tube of antibiotic ointment and handed it to Mila. "Put that on your hurt leg three times a day to prevent infection."

"Thanks," Mila said. "What are you, a guardian angel?"

"No, I am a man who likes to take care of beautiful legs. *Adiós*."

We watched Alberto cut through campsites toward the gate, whistling a song I didn't recognize in so lovely a tone I swear I could have swiped the notes right out of the air.

Except for a quick dip in the ocean, Mila and I spent the rest of the afternoon close to home. By evening, I'd damn near regained my full strength. We showered, changed into clean cut-offs and T-shirts, rinsed our lunch plates in the laundry sink next to the toilet stalls, and then set off for town. First we went to the *farmacia* to return Alberto's plates.

Alberto wasn't there, but the young assistant behind the counter took the plates from me like he was used to silly gringos whose actions didn't make any sense. Next, we stopped off at the canopied restaurant for dinner. With two of Escondido's five restaurants gone up in smoke, and a third refusing to seat tourists, we had to stand and wait in a short line of people beside the road for the next available table. Not long into the wait, a small drama unfolded across the street at the restaurant turning away *Norte Americanos*. One of two longhaired gringos passing by in the road pointed at the cardboard *no hippies* sign nailed to the front railing.

"Hey," he called out to a waitress, "you got lots of empty tables. Our money not good enough for you?"

The waitress ignored them with a haughty air, pouring coffee for an Indian man. The second longhair pulled out some peso bills from his wallet and held them up temptingly for the woman to see.

"Too afraid our *gringo* will rub off on you?"

Still ignoring them, the waitress disappeared behind the kitchen curtain at the rear of the restaurant. Immediately afterwards, a short, muscular, middle-aged woman charged out from behind the curtain and went over to the railing. Glowering at the hippies, she made a sharp hissing sound with her lips and gestured emphatically with her hands for them to *shoo* if they knew what was good for them.

"OK, OK," said the first longhair, "don't get all uptight. It's cool. Food smells better across the street, anyway."

Mila looked at me indignantly. "Did you see that?" We'd already moved closer to the front of the line. "That's not right. Someone should rip that sign down."

"Not right?" I said. "Think about it. A girl's dead. We're lucky *anyone* in this town will feed us."

Soon we got the table closest to the road and farthest from the kitchen. The young waitress took our order and served our food with her usual indifference. As I picked my red snapper's skeleton clean, I eavesdropped on dinner conversations at the other three tables. From the couple to our left:

"I still don't get why someone would do such a horrible thing?"

"Ya got me, Jennifer. Let's hope he's got a conscience and turns himself in."

From the two guys across the middle aisle from us:

"All it takes is one bad apple to ruin it for everyone else."

"Hey, do I look like someone who traveled two thousand miles so I could take the blame for a bad piece of fruit?"

And from another couple at the table nearest the kitchen:

"Maybe we should show our respects and go to the funeral."

"Honey, leave it alone. These people would probably bury us in the same hole with the girl. God, what's taking so long around here? I guess you order first, and *then* they go catch your fish in the ocean."

Something else was oppressively different than usual. As if music had been outlawed, no one in town was slipping pesos into any of the restaurants' jukeboxes.

After dinner, on our way home down the road, Mila asked, "How did we get mixed up in all this?"

"You thought Cowboy was cute, remember?"

"Please don't remind me." Now a contrite woman if ever there was one, Mila leaned against me as we walked. "I can't stand feeling this responsible for what happened to Consuelo," she said. "Jay's the one who did it, not us."

"You feel responsible because you care," I said, putting my arm around her shoulders. "*Caring* is the penalty we pay so that we can call ourselves decent human beings. If I honestly thought you didn't care, I wouldn't love you." Mila stopped and stared at me with an expression I can only describe as resentful. Then she hugged me so long and hard I took it as a plea for me to save the better half of her deeply conflicted self.

We made it back to our hammocks with an hour of daylight to spare. I picked up my book again and lost myself aboard the Pequod. That kamikaze vessel was just then gliding past the Bashee Isles and into the Pacific, "*whose gentle awful stirrings,*" according to Ishmael, "*seem to speak of some hidden soul beneath . . .*" I looked off to that same ocean not more than fifty yards away. Damn, old Melville sure had a way with the words.

Light blended into the shadows of dusk. All day long, Jay had been like a darting tracer in the far corners of my peripheral vision, never there when I turned to look. Now I allowed myself a glance in the direction of the cowboys' campsite. No one there. Smart, I thought. Layin' low.

Early into the night, I awoke and looked again. Two figures moved about on the edges of a small campfire's eerie ring of light. One squatted and toyed with a long stick, slowly lifting and lowering the burning end of it in and out of the obedient flames. Putting the stick down, the figure suddenly rolled backward onto his shoulder blades, legs straight up in the air, and flipped to his feet. His sheer physical agility, far beyond my own, gave me the willies. He picked up his stick again and brought the flaming tip close to his entranced narrow face. In that flickering ghoulish light, he looked as much primordial as he did androgynous. Then the stick's flame snuffed into an orange ember glow.

Closing my eyes, I told myself that Consuelo was counting on me.

CHAPTER 9

HIDDEN PLACE

The next morning, a snort awakened me. From high atop a chestnut horse, Alberto cut a rugged figure in his cowboy hat, boots, and denim getup.

"*Buenos días*, my lovebirds. Perhaps 'the morning' means something different in English than in Spanish?"

The stallion lowered his head, looked me over in my hammock with one of his looming skittish eyes, then jerked his head up and snorted again, none too impressed. Beside Alberto, dutiful Pedro stood holding the reins of two more horses, one speckled gray and the other jet-black. Stretching, I muttered, "What time is it?"

Before Alberto could answer, Mila awoke in her hammock, took one look at the three imposing creatures in the middle of our campsite, and let out a frightened gasp.

"Ah, Sleeping Beauty, do not be afraid," Alberto said. "My horses are very friendly. It is not their fault that Prince Big Al forgot to wake you up with a kiss."

Mila groaned, then lifted her head slightly. "Scared me half to death." All around us, the trailer park inhabitants were in high gear—a woman dousing a breakfast fire with a pan of water; a newly arrived couple pitching a tent; others traipsing to and from the ocean as if normal, daily, vacation routine were the best cure for the trouble in town. A few stared our way at the handsome steeds.

"We overslept?" Mila asked.

"Looks that way," I said, swinging my legs out of the hammock.

"It is 10:15," Alberto informed us. "Time to shake the lazy bones. Get dressed and be sure to wear long pants and a long-sleeve shirt. It can get cold in the mountains. I will meet you with the horses at the gate." He picked up his reins, and Pedro, ever watchful of his employer's cue, tightened the slack on the other two horses' reins, ready to follow.

"Remember," Alberto said, grinning, "people who think they are the descendants of the pyramid-builders do not like to be kept waiting."

* * *

We were out of town and on a dirt trail well into the brown grassy foothills before I got the semi-hang of staying in the saddle. By then Black Beauty had sized up my lack of equestrian talent and decided that no matter how hard I spurred his flanks with the heels of my hiking boots, he preferred to stay a couple of lengths behind Mila's horse. Up the hills we snaked with Alberto in the lead. He had assured us that he had packed everything we would need in his saddlebags. Stunning views of a glimmering ocean grew further away until it lay below the gauzy humid mist of *tierra caliente*, "hot country." The air had turned cool and dry. Here the stunted grass appeared mowed, the hills more rocky and severe, and the approaching wall of forested mountains less impenetrable. An orange butterfly flitted and swerved, tagging along like a mascot. We saw not another soul, but signs of human habitation and farming were everywhere. In flat clearings, large earthenware pots lay on their sides, left to dry in the sun. Broken dried cornstalks from terraced crops—*milpas*, Alberto called them—covered hillsides so steep I wondered how anyone had harvested the ears without tumbling to his death. On other hillsides, too much cultivation had eroded the soil; the swaths of sheer rock left behind looked like scar tissue on the landscape.

A flock of green parakeets cut the sky, temporarily blotting out the sun. Alberto's melodious whistling echoed off the craggy walls of a gully. I thought it a tune rooted in the rich romantic lore of Spanish culture, but then I recognized the commercial repetitiveness.

"Theme song to the TV show *Bonanza*," I yelled out. "Where'd you learn that?"

"Do you think we are so backward in Mexico that we do not have television?" Alberto called over his shoulder. Again the whistling.

"*I Love Lucy*," Mila said. It became a game as we clip-clopped out of the gully, up and down more hills, and into the mountains' curtain of shadow.

"*The Dick Van Dyke Show.*"

"Very good, Big Al." More whistling.

"*Petticoat Junction*," Mila and I both shouted at the same time.

"The tie goes to the *señorita*," Alberto said. "Here is a tough one."

It took me only a few notes to identify the song.

"*Mighty Mouse.*"

"Ah, Big Al, you and I need to spend more time in the saddle and less time in front of the tube."

We rounded a tall jut of rocks and came upon a white mare with no meat on its ribs. Calmly grazing in the middle of a grassy stand, it didn't seem the least bit fazed by a severely broken front leg. With the bone snapped cleanly near the bottom of the foreleg, ankle and hoof hung by a bloody thread of muscle.

"Poor thing," Mila said. The horse took a couple of stumbling steps, looked about dumbly, then began grazing again. Alberto led us on as if he were used to seeing casualties in the hills. Have to shoot it, I thought, and whether from the change in altitude or the gory sight of the horse's wound, I suddenly felt lightheaded with the sad pitiful sensation of shedding my entire life's experience. It would be of no use to me wherever I was going.

We dismounted and ate lunch on a flat ledge of rock by the side of a trickling brook. With my stomach growling from having skipped breakfast, the beefsteak sandwich on a *torta* roll and bottle of water supplied from Alberto's saddlebag tasted like a gourmet meal. Then we were on our way again, slicing between two mountains and into dark, lush forest thick with ferny vegetation. Birds screeched and cawed, announcing our arrival. Creeping philodendron vines of heart-shaped leaves circled up tree trunks and hung from lofty branches in long tangled ropes that looked strong enough to hold a man's weight. We trailed through a winding pass, zigzagged up the side of a mountain, and emptied out onto a dirt road—"highway," Alberto called it—that eventually wound over the mountains to the state capital city of Oaxaca. Clusters of wild banana trees defied all odds of survival by thriving in hazy shafts of sunlight penetrating to the forest floor. Bushy coffee plants, their dark beans ready for harvest, camouflaged themselves in undergrowth beneath *mulato* trees— so named for the Indian/*mestizo* color of their bark. We passed several lone *campesinos* squatting by the side of the road waiting to catch a ride. Dressed in floppy straw hats, all-white peasant clothes, and *huarache* sandals soled with the recycled rubber from car tires, each *campesino* stared at us as if thunderstruck, then burst into a smile and shot his hand up more like a salute than a wave. It was a far cry from the Indians' negative reaction to *Norte Americanos* in Escondido. I had the distinct feeling that every bend in the road brought us into another world more remote than the one before it. A third-class bus, full to the brim and topped off with a couple of brave souls clinging to the luggage rack on the roof, tore by from the opposite direction, startling the horses. It left behind the stink of its black exhaust. Up we went into the clouds and chill of *tierra fría*, "cold country." Like something out of a Dracula movie, wispy fingers of stationary fog hung low enough for me to reach out and touch.

"This is spooky," Mila said.

"It's freezing," I added. Only a few hours away, people were sunbathing on the beach in Escondido.

"Do not worry," Alberto called out. "This will not last long." He started with the whistling again. Mila beat me to the punch.

"*Addams Family*."

Should have known that one, I thought. My pop-culture security blanket drifted into the dreamy fog of the cloud forest. The road turned jagged with rocks. Then, just as I thought the horses would buck in protest, it smoothed out again into red packed dirt. The higher we traveled, the thicker the fog, until I could barely make out the swishing tail of Mila's horse up ahead.

"Alto!"

Black Beauty stopped alongside the other two horses. We were surrounded by a dozen or so soldiers, all of them wearing long, American World War II army-surplus coats and holding M-16 rifles as tall as themselves. Their determined youthful faces and too-big helmets made them look like boys playing a game of war.

"What's going on?" I asked.

"The army," Alberto said.

"What do they want with us?" Mila asked. Before Alberto could answer, we saw the cab door of a troop truck swing open, the shape of the vehicle barely distinguishable in the fog at the side of the road. Out stepped a portly man who, by privilege of rank, must have been keeping warm inside. Coming toward us, he barked an order, and the boy-soldiers obediently parted for him.

"Stay calm," Alberto said.

I noticed the sergeant stripes on the portly man's sleeve as he stopped next to Alberto's horse and barked another order.

"Get down," Alberto said. Doing exactly what we were told, Mila and I managed to dismount without falling on our big-city faces.

"What's going on?" I asked again. Alberto looked at me over the rumps of our horses as if to say, *Not now*. In that dim, hauntingly surreal setting, I tried to shake off my lightheadedness. The sergeant unbuckled the straps on one side of Alberto's saddlebag and began pulling things out of it—water bottles, a plastic bag full of goat cheese, and a second one full of torta rolls. He flexed his authority by dropping each item carelessly on the ground. I made the mistake of glancing for too long at a soldier close to the sergeant. Puffing himself up, he aimed his gun at me, finger on the trigger. There's nothing quite like staring down the barrel of an M-16, and I quickly looked away, feeling the unnaturalness of trying to act natural. Another soldier flicked his tongue suggestively at Mila. Still another one picked up a long stick by the side of the road and used it to scratch letters in the dirt a few yards in front of the horses. To a trooper they were a disciplined lot. Deep in the forest, an animal yipped and howled in protest of our violated civil liberties.

The sergeant unstrapped the second saddlebag and began dumping items from it—sweater, first-aid kit, flashlight. He retrieved Mila's small purse that Alberto had stowed for her, opened it, rummaged his hand through the contents, and pulled out a tampon. He held it up for a better view.

"*Qué es ésto?*"

"*Cosas para mujeres*," Alberto answered politely.

"Do you mind?" Mila said, restraining her voice. The sergeant, showing his country-bumpkin limitations, still didn't get it. He tamped the paper-wrapped cylinder against the saddlebag, then ran it past his nose, taking a long sniff like a cigar connoisseur. He frowned. Obviously not his brand.

"*Son productos femeninos*," Alberto said, his tone one of being careful not to condescend. Whether the sergeant understood or surmised that he should understand wasn't clear, but without changing his official expression he shoved the tampon back into the purse, then the purse into the saddlebag.

"*Váyanse!*" He headed back to the warmth of the truck's cab. The soldiers, several of them looking crushed that a rare break in their dreary boredom was about to end, moved aside. Alberto began picking up the dropped items and repacking his saddlebags.

"Get on your horses," he said. When Mila had trouble mounting, I boosted her with a hand on her butt—an innocent gesture that instantly triggered kissy-kiss sounds from a few of the hard-up soldiers.

"Losers," Mila said quietly, sliding her foot into a stirrup. Just before we rode off, I looked down at what the soldier had scratched into the dirt with his stick. Even with the letters upside down, I made out a Spanish word I'd learned from Latino friends in high school—*puta*, meaning *whore*.

Riding side by side with Mila in the middle, we vanished into the fog and around a twist in the road. I expected Alberto to tell us that he'd had everything under control, but when he finally broke the silence, he said, "That was scary."

"Not to mention embarrassing," Mila said.

"Yeah, what's with the tampon brigade?" I asked.

"The army is fighting with guerrillas in these mountains," Alberto said. "The soldiers were searching for smuggled weapons."

"Guerrillas!" I said. "What guerrillas? You mean we're horseback riding in the middle of a fucking revolution?"

"Ah, Big Al, what does *fucking* have to do with *revolution*? You butcher the English language. The guerrillas are few and do not care about us. They spend most of their time running away from the soldiers. I would not take you anywhere unless I thought it was safe. You can fucking count on that."

"What's the guerrillas' beef?" I asked.

"*Beef?*" Alberto looked at me like he didn't follow. "A cow is a cow."

As Mila and I laughed, the fog seemed to soak up our voices.

"What I mean is, *why* are they fighting?"

"The same reason the peasants always fight since the days of Zapata," Alberto said. "Land. They want the government to take the land from the rich and give it to the poor. God only knows what they would do with it."

"Maybe grow food to feed their families," I suggested.

"Roman, it's not our business to tell him how Mexico should be run," Mila said.

"That is all right," Alberto assured her. "I was once idealistic like Big Al, fast to speak from the heart and full of the anger of the common man. If you do not have experience with ignorant illiterate people, it is easy to think that helping them is simple. We learn the hard way that this is not true. For example, if I give a sick Indian medicine and tell him to take one pill three times a day for six weeks, he will think to himself, Why not take all of the pills at once and be cured in a day? Then what have I done? I will tell you. If the medicine is strong, I have killed the Indian. You can give an Indian land, but if you do not teach him to drink only clean water, he will get the intestinal parasites and lethal diseases. Congratulations. You now have a dead Indian who owned land. And if he is lucky enough to survive the bad health caused by his own bad habits, how do you expect him to compete with the modern farms of the big landowners? The Indian will slowly starve to death. Sad but true."

"Sounds awfully paternalistic to me—not to mention racist," I said. "And don't forget about the outer space men. If you're right about them helping the Indians build the pyramids, they could come back any day now and side with the guerrillas. From what I've seen, the Mexican army is no match for laser guns."

"Ah, Big Al, that is funny. Just remember that it was not a Mexican who said, 'The only good Indian is a dead Indian.'"

Alberto grinned as if satisfied he'd given me plenty to think about, then clicked his tongue in a giddy-up signal to his horse and pulled into the lead. Mila laid one of those you-were-rude looks on me.

"Hey, I was just talking politics with him," I said.

Mila giddy-up clicked her tongue. I'll be damned if her horse didn't obey, leaving me behind in my own fog-shrouded isolation. I listened out into the forest for twigs snapping under the feet of guerrillas sneaking up on us for an ambush, but all I heard was Alberto whistling the theme song to *The Andy Griffith Show*.

Soon we turned off the road onto a trail that tunneled through overarching brush and trees. A mile or so in, the horses, playing follow the leader, began to canter, then flat-out gallop. Faster and faster we went, pounding hooves hushed by a soft bed of soil. Branches stabbed out of the gloomy murkiness to swat me from the saddle if I didn't look sharp and duck. I heard Mila's exhilarated, frightened shriek, then the trail dipped suddenly and— "Oooooh shit!"—the bottom dropped out of my stomach. We were climbing, weaving left to right, and dipping again. My hands clung to the reins, legs snug against Black Beauty's flanks. I charged on, a foreboding universe sailing past at breakneck speed. Could get used to this, I thought.

The horses' finish-line kick didn't last long. Black Beauty slammed to a halt, damn near sending me head over heels to the forest floor. When I'd regained my equilibrium, Mila was right there next to me on her horse, hand on her heart, catching her breath. Flushed and looking radiantly alive, she said, "Let's do that again!"

I'd never seen her more beautiful and wanted to jump her

bones on the spot. Meanwhile, Alberto slowly rode up and down a short stretch of the trail once, twice, three times, both he and his horse scouring for something in the brush.

"Here!" Plunging into the fog, man and beast vanished. A moment later, Alberto called from the other side of the void. "This way."

I watched Mila, too, plunge off the trail out of sight. I heard another one of her exhilarated, frightened shrieks, then giddy laughter, followed by, "Wow! Come on, Roman!"

I spurred Black Beauty. He didn't move, snorting to remind me that he moved solely to the beat of his own drum. Then he leapt into action, diving down a steep hill. Thrown far back in the saddle, I thought I was about to flip over when I felt myself *whooooosh* through a wall of a warm air and into a valley bursting with sunlight. Black Beauty leveled off, stopped beside my fellow brave explorers, and snorted again as if to say, *Satisfied?* Talk about one hell of a fork in the trail. My eyes adjusted to the brightness. The stationary fog bank we'd just emerged from held fast to a ridge of forest and extended straight up into the western sky.

It was weird.

"How the hell can fog just sit there like that?" I asked.

"The weather does strange things in the mountains," Alberto explained.

"Very strange," Mila said, taking in the view. By use of water irrigation or sorcery, corn—chin-tall and abundant even though out of season—had turned the valley into one big steep bowl of manicured green. Far below, a church, huge in comparison to the surrounding labyrinth of white stucco dwellings, reflected a mesmerizing rosy glow off its smooth masonry. From north to east to south, I must have counted five distinct weather patterns over the mountains—everything from a dark brewing storm to rows of puff logs to a desert of rippling white dunes. Through a hole in a cloud moving slowly as a dirigible, fanning beams of sunlight, so solid I bet I could have shimmied straight up one of them and shaken hands with God, tracked across the other side of the valley's cultivated slopes. If a road led into the valley, I saw no sign of it.

"What is this, Shangri-La Mexican style?" I asked. At any second, I fully expected to hear a choir of angels.

"Very few people know about this town," Alberto said. "Trust me, you will not find it on a map. It is hidden."

I was about to accept Alberto at his word, when I caught my gullible self. "Yeah, right. And the Easter Bunny humps the Tooth Fairy."

Alberto looked at me as if he were trying make heads or tails of that last statement.

"The bunny humps the fairy?"

"Forget it," I said. I wanted to know the name of the town, or ask how the Indians had pulled off sneaking a Catholic church complete with two bell towers into a valley without anyone noticing, but I let it drop, not about to give Alberto the satisfaction of bullshitting me further. Besides, he probably would have told me that the warm wall of air we'd passed through was a protective force field left behind by the outer space men.

Alberto shrugged as if to say, Believe whatever you want to believe. Snapping his reins, he started riding down the trail that slithered to the valley floor.

"My dear, sweet, cynical Roman," Mila said, smiling wearily. Then she trotted off on her horse after Alberto. *Hidden* my ass, I thought. I snapped Black Beauty's reins. He didn't budge.

"Move it, ya big mutt."

Black Beauty twitched a family of pesky flies off his ears, lowered his head, and began plodding toward town.

* * *

We clopped down a narrow dirt street, not a single soul looking out from a window in one of the small houses with flat asbestos roofs. Soon I picked up the faint sound of what I can only describe as musical yelping. I assumed it to be the Indians' tribal brand of singing.

"We are in luck," Alberto said. "There is a fiesta."

"What are they celebrating?" Mila asked.

"Ah, who knows—this god, that saint. The Indians mix the old ways with the new."

The closer we got to the center of town, the louder the yelping. We turned a corner and ran smack dab into the *zócalo*—the town square. At the other end of it, in front of the church, as many as fifty men, all of them wearing green satiny vests over their white peasant clothes, were yelping so fiercely to the sky I felt the hairs on my arms stand on end. They would suddenly stop and start again as if on signal. A gang of squealing children chased and dodged through a crowd of spectators and around a water fountain tiered like a grand wedding cake in the middle of the *zócalo*. A couple of boys whipped tops on the trampled-smooth dirt, competing to see whose top would spin the longest. Women dressed in long black skirts and elaborately embroidered blouses every color of the rainbow went about daily chores—some hauling bundles of firewood on their backs, others lugging tied-up burlap sacks with a turkey poking its head out from a hole. Red-, green-, or purple-striped *bolsas* hanging from people's shoulders would have sold for a pretty penny in trendy Chicago boutiques. Elderly men squatted by grills, roasting ears of sweet corn over white-hot coals. People seemed reluctant to meet my eye, like they were scared I'd put an outsider's whammy on them. Could get ugly fast, I thought.

We'd just dismounted, when a man rushed up to us, snatched the reins of our horses, and without so much as a nod to Alberto, led them on the run down another street.

"You know that guy?" I asked Alberto.

"I do not think so, Big Al."

"Then I'd say that was an awfully bold horse-napping."

"You can't be serious," Mila said. "How are we going to get home?"

"Please," Alberto begged of us, "what do you think this is, the ghetto? I am sure that he will take good care of the horses for a fair price. Come, let us see if we can get permission to go inside the church. Remember that we must show respect. These Indians are not used to tourists."

"Maybe we should skip the church," Mila said. "People have a right to pray without feeling like they're under a microscope."

"Yeah," I added. "No point offending anyone."

"The worst that can happen is that they will kill us," Alberto said. "Follow me. This is not something that you want to miss."

We weaved through the festival crowd and across the *zócalo*, then circled around the yelpers to a set of wooden church doors big enough to use for spare parts on Notre Dame Cathedral. Indians going in and out would pull and push on iron ring-handles with all their weight, shutting the doors firmly behind them. Just as Alberto reached for one of the rings, a short man blocked his hand with a staff and moved in front of us.

"*Qué es el problema?*" Alberto asked.

A brief verbal exchange ended with the man yelling something at Alberto in a blustery show of authority. Then he disappeared inside the church, and the door clanked shut.

"Who's he?" Mila asked Alberto.

"He is like a policeman. That is why he carries the stick."

"Some policeman," I said. "Not much of a dress code. Wears the same white pajamas as every other dude around here. So the answer's *no*?"

"Big Al, think positive. He and I are negotiating."

A moment later, the door cracked open, and the policeman stuck his head out. Motioning with his hand for us to act fast, he made it clear that he was putting his ass on the line with the powers that be.

"Hurry," Alberto said. As we hustled inside the church, I saw him slip the cop a twenty-peso bill. Apparently, *la mordida* comes in handy even in hidden towns.

Our newly acquired friend took off like he had a reputation to protect and disappeared through a door in a corner of the sanctuary. I've never seen a similar house of worship. Clouds of pungent smoke drifted up into fingers of light shooting down through stained-glass windows near the domed ceiling. The pews were missing, straw scattered on the open stone floor. Statues of saints, their faces painted in expressions of the worst suffering imaginable, lined either sidewall. Among them, Jesus and the Virgin Mary were lost in the crowd, while John the Baptist, his hands cupping a depiction of water, took top billing on the altar. Families and individuals had staked out small praying areas by clearing away the straw and marking boundaries with sticks of burning incense and neatly lined-up bottles of Coca-Cola, Fanta orange, Squirt, and other flavors of brand-name pop. The place resounded with the many voices of people praying in whatever style floated their boat. One man salaamed and chanted to John the Baptist. A woman sat rocking and murmuring to the Apostle Paul. Another man, kneeling in front of a statue I assumed was Peter because of his long, flowing, gray hair, vacillated between fist-waving anger and repentant weeping. Beside him, his wife and three children lay like fallen dominoes with their heads in each other's laps, snoozing. Across the sanctuary and to the far right of the altar, a young mother sat against the wall, munching on a sandwich and breastfeeding her newborn. Without a priest in sight, the closest thing to someone in charge was a man walking around dispersing fresh straw from a bag similar to the kind paperboys wear.

"This is wild," Mila said quietly.

"You have to keep in mind that the Spaniards were very shrewd and built the churches right on top of the Indians' religious temples," Alberto explained, barely above a whisper. "That is why these people have everything mixed up. They will sometimes stay here for days, praying to heal the sick and for the good harvest."

"If the Spaniards built the church, then how can this place be hidden?" I asked.

"The Spaniards built many churches in Mexico," Alberto replied. "It is easy to lose track of one." Again, his smile told me that it was of no consequence to him what I did or didn't believe. Of all the ecclesiastical questions I could have asked, one ate at me the most.

"What's with all the pop bottles?"

I expected Alberto to give me some cock-and-bull story about how pop, at a premium in town because so little of it could be smuggled into the hidden valley from the outside world on horseback, was considered a worthy offertory gift to the gods, but he simply informed me, "If you pray all day, you get thirsty."

"Didn't think of that," I said. "So tell me, have these people dropped human sacrifice out of their repertoire? I'm not exactly into having my heart ripped out of me while it's still beating."

"Ah, Big Al. *Now* who is not giving the Indians credit?"

"Just kidding."

"He told us to show some respect, remember?" Mila said.

"OK, OK, but I think we should at least ask John the Baptist who the hell he thinks he is trying to fill Jesus's shoes. What would the Pope say?"

"The Pope is far away," Alberto reminded me. "And as it is common in all cultures, what he does not know will not hurt him."

People seemed to take little notice of us, but someone with pull must have complained. The cop returned shortly and, as if all bets were off, began yelling angrily and gesticulating his staff in our faces.

"We must leave," Alberto said urgently.

The cop shooed us out a front door and into the bright, reassuring sunlight. The door clanked shut.

"Interesting?" Alberto asked above the Indians' yelping.

"You can say that again," Mila said. "Am I wrong, or did we almost get in big trouble?"

"I am never sure with these people," Alberto said. "That is part of the fun."

"Should have nabbed one of those pops on my way out," I joked. Despite all my wisecracks, the church's topsy-turvy atmosphere had left me feeling strangely invigorated.

Circling back around the yelpers, we went over to one of the benches lining the *zócalo* from where we could watch the festival. Alberto disappeared into the milling throng for a moment, then brought back three of the biggest pieces of roasted corn on the cob I've ever seen, passed them out between us, and sat down next to Mila. I bit into the corn.

"Ummmm. Thanks, man." I'll have to admit I was beginning to take Alberto's generosity for granted. "Now *that* is sweet."

"And so tender," Mila said with her mouth full.

The Jolly Green Giant Corporation could not have scripted a better TV commercial. We finished off our snack and, as seemed to be the custom, tossed the cobs on the ground. A fruit vendor came by pushing a two-wheeler cart piled high with pineapples, mangos, bananas, and assorted other fruits.

"*Piña, por favor*," Alberto called out.

The vendor, his face lost below the floppy brim of his straw hat, set the cart down in front of us, grabbed his machete off a hook, and placed a pineapple on a cutting board. Using fast, amazingly accurate strokes for so big and clumsy a blade, he hacked the bumpy skin off the pineapple without wasting any of the meat, then cored, sliced, and evenly distributed the pieces into three waxy paper cones. He handed them to us, took Alberto's money with a humble nod, and then went on his way with his cart. I grabbed a chunk of pineapple and popped it into my mouth.

"Ummmm, talk about *juicy*."

"Try getting a pineapple this good in Chicago," Mila said, and licked her sticky fingers.

"Poor *Norte Americanos*," Alberto said. "You are—how you say—deprived."

Near the water fountain, a *campesino* held a fireworks rocket the size of a javelin. He lit the fuse with a smoldering punk, then heaved the rocket into the air. The booster ignited with a *shuuuu-uuuuush*, the rocket zipping higher and higher into the sky. Then just as I thought it was lost in the stratosphere, a report *boomed* across the valley.

"Cool!" Mila said.

"Yes, these people are very good with the fireworks," Alberto said.

Other *campesinos* on the *zócalo* launched rockets, the crowd gazing skyward. The yelpers responded to the explosions with a second wind of louder yelping. A man raced over to us holding what looked like a stone cylinder the size of a hand grenade. We soon found out that the hollow center of it was packed with explosives. He raised the cylinder high in the air with his bare hand, used a punk to light the fuse, and *KABOOM*! My fruit-munching partners and I damn near sent pineapple flying everywhere. The cylinder had absorbed the explosion's impact and left the *campesino's* hand still attached to his body. He looked at us with a thrilled expression, nodding vigorously as if to ask, Did you like that? Then he darted off into the crowd.

"My ears!" Mila laughed.

"Yeah, ringing like it's Sunday," I said.

"We have been officially welcomed," Alberto pointed out. He relaxed against the bench and breathed deeply as if the beautiful day belonged to him alone.

I ate a few more pieces of pineapple, each one juicier than the last. Something knocked against my boot. Looking down, I saw a wooden top caroming back and forth between my feet. Then it wiped out in the dirt. I picked up the toy and glanced around for its owner. A young, brown-faced boy stepped forward timidly. If cuteness could kill, I'd have already been dead. He must have on-purpose-accidentally sent the top in my direction.

"*Hola*," Mila said, bending down close to the boy. "*Como se llama?*"

The boy hesitated, smiling shyly.

"Felipe."

"Don't look now, Mila," Alberto said, "but you are being adopted."

I handed Felipe his top and pantomimed for him to show me how to do it. He expertly wrapped the top with a string, knelt down, and with a hard, whiplike pull of his arm sent the top bouncing and spinning on the ground. The ice broken, other kids swarmed over to us, giggling and vying for attention. A little girl leaned on Mila's thigh with her elbows like she'd known Mila all of her life. Felipe and several other boys thrust their tops out for me to give one a try.

"No, no, no," I politely waved them off.

"*Sí, sí, sí,*" a boy returned. The swarm giggled.

"Go on," Alberto said. "Show the *niños* what a Chicago gangster is made of."

Bowing to peer pressure, I handed Mila my paper cone and grabbed one of the tops with a string already coiled around it. The swarm stood back to give me room. Squatting close to the ground beside the bench, I yanked on the string. The top jerked over my shoulder, got tangled up, and fell to the ground. Kids shrieked in laughter.

"My turn," Mila said.

On her attempt, she sent the top sailing across the *zócalo*, almost beaning an old woman in the head. Again the shrieking innocent laughter. A boy dashed off to retrieve his toy.

"You can both forget about the gold Olympic medal in top spinning," Alberto said.

"Yeah, might kill someone," I said. For safety's sake, Mila and I called it quits, sat down on the bench, and resumed work on our pineapple.

"*Es peligro*," Alberto told the children.

"No, no," said Felipe, "*es duro*." He and three other top aficionados, only too happy to show off and prove to us that a top was neither dangerous nor hard to use, whipped their arms and sent their tops spinning on the ground again. Other kids watched Mila and me finish off the fruit as if our every move were a thing of wonder.

"*Como se llama?*" I asked a little girl.

"Cristina."

"*Como se llama?*" Mila ask another child.

"Pablo."

A boy turned the tables on us.

"*Cómo se llama?*"

"*Me llamo* Roman."

A few of the kids repeated my name, then giggled like the feel of it tickled their tongues.

"*Me llamo* Julio."

"*Me llamo* Pepe."

"Mila."

"*Señor* Huerta."

"María."

"Carlos."

We finished with the name game and moved on to a lesson in counting in Spanish. If Mila or I mispronounced or skipped a number, the kids would erupt in slaphappy laughter and correct us. Adults on nearby benches had begun to watch us as if curiously amused. Around the *asientos*, I noticed a boy—thin, smaller than the rest, and no older than eight or nine—in the back of the group. He was playing with a toy I'd never seen before.

"What is that?" I asked Alberto.

"It is called a *bolero*."

"*Como se llama?*" I asked the boy. He shouldered through his friends up to me.

"Angel."

His *bolero* was made of a wooden block the shape of a soda can, a piece of string a couple of feet long, and a small wooden dowel. One end of the string was knotted through an eyelet at the top of the block, the other end tied around a groove in the middle of the dowel. Holding the dowel in his hand, Angel swung the block up and around in a loop so that it spun with just the right head-over-heels rotation to land, by means of a small hole in its base, skewered on the dowel. He did it consistently over and over, then gave the *bolero* to me for a try.

Looked simple enough. I swung the block but only managed to glance the dowel off the side of it. The kids laughed uproariously. I tried again. Not even close. Again. That laughter was beginning to give me a complex.

"Hang it up," Mila teased.

"You must concentrate," Alberto coached.

Countless frustrating tries later, I passed the toy to Angel for another demonstration. Watching closely, I observed that as he swung the block, he would give the string a slight well-timed jerk to get it to turn over mid-air and land back onto the dowel. Kid's a fucking *bolero* Zen master, I thought. He passed the *bolero* back to me. I gave it another whirl. Closer. Again. Closer still. A good ten minutes later, the kids had stopped laughing, respecting my perseverance.

"Give it a rest, sweetie," Mila said. "I'll still love you."

Too late. I was a *bolero* addict. Finally, by sheer force of will, I did it.

"Yeeees!" I thrust the *bolero* high over my head. Then to cheers from the kids and applause from a host of adults on other benches, I hammed it up with a celebration strut.

"Now will you give the poor kid his toy?" Mila asked.

Soon after that, the entire kid-pack ran off as if alerted to bigger and better entertainment somewhere else across the *zócalo*. We watched the festival scene from our bench.

"Hey, check out the birds," Mila said.

A man with two huge birds, one perched on each of his shoulders, came gracefully toward us out of the crowd. I'm no zoologist, but I'd say that the creatures—green everywhere except for their yellow heads—were card-carrying members of the parrot family. They were magnificent all right, their preened tail feathers covering the man's back like he himself had wings. He stopped in front of us and smiled serenely. I was probably projecting the comparison, but I thought that his sharply beaked nose gave him a look of kinship with his pets.

"What's he want?" I asked Alberto suspiciously.

"To share his birds with you, what else?"

The man, tall by Indian standards and, though not old, slightly stooped, as if his shoulders were built to better accommodate perches for his birds, flourished his arms out to the sides. The parrots tightrope-walked to his wrists.

"Can I touch them?" Mila asked.

"Of course," Alberto said.

Mila got up from the bench and petted one of the birds on its feathery shoulder.

"Oooo, soft."

The parrot looked at her with his small, enigmatically tranquil eyes, then bobbed down and clamped its beak on her wrist.

"Hey!" She yanked her hand away. "He bit me!"

"Do not be frightened," Alberto said. "That is the bird's way of testing to see if you are a strong enough branch for him to stand on."

Mila tentatively reached her hand out again. After another taste test, the parrot hopped on board her arm.

"He's heavy." Mila stroked the bird's crown. Judging from the childlike happiness on her face, the bird had succeeded where I had failed. It stayed perched on her long enough to be considered polite, then hopped back onto his master's wrist. Without warning, the Indian threw up his arms, and the parrots, flapping powerful wings, lifted off into the sky. Soaring in tandem over rooftops, they circled the *zócalo* and returned with a braking, stormy flutter to the man's wrists.

"Whoa!" I said. "How'd he teach them to do that?"

"With patience," Alberto said. "Just like you with the *bolero*." Something caught his attention in the street. "Ah, there is the stable-man with the horses. He knows that we do not want to get caught in the forest when it is dark. Let's—how you say—make prints."

"*Tracks*," I said. "Already? We just got here."

"Can't we stay a little longer?" Mila asked. She was running her fingers down a parrot's tail plumage and seemed to have lost any fear of the animal.

"We got a late start, my friends," Alberto said. He stood up, went over to the bird man, and slipped a ten-peso bill into his hand. Then he smiled at us and ironically added, "That is the problem with you *Norte Americanos*. You are always on lazy *gringo time*."

As I mounted Black Beauty, the stableman held her steady by the bit. With Mila and Alberto on either side of me, we clopped our way out of town.

The street quickly turned deserted, the yelping fading behind us. Why did I feel such an overwhelming heavy sense of loss?

"Roman!"

I looked down and saw Angel running along beside me, reaching up with the *bolero* clutched in his hand. For a moment I thought he wanted me to stop and play with his *bolero* again, but then I understood. Those who have never had a child offer them a toy as a gift do not know the true meaning of the word *honor*.

"No," I said emphatically, waving the boy off, but he kept pace, staring up at me as if determined to prevent a dreadful wrong.

"Take it," Alberto said.

"I'd feel like a criminal."

"You do not want to offend, Big Al."

"Roman, he's going to fall and get trampled," Mila said.

My eyes welled up with a familiar scratchiness. A fucking toy, I thought. Angel was beginning to pant. To save us both, I leaned down and snatched the *bolero* out of his hand. He broke into a smile and stopped in the middle of the road, waving good-bye.

"*Gracias!*" I yelled over my shoulder, hoping neither Alberto nor Mila noticed the cracking huskiness in my voice—"*Gracias! Gracias!*" Black Beauty's jostling gait forced me to turn back around in the saddle. I looked at my prize possession. The wooden block was burnished with geometric Indian designs, the lacquer on the dowel worn by Angel's disciplined hand. Then I slipped the *bolero* through the neck of my T-shirt so that it dropped and nestled against my belly.

"Pretty sweet of him," Mila said.

If I so much as had to wipe at my eye once, I was going to disown my pathetic self. The sun, inching closer to the stationary fog bank high atop the valley's ridge, showered us in a clarity so blinding I had to squint. Alberto pulled down on the brim of his cowboy hat.

"Big Al," he said, "it is fun to watch you fight yourself." He clicked his tongue and rode ahead. Black Beauty slowly fell behind Mila's horse. I concentrated on getting an emotional grip, the *bolero* jiggling against me inside the T-shirt womb. Suddenly I heard powerful fluttering, felt a dusting brush against my cheek, then a two-footed clamp on my shoulder. Up ahead Mila let out a shriek as the other giant parrot landed on her shoulder.

"Scared the shit out of me," I said. I twisted my neck to get a look at my new hitchhiker companion. The bird eyeballed me with that puzzling stare of his. I glanced over my other shoulder. Angel was gone, but the bird man, far down at the end of the street, bowed with a dramatic sweep of his arm.

"He's giving us his birds?" I called up ahead to Alberto. "I don't even know what they eat. How will we get them through customs?"

"Remember the patience," Alberto said, leading onward. "You will see."

Sure enough, when we reached the bottom of the final steep rise, the birds took flight.

"Awww," Mila said. "And they were so cute."

It was just like her to ignore the complications of the future.

"That is what I thought," Alberto said. "The birds are devoted to the man. It is a beautiful thing."

We watched the parrots soaring down over the maze of rooftops, until they landed on one of the many dots in the *zócalo*. At that distance, the rocket explosions sounded like popguns.

"Bye-bye," Mila said longingly.

Alberto charged on his horse up the rise and into the fog. Mila followed after him. When she'd made it to the top without tumbling off her horse, I heard her laughter. That heavy sense of loss threatened to crush me. Fuck feeling responsible for Jay's sins. Fuck whether or not Mila and I lived happily ever after. Fuck school, fuck it all. Why not stay in the hidden valley forever, become a *bolero* Zen master, feast on roasted corn and pineapple, salaam to a statue of John the Baptist, train parrots to do tricks, fling rockets, and master the fine art of yelping? By the time anyone found me, I'd have assimilated so thoroughly into the local culture that my Indian brothers and sisters would elect me honorary chief.

Alberto was whistling another vaguely familiar theme song. It irked me to no end that I couldn't match the tune up with its TV show partner.

"What are you waiting for?" Mila yelled down.

My hands squeezed the reins. Black Beauty must have read my mind. With a wisdom far greater than my own, she whinnied, reared up, and stormed the rise. Doubled over and clinging to the saddle horn, I passed through a cool damp *whooooosh* and returned, for better or worse, into the fog.

CHAPTER 10

SHARK ATTACK

Road-weary and butt-sore, we made it home from *tierra fría* to Escondido's breezy heat just in time to see the evening sun turn the ocean into a sheet of jeweled frosting. Pedro, on the sharp lookout, met us in the road by the trailer park gate and led the horses away. At a card table in the small, canopied restaurant that was crowded with tourists, the three of us finished off red snapper dinners, compliments of Alberto. We'd hardly spoken a word to each other since the beginning of our slow descent from the foothills. Already, tourist-talk from other tables on such hot topics as suntan maintenance and where to buy the cheapest *liquada* drink in town, threatened to reduce the emotional wringer I'd gone through in the hidden valley to nothing more than silly. I picked the *bolero* off the table and rubbed my thumb over the burnished designs, trying to keep a spark of the object's importance alive within me.

Alberto crumpled his napkin, dropped it onto his plate, and said, "So, my friends, what did you think of our little adventure?"

"Interesting," Mila said.

"Only interesting?"

"More than," I told Alberto. "Thanks. You really saved our vacation."

"I would like to think I saved much more than that."

I assumed Alberto was referring to keeping Mila and me out of harm's way from Sánchez and other locals set on revenge, but now I'm not so sure. Perhaps he got a mentor's kick out of watching me stumble toward discovering something about myself—something he'd seen in me that very first time I'd walked into his *farmacia* with a stomach ache. Mila reached across the table and gave Alberto's hand a couple of grateful pats. I looked to the restaurant on the other side of the dusty road.

"At least they took down the *no hippies* sign over there. Maybe Escondido dodged a bullet after all."

"For once you are more optimistic than me," Alberto said. "Do not let people's compromising for the sake of economics fool you. Money makes the world go round, but the blood is always thicker than the cash."

A trampled bouquet of red bougainvillea lay in the road out in front of the *farmacia* next door, perhaps a remnant of the funeral procession to the cemetery earlier that morning. The name *Consuelo* hadn't come up once during our trip in the mountains, and it occurred to me then that we'd all been avoiding the subject.

"When is your flight?" Alberto asked.

"Tomorrow," I said. "One o'clock."

"That is good, Big Al. Not much time."

"Enough," I said. The word had slipped out like a challenge to myself to set things straight in that town.

"*Enough?*" Alberto asked. "Enough what?"

I rubbed the *bolero* harder, the ball of my thumb getting sore. Alberto waited for an answer.

"You mean enough time to say good-bye to people," said Mila, to the rescue. "Right, Roman?"

"Yeah, sure. That's what I mean."

"Say your good-byes close to your campsite and stay out of Sánchez's sight," Alberto warned. "And please, no more—how you say—*hanky-panky* on the beach tonight."

"Learned that lesson," I said.

"Jesus, Roman." Mila was none too pleased. "You told him? Does the word *private* ever come out of that big mouth of yours?"

"Do not worry, *señorita*. The Latin culture understands passion.

Tomorrow I will pick you up in my Jeep and give you both a ride to the *aeropuerto*—eleven o'clock to be on the safe side."

"You've already been too kind," Mila said. "We can take a taxi."

"Really," I agreed. "It's just a ten-minute ride."

"Not to scare either of you, but when the *Jefe* decides he does not like someone, it is a good idea for that someone to have me for a chauffeur. I will make sure that you get on a plane instead of into a jail cell."

"Since you put it that way, we'll be packed and ready to roll at 11:00," I said.

Just then, a hulking figure in the road cast a shadow over our table.

"Howdy, y'all."

Otto, at his green-under-the-gills worst, ducked beneath the canopy and stood hunched before Alberto like he was self-conscious of his own intimidating physique. A whiff of his stale booze-breath nearly knocked me out of my chair. Dried white gunk in a corner of his mouth, scabby wound looking like a worm tangled in his eyebrow, he struck me as a man who'd hit bottom.

"Sorry to interrupt, but, well, see, do you think, that is, I mean, umm . . ."

I was about to tell Otto to spit it out, when he finally got around to what he was after.

"I really 'preciate all you done, Alberto—loaning me money to eat and letting me stay in your trailer park for free. My folks'll be wiring that cash any day now, and I was wonderin' . . . just to tide me over . . . if you could . . ."

"How much?" Alberto reached into his jeans pocket and pulled out his wad of pesos in bills. "I trust you are good for it, my friend. Escondido is no place to be on a diet."

"Well, I wouldn't want to . . ."

"It is a loan." Alberto peeled off five twenties and one fifty. He handed them to Otto. "That brings your total to three hundred pesos."

"I really 'preciate this." Otto smiled apologetically. "Hunger's a bitch, if ya know what I mean." He folded the bills and stuffed them into his frayed cut-offs.

"What about your friend?" Alberto asked. "He needs to eat, too, no?"

Otto's expression turned cold. "Don't have nothin' to do with Jay no more."

"Why's that?" I asked.

"Differences." As if he were reluctant to get into specifics, Otto looked off toward the kitchen. "Let's just say we don't have a whole hell of a lot in common."

He *knows*, I thought. As the waitress brushed past Otto with two plates of food, a jab of her elbow to his ribs told him that he was cramping her style.

"Subtle, ain't she?" Otto said. Then to Alberto, "If it's just the same with you, I've moved my stuff to another campsite down the row."

"I have plenty of campsites to spare these days," Alberto said. "I am sorry to hear that you and your friend have had a—how you say, *breakup?*"

"Good for you, Otto," Mila said. "You don't need Jay. None of us do."

"I am missing something?" Alberto asked. Conveniently, no one answered him, and he let it drop, covering his mouth with his hand to burp. "Pardon."

Otto stood there like he wanted badly to say something, then decided against it. The waitress jabbed him again on her return trip to the kitchen.

"Guess I better get out of the way before she decides she don't like me. Y'all have a nice one." Otto ducked from under the canopy and headed across the road slowly like he was concentrating on not staggering.

"A shame," Mila said as the three of us watched Otto step into the restaurant that had previously been off-limits to hippies. "Seems like a good guy. Too bad he's an alcoholic."

"Hope you don't mind your money going toward a liquid diet," I told Alberto.

"Ah, Big Al. I do not tell people how to live their lives. I only do what I can."

"Might want to do less for some people," I said.

"What?" Alberto hadn't heard me clearly over a taxi going by, its muffler on its last leg.

"Nothing," I said. In the other restaurant across the road, Otto, at a front table along the spindled railing, raised his arm to get the waitress' attention. Before long he had a beer. He brought the bottle to his lips, tossed his head back, and chugged it dry. Beyond him, beyond the tops of palm trees and the lighthouse at the tip of the bay, a forgiving sun was loosening its grip over the ocean, sinking into a world of shades.

* * *

Again, with all due respect for historical facts, as well as respect for what I can see in spite of my limitations, I say that it happened like this.

It's late, Escondido dark except for the glare of lantern light bleeding into the road from a restaurant. The waitress, probably an elder daughter in a family-run business, is fed up with hiding in the kitchen so that her drunken last customer will take a hint. She pokes her head out of the curtain and yells across the dining area, "*Ya cerramos!*"

Slumped in his seat, chin resting on his chest, Otto glances at the waitress out of the tops of his shit-faced eyes. He's closed enough bars to translate her drift.

"Awwww, jus' ooooooone las' beer. Too damn purty be bitch. Love ya. Love ya more any goddamn woman . . ." He fumbles getting his hand into his pocket and pulls out what's left of the pesos from Alberto's loan. He lifts the bills high up and lets go, the bills fluttering down over a forest of empty longneck beer bottles on the table.

"All yours. Money fer my honey. Hey, looooooooove poet. Most beau'ful woman. Wan' marry you, goddamnit. Don't believe me?" Otto slides out of the chair to his knees onto the dirt floor and holds his hands out like a desperate beggar. "Toe'ly serious. Love ya so damn much . . . hey, where you goin'?"

The waitress has had enough marriage proposals from wasted customers to translate Otto's drift. Behind the closed curtain, there's a quick exchange of Spanish in the kitchen, then the double-wide mother whisks the curtain open and steps into the middle of the dining area ready to do battle.

"*Está borracho! Váyase a la casa!*"

"Awwww, wuz matter?" Otto stumbles and rocks to his feet. "Marry you, too, goddamnit. Think I'm drunk? I ain't drunk. Fuck you *I'm* drunk."

Big Mama isn't amused. She reaches over to a lantern hanging from a hook on a support beam, turns the key, and shuts off the flow of kerosene. The pair of brilliant white mantles extinguishes to red-hot glows, the dining area shrouded in darkness except for a path of light coming from the kitchen. One of its sharp edges cuts Otto down the middle as he sways.

"*Lárgate!*" Big Mama pounds back into the kitchen and whisks the curtain shut again. Now the darkness, broken only by a bar of light on the floor beneath the curtain, is intolerably final.

"Go ahead, rip my damn heart out. One las' beer kill ya? Tomorrow I'm new man. No more drinkin'. How's 'bout kiss? Ain't leavin' 'out a kiss."

Otto hears the sweeping of a broom on the kitchen floor, and far beyond that, past the restaurant and down a slope through a stand of palm trees, the surf hammers the shoreline.

"Drawers gold-plated? Shouldn' play man's love. Marry ya both, goddamnit. Fuckin' sickness, fuckin' health, fuckin' death do part."

Glasses clink and knock as they're stocked on a kitchen shelf.

"Awright, have your way. Takin' love home. Sat'fied? Don't mean trouble. Sorry."

Otto staggers into the middle of the road, swings recklessly in an about-face, and stops. Standing with one shoulder held awkwardly high like his armpit is hung up on an invisible clothesline, he calls back to the restaurant, "Sorrrr-ry." He weaves down the road toward the trailer park and into spinning blackness.

"Darker'n whore's hole," he mutters. He continues on blindly, veering off the road a few yards shy of Pedro's hut next to the trailer park gate. His foot snags on something and, tripping head-first, he's nailed by a punch that splits open the wound running through his left eyebrow. It's a tough call sober much less drunk whether or not you've blacked out in pitch blackness, but the next thing Otto's aware of is crawling on all fours in the dirt, the enemy poking, scratching, jabbing, and hemming him in from all sides. "Som'bitch!" Wobbling to his feet, he whiffs with a couple of wild counterpunches—"Kill ya, goddamnit!" Fists poised, he waits for another attack, but the enemy, picking and choosing his openings, is no fool. Slowly, Otto drops his guard and peers into the black void. Eyebrow tingling, a baffling caress runs down the side of his face. *Raining?* He rubs a hand in smeary circles over his wet cheek, then reaches out to see if the enemy is still there. The hand hits something made of hard concentric ridges, and he quickly withdraws it.

"Fuck *me,* motherfucker? Messin' fire, goddamnit! Git!"

In the morning, Pedro will step out the back door of his hut into the weedy undergrowth to take a whiz. He'll unzip his fly, glance up, notice a bloody handprint on the trunk of a palm tree, and wonder if it has anything to do with the loudmouth gringo who woke him up in the night.

Otto stumbles on, new adversaries scratching and clinging to his bare legs, others testing him with a bump to the shoulder. "Le'go," he slurs at one. "Piece a me?" he challenges a second. "State fuckin' wrestling champ," he warns a third. Suddenly, he's in the clear, slogging through sand, the sound of the pulverizing surf close by, and a star-studded careening sky up above. He comes to the shoreline and follows the wet compact sand in the wrong direction from the trailer park. "Where the hell . . ." With the help of the universe's dreamy glitter, he sees white roaring lines glide at him out of the blackness, each one spreading into a sheet of hissing foam that nips at his flip-flops, then retreats. Loneliness clutches and thrums in his chest. Run a few miles tomorrow, he thinks. Wrestling shape . . . school. Coach said, *Door always open.* He wishes he had someone to share the good news with, then remembers why he doesn't. Crazy Jay. Kept tellin' him, One of these days . . . Braggin' 'bout it like I'm supposed to . . . Girl's dead! Don't he feel . . . No friend of mine. Likes fire so much, have fun in hell.

Otto stops, stretches his arms so that he's taut as a full sail, and lets the salty breeze rush over his face and limbs. Out across the bay, the lighthouse blinks in a secret code. He howls to the stars—"Hooooooooooome." Soon as *Mañana Insurance* coughs up his money, he's gone.

A little ways down the shoreline from where Otto has just come, something catches his attention. Dark playing tricks? A group of shadows—dissolved into the blackness as much as real—huddles, separates, and huddles again. Following him? Shoot, Otto thinks. He head-counts three, maybe four. Pussies. He's whupped ass against worse odds. Without another beer, he'd rather call it a night. He starts up the beach again. A few minutes later, still no trailer park. He stops, looks around for a familiar marker without any luck, and notices that the shadows, also at a standstill, are a little closer than before. Five? Hell, maybe they wanna party. Nah, big day tomorrow. Pupils fully dilated, Otto sees across the empty no-man's land of beach to a looming wall that must be the start of the countryside's thick, tall underbrush. There's a wide break in it. Road? He leaves the shoreline. Loose sand tugs off one flip-flop, then the other. Halfway to the break, he glances over his shoulder, damn near losing his balance. Closer still, but in no particular hurry, the shadows seem inextricably tied to him. Maybe they're lost, too. This keeps up, he might as well say *howdy*.

It's a road all right, the ground turning firm underfoot. Otto passes one hut, then two more. Trailer park? Where'd all the huts come from, and how's he supposed to recognize which one's his? A stampede of footsteps comes up fast behind him, and before he can turn around, the tire-tread sole of a *huarache* slams into his tailbone, knocking him to his knees. He's surrounded.

"Hey, man, what the fuck's problem?" Otto says. "Ain't lookin' trouble. Got beer? He hears a *shooop!* and sees a long blade of reflected starlight wing past the tip of his nose. "Hey,

man, machete? Dangerous shit, no need to get all . . ." *Shooop!* A
diagonal slice in his Red Cross, lifesaver, tank top exposes a sting-
ing wound from breast to sternum to ribs. "Careful, man! Hurts!"
Bobbing and ducking more flashes, Otto holds up his right hand
for protection. "Amigos, man. *Como estas?*" *Shooop!* There's a
sharp, fleeting twinge of pain in his hand, just enough to make him
reach over and investigate with his left one. What the . . .
"Fingers!" Otto screams, nothing but numb, bloody-tipped stubs
of descending length for the hand's last three digits. He frantically
paws around in the dirt with his good hand. "Help me find . . .
Don't hurt, please, please, PLEASE!" A *shooop!* fans his ear. With
the sudden furious will to live, he lunges, wraps his arm around a
shadow's knee, and drives against the leg with his shoulder, exe-
cuting a sweep-leg single takedown. He's clawing on top of his
squirming foe when a blade digs lengthwise into his muscular
back—"Ahhhhhhh!" He logrolls in the dirt. *Shooop!* Reverses
directions. *Shooop!* Reverses again. *Shooop!* Spinning up onto his
knees, he holds out his mutilated hand, sobbing, "Got the wrong . . .
please . . . didn't mean . . . beggin' ya."

The shadows hesitate. A couple of them begin to argue in
Spanish. It doesn't last long. In the distance, the continuum of the
surf passes judgment.

"*Adiós, muchacho.*"

No matter how hard I keep rubbing my hand over my forehead, I am unable to stop the mental film footage of the event.

Shooop!

From crown to forehead, the blade wedges snugly into Otto's
skull and steadies him sure as a holy man's hand. His eyes bulge.
The shadow yanks his machete free. Otto topples forward, nose
smacking the ground and turning cartilage into pulp. He shares a
moment of profound silence with the shadows. A wheezing gurgle
rattles in his throat. He's ready.

It's like static fizzling. Then Otto jettisons up into the won-
drous, infinite, starry umbrella. He hovers looking down upon the
many, far-flung, terrestrial beacons and pinpoints Oklahoma City
due north of Dallas. Why go home? Mexico City, Vancouver,

Buenos Aires, New York, across the black ponds to London, Brisbane, Paris, Dakar, and Tokyo, all of humanity's safe harbors are but a thought away. Time for some real traveling.

2

The next morning, Mila and I awoke to the hubbub of people abandoning the Escondido ship. All around us, hippies rolled up sleeping bags, struck tents, stripped clothes from lines, packed belongings into cars and vans, and proved themselves to be a model for orderly community-evacuation procedure.

"Skip the shower, let's blow," said a guy from a campsite somewhere behind me.

Then a mother's shrill voice coming from the suburb across the trailer park, "Ellen, if you don't go find your brother this instant, we're leaving you both behind!"

From opposite quarters, car doors slammed and ignitions turned over. A red VW hatchback that had seen better days puttered and bounced down our lane, then turned the corner and lurched—the result of an anxious foot off the clutch—toward a small traffic jam by the gate. Mila sat up in her hammock, rubbed sleep from her eyes, and stared out at everyone leaving for a party we hadn't been invited to.

"What's going on?"

"Beats me." I swung out of my hammock, toes squishing into cool sand. All the more saddle sore after a good night's sleep, I stood there stretching my neck to work out a crick. The George S. Patton look-alike—country-club dapper in his plaid Bermuda shorts, white polo shirt, and khaki ball cap—came at a jaunty clip down the lane past our campsite.

"Say!" I called out. Grizzle-faced enough to be a veteran of the battles at Gettysberg, D-Day, Iwo Jima, and the fall of Saigon, all rolled into one, the general stopped to see what I wanted. "Where's everyone going?"

"Where's everyone going?" George repeated. He scowled with

Patton blood-and-guts disapproval. "Jesus H. Christ, boy. What cave you been living in? Locals killed a gringo up the road off the beach." Assuming that cave-dwellers lacked a sense of direction, he pointed toward the same road where Mila and I had gone hunting for the beach *bandido*.

"*Killed*?" Mila asked. Judging from the blind-sided disbelief on her face, she'd snapped fully awake. "Who? When?"

"Last night," the general said. "Guy by the name of . . ." Thinking hard, he used a finger to push the bill of his cap higher on his age-spotted forehead. "Must have heard it half a dozen times this morning. Something German."

Numbing dread swept down my face. I filled in the blank for the general.

"Otto?"

"Yeah, that's it—*Otto*. Big guy, they say. Hacked him up with machetes. Uh-oh." It must have occurred to Patton that he might have put his spit-and-polish foot in his mouth. Lowering his voice, he asked, "Friend of yours?"

The way the news lodged and swelled in my throat shocked me as much as the news itself. I looked past the general to the beach as if hoping to see Otto's distant figure materializing out of the dazzling white brilliance. Then my gaze fell to my backpack leaned against a palm tree at one end of the hammock. The *bolero* handle dangled on its string from the pack's loosely closed top flap. Silly as it sounds, I was certain that had I given Otto the *bolero* as a gift the last time I'd seen him alive, the magical powers of the place it came from would have shielded him from harm. The missed opportunity to change his destiny crashed within me. Dumb-fuck cowboy, I thought. Meant well. Didn't deserve . . . I glanced at Mila to confirm that the general had indeed confirmed my worst fear. She flung herself back into the hammock. Her tight-lipped expression walked a thin line between anger and the flood-gates of grief.

"We met him a few times," I told Patton. He must have thought that didn't qualify as a reason to spare us any of the scuttlebutt. Locals had found the body shortly after dawn. Gringos up

early for a swim saw men parade it on a stretcher down the beach
to the *policía* station. "Didn't even have the decency to cover him
with a sheet," said the general. Skull split in two. Chopped off fingers. Chest slashed. A bloody mess. "Think someone's trying to
give us tourists a hint?" the general asked. "Take a look around.
Worked, by golly. Otto's buddy is at the *policía* station right now
identifying the body."

"Jay," Mila said. Then quietly to herself, "Hope he's happy."

It crossed my mind to get in a dig by telling Mila that I hoped
she was happy, but Otto's death had knocked the *digs* right out of
me. George, too self-absorbed in his gossip to let a minor inter-
ruption stop him, yammered on. Two Indian women at a restaurant
in town said that Otto was stone drunk and on his knees asking
them to marry him before they'd kicked him out. Then the general
stepped closer to me. Whispering like a man hot on the trail of a
conspiracy that put his own life in danger, he said that Pedro had
shown him a bloody handprint on a tree out back of his hut.
"Now how do you suppose it got there? Killed Otto one place and
then dragged the body to another to throw off the bloodhounds?
Take the damn F.B.I. to figure that one out."

I found myself distracted by the large craggy pores on the general's nose. Who says you can't kill the messenger?

"Smart money has it that the *Jefe* is as crooked as a pregnant
nun," he went on. "Mean *hombre* like that is either Mr. Machete
himself or a close cousin—take your pick. Yep, he'll drink a couple of shots of mescal, call it 'case closed,' and send Otto's folks the
bill for a coffin and shipping. And forget about the U.S. embassy
bureaucrats making any waves. Think they want a big to-do? Pah!
Maybe in a month or so they'll send some people down here from
Mexico City to break their necks looking the wrong way for evidence. Score's always the same no matter if it's Mexico or
Timbuktu—polly-tics and public relations before justice."

The general stood up straight, looked out over a trailer park
already well on its way to becoming a hippie ghost ghetto, and
shook his head at the pitiful sight of refugees on the move. A
mobile home camper, big enough to pass for a country unto itself,

slowly inched past the toilet and shower stalls, dipping and rocking over uneven ground.

"Can I give you kids some advice?" Patton asked.

"Sure," I said, my flat tone implying, *if you must*.

"What happened to that poor little girl put these locals on the warpath. Mexico's a big place full of nice beaches. Don't be the last palefaces in Escondido to turn out the lights."

With a wink that seemed to say, *We're all in this together*, the general resumed his jaunty walk down the lane toward the suburb. I watched his backside with an urge to pick up anything handy and bean him with it. Looking the other way past campsites, the beach, and out over the curl and plunge of waves riding to shore, I took a deep breath that felt insufferably shallow.

I climbed back into my hammock. Through palm fronds up above, the sky over a paradise gone mad looked artificially injected with an extra dose of blue pigment. I waited for Mila to say something, anything, but she must have been afflicted with the same vocal-cord paralysis that I suffered from. Finally, without taking my eyes off that sky, I said, "Un-fucking-believable."

No response from Mila.

"Two people dead."

Still no response.

"Sure has been nice getting away from it all. Sun, beach, great seafood, murder. Whoooo-boy, can't wait to do this again. How 'bout you?"

Still nothing.

"Dead, just like that. You were right. Fuck playing it by ear. If I'd done what I should have done in the first place . . . Time to let Alberto in on what Jay's been up to. If it wasn't for that asshole . . . We owe it to Otto, Consuelo, the kid they jumped on the beach, the whole goddamn town, not to mention owing it to ourselves. That's a shit-load of owing, if you ask me. Sánchez wants to prove he's got a big dick by throwing me in jail, fine. Alberto's no dummy. He'll know what to do."

I didn't hear Mila get up from her hammock and come over to mine. She pounced on me, straddling my waist and wedging her

knees and feet into the fishnetting for balance. "Hey, what . . ."
She'd already grabbed my wrists and pinned me. "Get . . ." I spit
her hair out of my mouth, "the fuck off!" Blame it on the element
of surprise, the fear that too much commotion would flip both of
us out of the hammock, or the possibility that Mila had been
drinking vitamin enriched Ovaltine, but hard as I strained to win
yet another boy/girl wrestling match, I couldn't budge her. Thank
God no one was there to take a picture.

"Don't even think about it!" Mila yelled.

I stopped struggling. "Think about *what*?"

"Opening your big stupid mouth, that's what."

"Wait a second." She'd done a complete 180 on me. "You're
the one who suggested we go to Alberto for help in the first place,"
I said.

"That was two days ago, Roman."

"Yeah, and because we've kept our mouths shut there's now
two very dead people. We can't just—"

"Oh yes we can," Mila said. "You want to be number three?
It's a little late to play hero. And exactly what is it you think
Alberto can do to ease your conscience? Maybe ask one murderer
to arrest another murderer? Sánchez and Jay are two scums in a
pod. Don't believe me, go ask Otto. Oh, I forgot. He's dead. Must
have accidentally fallen on Sánchez's machete. That what you
want, Roman? To be a fucking dead hero?" Mila let go of me and
started batting my face with her small fists. Her sharp blows kept
sneaking through my leaky defense.

"Cut it out! Crazy . . ." A sweep of my arm caused the
inevitable. Mila went flying, the violent to-and-fro swinging of the
hammock tossing me after her. I twisted mid-air to avoid flatten-
ing her, then crashed hip-first to the sand. Sprawled face to face
with her and tangled in her limbs, I saw what I can only describe
as her startled look of realization. Then she gasped and burst into
tears. She'd had more than the air knocked out of her. She collapsed on top of me, burying a hot wet cheek against my collar-
bone. Her heaving sobs shook the both of us. I looped my right
arm around her.

"Don't cry."

A lot of good that did. Already Mila's tears were soaking through my green Fruit of the Loom T-shirt.

"It'll all work out," I said. "You'll see."

"No, it won't," Mila sobbed.

"Yeah, it will."

"Won't."

"Will."

Without so much as lifting her head, Mila jabbed a fist into my lower ribs.

"*Ooof!* OK, OK," I said. "We're totally fucked. Satisfied?"

As we lay there, Mila's sobs changed to sniffles. Bending my left arm back for a pillow, I floated in the pure, oblivious contentment of holding her. From the great, irrelevant beyond, a Coleman stove lid banged shut, then the rattle and *clip* of its latch.

"Can't get away from it," Mila said.

"Get away from what?"

"The curse of my half-*kraut* family."

"What curse?"

"If it's not my grandfather beating the shit out of my mother, it's the Nazis pointing machine guns at Tati to get him to work like a slave building tanks. Then there's his drinking, and don't even get me started on my fucked-up childhood. Jay and these Mexicans are nothing but another page to a tragedy that never ends. I'm doomed to a life of misery."

"Hmmmm," I said. "That's some serious shit. Kinda has a ring to it. Stay tuned to the next exciting episode of *Doomed to a Life of Misery*." I absorbed another jab to the ribs—"*Ooof!* OK, OK, let's look at the bright side. Maybe the curse got left behind in Chicago. Maybe curses can't get visas."

"Don't hold your breath," Mila said.

With a long exaggerated inhale, I did just that. It took Mila a moment to get the lame joke, then, "*Ooof!* Damn, woman, will ya go easy on the brutality?"

"Forget it, funny boy. You're not kidding your way out of this."

"I'm just trying to cheer you up."

"Well, you've got a funny way of doing it. What's this really about, anyway—preacher kid's guilt?"

My contentment raft sprang a leak, and I flared, "That has nothing to do with anything!"

"Well, that's good," Mila said, "because the last I heard, even socially conscious liberals like your father appreciate it when their sons come home alive."

"Who said anything about not coming home alive? You do the right thing, things have a way of turning out for the best."

"Not where I come from," Mila snapped. "Where I come from, you do the right thing, things turn out fucked. Jesus, you're naïve! If it's not guilt, what is it then? Getting even with Jay? So what, I fucked him, who cares?"

"*I* care." The anger coiling in my chest and arms left no doubt which one of us was the physically stronger.

"Guys," Mila stated wearily, as if the subject deserved no further explanation. "You all think the world rotates on what we let you do with your dicks. Jay's nothing to me but a piece of regrettable meat. How many times do I have to say it—I'm sorry, I'm sorry, I'm sorry. Haven't you ever done anything stupid in your life? Haven't you ever been scared?"

"Of *what,* for Godsake?"

"*You*, Roman! Scared of loving you and getting married and having babies and buying a house with a white picket fence and planting goddamn tulips in the garden and knowing that maybe, just maybe, I'll end up happy."

"Oooo," I said, "that's scary, all right. Just thinking about happiness gives me goose bumps—oooo, brrrrr, cold."

"Go ahead and joke. You're not the one who's cursed—a spoiled pig-headed brat, perhaps, but not cursed. Count yourself lucky."

"*Lucky*?" I asked. "Try being in love with a goofy cursed broad sometime."

"Try *being* the goofy cursed broad," Mila said. "You think I enjoy this? It's not my fault it's less scary to fuck up sooner on purpose than to fuck up later by accident. All I can promise is that I'm willing to try. I love you so much. Keep your mouth shut and get on that plane with me. Please."

I went very still.

"What are you talking about?"

More sniffling.

"You're asking me to marry you?"

"I think so," Mila said.

Talk about playing a trump card. Everything I'd hoped for— give or take the tulips and picket fence. I'd been down that dark suicidal road of optimism before with Mila. I thought about it. *Really* thought about it. I was the only man who understood and cared about her—the only man strong enough to go the distance and prove that it was safe for her to love me. Let those who would call me a fool stand aside.

"OK," I said. So much for agonizing. "Here's the plan. We shower, get some breakfast in town, come straight back here, and be ready to ditch this place the second Alberto comes to pick us up to go to the airport."

I felt Mila's tight hug of gratitude, then the heave of a new sob more withheld than audible. It made perfect sense. The cursed have their own unique way of internalizing happiness. I ran my thumb and finger along the muscular furrows on either side of her spine. The impulse to get up, to move decisively, twitched my cheek, then all ten toes. Not far away, a bare-chested camper yanked on an aluminum pole supporting the front of his orange pup tent. Mortally wounded, the nylon shelter collapsed into a sorry heap on the ground. Everything you wanted, I thought.

So where was the relief?

* * *

Call it my imagination, but our young waitress at the canopied restaurant seemed more prompt and solicitous to our dining needs than ever before—perhaps her way of extending her condolences to the tourist community. Then again, with the town practically deserted of North Americans, it's not like she was swamped dividing her attention between Mila and me and a single other customer. After finishing breakfast, we returned to a trailer park hit hard by gringo flight. With the entire suburb's fleet of mobile homes gone, only a skeleton crew of the stoutest, laziest, or foolhardiest hippies stayed on. Beams of sunlight, muted by interlocking swaying palms above, shimmered on the sandy floor in a gliding, watery illusion. Nine-thirty, according to Mila's watch, Alberto not due to pick us up for another hour and a half.

"Might as well grab a shower," Mila said, pulling her towel off the clothesline. I lifted an arm and took a quick whiff of armpit.

"Phew! Better, or they won't let me on the airplane."

Later, squeaky clean and back from the showers, Mila and I looked like the peasant Bobbsey twins in our change of white, embroidered Mexican wedding shirts and painters' pants. How Chicago would ever withstand so much *cool* stepping off one airplane was beyond me. We untied the hammocks, clothesline, and stuffed belongings—soggy towels and all—into backpacks, ready to haul ass at the beep of Alberto's horn. Using our packs for cushions against the trees that had supported my hammock, we sat down and tried to pass the time reading books. In that damned-if-I-do-damned-if-I-don't guilt-ridden state, my attempt at literary concentration didn't last long. Fuck this, I thought, caring not one iota about Ahab's inability to forgive and forget, much less an overgrown white whale's bad-ass attitude, and I slapped the book shut as if to obliterate the seafaring oceans of the world. Mila stared with pinched concentration at the copy of *Fear of Flying* open on her raised knees. She was down to the last few pages of the story. Suddenly, from the direction of the trailer park gate, Jay's twangy shouting drew the undivided attention of everyone left in the trailer park.

"Kilt him! My best friend! Like a brother to me! Murdering Mexicans!"

Lean as a toned dancer in his gray tank top and short-short cut-offs, Jay stumbled and lurched across empty campsites like he was too drunk or too grief-stricken to walk a straight line. Bullshit,

I thought, smelling the stink of his opportunism. I started to get up, ready to inflict serious cowboy damage.

"Don't," Mila said, holding her hand out for me to stop right there. "He's not worth it."

"The fuck he isn't," I said, but having already hesitated, I sagged to the ground again, sticking to our plan of playing it safe.

"Who's gonna stand tall?" Jay shouted. He stopped in the middle of the trailer park and raised his fist high in a *power* salute. "Protect our own, goddamnit! Fuckin' U.S.A. all the way!"

People, recognizing bad news when they saw it, picked up wherever they left off. A small boy, squeezing his dick with his hand to keep from peeing his shorts, was led by a woman into one of the toilet stalls. A young couple resumed their barefooted trek toward the beach. Someone popped an 8-track tape into a vehicle's cassette player, and Bob Dylan's "Lay Lady Lay" imposed the wrong melancholy mood on everyone. With no rush of hippie volunteer troops heeding the call to battle, Jay dropped his fist, huffed contemptuously, and lurched ahead. A few campsites away from where I sat, he came up to a longhaired Rasputin-looking dude on his hands and knees as he rolled up his flattened tent. Jay teetered over him.

"How's 'bout it, man? 'Revenge is mine sayeth the Lord!' Shoot, best defense is a good offense. Either we send a message to the beaner bastards now, or wait for them to pick us off one by one later. Don't believe me?" Jay let out a war-whoop to the sky— "Whaaaaaaow!"

Rasputin, listening up at Jay with a one-acid-trip-too-many stare, now went right back to rolling up his tent. Jay huffed and moved on. He swung his fist as if vowing to go it alone. "Eye for an eye! That's what the Bible says, goddamnit. Wake up, ya bunch of pussy, chickenshit, insult-to-the-white-race faggots!" A sharp swerve to the left put him on a collision course with Mila and yours truly. She must have seen something in my eyes.

"Don't," she said again.

During the sequence of what happened next, it's a wonder my anger didn't levitate me onto my feet. Damn if Jay didn't stumble right through our campsite. Bolder still, he paused between the trees Mila and I were leaning against. By his wibble-wobbly drunken manner, you'd have thought he didn't notice us. Then, for a split instant that must have been intended for our benefit alone, he broke character and smirked at me, then at Mila.

"Whaaaaaaow!" Message delivered, he lunged and stumbled across the lane in the direction of his campsite a couple of rows over. "Kilt my best friend in cold blood! Chickenshits! If you ain't with me, you're agin' me! Ain't nothin' down the middle of the road but a yellow streak!"

"Faker," Mila said quietly. "How could I be so stupid?"

Half a dozen smart-ass comments rolled to the tip of my tongue, but instead I told her, "Can't beat yourself up forever. We'll be on that plane soon."

Mila looked at me, eyes watering with what—gratitude? Self-loathing? Fear of our future bliss together? It was best not to guess.

Lo and behold, the same moon-faced, mothering woman who had fed the starving dogs under her restaurant table came out of the trailer park woodwork and approached Jay.

"Please don't talk like that," she said. "There's plenty of nice Mexicans. Poor guy. You're just upset about your friend, aren't you? Need a hug?" As she leaned into Jay, he crumpled against the healthy-helping of cleavage spilling from her neon-pink bikini top.

"Cold blood," Jay sobbed. "My best friend. Nobody cares."

"There, there." Jay's concerned new aquaintance patted him on the back. "I care. If anyone's due for some good karma, you are."

"Yeah," Jay said, prolonging the hug like the idea of playing his cards right to get into the babe's pants had just occurred to him. "Sure could use some good karma."

As if the woman's hug had signaled to others that all Jay needed was a little love and attention, a handful of the skeleton crew wandered over from different places and gathered around him. From my short distance a few campsites away, I listened in on the conversation.

"Tough break, man."

"Scary."

"Like a brother. Always there for me."

"Poor thing. You shouldn't be alone. Buy you breakfast?"

"Sure would 'preciate it."

"Think Sánchez had anything . . ."

"A *pig* like that? What do you think?"

Life is full of coincidences. At that exact moment, the man with the badge and mirror sunglasses came with a bowlegged strut down the lane. Ignoring Mila and me like we were nothing more to him than yesterday's irritant, he stopped mid-point between us and the group of hippies. One of the taller guys spotted him and must have told the others to *zip it*, eyes turning to the *Jefe*. Frowning, Sánchez shook his head with paternalistic, wearing-thin patience, then motioned with his hand for people to step away from Jay. The cancerous cell isolated, he wiggled a finger for Jay to put himself front and center. Damn if Cowboy didn't sober up and walk a straight line. Moon Face and the others scattered. Sánchez threw a friendly arm around Jay and led him down the lane to the next empty campsite for better privacy. There, close to a rusted, cast-iron barbecue pit, they faced off and became involved in what I interpreted as animated hushed negotiations. Who says that in a marriage of convenience the left hand has to know exactly what the right hand's been up to? A minute or so later, just about the time negotiations must have been entering the delicate stage, that tow-headed kid with a mean streak, butt-naked and dragging a palm frond as long as he was tall, toddled up the lane and over to the two men. His fair-skinned sunburn gave him the rosy-cheeked look of a disgruntled cherub. Perhaps familiar with Sánchez from previous encounters, the boy poked at the *Jefe's* trouser leg with his branch to make his presence known. Interrupted, Sánchez looked down, then broke into a grin.

"What are you, *niño?*" he asked. "Very brave, no? Maybe you grow up to be a *Jefe*—heh-heh-heh-heh-heh."

Judging from Jay's annoyed expression, he wanted to boot the upstaging kid in the tush. The boy, grinning himself, poked

Sánchez in the thigh with his branch again. Then he took the game a step further by whipping the branch across Sánchez's knees. What had been threatening to other kids in the trailer park was no more than amusing to the *Jefe*.

"That is a good little man," he said, reaching down and tousling the boy's sun-bleached hair. "You are very strong!" He went back to his negotiations with Jay. The kid must have recognized a kindred spirit when he saw one. He stayed close to Sánchez, staring up at him with those shockingly blue, hardened, astute eyes.

Soon the deal was done. Jay started nimbly across the trailer park toward the gate. A swing of his fist showed anyone watching that he was no man's pawn, but he kept his mouth shut for a change.

"Where's he going?" Mila asked.

I shrugged, her guess as good as mine. Sánchez, having nipped organized dissension in the bud, took off his sunglasses, the better to communicate with the gringos and gringas warily observing him from the relative safety of their campsites.

"My good *Norte Americanos*," he addressed one and all. "Last night a *turista* go to the beach to buy drugs and was killed. I have investigated. The dead man is the man who make the trouble with the fires and kill the girl. Now that he is got what he deserves, there is no reason for you to leave our beautiful Puerto Escondido. Stay, enjoy the sun, the ocean, our hospitality. Mexico is safe for the people who do the safe things. If you have the complaint, my door is open." He looked about, giving anyone ample opportunity to speak up. No takers. He slipped his shades on again, the mirror lenses reflecting the landscape of his domain, and smiled like a man who savors the joy of irony. "I, Roberto Sánchez, am here to serve and protect. Have fun."

Swaggering like he'd just graduated from the John Wayne School of Walking, he headed straight for the gate. The kid waddled after him but, unable to keep up with Sánchez in the lane, dropped his branch and bounced on his toes as if he were having an attack of separation anxiety. Perhaps developmentally delayed in speech, he let out a loud "Aaaaaaagh!" Sánchez didn't look back. The boy fell to the ground and sat there puffing up red, screaming, crying, fists banging thighs in what some would mistake for the throes of a temper tantrum, but which I understood to be a much more profound crisis.

"Brat," Mila said. "Does he even have a mother? Might as well be raising himself." She shifted her vision to Sánchez, already halfway to the gate. "Blame Otto for his own death and call it even. Makes me sick to my stomach."

Brakes squealed in the road. Through holes in the tall brush along the fence, I saw Alberto hop out of his red jeep.

"Look alive," I said.

"A little early, isn't he?" Mila asked.

"You won't hear me complaining." I was already up and stowing *Moby Dick* in my backpack. I watched as Sánchez and Alberto crossed paths inside the gate and stopped to exchange words. A cordial tip of the head from Alberto implied no more or less than, *Always at your service.* With that he continued on at a smart pace into the trailer park, while Sánchez went out.

Pedro, his boss-radar in full operation, rushed solicitously out the door of his hut, but when Alberto waved him off with hardly a glance, he stopped and assumed his Tarzan pose with buffed arms folded across his chest. He was at the ready if called upon. Alberto carefully sidestepped the boy still sitting in the lane, kicking, wailing, and looking rabid enough to bite anything within lunging distance. The mystified, disturbed expression on Alberto's face seemed to ask, *Maybe something in the child's Norte Americano diet?* He reached our campsite.

"*Hola*, my young lovebirds. You are both looking—how you say—*chipper* this fine morning." Then in a more subdued tone, "You have heard about Otto."

"Yeah," I said. "Been hearing nothing but him all morning."

"Ah, it is very, very bad." Alberto placed a hand over his pained heart. "I do not understand people who do not understand . . . Human beings, no matter where they come from, have a responsibility . . ." But here he trailed off, sparing us the moralistic lecture. "For your safety, I thought it a good idea to come early and let you spend your last hours in Escondido at the airport."

"Sounds good," Mila said, accepting Alberto's hand to help her up. "Sorry about the major dent in your business. I know you'll say it doesn't matter, but I think it's sad, anyway."

"Ah, *señorita*, money is not the most important thing in life." Alberto grinned wryly, adding, "*Almost* the most important, but not *the* most important." He gazed off toward the ocean. "Maybe if I had done more . . . to prevent . . . However," he said, looking back at us, "hindsight can be unfair. We do what we can."

"You certainly did," I said. "That's what counts." I hefted my pack and slipped on the shoulder straps. The sum-total weight of the vacation straightened my posture. Like the gentleman I wasn't, Alberto helped Mila on with her pack. She looked about sadly.

"Good-bye."

Defying rhyme or reason, I, too, felt Escondido's imprint tug longingly on my soul. Go figure.

Out on the road, Mila hopped in the jeep's passenger bucket seat next to Alberto; I kept the luggage company behind them in the carrying bed. I was in for a bumpy ride. As we roared off, I caught a glimpse of the toddler delinquent through the gate. He was dragging his branch and patrolling campsites, in search of bigger game.

* * *

If a field with its grass munched as short as a carpet by a small herd of goats can qualify as an airport, we arrived in a matter of minutes up through the hills north along the coast to the same airport we'd flown into five days earlier. A bald strip of red dirt ran down the center of the field and stopped just shy of a cliff's edge that overlooked the ocean far below. No doubt more than a few pilots circling their airplanes over the water and coming in for a landing had developed the wind-sheer jitters. Our jeep screeched to a halt near a thatched-roof shelter that was between the road and the airfield. When Alberto cut the engine, the clanging of goat bells, cawing of birds, and whirring of insects reclaimed the countryside. The place was deserted except for a couple of peasants under the shelter—mere teenage boys, by the size of them—laid out catnapping on either row of wooden benches. With straw cowboy hats pulled over their faces, they passed for dead. We hopped out of the jeep. Not to be out gentlemaned again, I lifted Mila's pack over the tailgate and helped her on with it.

"The turning of a new leaf?" Alberto asked me, nailing the idiom right on the head.

"Hey, where I come from, you can get into a lot of trouble by putting women on a pedestal," I said.

"Ah, yes, the *feministas*. I do not understand. The view is better from the pedestal."

"Nothing wrong with treating a woman like a woman," Mila said.

"And there's nothing wrong with women realizing they can't have it both ways," I added.

So as not to go *there*, Mila turned to Alberto. "You've been so incredibly kind to us." She kissed him on the cheek. "How can we ever repay . . ."

"A kiss from one as beautiful as you, *señorita*, leaves me in *your* debt." Then Alberto, holding up a hand to the side of his mouth and pretending that only I would hear him, whispered, "Are you taking notes, Big Al?" Mila giggled and planted another kiss on his cheek.

"Ah, *señorita*, please! Go before I must follow you as your humble servant to Chicago."

"I can think of worse fates," Mila said, rewarding Alberto with a well-deserved flirty smile. "Take care."

When Mila was almost to the shelter, Alberto, keeping his voice down, said, "You see? It is not so difficult to get a woman's attention. It is the holding it that is the hard part."

"The hard*est*," I said, lifting my pack out of the jeep and slinging a strap onto my shoulder. I extended my hand. "If you're ever in Chicago . . ."

"Too many gangsters," Alberto said, his firm grip putting my finger bones to the test. "I will stay here and help Escondido become the next Acapulco. It is a dirty job, but someone has to do it."

Then it occurred to me that this would be my last chance to ask *the* question.

"So, you think Sánchez killed Otto?"

Alberto stopped pumping my hand but didn't let go of it. From his look he seemed annoyed at my *Norte Americano* bluntness on so delicate a matter.

"It is not for me to speculate about the honorable *Jefe*. Why do you ask?"

"Just curious."

"Curiosity killed the cat," Alberto said, nailing another idiom. "This is no vacation for me. This is home. I have invested everything here. *Señor* Sánchez is a fact of life that a businessman like me must never fail to appreciate."

"But if you *were* to speculate."

At the time I took Alberto's frown to mean that he didn't think it prudent for him to accuse anyone of murder, but now I interpret it to mean that he thought I was being dense. Then he answered, "I would say that a man is innocent until proven guilty."

Either one or both of us started our hands to pumping again.

"Ah, Big Al, in Mexico justice works in mysterious ways. But I have to admit that Otto did not seem like the type who would kill . . ."

"Yeah, well . . ." I withdrew my hand. "Guess this is it. *Adios*."

I hadn't gone halfway to the shelter to join Mila on one of the benches, when Alberto called out, "Roman."

I turned around, heart skipping a beat, sure that Alberto had read me. The truth was his for the asking.

"Do you know what *Puerto Escondido* means in English?" Alberto let me hang on that gambler's grin for a moment. "Hidden Port."

"Really," I said. "Kinda like the hidden village up in the mountains. You people got more *hidden* around here than a game of hide-and-go-seek."

"Ah, my Chicago amigo, it is the same with you. When you learn to spend less time hiding behind the fast comment, you will find yourself."

"I wasn't aware I was lost."

"We never are," Alberto said. With a wink that to this day I believe was meant as a vote of confidence, he stepped to the driver's door of the jeep, whistling "*Santa María*" in so sweet and pure a tone that the melody seemed to resonate from the foothills themselves. He climbed into the bucket seat, shut the door, and turned the ignition key. I caught his attention long enough to tip him a finger good-bye before he roared off and disappeared around a bend in the road. A cloud of dust left in his wake slowly drifted out over the brush land and airfield, then settled along with my oppressive guilt in the mid-day heat. Fuck it, I thought. Same time tomorrow I'd be in my European Literature class listening to Professor Silverstein lecture on *Madame Bovary*. I glanced at the woman with whom I hoped to spend the rest of my life. She sat there on the bench pressing fingertips to temples, her eyes shut. Headache, I thought. By the time I got to her, she was digging a hand in a side pocket of her pack.

"Damn it! Where's the aspirin? Do you have it in your pack?"

"I'm not the aspirin freak, you are," I said. Letting the pack fall off my shoulder to the dirt floor, I sat down beside Mila, the rickety bench creaking in protest.

"Shit! If I don't take a couple before the pain gets too bad, my head will be splitting the whole fucking way home."

"OK, OK, calm down. Last I saw, you put them . . ." I reached into a different pocket on her pack and pulled out a bottle of Anacin. In a super-hero voice, I said, "Aspirin Man to the rescue." I popped the cap, poured out a couple of pills, and handed them to Mila. Then retrieving an army canteen from my pack, I passed that to her, too. With the help of a swig of water, she swallowed the pills, then closed her eyes again as if she were concentrating on banishing the pain.

"How come you keep getting these headaches? I'm telling you, you should go see a—"

"I don't need your professional opinion right now," Mila said, eyes still shut. "It hurts, OK? I just want to sit here quietly."

No reason to be a bitch about it, I thought. Then, *Easy. Show you care.* I slid my hand over her hands that were folded together on her lap.

"Anything I can do, sweetie?"

"No."

"Love you."

"Love you, too," Mila said. "Shhhhh."

"I mean I *really* love you."

No response. Letting my hand slip away, I left her to the privacy of her own pain.

3

Time snailed by. After an interminable period, taxis began to arrive one after another, depositing tourists and locals alike, all of them loaded down with luggage and bags stuffed with prized possessions and commodities. An entrepreneurial Indian father-and-son combo carried enough *bolsas* filled with goat cheese to feed all of Mexico City. Moon Face, apparently on the same flight, showed up lugging a backpack, her hands overburdened with essential carry-on items such as a clear plastic bag filled with seashells, starfish, and God knows what other plundered natural resources from the local environment. Taxi drivers gabbed in the road by their cars, leaning on fenders and hoods, waiting to shuttle the next load of arrivals into town. The two teenage boys woke up, made room for others on the benches, and proved themselves to be Aero Mexico Airlines employees by circulating and requesting to see if people's tickets were in order. Even under shade, the sticky heat swirled inside my head. I tuned out conversations happening around me. Then I heard the thud of a heavy burlap sack of coffee beans hit the ground by my foot. I looked down at it, then up at an old man with a full head of stark white hair and cloudy blue eyes, one upper eyelid droopier than the other. His rumpled white shirt and brown trousers looked as if he might have been trying to get one-day's-wear-too-many out of them between washings. He slipped off his shoulder bag and slowly sat down at the end of the row beside me like he took the warning *Fragile, handle with care* personally.

"Didn't mean to startle you," Old Timer said with a been-there-done-it-all smile. "Had to remind that coffee who was boss before I went another step."

"No problem," I said.

"Going home?" he asked.

"Yep. Chicago."

"Nice city, Chicago. Spent a few years there. Cold, but nice."

I lost him to a trip down memory lane as he stared to where the road dipped beneath the top of the hill we were on. He returned shortly, and said, "Worked in the Pullman factory on the south side after the war. Yeah, good times. Depression over, no more worrying about having a roof over your head or food in your belly. Had to put an end to that cold, though. Man-oh-man, used to cut right through me no matter how many layers of clothes I wore. So I moved out to Seattle and went to work for Boeing. Retired down here after the wife died. You got yourself a steady retirement check every month, you can live like a king—servants, the whole bit. Been here going on twelve years."

"Suits you, huh?"

"Oh, yeah. Nice little town, Escondido. Keeps growing right out of its socks. Heard we had a little spat of trouble lately, but that'll blow over. Can't stop progress. If Escondido's anything, it's a work-in-progress."

Mila had taken her book out of her backpack and opened it to read, a signal that even though her headache was better, she wanted no part of idle chitchat with a stranger. On the airfield, the herd of goats, as if they'd all come to a unanimous decision that the grass was indeed greener off to the left, was moseying with bells clanging toward a new area. The Midwesterner within me had to ask the man, "You ever seen any sharks around here?"

He didn't answer, staring past the other row of seated passengers, the airfield, to far beyond the cliff's edge where long threads of clouds were stretching into diaphanous bands over the sky's western frontier. Hard of hearing? I wondered. Then he turned those droopy, off-balance eyes on me. There was a speck of something troubling in them.

"What makes you ask?"

"I don't know. I've always had this morbid fascination with sharks. Ever seen one?"

By the way Old Timer looked away again, I thought maybe he thought my question too touristy to deserve comment, but then he said, "Once. Years ago. Big fish, maybe six feet long, in shallow water right near town."

"Really. What kind?" Out of the corner of my eye, I saw Mila put her book face down in her lap, drawn into listening.

"Mako, Tiger, Lemon, Bull—shark's a shark to me," the stranger began. "It was sunset. That's when I've always liked taking a walk along the beach, all those beautiful colors hanging in the sky and reflecting off the water. Can't beat the show or the price, that's for sure. Escondido didn't have tourists to speak of back then, the whole beach to myself except for a group of three or four boys riding waves and a couple of fishermen netting minnows in the surf. What they do is stand in water about waist deep, twenty or thirty feet apart, holding either end of a net. Then they move to shore closing toward each other, but not too fast or the whole school will get spooked and swim out of the trap. These fellows were in the middle of herding those fish, when I see a dorsal fin glide by a yard or so behind them without them even noticing it. Doesn't so much as make a ripple in the water. I stop, but by the time I've shaded my eyes, the fin's gone. I'm thinking, Eyes playing tricks on me? Then there it is again not far down the beach, cleaving a circle around the heads and shoulders of the bodysurfers, so close that any one of them could have stuck out a hand and petted it. How human beings can miss seeing something that big and dangerous is beyond me, but not one of them hightails it to shore, probably distracted talking to each other or keeping their eyes peeled for the next big wave. And me? How can I justify it? I'm standing there on the water's edge, part of me so afraid for those people that my hands are shaking, the other part so detached I'm leaving it to the next guy to sound the alarm. But there is no *next guy*.

"That shark makes its move, fin shooting straight for the fishermen. By now they're in water not much above the knee, and those minnows, with no place to go but the shore or the net, are splashing and jumping out of their skins. I find my voice, screaming, '*Tiburon! Tiburon!*' Too late. *Voooom!* You can't begin to imagine the power of a creature like that. The sheer force of the hit knocks one of the men I don't know how many feet out the water. I can still see him falling through that red ball of sun behind him, one leg gone from the knee down and a glazed *where am I* look on his face. Funny, but in my memory his splash has no sound."

"Wow," I said. "Scary." A vague identification with the man's inability to scream out before it was too late poked and prodded in my bowels as much as any fear of sharks.

"He died?" Mila asked.

Old Timer grinned sadly and gave a quick noncommittal tilt of the head.

"The other fisherman didn't even notice the net had gone slack in his hands until he'd taken a couple more steps into shore. Then he turns around and sees his buddy flailing in all that red water and runs like hell out to save him. I can't say I remember following after him, but the next thing I know there I am helping to pull that poor guy out of the water, too. What a shame, him lying there in the sand quivering, going more and more into shock, blood spurting like a fountain from severed arteries. I whipped off my shirt and used it for a tourniquet, but a lot of good that did. His friend was kneeling over him blubbering and trying to explain what happened. One look at that ragged stump of tendons and bits and pieces of muscle and you knew the man was too far gone to grasp any concept of *shark*. Not a pretty sight. He tried to say something, but his teeth were chattering so bad I couldn't understand. To answer your question, by the time I'd run to the *Seguro* in town and brought the nurse back with me, he'd bled to death. The next morning, someone found his chewed-up leg washed ashore on the beach. Guess that shark was just out for a taste-test."

"Lovely," Mila said. "Probably give me shark nightmares for a week."

"Sorry." The stranger grinned apologetically. "If it makes you feel better, a marine biologist told me that the shark must have mistaken the leg for a seal or another fish. He also said that there's an average of only fifty shark attacks a year worldwide and that it might be another two thousand years before a shark takes a chomp out of someone anywhere near Escondido again. But I'll tell you what, once you've actually seen a shark attack, you're not in any mood to play the statistics game or hear a lot of shark excuses. I just hope those fifty people every year have a better man than me looking out for them when it happens."

The old guy stared off at the bands of clouds over the ocean like he was tracking their encroaching progress.

"Never a day goes by I don't see him. One second he's catching minnows, the next he's falling through that sun already good as dead. How could I have waited so long to scream out?"

"Probably from the time you first saw the fin until the attack happened, it was a lot faster than you think," I said. "Anyone could have froze."

"Yeah," Old Timer said, "probably."

I should have thought of something more to say, but selfish as it may be, I needed comforting every bit as much as him.

"*Boleto?*" One of the Aero Mexico Airlines workers stood before us with his hand stuck out. Old Timer, Mila, and I produced tickets from our luggage. The teenager looked them over, returned them with indifference, then moved past Mila to a pint-sized Indian granny who could have fit in my backpack and flown for free. Mila picked up her book again, excusing herself from the conversation by reading.

"If I learned anything from the experience," said the stranger, "it's that there's a few things worth making sure that your voice is heard." With a slow turn of his head, he laid those disturbing eyes on me. Then, as if attempting to wipe the slate of his regret clean, he asked, "So, you ready to face that Chicago cold?"

I sat in so deep a funk, I could not have begun to guess how much time had passed. Focusing on a patch of the red dirt ground just beyond the tips of my outstretched feet, my vision began to blur, then went into a slow dizzying spin. Breathing all but stopped. When I finally came to my decision, I snapped out of the reverie and took a quick glance around. There was standing room only left under the shelter.

"What's your watch say?" I asked Mila.

"Quarter past twelve."

"I'm going back to town."

"You're *what?*"

"Take my backpack on the plane with you. If I'm not here, go without me. I'll catch another flight."

"Roman!" Hands can't move any faster than Mila's did, one clamping my thigh and the other my shoulder. "Don't you dare! You do and I swear I will never, ever—"

"I got some unfinished business," I said. God bless clichés. I pulled free from Mila's clawing grasp not once but twice on the way to my feet. Then, before she could have the presence of mind to give chase, I brushed past the startled Old Timer.

"Roman!" Mila screamed. "You want to rot in a jail?"

Out from the shelter and into the blazing heat, I didn't have to turn around to hear that conversations had shushed.

"If you're lucky enough to make it to jail alive! Stupid idiot! Don't leave! I love you! Please!"

"Escondido," I told a taxi driver, a man so skinny and deflated he must have had an air leak. With a fare on the line, he bounced up from leaning against his cab's front fender, swung open the door, and climbed in behind the wheel just as quick as I climbed into the backseat. I refused to look out my open window to see how far Mila had followed after me.

"You're throwing your whole life away! Us! There's not going to be any second chance! If you want to get married, this is it! Do you hear me, Roman?"

Tires spun, kicking up a ruckus of dirt. Then as I careened around a bend, I heard Mila's fatalistic cry.

"Roooooooooman!"

* * *

Holy shit. What am I doing? The macho-fast, twisting, skidding taxi ride down the hills tried to bounce and knock a change of mind out of me. No going back. It might have been past 12:00 for the rest of the time zone, but for this fool it was high noon. I needed a plan. Nothing but the same-old-same-old came to mind: *Play it by ear.* Walls of brush cloaked in suffocating philodendron vines whizzed by either side of the road, breaking for panoramic snapshots of the dry, brown-splotched countryside. The driver, smiling in the rearview mirror and flashing yet another Mexican's gold tooth, snickered—gratuitous commentary on my very public woman problems.

"Hey, do I make fun of your teeth?" I asked. "Then shut the fuck up." Tone got the message across, but even though the cabby cut his snickering short, I suspect he took his revenge by adding a few more miles-per-hour on the speedometer. He fishtailed the next turn and nearly sent us flipping and tumbling down a steep hill. Gold dingle balls fringed around the windshield bopped spastically on strings. A Madonna figurine hanging from a strand of rosary beads off the rearview mirror twirled in a jig. We passed a thicket of mango trees, the green palm-sized fruit just beginning to take recognizable shape. I checked for cash in the pockets of my painter's pants—almost thirty-five pesos in crumpled bills and spare change. If I didn't end up in jail or dead, I'd have enough money to pay for a taxi ride back to the airport. The absurdity of thinking that far ahead struck me as funny, and I shoved the money into a pocket again, then braced against the seat. A heart-pounding rush of unlimited freedom left nowhere to hide.

We bottomed out on the coastal flat, whipped around a bend, flew past the *Seguro* hospital, and took one more reckless turn onto Escondido's main drag. A ghost returning to haunt the scene of his former unresolved life must not feel any differently than I did. Not wanting to have to explain my reappearance to Alberto, I slumped low and waited until we'd past the *farmacia*.

"*Alto.*"

The driver slammed on the brakes and tossed me so far into the front seat I could have kissed the dashboard before I was flung back again. He looked innocently over his shoulder as if to ask, Is there a problem, *Señor* Hippie? Then, all business, he stuck out a hand.

"Quince pesos.*"*

Deposited in the middle of the road, I ate the taxi's farewell dust.

At first glance, Escondido was deserted except for the shadowy movements of locals inside restaurants and shops. The town seemed to be catching its breath before a new wave of tourists rolled in. An insect-humming quiet listened for my next move. Where would I go looking for Jay first?

"Whaaaaaaow!"

Chance is one thing, divine providence another. The signature scream had come from the restaurant up the street across from the *farmacia*.

"How many times does a man have to ask for a dang beer to get some dang service in this shit-hole?"

Stay loose, I thought. Tight as a snare drum, I marched post haste so as to minimize the possibility of Alberto seeing me. In the middle of the restaurant's otherwise empty dining area, Jay sat at a table with his bare feet propped comfortably up on it like he owned all of Mexico.

"Yoooo-hoooo!" he yelled toward the kitchen curtain at the back of the room. Underneath the curtain's bottom hem, two sets of woman's calves moved about—one stout and gnarled, the other shapely and smooth. The legs probably belonged to the same Indian tandem that had last seen Otto alive in town. Either busy with chores or intentionally letting Jay cool his heels, both mother and daughter must have considered their mouthy gringo customer to be of secondary importance.

"Will one of you shake your fat butt out here and bring . . ." Spotting me coming through the opening in the restaurant's spindled railing that served as a doorway, Jay leapt to his feet, metal folding chair banging to the dirt floor. As he stood with hands at the ready to break me in two, half a dozen or so empty beer bottles quaked on the table in the aftershock.

"Easy, amigo, easy," I said. "Just wanted to let you know there weren't any hard feelings before I take off for the airport."

"Really," Jay said, stalling to get a foothold on my intentions.

"Really," I said. "How's about a good-bye beer?"

Jay looked at me as if to say, Who the fuck are you trying to kid? Then all slippery grin, he reached down to pick up his chair without taking his eyes off me. Unlike earlier at the trailer park, they showed the bloodshot signs of a beer-buzz.

"Why sure, amigo." Grabbing his seat again, Jay kicked the chair across the table from him out for me to join him. I took him up on the offer, then reached into my pants pocket, pulled out the pesos, spare change and all, and slapped them on the table.

"My treat, friend."

"Hell, no," Jay said. "You've already given me more than any man oughta." That grin tested my limits. "This one's on me."

"Is that right?"

"That's damn right."

"Shoot," I said, borrowing one of Jay's favorite words. "No reason for two grown men to let a woman get in the way of friendship."

"And a mighty fine piece of ass she was," Jay said.

It took every ounce of self-control I had to ignore the taut twisting cord in my gut and muster the wherewithal to say, "I'll drink to that. What's a gringo have to do to get served around here—stand on his head until he changes color?"

"Ain't that the truth." Jay yelled at the curtain, "*Dos* beers, you lazy-ass bitches! Else I'm coming back there and won't be leaving till after I've used one of y'alls assholes for a bottle opener, *comprende?*" Then to me, "What did I tell you way back when—dumb as oxes."

"Yep, you were right, I was wrong. Sure is nice of you to buy me a beer."

"*Buy?* Hell, amigo, when you're with me, everything in this town is on the house. Sort of a deal I worked out with Sánchez."

"What kind of deal?"

"That's between me and him," Jay said. "Question is, what the hell you think is between me and you?"

The daughter appeared at our table with customary sullenness. She slammed two bottles of beer on the table, foam bubbling out of the rims and dribbling down the long brown necks. If I'd learned anything in Escondido, it was the reason for the locals' bad attitude.

"Between us?" I asked Jay, as the daughter left without a word for the kitchen again. That taut cord twisted another turn. At my own expense as much as it was at Mila's, I said, "I thought we'd already agreed on that: the finest piece of ass in the civilized world. Did she give you the *Hoover* treatment?"

Jay hesitated like he didn't follow my meaning.

"The what?"

"You know, *Hoover*—as in *vacuum cleaner*? That girl can suck the chrome off a bumper. Tell her to suck harder, and she'll suck the bumper right off the car."

"Sounds dangerous," Jay said.

"Yep, but it's a danger a man can learn to live with."

"I'll sure as shit drink to that," Jay said. "Truth is . . ." and here he dropped a little of his guard, tilting back in the chair ". . . she got cold feet in the middle of things, or maybe I should say *cold pussy*." He reached up, and with a reflective, creepy lust in his eyes began twirling a lock of his stringy hair around a finger. "Pussy ain't no different than a spirited filly. Got to break it in to the saddle before it can enjoy a nice, long, hard ride. Believe me you, I'd have that hot little bitch screamin' a different tune in no time." He stopped with the hair twirling and raised his beer for a toast. "To pussy."

"Here, here," I said, returning Jay's bottle salute with my own. "To pussy past, present, and future. The wetter the better."

We each took a swig. Jay propped his feet up on the table again. Between his beer-buzz and our getting down in the boys-will-be-boys gutter, he seemed to have relaxed. There was no room for mistakes.

"You know, amigo, it's a real shame you and me got ourselves off on the wrong foot," Jay said. "Gonna get awfully lonely round here without you and Otto, poor bastard. Truth is, much as I liked Otto, I see a whole lot more smarts in you."

"How so?"

"Well now, I don't know as I should trust you *that* much."

"Awww, come on. Not like we're ever going to see each other again. Drink up. Next one's on me."

"Already told you Sánchez gave me carte blanche in this town. Might call it *payment for services rendered*."

"Services?"

"Yeah," Jay said. "Good a name for it as any. Works like this: Scratch my back, I'll scratch yours."

"I'm listening."

"I'm sure you are, amigo. I always thought of you as in my league, so to speak."

With a nod that thanked him for the dubious compliment, I raised my beer to toast again. "To our league."

"Here, here," Jay said. We each guzzled another swig, then he let out a quenched, "Ahhhhhh. Never thought I'd learn to like this Mexican piss. Amazing what a man deprived of respectable alcohol can adapt to. You and me, we're similar. We adapt. Survival of the fittest, you might say. Otto on the other hand, well, he couldn't quite make the same evolutionary jump. I offered him the chance to be partners with me in teaching these beaners a thing or two about messin' with the wrong gringo. Maybe after I'm long gone, it'll dawn on them that they oughta think twice before they throw a man in jail, make him pay bribes out the whazoo, total his truck, and then leave him to starve to death in this Podunk town. You'd think Otto would jump at the chance to get even. Problem is, he traded his potential for the bottle a long time ago—nothing but mush for brains. He kept saying he don't want no part in it, so I'm like, fine . . ."

Jay's voice trailed off, a flash of worry crossing his face. Then he grinned, and added, "Don't forget, amigo—my word against yours."

"Hey," I said, shrugging, "not like anyone in Chicago cares."

"You ain't in Chicago *yet*."

"Speaking of which . . ." I casually lifted my bottle, then shook it around in circles, watching the beer slosh inside. "I better drink up. Don't want to miss my flight; already had to come back from the airport once because I lost my passport. Found it in the sand at our campsite. Lucky."

"Yeah, I saw you and Mila head out of town in Alberto's jeep," Jay said, eyeing me suspiciously. "I was wondering what the hell you were doing back here."

"Now you know."

We each took a couple of more chugs off our beers. Then, whether he'd bought that I would be of no threat to him from the far-flung distance of Chicago, or that he simply had a criminal's psychopathic need to evasively brag about his accomplishments, he said, "I went it alone, all right."

"You did, huh?"

"Yes, indeed."

"The boy on the beach?" I asked.

Jay's grin said it all.

"The fires?"

Jay looked at me as if to ask, *What do you take me for?* Then he glanced to either side of himself to double-check that we were having a private conversation in an empty restaurant.

"*Suppose* I did," he said.

As off-handedly as I could, I answered, "Then I would have to suppose that Consuelo's dead because of you."

"That's one way of supposing, amigo. Another way is to suppose that girl would still be alive if her parents hadn't been too damn stupid to find her and push her out a window. And let's face facts. It ain't like selling tamales on the street is any life of leisure to look forward to. The way I see it, the *somebody* that set that fire did that little girl a favor in the long run. But does Otto see it my way? Nope. He gets all moral on me and says he's going to go to Sánchez and tell him everything he knows."

"And what *did* he know?" I asked.

"Nothin' much. And wouldn't be right for me to repeat what he supposed he knew. Might start a vicious rumor." Jay let me chew on that for a moment, tilting back and forth in his chair. "Now here's where the *fittest* aspect comes into play," he continued. "Let's suppose that Otto procrastinates about whether or not he should really go to Sánchez, whereas somebody else hightails it over to the *policía* station and tells Sánchez *his* theory on who's been causing all the shit around here. Might take some fast talkin' to get a mean old *hombre* like Sánchez to believe that the somebody had come to him just as soon as he'd caught wind of the situation, but it can be done. I guarantee it."

I felt something flooding my chest. Measuring my words, I asked, "You told Sánchez that Otto did it all?"

"Careful there, amigo." Jay said. "Next thing you know, you'll be supposing that Sánchez kilt Otto, and that's an awfully dangerous accusation to be making when the *Jefe's* got home-field advantage. It is sort of funny, though, that all of a sudden Sánchez is worried about a hothead like me stirring up a gringo rebellion that might go international-incident on him and bring a lot of people down here asking a lot of questions. Yep, he sure does know how to oil the squeaky wheel. Seeing as how he's got everyone in Escondido taking such good care of me, I would hate to think that he had anything to do with killing my best friend."

There is no excuse that until that moment, I hadn't fully appreciated Jay's capability. As nonchalantly as I could under the circumstances, I straightened up and took a sip off my beer.

"Shoot," Jay began again, "we all make choices in life—you, me, Otto, everyone. Nothing happened around here to nobody that didn't deserve it, exceptin' maybe that girl. I don't understand beaner logic. They pick a war with people, then they get all bent out of shape when one of them gets kilt by accident. I suppose even that boy on the beach brought it on himself. He wouldn't have gotten his ass kicked half as bad if he hadn't done something stupid like, say, spit on somebody."

There are repulsions you just can't hide. Jay read my face.

"Little late to get all moral on me now, pretty boy. You must take me for a jackass. You *think* you're acting, pullin' a fast one, but you ain't. I cut you to the quick, and we both damn well know it."

"Really," I said, lifting the beer to my lips.

"Really," Jay said. "You don't do nothing but look out for your own hide same as me. I just break a few rules to let people know that if they don't heed my bark, they'll have to suffer the consequences of my bite. Besides that, we ain't so different. I guarantee it."

A righteous, single-purpose calm came over me. It was time to be different.

"You got me there," I said. Draining the last of my beer, I noticed a couple of geckos defying gravity by playing an upside-down game of tag on one of the thatched roof's support beams. From the kitchen I heard what sounded like a raw onion being chopped with a knife on a cutting board. I brought the empty bottle down to my lap and began peeling the soggy Sol brand label with a fingernail. I remembered the wise words of my high school philosophizing buddy, Jesse Wilks. "*White boy, a good fight is over in three seconds.*" Slowly, so as not to attract Jay's attention, I slid my feet out of my flip-flops and drew them in until my legs were squarely underneath me.

"Not bad for piss water," I said. "Sure I can't buy you one before I leave?"

"If it makes you feel better." Jay drained the last of his bottle and added it to the collection on the table. "Your money, pretty boy."

"*Señorita*!" I yelled at the curtain. "*Cerveza, por favor.*" Then to Jay, "Twenty pesos says she doesn't get here before midnight."

"Shoot, that's a loser's bet. Do I look like a loser to you?"

I matched Jay slippery grin for slippery grin. "Can't say you do."

"Mighty nice of you," Jay said. "Hey, did you hear the good news? That damn *mañana* insurance company finally wired my money. Guess with Otto gone, it's all mine now. Don't even have to spend it. Think I'll stick around Escondido and let these beaners treat me like a king for a week or two. That oughta make things about even, wouldn't you say?"

"Yeah," I said. "No sense getting greedy. *Even* is good enough for any reasonable man."

What I did next was so cheap a sucker move I'm proud to say it worked. Glancing over Jay's shoulder, past the restaurant's railing and into the road, I suddenly trained my eyes as if they'd landed on something extraordinary.

"Damn, check out the titties on that one."

In the instant that it took someone of Jay's superior intelligence to look hard to his right, I have no memory of diving across the card table and in one fell swoop cold-cocking the meaty end of the bottle across the left side of his face; there is only the spray of glass, his yelping scream, and both of us on the ground with me on top, bashing away with my fists. The term *seeing red* literally means just that. Beyond my tunnel vision, the mother and daughter's shrieks put the sleepy town on notice. Jay, blinking away glass shards and blood running down from a deep gash on his forehead, tried in vain to block punches and snatch hold of anything from my hair to my crotch. Without remorse or mercy, I pummeled that despicable wounded face, silently counting, One, two, three . . . A limber leg hooked underneath my chin, pried me backward off of Jay, and onto the overturned mangled piece of scrap metal that had once been our table.

So much for Jesse's idea of a good fight.

Losing the mad scramble to our feet, I found myself being shoved in a backpedaling, off-balanced run clear across the restaurant. I clutched at Jay's tank top for dear life, spun him around, and gave him the honor of crashing through the railing first. Seams on my wedding shirt popped and ripped as we turned rungs into kindling wood, flew stumbling out into the middle of the road, and hit the dirt in a rolling flailing mess. A twisting yank to my wrist smelled like the doom of an arm lock. I quickly slipped it, sprang up, and began stomping Jay's head with my bare foot.

"Murdering-ass" *stomp* "loser" *stomp* "racist" *stomp* "touch my woman" *stomp* "motherfucker!" *stomp*.

In the heat of battle, it's easy not to realize that you're spraining your foot more than denting your opponent's skull. I heard more than saw people running toward us from all sides to watch the gringo main event. After several failed attempts, Jay's hands caught hold of my abused foot and sent me spiraling to the ground. He must have done that agile flip to his feet, because when

I looked up from my new vantage point, he was towering over me with nothing but blue sky all around him. He held a switchblade poised in his hand. *Fuck.*

Blood grotesquely painted the side of Jay's face, his badly ripped shirt and roughed-up chest caked in dirt. A large strawberry scrape oozed on his knee. Whether drunk, rattled, overly confident, or in the mood to prolong his idea of fun, he let me scramble to my feet again. We circled, my hands held out defensively, Jay slowly stirring the pressurized air between us with the knife. From the looks of his smile I could only hope that he'd been watching too many movies. He lunged. I jumped back, the swipe of the blade coming within an inch of my stomach.

"Getting' shy on me, pretty boy?"

Another swipe breezed one of my palms. Still another whizzed past the tip of my nose. Somewhere in the peanut gallery, a woman's nervous laughter brought home the deadliness of the moment. Run? Where would I go? I was about to make a play for a railing rung in the dirt behind Jay so that I could at least club him while he stabbed me to death, when Alberto, dressed in his white pharmacist's jacket, streaked out of the crowd and into the ring. Jittery on his feet like he feared Jay might take a swipe at him, he said, "Fight if you must, amigo, but drop the knife."

It all happened so fast. I didn't waste time to think. Aided by Jay's momentary distraction as much as by my lucky aim, I kicked the knife out of his hand. It landed on the ground by Alberto, who stepped on it, then just as quickly slid it with his foot behind him and into the crowd. He jumped in between Jay and me, held out his arms like a referee breaking the action in a prize fight, and yelled, "Fair fight!" Then backpedaling into the crowd again—"*Peléen limpiamente*!" Had Alberto caught me at a more convenient time, I'm sure he would have asked me what the hell I was doing back in town.

I staggered Jay with a right cross to the jaw. Preferring wrestling to boxing, Jay charged and took me down with a flying tackle. Next thing I knew, he was on top, throttling my neck and banging my head against the ground. Coughing, gagging, the thuds from the head blows resounding in my ears, I distinctly remember thinking, *Losing*. Beating and scratching at his chest, I clamped my other hand over his face, pushed, and by sheer accident slid my thumb into the deep gash in his forehead. Then not so accidentally, I dug in with my fingernail and ripped down.

"Ahhhhhhh!"

I swatted, whacked, and bucked Jay off of me.

It doesn't take long for a couple of lean hippies to tucker out. We were on our feet again, and my lungs clawed for oxygen. Without letup, we rumbled up and down the street punching, clinching, grappling, tripping, slamming, tussling, and slugging free of each other. The crowd moved with the shifting of our storm, people reacting to hard connecting blows with *Oo*'s and spectator rooting that needed no translation. I tasted blood from a split fat lip, my face one big hot bruise. Fists lead-heavy, throat raw, I knew I couldn't last much longer.

Ending up in front of the *farmacia*, we abandoned complicated self-defense strategies, such as ducking, and stood our ground exchanging wallops in a brutal contest of who could dish out and take what.

Whomp!

Whomp!

Whomp!

Whomp!

My vision fuzzed up around the edges. Legs gone, I was blacking out and throwing punches on instinct alone. Swaying but refusing to topple, I got a glimpse of Alberto somewhere in the crowd behind Jay. His imploring look of encouragement seemed to say, *Finish him!* I reached low, then coming up with the collective power and timing of every muscle and sinew, my fist caught Jay square under his chin and snapped his head back. As he crumpled to the dirt, I dropped to my knees cradling my battered aching right hand in the palm of my left. Jay tried to get up but lost his footing. He tried again. Same result. Conceding nothing, he spat a mouthful of blood in the dirt. It was over.

I glanced at the crowd all around us. On many of the peoples' faces, the thrill of the violent spectacle had already begun to dim.

A woman, perhaps noticing a small boy next to her for the first time, protectively shooed him away and down the street. The sleeves on my wedding shirt hung by threads, my painter's pants trashed with dirt stains, blood, and various rips. So much for looking cool in Chicago. I hung my head and concentrated on breathing. Someone's shadow fell over me. Then a white hanky appeared in front of my eyes.

"So, Big Al, *cómo estás?*"

"*Estoy bien.*" Taking the hanky from Alberto, I dabbed at tingling abrasions on either cheek, then to my split lip.

"We meet again," Alberto said.

"*Sí,*" I replied.

"May I ask you a question?"

"*Sí.*"

"Why are you here?"

I pooled a few more breaths, then with a nod in Jay's direction, said, "He did it."

"Buuuullshit!" Jay howled. Gasping for air, he managed to sit up on his hip. Then he slumped forward and braced his arms against the ground to keep from collapsing. Stringy hair stuck to his bloody face, I could only hope that I didn't looked as pathetically torn up as he did.

"Did what?" Alberto asked.

"The fires . . . Consuelo . . . boy on the beach."

"His word against . . ."

"One at a time," Alberto said, holding his hand out for Jay to wait his turn. Then to me, "How do you know?"

Fudging on the truth, I said, "He admitted it."

"Damn liar!" Jay screamed.

"But . . ." Alberto looked confused. "I let him stay in my trailer park for free. Why would he . . ."

"Long story," I said. "Starts with what some federales did to him and ends with his wrecked truck. Should have told you days ago. Sorry."

I didn't have the breath to explain to Alberto that I would have come forward sooner had Sánchez believed in a Witness Protection

Program. I expected and deserved the full brunt of Alberto's anger. In spite of the language barrier, people in the crowd must have sensed that all was not over—no one stirring.

"This is true?" Alberto asked Jay.

"Hell no! Why are you . . . Oh, I get it. This your idea of *fair*, Alberto? You two against me?"

"I am not against any man," Alberto said diplomatically. "I am only asking you if—"

"First you people kill my best friend, then you want to pin that girl's murder on me. Think your cheap-ass, trailer park welfare makes that OK? Huh?" Still winded, Jay paused for air. He stared malevolently up at Alberto. "You ain't nothin' but a big shit in a small toilet. Underneath all that money, you're just like every other—"

As if it suddenly occurred to Jay that he'd revealed more about himself than he'd intended to, he stopped right there. I finished his sentence for him.

"*Beaner*. You were about to say *beaner*."

"I didn't say no such thing!"

In a play for sympathy, Jay retched like he was choking on his own blood. Alberto must not have bought it.

"Ah, yes, *beaner*," he said, and seemed to absorb the racial slur with the same dignity he absorbed everything else in life. "That is a word that says a lot about the person who likes to use it." Then turning to me, his stern expression changed into a big smile. He offered me his hand and helped me up. Hobbled by a bruised heel and sprained big toe on my right foot, I stood listing severely to the left.

"Did I not tell you at the *aeropuerto* that I had faith in you, Big Al? Maybe you are right, maybe you are wrong about . . ." Alberto looked down at Jay like he was letting his disdain stretch the limits of his English vocabulary, "this pathetic human being. What matters is that you cared enough to come forward. Better late than ever."

"Never," I said. "Better late than *never*." Relieved, I felt my lungs loosen.

"Ah, *Inglés*." Alberto shook his head. "I would like to catch the son-of-a-whore who invented it."

Jay lurched to his feet.

"Not so fast," Alberto told him. "I am sure that *Señor* Sánchez, another beaner, will want to have a few words with you. It is my understanding that he has a way of getting to the bottom of things."

Perhaps thinking he could bluster his way clear of suspicion, Jay yelled, "Fuck you, Alberto! Ain't no one with balls big enough on his best Sunday to keep me in this two-bit town. Sánchez wants to talk to me, he can look me up in the U.S. of A." Then he turned to the crowd. "Get outa my way!"

The locals looked to Alberto for a translation. When he didn't give one, they stayed put. I watched disgust and then pity cross Alberto's face. Ever the gentleman, he calmly said, "My poor, ignorant, young man. If what Roman says is true, your U.S. of A. days are over."

Just then, an *hombre* whose balls were a tight fit in his pants on his worst Monday, much less his best Sunday, arrived late on the scene and pushed his way through the crowd. Mirror sunglasses flashing, he stopped and looked back and forth between Jay and me, taking note of our beat-up appearance.

"Tsk tsk tsk. What have we here, *muchachos*? A disturbing the peace. You are both under arrest. A few days in jail will teach you to love your brother gringo—heh-heh-heh."

Alberto began speaking to Sánchez in emphatic Spanish. He hadn't finished before an angry murmur traveled through the crowd, followed by people shouting at Jay.

"*Mátenlo!*"

"*Gringo cerdo!*"

The minor detail of no one having any hard evidence against Jay aside, it appeared that many of Escondido's esteemed citizens wanted to lynch on the spot a gringo accused of killing Consuelo.

"*Mi Consuelo!*" On the outer rim of the crowd, a short, thin, enraged man whose hands were wrapped in gauze bandages strained to free himself from two other men struggling to hold him back.

"*Mató a mi Consuelo! Asesino!*"

A raw burn wound covered most of his forehead and ran up into his singed hairline. With that drawn, inconsolable face, he could not have been anyone other than Consuelo's father.

"*Ahora la va a pagar!*"

"This is true what *Señor* Huerta tells me?" Sánchez asked, stepping over to Jay.

"Hey, no need to get all hasty," Jay said, waving his hands in front of himself like he could explain. "Awfully convenient that pretty boy here is so quick with his vivid imagination. I saw him take a machete and say he was gonna go fuck himself up a Mexican. Don't sound like someone so innocent to me. Who's to say *he* didn't light them fires? I was on my way to tell you that when he jumped me."

"I never did anything with any damn machete," I said, sticking to the truth that counted.

"Liar!"

Right when I thought that either Sánchez or Alberto would want to press me for more details about my past vigilante indiscretion, Sánchez removed his sunglasses, folded and slipped them into the breast of his uniform, and leaned in closer to Jay.

"Yesterday you tell me one thing, today you tell me another."

"Well, yesterday I thought—"

"If you lie then, why should I no think you lie now?"

"Let's calm—"

"And you take the people's free food and *cervezas*?" Sánchez asked.

"Just hang on a second," Jay said. "What say you and me go on over to the *policía* station for a private chit-chat to work this—"

It's not so much that I think Sánchez felt inclined to believe me, as it is that he seemed to have his reasons for doubting Jay. With the fury of a man unaccustomed to being someone else's pawn, Sánchez grabbed Jay by the hair on the top of his head, yanked down, and slammed a knee into his gut, dropping him on the spot. Coughing, gasping, and clutching his stomach, Jay squirmed and rolled in the dirt. "There is your chit-chat,"

Sánchez said. Then he leveled his furious stare at me. "How about you, *muchacho?* Want to chit-chat? What did I tell you will happen if you wait to give *información?* I think I will fuck up a gringo."

Alberto, running interference, moved in between us. A few inches shorter than Sánchez, he stretched to meet Sánchez eye to eye and thumped chests with him. The two Godfathers of Escondido began screaming at each other with such rage that I suspected their mutual hatred had a long history to it. Behind them, a husky man with a boyish round face rushed in and landed a swift kick to Jay's kidneys. I recognized him as the owner of the first restaurant that had been torched.

"Motherfucker!" Jay spun up onto his knees and lashed out with a punch, but the man, too quick, had already retreated.

"Chicken?" Jay yelled. "Come and get it!"

A woman snuck up behind Jay and boxed his ear. He whirled and lashed out too late again. Cooler heads in the crowd seemed to be arguing for calm with neighbors. Apparently, Escondido's split personality did not start and stop with Alberto and Sánchez alone. Someone struck a blow to the back of my neck. When I turned around, Pedro was protecting me by warding off a *campesino*.

"*Ese desgraciado es un cobarde!*" the *campesino* yelled. "*Mátenlo también!*"

A taxi slammed to a halt in the middle of the road beside all the ruckus. Mila flung open one of the car's back doors and jumped out.

"Roman!"

She ran toward me, shoving people out of her way. When she reached me, she stopped and looked me over, horrified. On the puffy-red-eyed verge of tears, she lifted her hand to touch my mauled face, then withdrew it as if afraid of hurting me. I repressed an urge to gush about how happy I was to see her.

"Just a scratch."

"Stupid fucking idiot."

She loved me, all right. Her conflicted look of relief and resentment swept aside any chance of tears. Jay, still on his knees and hunkered down in anticipation of another local's attack, must have assumed that Mila had shown up to corroborate my version of things, because he yelled, "Slut! You don't know nothin'."

"Better a slut than a redneck murderer slut," Mila said.

Hey, *slut semantics* aside, where did Jay get off insulting my girlfriend? I limped forward with the intent of dishing out more cowboy punishment, but before I could take a second step, something happened that saved me the trouble. Consuelo's father wrested free of the men restraining him and led a charge of locals. Scuffling for position, they began to stomp, trip, slap, and pummel Jay from all sides. Through the kicked-up cloud of dust, I saw him crawl, falter, and crawl again in a futile search for an escape route.

"Motherfuckers! All . . . you . . . goddamn . . ."

Sánchez, perhaps concerned with the mob's challenge to his authority, quit shouting at Alberto and started pushing, yanking, and flinging people off of Jay. The next thing I knew, Alberto had me in a bear hug. In an impressive display of strength for a man half my size, he uprooted and carried me bent over his shoulder to the taxi no more than fifteen feet away. Then he transplanted me firmly on the ground again.

"Get in!"

I hadn't even pulled my last leg through the open door before I heard Mila's piercing frightened shriek, then saw that Pedro was stuffing her into the car on top of me. I slid over on the vinyl seat to give her room. The door slammed shut. Alberto leaned his head through the open window.

"*Adiós*, my friends. Never come back here."

The second he pulled his head out from the window, the mother/daughter tandem were in his face yelling and pointing back and forth between me and their restaurant's busted railing and mangled furniture. It didn't take a rocket scientist to figure out that they wanted to know who was going to pay for the damages. Alberto reached into his trousers, pulled out his wad of bills, and began peeling off pesos. In the choking dust behind him, Sánchez took a time-out from manhandling people off of Jay and glanced in my direction. If I'd been under any illusion of escaping without his knowledge, his scornful look of utter loathing set the record straight: *Next time, muchacho.* Jay, swallowed up and lost in the middle of the mob's vicious stomping melee, let out an agonized moan.

"Hippie *cochino!*" screamed a woman.

"Have fun!" Mila yelled from her window at Jay.

A Good Samaritan tossed my flip-flops through the other open window beside me, then darted off before I could see who he was to thank him.

"*Aeropuerto!*" I shouted at our driver, the same man who had once blown a lewd kiss to Mila from his taxi.

We tore out of town and swerved around the bend overlooking the ocean. With a little luck, we had an outside chance of making our flight. Sinking low into the seat, I was about to thank Mila for coming to my rescue, for proving her love beyond a shadow of my unfair doubts, and to suggest to her that maybe, just maybe, we made a pretty good team.

"Stupid, stupid, stupid! . . . Can't believe you . . . Teach you to leave me like that at the airport!" No matter where her fists peppered me, she struck a bruise, scrape, sprain, or otherwise damaged goods.

"Hey!" I said, trying to fend her off. "Stop it! No one asked you to come and save me."

"Selfish, fucking, asshole bastard!" Mila yelled ". . . Expect me to trust . . . Fuck you, fuck you, fuck you, FUCK YOU!"

I finally circled my arms around Mila. As her fists slowed but continued pounding against my spine, I pulled her close to smother her contradiction as much as to comfort her.

* * *

When our driver dropped us off at the airport, a small twin-engine plane that didn't look much younger or bigger than the Spirit of Saint Louis sat parked on the airfield, its propellers at a standstill. The herd of goats, disciplined public servants, had removed themselves to munch on a far corner of the field. I hurriedly limped to keep up with Mila the short distance from the road, past the shelter, to the portable stairs leading up to the plane's door at the rear of the fuselage. The two teenage Aero Mexico employees were crouched down by one of the plane's balloon tires trying to get the hose from a tank of compressed air to connect with the tire's valve. After several failed air-hissing attempts to pump up the sagging tire, the boy with the hose shrugged and smiled at his friend as if to say, Hope she makes it. Yeah, I thought, gingerly following Mila up the stairs. Let's hope.

I saw that our backpacks were stowed with the other luggage in the cargo-hold—a small space behind seven passenger rows. We passed by the old timer, the pint-sized granny, and Moon Face. They all stared at me like they were wondering what buzzsaw I'd run into. At the second row from the front, we squeezed into the last empty seats on the plane with Mila by the window.

"Made it," I said, buckling in.

"No thanks to you," Mila replied, buckling in herself.

So that was how it was going to be. Chilly. And what had I expected from her—a hero's medal?

Outside, I heard the stairs being rolled away. Through a doorway a few feet in front of me, a couple of young pilots—looking smart in their uniforms—joked and clowned with each other in their cockpit seats.

Contact. Propellers coughed and whirled. We slowly taxied to the east end of the field. Blades roared into a deafening hum, and we were off. Every soul on board pressed into his seat, resisting the do-or-die approach of the sheer cliff drop-off at the other end of the short runway. In the nick of time we soared out over the glare of beaming ocean, circled, then headed inland toward the cloud-forested mountains and the city of Oaxaca on the other side of the range. From there Mila and I would catch a jet to Mexico City, and finally a jumbo DC10 to Chicago. Air-pocket turbulence was making for a bumpy, jolting ride.

"Earth to Mila," I said. "Come in, Mila. Over."

She turned from staring out her window to eyeing me sullenly.

"Yeah, you got that right, Roman. Over."

"Hey, relax. We pulled it off. Doesn't it give you satisfaction